I0631762

ADVENTURES OF A NAKED GIRL

Song Courson

ISBN 978-0-934546-68-3

Universal Workshop

www.UniversalWorkshop.com

Foreword

This fool book was sent to us because of its many references to the stars and especially the moon. It does have some of the extravagant qualities claimed in the "Review" or letter of recommendation by someone suspiciously friendly to the author, which is used here as an introduction. And I rather like the mis-spelt version of my name in a footnote near the end—in fact I#d like to adopt it.

Guy O'Howell

Introduction
"Clothed in names alone":
Applepeel according to herself

Reading this too-short novel is an activity less like reading than like taking a swim, strolling on a sunny hilltop, sprawling on cushions, eating a chocolate, sneezing luxuriously, or (let's face it) masturbating.

It has been circulating since, apparently, late 1987 in paper and electronic versions. One reader of my acquaintance called it "maybe the sexiest book ever, but certainly the richest, deepest, funniest, most beautiful, most civilized, most good-natured sexy book ever." According to another it is "the book that will give pornography a good name— 25 times more fun than *Candy* and 265 times more intelligent."

Exaggerations, and there are less friendly comments to be made too. But I had the feeling that you can't compare this with the run of good novels that make minuscule points about modern American life: you have to compare it with Rabelais for license with reality, Shakespeare for rhythm and luxuriant vocabulary. The springs of the delight are laughter, shrill eroticism, daring and ironic use of language, and, above all, the girl herself. She'll become a universal darling, the latest heiress of Helen.

There is no kidding about the hair-raising title. Applepeel is an eighteen -year-old with enough sex appeal to cause "social and climatic consequences" even before she finds herself wandering the world without her clothes. (Actually, through most of her adventures she is only half naked.)

Her adventures come thick, fast, strenuous, and improbable. They include being communally tickled, auctioned in a marketplace, tied up in a cat's-cradle of ropes, scrubbed by washerwomen, having to pose as the statue of a goddess, undergoing a public "Bellywedding" to a god, and walking naked yet unnoticed through a crowd—because they are staring up at balloon effigies of herself. She fights three "Battles of the

Britches" or bluejeans (stealing them from a boy, struggling to pull them on, and begging for help in stripping them off because she imagines they are on fire); she is immured in a school that is a caricature of perversity; in one epic night that leaves the strongest reader breathless, she is chased around a red-light district, snatched up in a helicopter, dropped from the sky into a duckpond, punished with "detailed spanking," abducted by pretended parents, and locked in a traveling coach with her "long-lost enemy" (result: the longest stripwrestle in history). Constantly in peril from ravenous males (in a prison cell, a restaurant, a state brothel), she achieves hairbreadth escapes *almost* every time, by wit, luck, pluck, and sheer gymnastics. She yields her virginity only when she chooses, and ends—well, let's not tell it all, but she ends on top.

Yet the text is far from naked action. One can imagine generations of students finding material for dissertations in the *motifs* from which it is woven.

For instance, names. Names are rich and thematic and strengthened by their variations. Applepeel herself has no name but "I" until well on in the story, yet eventually she gets called, fairly naturally, by more than fifty! (Not counting the personal names that her devotees apply to parts of her body.) Her "real" name is Felicity Jane Pepper, or Fristy for short.

There are chains of sound-association that run through the book, sometimes mingling with each other. One, for instance, is built around the syllable *og* and includes the hilarious neologism *oligogamous*.

Another small motif involves the words *shade* and *side*. There is no flab in the writing: words are repeated as little as possible; sentences, though dense with material, are stripped to their material only; particles, modifiers like "very" and "rather" and "maybe" and "usually," padders like "there is" and "the fact that," even auxiliary verbs, are almost absent; rhythms are definite and assertions simple. This economy is set off by an exception ("one of the exceptions that improve the rule"): Applepeel has a speech-tic, a slight retreat into understatement, wordiness, and empty idiom: too many times to be accidental, she says (e.g.) "a shade rash" or "on the intimidating side."

And there are the motifs of moon-lore and moon-worship (Applepeel's fate becomes so entwined with her guardian moon-goddess—Tashartris—that she seems to become the goddess's statue, daughter, impersonator, successor); of a species of art called Hearthstoppers; of internal thoughts that turn out to have been spoken or at any rate understood by others and, conversely, startling things said aloud that turn out to have been mercifully inaudible; of the language of bodily noises used by the Mongers (the quasi-human tribe of peddlers to whom Applepeel is sold); of anatomical miracles caused by the stress of lust for Applepeel ("Their own erections blocked their view"); of topology; of sculpture; of Eden and Lilith and Adame . . .

But the themes most worth tracing are the many aspects of Applepeel's own exuberant personality: her resistance to her attackers in a spirit mainly of play, her inclination to yield to the more forlorn or unlikely or "bewildered" of them, her "Table-Turning," her forgiving-ness, her occasional rapid lurches of mood between laughter and senti-ment and fury, her vegetarianism ("You've already been caned every day for refusing to 'eat corpse'"), her acrobatic vigor, her kid-like propensities (such as for getting muddy), the mysterious color of her hair and of a kind of apple called Arkansas Black, her need of sleep and ability to doze even in moments of tumult or peril, her love of fresh air and the depraved "heat-dreams" she gets if compelled to sleep under coverings, and her instinct that all is not far from being "okay."

A story consisting of incessant narrow escapes from rape can scarcely claim to be ethical. Yet the welcome and radical difference between this and most pornography is that the female is in no way despised: she is cherished.

Applepeel's grammar takes some shortcuts, but the language she speaks is not that of the masses. You don't absolutely have to keep a dictionary at hand, but it is worth stopping to find out what she means when she says things like "the architraves of my breasts" or "the crunode where the curves collide."

Not to be found in dictionaries—yet—is the sexual vocabulary she introduces: *sitch, stalk, sweedle, lipple, supplaud, clevel* (short for *cleft-veil*), *ool* . . . The invention that will surely stick is *glush.*

There are sentences that will make their way into future dictionar-ies of quotations:

> It had been refreshed by rains like a plant. How neat a kit for living! [Applepeel contemplating her body]
> Nowadays you can't tell music from engine trouble
> My head sank back, and my evemound rose, groved and grooved, like the world from the flood [Applepeel falling asleep in the bath]
> "Everywhere men, imagining her, are able afresh to swive their wives"
> And where is the mary, the essence-of-gender, the shehood, the hership?
> Why aren't there stronger words for laughing, and more *voicy* ones?—has no one ever really laughed before me?
> To raise me ever again from this bed was going to take an act of will, if not of Congress

"Thou shalt not commit infantry, as the private said to the general"
The rush of fright through my system had done it so much good that I
wanted to go sky-diving again

—and others whose humor is prepared by what leads up to them:

"Sir," I added, but it didn't do a whole lot of good
He was desperate because I had been debagged but not Debriefed
"But it might hurt, and that would be against the house rules"
"Hardly," I said. "Useful, maybe"
And there ahead, coming along the sidewalk, was a crocodile

And perhaps best of all:

"Vitality," he grumbled

—or more fully:

"Luck nothing. Vitality," he grumbled; "I should have known; you've got
enough to keep any *ten* alive" [spoken by the suicidal lawyer who makes
Applepeel take a death-jump with him]

That's it. Sheer shining vitality is what makes Applepeel so magnetic.

What is *literature?* The term should not include all that is printed, but
should not exclude the epics of preliterate peoples. And so a definition
by linguists is that literature is discourse which a society deems worthy
of repetition. Nowadays there is so much to read that very little is *re-*
read. Much of this story, I suspect, will be.

Though it seems a little book, perhaps because its heroine is a kind
of articulate baby, it is actually, at nearly 300 pages, not so little; but
after the first few chapters it becomes so tempting that one glides on to
the end. And then there is nothing for it but to go back and dwell again
on the pleasures of, say, the "Overhearing" episode (the one in which
Applepeel listens to men who think they are listening to her being ravished, while they are really listening to the grunts of the man she has
bound and gagged); from which it is difficult to refrain from gliding on
again . . .

But taking the novel in any way seriously reveals that it is not such
easy reading: that it sets us problems. Primary, of course, is how something can be, or can dare to be, at the same time energetic pornography
and high literature; or why. It is as if the author has tried to trap us into
quoting, in anthologies and English classes, beautiful passages that we
forget are obscene.

Or it is himself for whom he has set up these perverse challenges:
to mix slapstick and smut with nobility in such a way that they cannot
be separated; to lavish not only rhetoric but philosophy (the Thorotouch, the Sixteen Sleeps . . .) in contexts where they cannot

respectably be quoted. Also to make a first-person narrator present herself as the most adorable person in the world without our even noticing the difficulty; and to have us suspend our disbelief despite shameless unrealism. While the knight is struggling out of his armor with the intent of deflowering her, "from time to time I had to help him with a hard-to-reach zipper or point out that he was using a metric wrench on an English nut"—anachronism is deliberately made inextricable.

A preface to one of the versions claimed that "The general subject is the problem of beauty." That is ridiculous. There is an encyclopedia's worth about female sex-appeal and a surprising amount about the natural beauty of woods and weather. But beauty is much more than the sum of Woman and Landscape; it may be that all judgments of the good are aesthetic. This novel is not a contribution to aesthetics; it is at most a symphony of variations on the concept of "girl." Its only grappling with a "problem" is Applepeel's occasional wondering about why she is so singled out.

An even book it is not. A politically-correct book it is not. A professionally constructed book it is not. (There are claims that it must be a composite product, like a folk-epic or *The Miracle at Kahburg*, the pederastic "opera" that once circulated in Cambridge University: some parts *cannot* be by the hand that wrote other parts.) A realistic book it is not. "This is a remarkable book," boasts the preface, "and one of the remarkable things about it is how badly it starts." This is embarrassingly true. The kind of browser who opens books at random will be hooked almost anywhere, but the kind who starts reading at page one may say "This is crazy!" and give up before reaching the first inspired inventions.

Indeed, one of the notorious features of the book is that it *has* no beginning. It seems the beginning was considered so bad, by at least one reader, that it was simply dropped from the copies that were passed on. There is a "Preface," but then the story starts with what is presumably Chapter Two. (Or Three—the chapters are not numbered, so it is uncertain how many have been lost.) There is a tradition that the lost chapter was called "Spectacular Event"; and, from clues scattered later, one guess as to what happened in it is that Applepeel, at her May Eve birthday party, was mistakenly arrested for indecent exposure, whereas what was really exposed—and then destroyed by falling from a rooftop—was a model of her made by a spy. There have been other theories, and spurious "First Chapters." In any case, the early chapters that remain are not much less absurd.

This has to do with the way the thing originated. The claim is that it was started as a mere amusement, intended only for the eyes of a girl-friend, who had said "Let's write some pornography!" Then by stages it "took off," as Applepeel came alive in her creator's hands. It might be a pity to remove the traces of this spontaneous genesis, even if a better opening could be written. (As Applepeel hints it could: fending off her friend Saxie's questions, she suggests a half dozen other beginnings for her descent into nakedness, some of which would have made for a more gradual striptease.)

Presumably because of the pro-female bias—the mockery of all the males in the story—there is a rumor that "Rev. Hourn Gregory"* was actually a woman. This to me is out of the question. It is a male fantasy. (Though a female reader may enjoy imagining herself as Applepeel.)

Yet Applepeel *has* taken on a life of her own. Salvador de Madariaga said that there are four live men created by men: Hamlet, Faust, Don Quixote, and Sancho Panza. Perhaps this company is now joined, none too soon, by a female.

—Michal Drawwater

---

* Name apparently retained from a previous edition attributed to this person.

A UDACIOUS READER! you are in for a dose of merry lechery, without redeeming social value though with a redeemingly amiable character (the girl). It won't do you any harm—it has already done me a lot of good, for the medical profession is now almost agreed that laughter promotes health and adds to the length and sheen of life.* The same is probably true of erections; and fantasy too has its tonic function, so that no feminist need be reluctant to imagine herself in Applepeel's skin.

I started this one October day to amuse my friend Gift, or to head off her suggestion that we should write some pornography together. She may have envisioned a love-story with raunchy details, and looked at me a shade strangely after the first instalment, though she still has it in the pocket of her car and is no less—etc. However, the answer to the expected question of "Have you written any more of your 'pornography'?" which should have been "What?—oh, that!—no, of course not, forgotten all about it" turned into "As a matter of fact I did—couldn't seem to stop—it took on a life of its own . . ."

This madness overwhelmed me at the worst time, an October when I should have been, in fact was, spending days and nights striving to finish a sober and vital and enormous task, when it was disastrous to be doing anything other than working, throwing myself flat on my face till endurance returned, and working again. Yet here I was, postponing grave endeavors for a minute to take down Applepeel's latest disclosures, and coming to my senses an afternoon later still in her infectious

---

* Scientists have discovered this yet again. Research published in the journal *Heart* shows that it strengthens the diaphragm and has no known negative side-effects. Blood flow in the brachial arteries of twenty healthy volunteers who watched *King Lear* improved when they tickled each other. The two known cases of people who died laughing are the exception that, as Applepeel says, "improves the rule." "We don't recommend that you laugh and don't exercise, but you should try to laugh on a regular basis. Thirty minutes of exercise three times a week and fifteen minutes of laughter daily will probably save you," said "a humor therapist at Maryland University."

company. But I was having fun and that was not, after all, so reckless a policy; it substituted for sleep in keeping me sane, or at any rate in fine spirits. Thus in a couple of weeks most of this spilled out, though ever since it has been hard to refrain from going back and tightening the verbal screws.

Though I say it myself, this is a remarkable opus, and one of the remarkable things about it is how badly it starts. If you don't agree, wait and see how it goes on getting better until it is, in long patches, gorgeous. This happens because, like not a few other classics, it was begun as an idle diversion and then took off. You can hardly be expected to believe in Applepeel in the beginning, but she comes to life somewhere about the time she is scrubbed by the washerwomen, or earlier, at the moment when, tied hand and foot, she starts to fight back and "turn the tables"; and before long she will become for you, as for me, one of the most cheerful of life's realities.

Perhaps you would wish her to start, at least, as a twittering innocent who could be shocked and shamed. Well, she is sheltered, mother-trained, clothes-muffled, and ticklish; able to feel surprise as keenly as anyone; she can be panicked, enraged, bewildered, or embarrassed; she can even, with a little extra push, be shocked or shamed. But these emotions are so short-lived that suspicion is cast on their sincerity. Virginal she starts (and almost remains), but in view of her development it is too late to pretend that she could ever have been demure, helpless, squeamish, or even particularly attached to clothes.

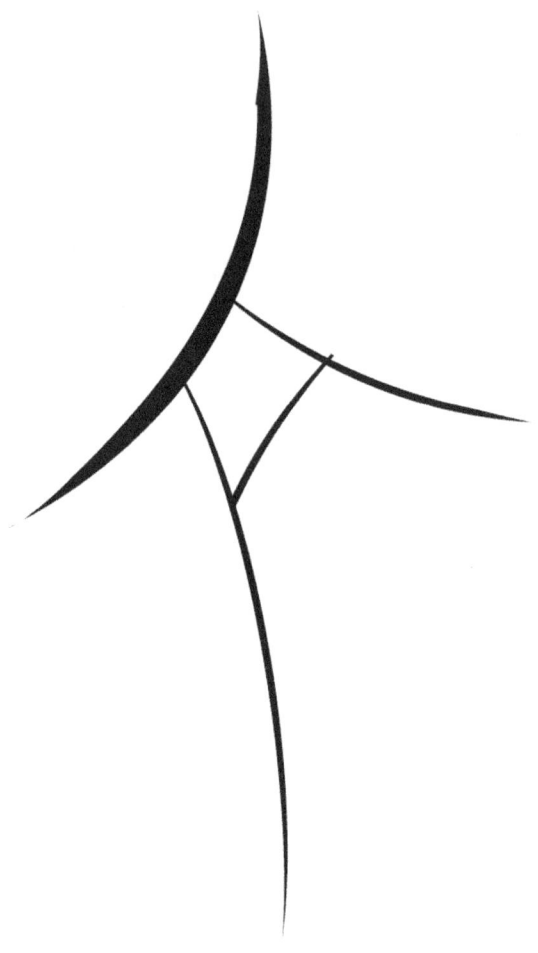

Chapter 2?*

I became aware of lying in a boat, and, eyes shut, smiling at something: smiling at relaxation. This must be the feeling that fills my body when it is asleep. When I'm awake I'm on my feet. As I was not on my feet, it must not yet be morning. And so something unaccustomed must have brought me awake. No doubt the being in a boat.

No, wait, not a boat: the air around was stagnant. I was in a bed, a sagging one. I put out a toe to find who else was—struck a wall. At that I opened my eyes. They saw nothing: and I remembered that I was in the depth not only of the night but of a jail. Things grew from the dark: first, the orange clown-suit they had given me. I had thrown it on the floor with the blankets. (I was of course far too hot, and everything that followed could have been one of my heat-dreams. Though heat-dreams are even more.) Then emerged a pale square: a small high window. Which direction was anything, and how much of the night had passed? I thought, I'll climb up and look at the stars; or see if the moon has risen, which it would at midnight.

The window would have been hard to reach, if it hadn't been in a corner. It opened south, and I could see a horizon of housetops with moonlight from the left. Above them already reared the stars of the Scorpion. The time was about two! Where was my apology, my release? Or could I really be guilty? Did you get life for what I had done?

Now this window had no bars. Why? It opened into a sunken space, but this seemed to be near a street. What was the catch? Maybe there would be something else, a chainlink fence, a moat. But surely I couldn't lose by squeezing on through to see. And I was going to, when I heard the lock of the door roll slowly over.

"Come on in! April Fool!" I called, or was ready to call. I waited a moment before calling, to see who was coming in.

A warder came in, but very quietly, and closed the door behind him, and locked it. I watched his dim form as he felt his way around. There was a lightswitch, why didn't he flip it?

He patted his way along the wall to the corner, and passed below me, patting his way along the next wall. Just before reaching the bed

* See the Introduction for a theory of what might have happened in the lost opening chapter or chapters.

he tripped over the pile of blankets. He stifled a curse and picked himself up. He found the bed. Then what did he do? You may not believe this. He took all his clothes off, except for his boots, and laid them down very quietly.

Now this was food for thought. This was some clue. This could not be just coincidence, this second shedding of clothes. Surely these two events, though contrasting—one on a rooftop, one underground; one mythical, and one all too verifiable—must in some way connect and lead to a solution of the puzzle.

The man's body was white, so I could make it out better, though I couldn't quite understand it. He began again to pat the bed. He touched it at first very cautiously indeed, and then he paused. He slid his hand over it; slow, then faster. And then he straightened up and swung his eyes once around the cell and raised them and saw me.

"Fur Karooka!"

His voice was like a shovel going into sludge. After this it sank to a whisper like a crackling of tobacco pouches.

"How in the hell did you get up there?"

"Why, I—"

He ran two steps and leaped.

I drew up my leg, and he only just missed.

His soles clattered to the floor. Though the leap had been a poor effort, he stood panting.

"Come on down," he said.

I thought about it.

Trying official sternness, he addressed me as Inmate, followed by a number. I had my suspicions about that.

He held up his arms: "Come *on*, I'll help yer down, it'll be all right," and on with persuasive phrases about how he wouldn't hurt me and what was I afraid of. His head was tipped back on his shoulders and below it his middle body wove about.

I answered: "I don't think I want to. I was thinking of taking a walk."

"Talk softer! You'll get in worse trouble if you try to escape."

"Try?—it doesn't seem difficult from here."

He shook his head and said, "They bolt the bed to the floor so you can't use it as a ladder, and they take out the bars so you can't hang a sheet around 'em, but they didn't think of a *bird*. No wonder you're unfrightnable. —Come on down and I won't tell on yer."

"You know," I said, "you're going to catch it too. That's a crime, what you're doing—being bare; I know because it's what I'm in for."

"Come down and let's do it together," he whispered.

"What's your name?" I asked.

"Furrock," he muttered.

I looked at him and he at me.

Then he curled over forward, and went down on his knees at the foot of the wall.

I had a feeling that before anyone other than me he would have had more care for his dignity.

"I'm going to have to go," I said. "Will you raise the alarm?"

He was groveling to the wall, stroking it. He licked it.

"Er," I asked, "when I go, will you raise the alarm?"

"Yes—oh—not if you—"

"Really? I'm only going home. Give me five minutes before you do it, okay?"

"Yes if you—"

"What?"

"Give me your clevel!"

"What's my clevel?"

"Your cleftveil."

"Oh. You really want that? All right!" And, fool that I am, I worked it out from under my skirt and dropped it to him. I can only say that the moon had moved out past a corner of the building and touched me.

I climbed up through the well, and found myself in a trash-bay, containing sacks and hoppers of shredded police documents. I was tempted to browse among them, and then I said, Get going, goof, they'll be out after you any moment! Then I thought, no, Mr. Furrock will surely wait ten minutes at least before, as it were, discovering my absence. So I lingered and pieced together a whole case about three postal workers and a parrot. Then I got a grip of myself and vaulted over the spiked gate into the street, crossed to the south side out of the moonlight, and ran east.

But when I came to a crossroads, I didn't take the way back to my house, where they would go. I turned to face the moon—took the way southeast to the edge of the town, and went out and sold myself to the Mongers.

Among the Mongers

THESE PEOPLE travel from place to place trading in whatever can be piled on a cart, such as hatbands, sketchbooks, china rabbits, elderberry wine, monoculars, family portraits, knitting-patterns, bottles of iodine, and old calendars; they carry fruit and vegetables in season, and they are willing to deal in jebels and chollops, though I didn't yet know what kind of sweetmeats these might be.

I didn't exactly sell myself to the Mongers—I wouldn't have had anywhere to put the money. I just had an idea of asking them for asylum.

In the fraying streets I encountered what I thought was my first Monger. I'll call him the Derelict Monger. He was a slight stooped man in a patched coat, engaged in prospecting trashcans.

When I asked him the way to the Monger encampment, he looked at me in silence, and then he shuffled up to me and threw his arms around me. There was a struggle longer than it needed to be (I didn't want to be rough with him) before I shook him off and said, "I can walk, thank you." It would have been easier for me to carry *him!* He thought some more and then led me down past a lumberyard and bushes to a hollow by a misty stream.

There was a shade-shelter, a flat roof of poles and twigs, with a lantern hanging from a corner, and a dense smell coming from a stew that went *clof-clof* on a brazier. Mongers even at this time of night were mending pans and plucking chickens. They looked slowly up at us.

The Derelict Monger halted at the edge of the light. He took my hands and lifted them above my head, as if I was a winner. I didn't resist; I thought it was a ritual. Leaving his skinny left hand to detain my wrists, he stooped down with his right and lifted my skirt.

The Mother Monger, sitting massively on a wicker chair, signaled: "Put it down." She preferred not to see the goods while haggling, especially if the seller thought them irresistible.

"She got no shred," said another Monger (they use the vulgar word for a clevel)— "why?"

"Thought she'd look better without it," said the Derelict Monger.

"She does."

"Well then—"

"Well then, get out before we—*geek*," a throat-slitting gesture.

The Derelict Monger dropped my wrists and began to shuffle backward. But I burst out: "Hey, aren't you going to give him anything, you rats?"

"No mam."

"Give him some supper!" I said. "Can't you see he's hungry?"

I advanced on them with my hands on my hips. They were used to women like this. They shrugged and steered the Derelict Monger back and sat him on a bucket and fed him.

"And what about me?" I said when I had seen to this. "Am I to stay with you or not?" They were speechless. "The night is well worn on," I said, "and so am I, and I'd like somewhere to sleep. Do you speak English?" I made a snoring sound.

They called up a little Mongress, and she and I walked away between the carts. Above us the moon climbed with tomorrow written on it. We came to what seemed to be a four-poster bed.

It stood out on the open ground under the moonlight, rather public, but it had curtains around it. She pulled them back to show me that there was straw on the boards, and here she said I could sleep.

I was sure I couldn't, because it was hardly what I was used to, and also because my emotions weren't in order; also because of my unwashed face, and my bladder (faintly ringing), and the bit of sleep I'd already had, and my nightgown—for, believe it or not, there was a time when I used to wear something even *in bed*. And yet more reasons, but no sooner did I begin to count them than I was asleep.

When I awoke, my good sense had caught up with me and I was ready to go home.

What had woken me was a ceasing of motion. The four-poster bed was really an open box on wheels, pulled by a tall mule. The high sunshine of the first morning of May sifted in through the curtains.

I parted them cautiously and saw wayside flowers, a hedge, a gate, a steep field, a nearby horizon. We had halted somewhere on a country road. No Mongers were in sight, though a smell and sound of frying told me they were not far off.

I wasn't tied. What was to stop me from slipping into the field and running? Soon I realized what was. While I slept, hands had removed my skirt.

I had been tied by an untying.

I have never, before or since, experienced such a powerful blush, even when there were eyes to see it. I knew myself at once terribly freed and terribly captive. Freed into a locked career, like a cannonball.

I sank back and lay cooling.

The panicky sting left, but the heat remained. I was sticky, after the night in the straw. I peered out again. On the bank where the sun had not yet licked it up sparkled the maydew. Here and there in it the little Sirii fixed me with their slowly changing colors. I couldn't resist it, I slid out and plunged my hands into the grass, and ran them over my face and down my body. It was so refreshing that I carried some of it to my tongue too; it was sweet. Because I didn't know it was magic, it was. I ran it behind my nails, and turned my fifth fingers in my earholes.

I heard a step, and dived back into the cart. The Younger Monger was coming by, a handsome swarthy nomad with a red neckerchief.

"You've taken my skirt!" I said.

"My sister is mending the ladder in it right now. How did that happen?—climbing out some window?"

"So you'll give it back?"

"Probably not," he admitted impudently.

"You've stolen it!"

"Taken custody of it. Fine quilted piece, we couldn't resist it; it'll fetch a good price in the souk. But we left your earrings on you."

"So you did," I said, feeling them. "Why?"

"Because they look so nice. They'll be worth more on you than off you. —Good day, citoyenne, are you ready for lunch? Have you any other needs?"

"Yes, I need clean straw."

I hoped just to tip out my soiled straw and receive a fresh bale through the curtains. But two urchins were sent clambering in. Even at seven or eight, they had the wizened Monger face, like monkeys, and I couldn't tell whether they grinned, as they drew the moist straw from under me and introduced the dry, with more frictive confusion than was necessary. It was hay of the pinkish *vulvul*-grass, curved slippery sheaves ending in clouds of seedheads.

I was surprised at myself for lying so comfortably on it, as we trundled on. When I was tired of lying, there was height enough to stand; and for exercise I seized a beam and pulled myself up to the roof, stretching my toes to another beam, and hoping that no Monger chose such a moment to put his eye to a chink of the curtain.

At this time they called me Cheyenne or Shy Anne—I'm not sure which was meant, since they sound the same. It could have been my other-tribeness they were mocking, or my reluctance to come out of the cart skirtless. In Monger body-language, or body-slang, it was one-hand-across-the-breasts-and-the-other-on-the-cunt, followed by two-horns-on-the-head.

I was already farther from home than I had ever been. We took byways into the hills to get safely away from my town. But it turned out to be a smugglers' route, and as we were going up a track on the shady side of a troop of beeches we were overtaken by an excise officer. The Mongers had time to gag me. After poking through trays of kerchiefs and candied dates and whetstones and log tongs, he said: "And that dray?" "Hay," said the Younger Monger, "you can see some of it sticking out." "And parsnips? I can see one of those sticking out too." This was my toe, which I had managed to protrude.

"Yes, hay, cores, rind—little consignment of fodder for lechers' troughs."

Lechers?—though I had farming cousins, I hadn't heard of those. Something like shoats or hoggets?

"Well," said the customs man, "I must satisfy myself you haven't stashed anything illegal under it." And he put his head in. I had rolled onto my front so as to conceal my worst; I looked back at him over my gag, but he never caught my eye or spoke. I yelled but through my bound lips it sounded like the calm bawling of a French horn. After thoroughly satisfying himself that there was nothing illegal *under* the hay, he withdrew.

"Applepeel, mainly; that's what I'll write. The duty on that is just two smackers a pound." Coins clinked. They were paying him (steeply, it's true) just for appleskins! Really, for jobs like this does the government have to hire the blind?

He went away with my hope of rescue. They took my gag off and I should have used every moment in praying or else in nagging my captors. But I'm not one to worry about calamities till they happen, perhaps because in my upbringing they never really had. So I let myself be lulled, and enjoyed what there was to enjoy—the grumbling motion, the gypsy pie, even the sensation of sprawling out before me (or behind me, depending on which way I was lying) the far half of my body, free of all obscuration, with ridgings of the hay between my legs, in the filtered glow of the sunshine. I knew that to be abroad in the world defenseless from the waist down was to be floating a river toward a cataract, but I never doubted that after it I would still be afloat. I knew the risk ahead was, approximately, that there might be touching of this body of mine, but when I tried it, using the hay to simulate a stranger, it didn't seem so calamitous.

The track climbed a valley head. At sundown we bivouacked on the high cool shoulder of a tor and they invited me out to the fire.

Portrait in the Fire

" NO, *SIRS*," I said.

"Look," said the Younger Monger (his name was Harrison Monger),

"you might as well relax while you can, before you're back among humans."

"Aren't you human?"

"It's generally supposed we ain't; subhuman is what it's generally agreed we is. Anyways we don't oolya." "Ool me, what does that mean?" "We doesn't bemate you. So don't be embarrassed. Just think of yourself as stepping out in front of your cat or your pet mandrill," he said as he handed me down from the cart. "Make room for her, sisters and brothers. Yes, warm your cunt or your glushes, whichever you like," he courteously encouraged me. His mother, Dereka Monger, great matriarch, gave me a sausage and a stick to toast it on.

On logs or cross-legged in the dust sat the dark Mongerly clan.

Some talked quietly by yawning to and fro among themselves; at the fringe a closer conversation was conducted in tickles, for these too are Monger sentences.

Aside from their language, they seemed like other people. I asked Harrison, "What's the difference between humans and Mongers?"

"They are the animals with hair around their brain," he said.

"Yes, but so are Mongers."

"Mongers is what I mean. Humans has hair around *part* of their brain—*most* of them does—and also their mandibles and secks and lymphnodes."

And I saw that, yes, his scalp ran into his eyebrows.

The blaze was huge: whole junipers leaned together at the middle of it, and bushes of furze exploded as they were thrown on. The Mongers were hiding from no excisemen in these hills.

"Do you have a fire like this every night?" I asked.

"No." For today was Beltane, the feast of the manhood of the sun.

"What are you painting there?"

An aunt Monger was sizing particle-boards and an uncle Monger was drawing an outline on one of them with a stick dipped in black axlegrease.

"These are things we sell a lot of; we need to build up our stock of them before we reach the warm country. They're used for blocking up fireplaces."

"Oh, yes," I said, "Hearthstoppers, we call them; we have one in our house. Lots of people use them in the summer."

"These are the only things we sell that we make ourselves."

"But, you know," I said, looking at the emerging design, "that doesn't look like feet. I thought they always had to have feet painted on them." Every Hearthstopper I had seen had those feet (sometimes winged), leaping away up the chimney.

"That's your traditional northern Hearthstopper," the Younger Monger explained to me. "Further south they don't have them Leaping Feet, they have the Woodshaving Woman."

And he told me that Hearthstoppers were invented by a young husband who was building furniture to please his bride. He built a settee, and the blond shavings he planed from the wood reminded him of something else; and so having next to block a fireplace with a board he drew a curvy figure, brushed on four patches of glue—scalp, armpits, *matter*—and shook the shavings over. His wife, even though she was a blonde, disapproved and threw it out, and only then did he paint the less provocative Feet on another board. But the Shavings Venus was pulled from the trashcan by a Monger passing along the back alley, and spread in southerly cultures, even where there are no fire-places.

"It makes good kindling if they decide to have a fire after all."

"Stand still," said the Uncle Monger. And I realized he was using me for model. Sometimes he held up an oily thumb to proportion me.

After a while he said: "Haw kay. Got the crotch and the head, now just take off them cloves and hold your arms up so I can do the armpits." (Mongers don't talk Human quite proper.)

"Uh-*uhh*," I said (meaning "No, that *isn't* cool").

And to show that the posing was at an end I walked over and looked at his smutty sketch. Though nothing but an outline, it was surprising-ly fetching, venereal, yet clearly me.

But it was flat, without bulk or sheen, though my body must have been rivered with hot light down its fireward verticals.

"Tell you what," I said, "I'll pose the way you want, if you'll add something that I suggest."

So I took off my shirt and breastlet and lent them to a little Mon-germaid, and stood with the fire on my right and my arms upstretched. Around me in the lurching shadows the faces were carved by flame out of the night. And from my fingers, as I raised my eyes, the sparks of the fire poured up to mingle with the stars of the Lion and the Lock.

So simply I had acquiesced in standing for the first time quite clothesless among spectators. But they're only Mongers, I told myself. In any case I was clamped where I was until the Uncle Monger finished my arms and torso.

When at length he did so, the Aunt Monger handed him the gluepot, and he daubed the triangle—or chraw yangle, as he called it— and the scrawls of glue around my blank face. "She ain't got no under-arms to speak of, but we'll pretend," he said, and dabbed it there too. Then they brought the sack of beautiful curly shavings and sprinkled them on, shook off the loose ones, sprinkled them back on till each of the four places was grown.

A Woman.

My right side was baked by having been kept to the fire. I walked over to join the admiring ring.

"Nice?" the Younger Monger leered.

"Yes," I said. "Not me, though, as I'm not blonde."

"No, that is a pity. Humans prefer blondes, we understand. Ain't that so?"

"Yes. In stories anyway."

"Now, what is your artistic suggestion? Will blond shavings do for it?"

"Yes, certainly, since they're to be highlights. Find me the longest ones, and press them out flat." Though I couldn't see myself standing in the fireglow, the extent of redness along the right of my arm and side and legs was a guide. Each long shaving, flattened, had a curve. I knelt and showed where they should go, and the Uncle glued them and pressed them. Two slivers, the semicircles of the last-dawn moon and of tiny Venus within, picked out my breast and nipple.

Now the hieroglyphic nymph now not only bristled in the right places, but bulged and gleamed.

"Holy coconut!" exclaimed several Mongers. "Beaut! She's inflat-ed! Will these sell! They'll cause the most excitement since the General Erection of 1963!"

(The Mongers have borrowed the habit of swearing, but they think a swear is Holy anything; so if something surprises a Monger, you can expect to hear "Holy carob! Holy crucible! Holy beadle! Holy croco-dile! Holy Roman Empire!"—at least.)

Hastily I stepped away and borrowed back from the little Monger-maid my breastlet and shirt, shaken with a slight doubt as to the non-humanness of the Mongers. But their emotion was commercial; they settled to making copies of the Firelight Woodshaving Hearthstopper, while I clambered back into my cart for the night.

I had little trouble with the Mongers. The two Urchins were the ones that came closest to exhibiting ordinary human mischief (perhaps they had a strain of ordinary human blood).

Sometimes I opened my curtains and sat with my legs dangling as we traveled. I had had in the past, like everyone, shame-dreams of half-nakedness; the real thing seemed more bearable, just as it is easier to cope with one's own pain than another's. Sometimes, since the Mongers took no notice and the hills were bare but for a remote dog or shepherd, I walked up and down the line of our caravan, letting beads run through my fingers or reading reeskay greeting-cards. There were plenty of skirts for sale if I had been able to buy one. The cart behind mine was loaded with what looked like fat plums, but though black they felt too hard to be ripe; and I hadn't had enough exercise to be hungry.

Story Mongerized

L IFE WAS interesting with the Mongers. I had problems to which I should have been giving attention, but I didn't bother because there were so many things to look at and listen to. I imagined traveling with the band for the whole summer, learning their lore, gaining acceptance as a Mongeress, escaping at last to write my Monger Monograph. So it was only toward the end of the second afternoon that I took a siesta in my cart and lay back and brought my mind to bear on my problems. First, how to escape. —Shelving that, I turned to something easier: what explanation, or lies, to have ready for when I did get home; or for that matter, when I encountered another human. I closed my eyes and had a couple of useful dreams about it.

When I opened my eyes I saw a tall haggard Monger who stood gazing at me. "Do you mind?" I said and began reclosing the curtains. But he invited me to come down for supper and stories.

"Stories?—good!" I said, jumping up. "Yes," he said as he led me into the ring by the fire, "we need to do some rehearsing. See, at the fairs when we've finished selling articles we sometimes sell stories too. I'm the one who keeps the stock up, and we've been in dry territories lately, except for you. We thought, how about you tell us your story."

"Gosh, I haven't invented one."

"But your story of what brought you out. What made a nice girl like you leave house and mother and fall in with the Mongers?"

"Oh, my real story—the story of me. But I haven't yet discovered that either. It was started by an as yet unexplained event." I told them about it.

"That's no good," said the Storymonger. "You can't leave the audience without a connection. Everything has to be neatly tied up, however crazy. You'll have to think of something better. You've got a beginning, you've got a end, all you got to do is find a middle. Tell the people how you came to be naked."

"I'm only half naked."

"All the better. They can come back for Part Two the next day."

"Look," I said, "if I'm to stand telling stories I want my clothes back. Storytelling is a respectable profession, yes?"

"Touché," said the Storymonger. "We'll worry later who gets to do the telling; point is, the theme's a winner for human markets. So give it a try. Get your clothes off quick or slow—stage by stage, or an explosion, whichever works prettier. Heave ho! One, two, three, go!"

"You talk as if it's like the broad-jump—just take off running and pick up speed and leap and shut my eyes and I'll get there."

"That's it. Start from some little thing that really happened and make a rush. You might accidentally hit on what you'd like to know."

"Okay, I'll try." I had expected to be a listener, not a teller, but this could be fun too.

I paced in front of them with my hands clasped behind my back, and said:

"Of course I wasn't born naked—"

"Great beginning, great beginning," murmured the Mongers.

"Of course I wasn't born naked; I lived pretty well clothed until my eighteenth birthday party, which was also to be the feast of my betrothal to Fortesant."

"Betrothal, what does that mean?"

"I hardly know, are you going to keep interrupting me? He was sitting opposite to me and he presented me with his gift, which was a pair of earrings (he should have given me an engagement-ring but he hadn't found one or someone had cheated him) and I tried to put them on. The fellow on my left helped me with one earring, and then the fellow on my right helped me with the other; his name is Richardling and he's a great cackhanded oaf. He fumbled it and the earring fell down my shirt, and he tried to grab it. And so Fortesant took a swing at him and there was a bit of a brawl."

"Not 'a bit of a brawl,'" the Storymonger prompted me, "'a terrible brawl,' or at least 'a regular brawl.'"

"No, it was nothing much, they never are. We were eating and chatting again a minute later. It didn't lead to anything."

"Exactly," said the Storymonger patiently. "Since you don't know what did lead to anything, this will have to, see?"

I tried to think. I sat down in front of them and frowned. But I couldn't see how these trivial highjinks could lead to the rushing into the garden and the strange accusation.

"Then forget that," said the Storymonger. "Skip it."

"How can I forget it?"

"Let's start by seeing if we can magnify this brawl, and these earrings. Where did your solemn admirer get them?"

"He said he got them from some pedlars."

The Mongers nudged each other.

"Let's take a look at them. Why are they called 'rings'?"

"I don't know," I said, "you're right: topologically they're spirals.

No, helixes. Turning opposite ways, so they're not the same as each other."

"Maybe you got them on the wrong ears and that screwed everything up."

"Ridiculous!"

"Beautiful, aren't they," said the she-Monger who returned them to me.

"Rather cheap," I said, "gold only on the outside, I think—they look greenish where they're worn."

"Beautiful. 'The guest on my left hung this sparkling thing to my earlobe. There was a hush, and every eye became fixed, as if discovering it for the first time, on the satiny skin of my cheek.'"

"'And when it came to the other earring,'" said another Monger, "'I had willing help from the guest on my right; but his hand shook, the ring cascaded into my corsage, his hand followed it, he— ' Did he take the chance to open up your shirt?"

"Oh, hardly!"

"This shirt, now. Where did you get *that?*"

"Anything wrong with it?"

"Well, it's one idiotic color."

"It *is* a shade excessive," I admitted.

"Excessive—it's bloodless, if you can say that of a green." There was general condemnation of my shirt. "Sapless," said another Monger. (Yet he wore an orange headband and I thought, is there such a thing as a too-much color in clothes?) "It needs to be a real green, a full-bodied green, then it'd go with that hair of hers." "Her milk has got into it." "No wonder they wanted to tear it off. 'Rummaging between my breasts, he pretended a need to disarrange my flimsy chemise. Whereupon my noble suitor sprang up to aim a blow, the table tilted, wine flew— '"

"We didn't have wine," I said, "my mother wouldn't dream of allowing it."

"'—wine flew, there were curses and crashes, the officers of the watch were in upon us; in a trice our hands were cuffed behind our backs— '"

"You got it," said the Storymonger; "and she was marched along the street with her shirt still off her shoulder, couldn't do anything about it—"

"And her earring spiraling down inside—"

"She's hauled before the Beak—"

"Judge Guilth (we know him), she doesn't expect no justice from him—"

"He cuts short the tipsy maunderings of the youths and goes straight for the root of the affray: the girl."

"A beadle measures the visible percent of her bosom. Anything more than forty-five is a felony, see—"

"'Aren't you ashamed, miss?' says the judge. 'No, sir,' she falters— 'Then stand up straight!'— 'If I do that, your honor, my nipples will pop out'— 'Cheeky girl! You're still trying to cause a riot. Clap her in clink.' Good, we got her in jail."

Sitting in the dust before the circle of Mongers, I was staring from one to another.

"She's flung in a gloomy dungeon and she sobs and strives to chafe her manacles on the stones, but all that does is shake her shirt down to her waist, so she puts her head on her knees and weeps herself to sleep." "And at midnight she's startled by the horrid sound of an 'acksaw. Yes, it's Fortesant and Richardling, sobered up and coming to rescue her. She pleads with them not to make things worse than they already are— 'Don't be such phunt-heads!' she tells them, but they are determined to snatch catastrophe from the jaws of inconvenience. Fortesant climbs in, he makes out her earring gleaming in the dark, he goes down on one knee. 'This isn't the time to propose,' she says, 'anyway, didn't you propose already?' 'I'm giving you a leg up to the window,' he explains."

"What about my manacles?" I asked. "You haven't got them off yet."

They waved as if to say "Mechanics! They can wait for the next version" and rushed on: "'The innocent don't run away,' says she — 'No,' he says, 'and that's how the innocent lose their, hm! innocence. Dost hear yon footsteps?—a prisoner, approaching with no legal intent.'"

"A jailer, you mean," I corrected. "They're not the same, you know. She's the prisoner, he's the jailer."

"Well, while you argue which kind of nogood he is, he's unlocking the door—a turnkey who plans to turn his key in *her*. So she scrambles through the winder, the jailer bursts in, he sees her hineys vanishing skyward and he makes a grab—"

"Never before has she felt a hand, except maybe that of her ancient nursemaid, touch any of her but her hand—"

"And so, Richardling tugging one way and the jailer the other, she comes free but without the inmost of her garments!"

(A complicated thought occurred to me. Can you dream about talking in your sleep?)

"Now this Richardling, he takes over. I see him hurrying her away, and her saying what about my beloved down there, and Richardling says, 'Don't worry about him, his dad's got influence, he'll get out tomorrow and with his virginity, which you might not have—be thankful you got away without losing nothing' (he doesn't know about her clevel)."

"But on the way home he draws her into an alley to claim a kiss."

"So she has to whang him on the head with a tile." (There was some tension between female and male Mongers as to the direction of the story.)

"Meanwhile, the alarm has been given, the streets are full of hue and cry—"

"What, all for one little humaness? No, there's just an officer on a horse and a bow-legged footman. He's the one who burst into the cell (his name is, say, Gorough), his eye has been blacked by Fortesant's fist, but he's got enough night vision left to spot her. He nudges the officer, the officer says 'Apprehend.' It's quite a chase, but they got her surrounded—"

"The cavalry blocks the alley and directs the operations of the infantry—"

"And now they got her tied across the saddle. Where do they take her?"

"Well, they *start* for headquarters, but they go by a lonely way beside the city wall. Her face looks not bad even upside down, and the fellow walks alongside it and says, 'Hello, my name's— ' McGurral, or what did you say his name was?"

"Gorough. And the officer says: 'Get away, what for does she want to know your filthy name.' 'Don't she look dainty,' says Gorough, 'arched over like that, between your legs?—sir.' The officer bends over her and he says: 'And my name, mademoiselle, is Commissioner Gottany.' She thanks him."

"What's this, introducing themselves? Don't be wet! Get on with it."

"'There's a quiet corner back there by a turret, sir,' says Gorough. 'It won't be quiet if she yodels,' says the officer, knotting his scarf around her mouth. 'Well,' he says nervously, 'take her down, we don't have much time, the watch will be coming.' 'Not till four,' says Gurrah, 'so may I make a suggestion? We'll leave her over the horse for a while, so pretty.' And he tells the officer: 'Take your time, sir. I'm so glad you're here, sir!' 'Yes, yes!' the officer mutters, 'I, ah—I'll begin.' And steeling himself to ignore her curses—" "She's gagged." "I know, but he knows she's cussing—he plays a second hand up her leg, all the way until it touches those frizzy hairs, see, that she's got."

"These?" I asked.

"Yes, it's interesting, isn't it, the other hairs that she's got aren't frizzy. And leaps back." "What leaps back?" "His hand, with an imprecation. 'Furrock!' 'Sir?' 'This is not a virgin!' 'Very quick of you, sir. I didn't think you was so edgicated.' 'This is a whore!' 'No, sir, surely not. You know what our best gurrels are like. Doubt she even knows what her cunt is.'"

"That's true," I said. "Until you told me, I thought it was a sort of boat."

"'A whore! She has no drawers on! The type that goes around with nothing on under, not even a shred, ready to throw her skirt up for the workers! Like this!' And he throws her skirt up so that it cracks like a sail before slumping across her stomach. 'I got to admit she's got no drawers on,' says Gorough. (He's got them in his pocket.) He says: 'Did you really have to have a vurragin, sir?' 'I don't want a whore!' screams the officer; 'she may have pox or pocks or some four-letter disease! Sell her, that's the best we can do with her, that's what she does with herself!' So they take her off the horse and carry her down the postern stair, out onto the grassy moat where the Mongers are camped . . ."

I caught my head nodding and jolted myself out of it just in time (don't think I missed anything; I guess I was sold to the Mongers at a fair profit for my hometown police). I got to my feet and clapped. The Mongers grinned shyly. "Was it any good?"

"Yes, you Mongerized my story nicely. I guess I could tell it that way."

"It wasn't a bit—nasty?" said the Storymonger anxiously.

"Oh no, why?"

"So you didn't understand it?"

"Not the details, but I got the general idea. You think I'm something to sell."

They fidgeted their feet. "That's all right," I said, "I knew that already, you're Mongers, you can't help it. I feel *I'll* win in the end, but anyway we'll play the game. —But now I've *got* to get to bed." "Goodnight," they said. "We'll see about part two of the story, tomorrow maybe."

My foolish serenity was broken on the third day. Descending into another country—whose ways were very different from mine, as I expected since I had been taught that human kind Romances and depraves as you travel south and east—we began to meet its traffic.

I was propped on my cushion, reading one of the paperbacks from the book-cart. It was a light tale of love, pleasant enough though scarcely realistic. I took little notice of the halt and the talking, till suddenly the rear curtain was opened.

I slapped the book over my, or down onto my junction, also with the other hand scooping some hay over me, and stared wide-eyed at the customer who stood framed in the sunlight. He had already seen, and he bargained bravely, but he was soon brushed off in expectation of higher bidders.

Our by-road came out onto the highway where folk were journeying in both directions, and I didn't again pick up my book with much attention. Sometimes wayfarers called out "Whatcha got there, friends?" and were answered quietly "Girl sans skirt; shilling a look" and were allowed a look a heartbeat long, but must have had no more shillings, for our wheels didn't even stop rolling. (Some of these glimpsers didn't give up, but followed along, hoping somehow to outwit the Mongers.) But now we came to a firm halt, and this time the voices were either side: we had met a merchant coming one way and a gentleman's retinue the other. The curtains along both sides went remorselessly back, and I was exposed in bright sun on a stage with two fronts.

The Hay

READY, I had mounded the hay over most of me. The audience didn't object. I learned that just a part of me—face or even foot—could suggest the whole envelope of my skin.

"Well, are you speechless?" asked the Younger Monger. The marquis massaged his jaw to unlock it and said: "A babe in a basket! A delightfully packaged gift." "Not quite a gift," said the Monger.

"If the face is a promise of the body," said the merchant, "I bid—"

The opening bids were already higher than I had thought numbers reach. But the Mongers stood looking at the sky as if they hadn't heard. There were second bids, a bit higher; then the Younger Monger spat on the ground and, turning, made a motion to the two Urchin Mongers who changed my hay. They ran and ducked under the mule's traces and came up through the curtain behind me and mastered my wrists, which they tied (with swatches of hay) to the forward posts. And now I knew that worse would not be long in coming. All looked benevolently on me (at least, they were smiling), breathless as I was and upbreasted on the cushion. The Mongers made a "Yes, go ahead" gesture, and the merchant stepped forward and flicked my hay aside.

In the same instant as the chorus of approbation, I desperately twisted over at the waist, saving my kneecap-side from ravishing eyes by pressing it into the hay.

An incoherent whoop from the marquis made me fear that this had been somehow rash. He doubled his bid.

"Now we're getting somewhere," said the Younger Monger, and glanced at the merchant. The merchant had been taken aback by the sudden rise, so the Monger added: "*She's ticklish,*" as if that was worth another twenty percent.

"Caught you out!" said the merchant. "You started by telling us she's never been touched."

"True."

"So how can it have been established that she's ticklish?"

At a further signal, the Urchins took up hay and showed.

Cries of joy broke out, and on each side the merchant and the marquis accepted the hay-sprays and reached in, at first taking turns, then tickling unceasingly and commingledly. Frantically I threw myself over to end the intolerably light caressings to my glushes, and immediately they were at my groin, and I threw one thigh across it, but that allowed them to tickle both over and under, and I threw up both thighs, and they tickled my crotch under, and I threw myself flat and the tick-lebreeze swept over my navel and started cuntward, and I threw myself over again, pleading and, through my distress, fountaining with laugh-ter.

Whichever face I turned up, the tickling was unendurable; but when I rolled on one hip they could tickle both: the marquis shed his seeds in my fur and the merchant nearly lost his whole stalks in my cleft; so I spun the opposite way—and found this was just what they wanted. Each time he saw my cunt anew the merchant raised his bid, and each time I writhed over the marquis invited the gods to see the shapes he saw, until they drove him to a bid which even I would have considered accepting.

The Younger Monger made a sign in the air like a conductor closing a symphony— (In the same moment the Mother Monger sneezed. You might have thought it was from the hayseeds we had set flying, but I knew it was a word in the secret Monger language of sniffs, belches, throat-clearings, and other bodily expressions that I've already men-tioned; and the Younger Monger went over to her and they conferred.) —the climax was reached, the merchant had given up, yet he and everyone tickled on, all the male and female Mongers for whom this was a last chance— (The Mother alone stood with folded arms, con-templating the throng and myself only as part of it. But she was said to be more than two hundred and twenty years old.) —and travelers who had alighted from their coaches to join. To tell the truth, the touch of the vulvul-grass, soft and thorough, like a cat's back, was not distressing to me any more, but rather the opposite; but they couldn't tell the dif-ference. All at last desisting, they wiped their brows and swore dazedly, closing their eyes to repicture my convulsions.

I couldn't speak—couldn't even sigh *"Ayhi . . ."*—so wished to wave my hand for the curtains, but it was tied, so waved one leg. The marquis took it from the air and with a sort of reverence held and kissed the foot of the body he had acquired. My first kiss, on a toe. And he did close the curtains; and I lay in cooling sweat and convulsions still subsiding.

He put in his head, which hung like a goofy moon as he clasped the curtains around it, simply staring down on me and saying "Aah . . ." Recovering his brains, he told me that he thought of buying the cart too, "of happy memories," hitching it to his carriage for the rest of the journey to his manor, and might let me live in it for ever.

I was too limp to move, and lay with my legs apart.

"Would you," he said, "lie as you lay before?—half over?"

"Why?" I said, beginning to shut my eyes.

"To let me see the parts I chiefly bought," he replied in an enigmatic pentameter.

"Untie my hands and I'll lie all halves over," I murmured.

He did, and I rolled slumbrously to my front, and dreamed of things that still fanatically caressed me.

Auctioned

BUT IN no time I was disturbed by an altercation. The Mongers had told the marquis: "No sale." They had realized how much they could really get for me, even if I wasn't a blonde.

They had learned that there was a caravansary ahead, where the turnpike met another at the fringe of a town, and if the marquis was prepared to offer a fair price he could do so in competition with the capitalists who would be lodging there.

The marquis and his retinue were noisier than the Mongers, but less dangerous. And soon I was being trundled through a gateway into a din of clamor and color. I kept inside my curtains, but I couldn't help peeping to see what the sounds meant. Porters were staggering to their feet under crates or letting them crash to the dust, goats were bleating and cocks cackling, slimy eels were being slung into tubs ("Come on, Bumfred, grab 'em—*ooweeoo!*—you're like a princess with a navvy's prick!"); everywhere, activity and bad language ("You dropped it on my toe, you son-of-a-camp-bed!"). There were entertainers too: in a corner of the yard the Society for Creative Anachronism mummed for a few idlers, and from the gallery, which ran on posts around the upper tier of the hostelry, the scream of a magnificent fat contralto sailed out over the crowd:

                                                                 beh!
     Ruuuuuuuuu
     Ru
          u
                         u
                                   by!
     Are you mad at your man?

We threaded our way across. The cart was backed up to a door, and the rear curtains were held open like a short tunnel to conduct me straight in without giving busybodies a glimpse.

But inside we came face to face with a human, bald and portly, carrying a receipt book in his hand and a pencil behind his ear. He was the caravansary manager. When he saw me, he first—or almost first—glanced nervously at the Mongers, to check whether he had permission to look me up and down; and then he looked me up and down.

I thought I was going to be sold to him, and he looked as if he hoped so. "Yur, we got a opening for a maid," he said.

The Mongers didn't deign to speak. They smiled and one of them took his greasy chin and gave it a squeeze. He turned yellow and backed into the room.

It had dark paneling and only one leaded window at the courtyard end. "V-v-vis is your reserved diningroom," said the manager; "will vese arrangements be satisfactory?" On a long table was laid a lunch of the kind of things that Mongers like and I can get used to. "Yes," said the Younger Monger; "but we got something else we need to arrange, you and me," and the two of them went away into an office. The rest of us took our places on the benches, me in the middle of one side, and began to apply our bad table-manners to the food. The Mongers seemed out of place indoors, and I felt more attention directed on me than usual from the row of sharp eyes.

It didn't deter me from eating, but after a while I said, "Fellas, is there something wrong? Otherwise, would y'stop staring?"

Sheepish, they shook their eyes loose, and one, a halfwit called Billy Monger, doubled down and took a look at me *under* the table.

"Billy!" I said, kicking him, "how primitive!" I knew the Mongers well enough that I could insult them and live.

The Younger Monger came back from making his arrangements and sat down on my right. "Well," I asked, "what happens this afternoon?"

"Horse-fair," he said.

"Oh, good, I like horses! Shall I be able to see them from here?" I got up and went around his back toward the window.

"Sure. You can even take a walk outside and pet them. Pretty things, horses and ponies."

"Why, thank you, that *is* nice!" I perceived that the Mongers had gone careless and I should be able to get away from them in the crowd. "What about you, you'll all be resting, won't you?—business all finished."

"No, it's our big time."

"But you haven't got any horses to sell, have you?" So far as I knew, the Mongers had only a mule or two.

"We have one very valuable filly," he said. — "Let's go." He went to the door and opened it for me. I almost stepped through, but halted, remembering my state.

"I'll need to borrow—"

The Mongers, rising in a body, propelled me through the doorway and twenty feet into the sunlight.

I was the Filly.

The first impression I had was not a sight-impression but a sound-impression. You could think of a momentarily bare stretch of sand, before the sucked-back wave crashes upon it.

Then my eyes took in the scene. It was materially different. The courtyard had been cleared of bales, barrels, carts, cages, and bicycles; only a few cabbage leaves and chicken feathers drifted in the dust. The street gate was barred and there was a police-lookout on the roof. I found myself alone in the middle. Alone, that is, in being female and being naked below the waist.

The throng surrounded me in a circle.

Sometimes I wonder, looking out of myself at the picture-show on my eyes: Is this the present?

How dreadful, how really dreadful! The Mongers had lied to me, but what was the use of taxing them with that when it was the least of their crimes. I got ready to scream—no, weep, wouldn't that be right?—and then I thought maybe I should whinny instead, and that brought on a risk of giggling, so I ended by keeping quiet. I even managed to shut my mouth tight, though I could feel the corners struggling whether to go up or down.

I had a circle of space to myself, not more than half a dozen yards across; then began the throng, and built up, like the breaking wave. The front row consisted entirely of millionaires, yet humble ones, for they were content to squat on the ground. Behind them stood drovers and ostlers; potboys and ragamuffins filled the corners, swarming up among the windowsills and roofbeams. There I stood, feeling roughly as you would expect, with my hands pressed to my maidenhead.

Yet this almost seemed unnecessary. The first of such of the exclamations as I disentangled, after the merely general ones ("Og-God Og-God! Now I can die!" . . .), were about my earrings, and my hair, and my face (though later there was more variety); and wherever I looked—facing apprehensively around for inward movements—the eyes rose to my eyes. And this must have been why the Mongers decided to hide my earrings, hair, and eyes and compel attention to the commercial level.

The ring shifted: the squatting millionaires shuffled forward. My space shrank, bringing their eyes nearer, but it also moved off center so that now I was under the rail of the gallery; the ring sat partly in the court and partly under the gallery, and I stood where sunshine and shadow met. But the purpose was not just to place me in a more variegated light. Two Mongers took my shirt and hoisted it. Up it went so that my chest came out below but my head and hands disappeared inside above, and there it stuck, on my chin and armpits. And they knotted the ends of the sleeves to the gallery beam.

I still had on my breastlet, so I was no more naked than before. In a strict sense I was less so, since my head and hands were now enveloped. But with my hands aloft, everything below was indefensible, and perhaps unpardonable.

I was tempted to give them a good show by struggling—as you know by now, I'm a bit too much of a ham. I could have made the sounds they expected, and entertained them with vain efforts to hide my cunt by the only body-movements available to me, lifting one thigh across it, rising on tiptoe to fold forward, even spinning and shaking as if to move faster than their eyes—fine dramatizations of panic, but on the ludicrous side. Especially as, though helpless, I felt privately secure. Through the fabric I could see them all faintly but they couldn't see me at all. My body hung ready for them to deal with in whatever way they were going to deal with it, but I was not responsible. It felt less me than a nerve extended from me.

So I stayed still and by merely crossing my ankles appeared (I think) quite at ease. There followed some discussion between the Mongers and their customers as to whether the pony's value was obvious or whether she needed to be put through her paces. The conclusion was yes to both. "Let's see her move . . ."

I saw the shadow of footsteps coming toward me. But it was only the Younger Monger; pretending to adjust the knot above me, he said quietly beside the stretched membrane of my shirt: "Hey, little Pony, we mayn't see you for a while after this. Been nice knowing you. Feel free to be our guest any time."

"Thanks," I said, shirt-muffled. "I'll look you up next time I want to be enslaved."

"Now this here ordeal of yours. It ain't as bad as it seems."

"Tell me about it!"

"It looks as if we're just raising the price on you, don't it? But you know what we're really doing?"

"No, what?"

"*Creating you.*" He touched my navel by accident and went off, and the two Urchin Mongers were sent out to show their art.

They had been issued with hotel feather dusters. These were a shade less excruciatingly subtle than the hay but stood up longer. Sometimes for variety they surprised me with a raffia fly-whisk, the insect crispness of its bristles not so much panicking my nerves as insulting them. They knew all the best places. They played tennis with me, the cuntickler sending me rebounding to the glushtickler. Then working together, one to each glush, or one to each groinchannel, they drove me to erupt my glushes or cunt as if offering them to the crowd or the sun; with bursts of tickling unsymmetrically and unpredictably placed they built me to festoons of involuntary dance.

And yet there was a mercy: so absorbed were all with the ticklability of my nethers that none suspected I had a part doubly ticklish. No one had had time to expose them, even think of them.

"Breasts!" came a call.

It was echoed in several quarters. So they rolled my breastlet up. It stayed around me, but too high.

Tickled my breasts! (Not only; the other brush still at my tail.)
They had discovered how to manipulate me into a flying wrestle with
the air.

"What's her name?" I heard someone ask. "I don't know—Lacy
when she's dressed and Lucy when she isn't"— "Hilaire," someone else
suggested, "judging by how freely she laughs"— "No, the Mongers have
a market-name for her—" It sounded like "Arrowheel" or "Grapplefeel"
but it came under my own next scream. It went around; everyone
knew my name but me.

"Not quite so high!" said the Younger Monger. He didn't mean my
legs, or the bids, or the bawling of the crowd; he was asking me to
moderate, as if I could, my volleys of vocalization. "You're drowning
the bids!"

The bids were too tall to be drowned. And now the Urchins were
directed to play me to each bidder in turn, around the circle and then
around again. They knew as they came to each which part of me he
wanted to be tempted with, so they spun me his way with applications
of the feathers, and there, by applications to the opposite part (and
always to the waist, and armpits, and the soles of my feet if I showed
them, and anywhere I was not just then expecting), they drove me to
seduce him until his bid shot up. I have to say the Urchins were dex-
terous. They now worked kneeling, so that those behind them could
watch the region being feathered.

The poor Urchins were tired. (Was I tired? No one asked, but I
wasn't. If I hadn't been so damn healthy I'd have been worn out and
they'd have had mercy—or might not have started tickling my health in
the first place. But though begging at the top of my lungs for this bath
of feathering's cessation, I wasn't really hoping any more than expecting it. It was intolerable, but it was intolerable fun. That's the way tickling is.) The Urchins were tired, or at least the offer of the bidders to
take their place was approved.

But only as reward for each raise of their bids. Their skills were not
as devilish as the Urchins', but I was too sensitized to respond any the
less. Two by two, paired according to their tastes, they tickled the
aspects of their tastes. Or one of all-embracing taste would take both
featherbunches, and take his stand at my side, legs apart, half-crouched,
glaring and snorting in an anticipative pause, the bunches atremble,
both at middle level; and they came shivering in toward my awaiting
rigidity; and one touched! and I broke toward the other; he oscillated
me!

He oscillated me until my oscillation-response gave out; then worked me up and down to make me ripple; slow cunning attention to one of my delicate hollows—sudden frenzy of cascades from neck to calves by way of cleft and shriek-drawing uprushes from knees to breasts. My writhing and shrilling implored him and heaven to stop his torments, while inspiring him to redouble them.

It would soon be too much; my laughing was mixing with hiccuping and beginning to sound like crying; but I was holding it off as long as I could because it would spoil everybody's afternoon.

He dropped the feathers; his bare hands came in, bowed like crabs.

"No touch!" barked the Younger Monger.

The hands paused, vibrating, just outside.

"I must . . . necessary . . ."

"Any touch, out of the bidding."

"Must—cup; must—hook."

"When you own them."

And he suggested a sum just higher, and in fact the highest number yet discovered.

The man crouched groaning with desire (to cup and to hook, whatever that meant; but if at this point someone, some guardian or teacher, had stood beside me and whispered to me, "*Now*, you slow learner, do you begin to have an inkling what 'desire' means?" I might have been able to answer "Yes, I—think so"). The tight brown hands, which I could glimpse under my blindfold, hovered so close that I already felt a whole hand-sized tickle from each through the hairsbreadths between; yet I had to force myself for the first time rock-still; the slightest tremble would have given myself into the hands, and at their real touch my pelvis would have exploded into motion in their grasp. Without relaxing the encasing hands he turned and stared at the Younger Monger, and gritting his teeth said faintly: "Okay." (What a bathetic remark to close the bidding with.)

The applause (actually it was a sigh, but with the force of a clap of wind) burst and instantly smothered itself as the crowd leaned forward, intent on watching cup and hook.

Rigged

B UT INSTEAD he passed out, and lay crumpled around my feet. I would have had more excuse, my suspense being at least as great as his. I've heard that people who are going to faint see a pink glow; inside my shirt-world the glow was amazing green, and when I shut my eyes it throbbed complementary carmine. But I don't faint or even swoon (the worst I do is lose attention and doze) so they needn't have worried. They carried me upstairs to a room and laid me on a bed. My sleeves were untied, I brought my shirt down to its proper place around my thorax, still they hadn't found me anything for my abdomen. I settled to rest, but this wasn't the purpose of shutting me in the bedroom. Through the door I heard the winning bidder talking with his agent, who was solicitously reviving him with a drink.

"She's worth it, but oh, I've ruined myself! How could I! Just when I thought I was getting older, too, and calmer about breasts and bottoms. It's true that a girl can drive a man crazy and even make him forget his arithmetic. Not to mention his business: I came here to buy a thoroughbred, but now I'll be kicked out of the Hunt."

"Never mind, sir, you've got something else you can ride."

"I think I may find—have you seen the way she bucks?—she's too spirited to ride bareback; before I can ride her I may have to bridle and saddle her. You know what I mean?" "Indeed, sir. I'll have the tackle ready." "I'll take sixteen hours on her—that's how long we have till checkout time—my last and only sixteen hours of heaven, and then all will be over, and it will be off to hell with me; I'll drown myself, I'm damned if I'll use rope." (This he said because he was, as it happened, a twine-merchant.) "I'll drown myself or go a-beggar, or at least look for a job, far from my native bourne. Say goodbye for me to my wife and aunt and the little ones, and tell the others how sorry I am that they must all be turned out on charity."

"No, sir, there is rope. —I mean there's hope. Take your sixteen hours, but meanwhile let me and Thog and Polliver seek out your disappointed rivals."

"I'm not sure I follow you."

"We'll draw up a timetable, and they can each put down a thousand for an hour."

"I see—of course! Just leave her tied, give her a rinse, and let the next in!"

"That's the idea."

"My fortune will be restored! That shows it's right in bidding to follow your feeling all the way!"

"At any rate for a renewable resource."

"How unfairly lucky can you be: I'll have her first and best—they'll each have their hour and pay for it—then I'll have her back, for ever! Free! At their expense!"

"And a little profit."

"It's right that she should earn back my costs, having made me pay so much."

"Yes, she can work on at it while you're sleeping, sir. A girl like that, pity to let her be wasted for a moment. And if I might respectfully request—"

"Yes, you shall have your hour a week, and Thog and Polliver too."

"Much appreciated, sir. But now I must hurry. Got to catch them before they jerk off on the image of her, as they're certainly about to do. We'll knock on their doors, try to get them after they start but before they finish. At such a time they'll pay anything."

This scheme I didn't fully understand, but it suggested that I was to be subjected to something, presumably tickling, for a day and a half. And immediately, for the door opened.

But it was a hag with a haggis—a kindly cookwife with a tray of nutritious food. "Now," she said, "Applepeel me darlint, eat all this and go to the bathroom well and sleep hard for an hour. Master Theopard's allowing ye an hour's readying because you've got a long stint coming. Ah, how I envy ye!"

"Envy me!"

"No, I don't envy ye—but I envy ye! He's going to feast on your, and so on, for a whole night and a day and a night non stop, him and twenty more of them, I'm told. They'll do terrible things to ye one after another as fast as they can think of them—none of which will hurt ye, but all of which will drive ye mad as a wildcat with rage and shame! Ah, it's a long time since I was in such risks, but I'm telling ye I was a nice little plump one once. Anything else ye need?"

"Just a feather duster."

For the hysteria of my skin couldn't just stop, it had to taper off. At first I could even tickle myself; it quieted into all-over soothing of myself, and (leaving my dinner uneaten) I slept sweetly till woken by the sliding-to of the bolt.

He was clad just in a copper jock, in case I kicked, and was carrying a small jar of lard (whose purpose I never did find out) and a complicated truss of ropes and snatchblocks. He had taken one of the

courses offered in modern general girl-arranging.   And I too had
enjoyed a bit of few-dimensional topology in junior high (lesson one: "If
there's more than one wire, cord, power-supply or data-cable, they'll
cross over the wrong way"—lesson two, how to fold a fitted bedsheet),
so I sat up and looked with interest at the loops, nodes, and bends. My
curiosity was my undoing, or doing up. For he took the chance to slip
something between my legs and catch it at my neck, and then he had
me fixed at three points (one wrist, as an anchor, to a corner of the bed,
the others—wrist and ankle—connected to each other behind my back
but otherwise topologically free) and could work at leisure, like a spider
securing a fly.

"I'm taking my time about this, you see," he explained, "because I
have fifteen hours in front of me. That's also why I'm not starting on
the touching." (Indeed he had remarkably mastered the frenzy I had last
seen him in, though a vein throbbed and his palm started toward my
belly and then clenched and stopped. A trembling finger made a
mistake in a slipknot but he caught it. He was a fanatically methodical
spider-man.) "It's worth doing well, don't you think? Then I'll be able
to enjoy you in every, absolutely every, way possible. It's been topologically proven that there is no attitude you cannot work a girl into, no
version you cannot induce her into, no combination of bodies you
cannot evolve, if you just get this rigged right."

"What's it called?" I asked him.

"Called?—I haven't patented it yet; a girlweb, perhaps, a nipulator,
a pussycradle! Now I'm coming to the cleavage hitch, it's the center-
piece, the key to the whole flexibility-in-helplessness. (I do hope we
can get you out of this tomorrow. I had it assembled by the ar-and-dee
department in my factory—if the worst comes to the worst we can have
them in to solve it—they'll be glad to see the use I've made of it.) There
we are: one more round turn and two half itches, ease the sheepshank
to allow play in the thigh, and I'll need to have an overhead connection—a traveler between the cupboard door and the curtain transom
should do it. Now I expect you think I forgot to remove those clothes
of yours—missed the stage, it's hopeless? No, this is one of the felici-
ties of the craft: the topology is such that I could take off your skirt and
stockings and clevel, supposing you had any, just as easily as I now withdraw these through the tangle. The blouse, or tunic—what's it called?"
"Just a shirt," I said, as it slipped away along my arm. "Shirt, of such a
happy color"—he held it up and answered it with a hectic grin— "it
almost giggles. You'll certainly look better without it." (The green was,
indeed, on the silly side of spectacular.) "And now out comes the dear

little breastlet, *floowhoosh*. Ah," and he gave a great swallow (Eve's Apple rising and setting) when he saw me perfectly naked.

I wasn't quite perfectly naked, with his device hanging about me like an exploded octopus. But considering how much of the network there was and in how many ways it held me, it covered of me astonishingly little. In fact the only parts concealed, by the rings of felt, were an inch or so of each wrist, shoulder, and knee. And these "clothes" of rope certainly did nothing to slow access between the world and my person.

"And I've been kind enough to leave you your earrings, haven't I? Ha! They make you *more* naked."

He walked around me to admire his handiwork.

"Excellent attitude," he said, "my compliments on it. By it you clearly invite me to Explore. My right hand will be the first to accept the invitation. I shall continue to a thorough Geography Lesson." I could see him wrapping himself around a simulacrum of me in the air.

"But my arousal is proceeding faster than it need," he said, uncurling and stepping back in contemplation.

"I don't suppose you have any idea of the ways I can upend and refold you. Just as a beginning: *now*, d'you see, your shoulders are on the bed but your glushes (otherwise known as chollops) hang free for me to updelve as I thuck you." ("Do what?" I wanted to ask—oh, suck he must have meant—he seemed to be a lisping spider. What would he mean about sucking, though? The only use for sucking I could call to mind was slurping water to make it taste even better—oh, and then there's that way you bite-with-a-suck when someone's given you a biscuit and forgotten to offer you a plate to catch the crumbs on.) — But the next moment I was flying through the air. "Quick application of fulcrum: *now*, shoulders still on the bed but rotated, you are stretched high up the wall with legs pointing at the corners of the ceiling and I can squat on your face while sipping the springs in this high wide valley—"

From down between his hairy thighs I piped up diffidently: "Mr. Theopard, don't you think it would be fair to start me with something simpler? I mean, up to now I don't even know what comes after kissing."

He paused only a moment, and continued as if I hadn't spoken (his words were upside down but I could still read them): "—Or *now*, with a simple fillip, I have you where I could conveniently ponder—that is, weigh—a pillow in one hand and a cushion in the other; I call these upper softnesses pillows and these lower ones cushions. (It helps that you're so light and *manipulable*, I can just throw you around. Woman in general is disappointing in that regard, she's such a lump that if you want to get at her another way you've got to either hoist her or ask her, which ignot what you want.) Or now again, with a somewhat less simple fillip, you are on all fours over me for a different sixtynine. Topologically related, yes, but each oh how superbly different in its advantages. Lying at ease under you, your sitch fixed in my gaze like a little star, your breasts swinging available for my palms as soon as I care to lift them! But this is too far along to be a beginning; presently I'll extend you in the Kite—the one where one heel alone reaches the floor and the other inner thigh so yearningly invites the first touch. But it's so pleasant to lie here, so close to the already celebrated Applepeel glushes, and I see one or two of the knots that need tightening."

And now I had cause to be thankful for my slight grounding in topology.

Topology

ANALYSING THE position (weft only, ignoring warp for simplicity), I determined that the virtual sheath involving (in the technical sense) my left leg in the same half-space as the ceiling was Moebius, not Bernoulli as he supposed, so that an "orange" harmonic plication of it would transform into an open, not a closed, pentagram. This was all the result of one little granny which he had inexcusably widowed. In other words, if I could manage to shake the cuckold's neck (a knot whose name must tell some story) over my left shoulder a way would be clear for me to dive my hand under his knee, slip it through the main bedloop, come back with three free ends (I would have to be quick), and merely let any two of them drop where he could not reach them without sitting up and hyperstretching the plaited halter, which would predissolve it and paradoxically consolidate his position. This I did. He went on talking for a while, not yet understanding that I was topologically free while he couldn't move a muscle.

It wasn't quite as simple as I thought. He was irreversibly immobilized, but I met unexpected difficulties in disengaging my wrists. The torque that I couldn't avoid exerting forced me back by small increments, like a house leaning, so that my underparts shuddered nearer to him. One of the silly little marlinghitches had jammed and simply would not give. For a while it seemed we were both firmly entangled in this Net of Vulcan, like guilty Mars and Venus, our nakednesses nowhere quite touching, our only hope also our dread: for the mocking gods to burst in.

But I didn't give up; I kept picking at the knots. I hadn't meant to reverse my nethers all the way to his face, but I would if that was what it took. The effect on him was distracting: he began to rave. I paid no attention to his sounds, intent on my work. They were at first grudging ahem-what's-this-oh-I-see-we'll-soon-have-this-sorted-out sounds, and then I-ahem-well-but-no-I-don't-think-I-quite-understand sounds, and then I-don't-believe-this-there-must-be-something-not-quite-right sounds, and then ha-ha-quite-a-good-joke-but-just-you-wait sounds, and then a-joke's-a-joke-but-enough-is-enough sounds, and then let-me-go-right-now-or-it'll-be-the-worse-for-you sounds, and then how-dare-you-how-fucking-dare-you sounds, and then oh-hell-oh-hell-oh-hell-oh-HELL sounds, and then pure (if that's the word) SOUNDS. He steadied himself to say severely: "I'll give you three. One . . . two . . ." I began to move in rhythm, and there broke out a bellow which made me think a train

was coming through the tunnel; and when I dipped my face to look
back under I saw that his eyes were starting from his head and his
tongue from his mouth. Catching my upside-down eye (between my
breasts), he reverted to articulation: "Oh please Applepeel Applepeel
darling darling please please! For gutsache backjustabitmore please
please! gotta lick! oh jebus let me loose or let me lick!"

And so on. It made me wonder how things looked from his viewpoint. I didn't, after all, have an exact idea of the appearance of that
scenery—I mean my underglushes and the roots of my grace-muscles,
flesh details, but whole sceneries from as close a viewpoint as his—I
could sometime in my girlhood have held a mirror under, but never did.
Did he see something to terrify him? He seemed annoyed at being so
close, yet annoyed at not being closer. He seemed going off his head.
But I couldn't help that, I had my own troubles. I had made a mess of
the running bowline, and when I tried to unravel it by taking it in my
teeth it dropped and caught under his codpiece. I snatched it up and
the whole thing came away like a beetle's wing. Out sprang a fleshy
process that much surprised me. It was divided into two parts of different formations, one of which was itself divided into two parts, and
all had started out of a black flowerbed of hair. I had the impression
that this outgrowth resulted from the stress he was feeling. It might be
an emergency. Should I call for a doctor? The process was growing up
toward my face. I didn't like it. I hoped to get away from it, but each
struggle brought me closer. And this too added to Mr. Theopard's agi-
tation.

He was beyond language, uttering an unbroken storm of horrible
slurpings. He rattled his body, trying to drive his head and his hips
upward. For my part I calmed and concentrated on my work. I was
only a beginning topologer after all and by now in my haste I too had
made many errors. I discussed the problems with him, hoping he
might help me reanalyze them and isolate my line of escape, but he
wasn't interested. In truth I didn't know what I was doing; and only
luck—or was it the still-clinging traces of the maydew?—slid my fingers
along the right choices. Now I was getting there, though each way-
station brought my face a little lower and my hips a little back (because
I was trying to get a submass of the network over my head). By the time
the breakthrough came, my mouth was so near to that process of his
that I couldn't help dribbling on it, and my hair was brushing its lengthy
flanks; and some of my cuntbeard was actually in his nostrils, so that
his splutterings culminated in a sneeze— "Retchyou!"—a sudden cool
spray in the chamber between my thightops.

"*Ayhi!*"—free! But for the moment I was exhausted, and rested where I was. And his expressions of frustration did not cease to worsen.

I rested on because I was curious as to the cause. No, I'll be frank, I began to guess what the matter was. And since he had intended sixteen hours of no mercy for me I lingered to inflict some minutes of no mercy on him. I sat up and not only poised my glushes as close to his face without touching it as skill could manage, but moved them in ways I didn't know I knew. After less than four seconds of this it was imperative to gag him.

While I did this with the flying thigh-reins from his contraption, my eyes fell on his stalk. (I had identified the cylindrical process: it must be what my little brother called a stalk or log or prong.) It was now about the bigness of a cucumber, and still waxing, but in color it had more of loganberry. I knelt beside it and examined it closely. I blew on it from several angles to see whether it would wobble. For it appeared to be a type of balloon, swelling tight and shiny, and kept straining to lift to me, flopping back to his stomach, bouncing, floating up again. At its upmost I englobed it.

My mouth surrounded it, still without touching it. Quite a feat, and a risky one. I heard his howl, as from far back in a cave. I took my mouth away and looked and there was cream beginning to well out of a slot in the tip. In alarm I hopped off the bed; and then it quivered and stopped welling up, and slowly dripped off. I watched with interest. "Hum-mazing." It wasn't like water; the drip didn't just fall, it lengthened as a thread till it stuck to his stomach; and then it sagged and stretched as his stalk kept sinking and heaving. He screwed up his eyes, and all his arms and legs tried to beat.

My dinner (of which something reminded me) was hardly colder than when it left the kitchen, since the room had become quite hot. I ate it sitting on the bed beside him. He opened his eyes to glare at me.

For dessert I picked up the last and only cool thing on the tray: one of those large round plums that must have come from the Mongers. I bit it and got a surprise: it was hard and tasted like—no, was—an apple.

I took it away from my mouth and looked at it. Its skin, which at first glance seemed a perfect glossy black, was in fact a red *so deep that it looked like black.* In places where it slightly flawed or lightened, the red gleamed through the black.

When that was discerned, it was a beautiful and mysterious object; and reminded me of I was not sure what.

But perhaps it was a shade old (funny, isn't it, that you can call an apple old at seventeen days but not a girl at eighteen years?): its white flesh was on the hard and tasteless side. I decided to bite no more.

"What is it?" I said, showing it to my captive. "I've never seen anything like it." The obstruction in his mouth replied something like "Aakhaakhaakh-hwalaa" and his eyes rolled up above my brow.

When I had finished eating I was in good spirits, and felt like teasing him some more.

I jumped on all fours over him again, but the other way around, as if I was going to kiss him. "Bother!" I said, "I can't, because of this gag you're wearing," and instead I gave him my breasts—almost. We shared an intimate tent made by my hair, glowing reddish in the touch of sun from the window—I, my breasts, and close under them his up-pleading eyes. I prickled both my nipples on his eyelashes, compelling them to flutter. "D'you think I could kiss them myself?" I asked him; and I tried lifting a breast to my lips, but it wasn't loose enough.

I laughed and whisked the warm tent open. Then I brought up my cunt, maneuvering it with more refined accuracy than had been possible with my glushes: I could look down and monitor the precise interval between fur and face. His tongue outdid itself and a corner of it oozed around the dam of his gag. He had a little vibration-range, which at first I allowed for; then, more deft and daring, I reduced the interval to a tolerance not only fine but constant: retreated before him but only just enough, readvanced as he sank back. I seemed to hover on the skin of his breath. So he stopped breathing, even tried to suck me to him; then despairingly blew, so as at least to see his wind affect the trees of the little forest. I noticed that it was lighter than the hair on my head—almost fiery. I stooped over and, tweezing my cuntlips apart, allowed him to share my own first examination of that labyrinth.

"Why, it's quite complicated!" I said. "A sort of fortification. You're nearer, can you see in *there?* And what do you suppose *that* little thing is for?"

He failed to answer. But I did make out the words he was trying to form at this point. They were: "I am Napoleon." I had heard that this is what men generally say when they become lunatics. That alarmed me and I eased off and stroked his brow, and he did calm a bit. I didn't really want to drive men off their rockers. Although, why not?—when sane they did nothing but pester me, so if I sent them all Harry-bonkers then at least a few of them might think of something else.

Well, the room was safe for fourteen hours—he had guaranteed that himself. I could have just curled up beside him for the night. I tried it for a while, but soon my eyes floated open: it was boring. I talked it over with him: "You don't seem to have anything to read, and it's too early to just lie. I'm afraid of absent-mindedly fiddling with you, just for something to do with my hands—I might tickle your tummy or pick up your stalk and sweedle it or something, and you wouldn't like that?" His neck strained in the corpse of a nod.

I'd seen the word *sweedle* in a naughty novel but I thought it just meant fondle or twiddle. If I'd known it meant *gam* I'd have realized I was going too far. It's one thing to give a fallen enemy a taste of hell, but it's another to put him in a torture-chamber with a view of heaven.

"So I think I must leave you now. You won't be mad at me? You won't spank me if you catch me?"

Listening close for one last message, I understood him to say: "*Put you in the pillory.*"

Ow! That didn't sound nice at all. It was time to be serious and make the most of my start. I found my topclothes and put them back on. Picked his codpiece up off the floor and parked it on his big toe. Unbolted the door, waved goodbye to him with my behind, and stuck my head into the corridor.

The Overhearing

N O ONE was in sight, but I heard footsteps approaching around the corner to my left and also up the stair to my right. I was trapped between them!

Not quite: straight opposite to me was a small closet. I ducked into it to wait for them to pass.

They didn't pass. They met before the door and halted.

"Hullo, Vardue, good to see you," said one nervously.

"Good to see you; hm. —This the door?"

"I beg your pardon?"

"Number one-forty-one? You know."

A pause and then a chuckle. "Yes, this is it!" A handshake. (Can you hear a handshake?—Yes, a sweaty one.)

"Keep your voice down, though. Here comes Forew. How many more?" "How are you?" "Fine, fine! And you?" "Fine." "So fine I cain't hardly stand it," said one in a smoker's croak. "And how's your wife?"— "Well, Waist not, want not, you know"— "Right. More waist, less greed. Excuse me, I'm dripping over my dung today." They were, it seemed, becoming crowded ("Ow"— "Sorry!"— "Sokay") and impatient ("Stime?"— "Still six till"— "Not quite: tentill"— "Still, too muchtill!"). Introductions— "Pleased to meet you"— "I'm fine, as I mentioned"— "What do you do?"— "Oh, I have Outlets. And you?"— "I sell space"— "I cover the Southeast" (I knew this brisk business type—the type who, as he strides around a corner, already has his leading foot angled to the right)— "J. Norman Jones" (as if that was enough to signify himself a C.E.O. with his frame hanging on the boardroom wall, whereas mere Joe N. Jones was a checkout wallah). "I'm a Consultant," claimed another, and another was a Constrictor or Expander, and another an Annalist, which sounded more interesting, but "Systems Analyst?"— "Of course. Systems and Services. Facilities Management Services; E-Services, that is"— "While we're on Systems, let's hear it for Applied Behavioral Systems"— "Capital . . ."— "Longtermcapitalmanagement"— "Liquid assets assessment"— "(Watch your language)"— "I'm in Quality Control"— "I'm with Fulfilment"— "Lifestyle counseling"— "Organizational Direction Dynamics Initiatives"— "Integrated Information Technology Solutions"— "Secure Scalable Network Platforms"— "Risk Retention Specialists (to Third-Party Administrators)"—and I realized that these (though I couldn't picture what it was that any of them did with their time when they weren't chasing me) were some of my disappointed bidders, no longer quite so disappointed.

"Well, so we know where to come tomorrow," said a fat fellow called Fafteloe, with itching eyebrows. "Well, better get some rest and be fit, you know! Good night."

"I don't know how I'm going to sleep," said a thin fellow called Skelcrow. "I don't know how I'm going to wait at all for fourteen hours."

"You're first? Lucky bugger!"

"First bugger after—after what's going on already."

"Oh yes! To think of it going on! Now! Her! She! *Applepeel!* He's in there with my darling Applepeel, doing whatever he likes, choosing lassholes—oh help, I can't bear it. Just the other side of that door! To think what we could see, if it wasn't bolted! Oh, describe to me the things we might see—oh no, don't!"

"I think I can form an idea—"

"Hey, maybe oughtn't to go ssquomting through keyholes."

"Don't talk about keyholes!"

"I never squunt through no keyhole."

"There isn't a keyhole. I'm just listening."

"Well, maybe oughtn't to listen either. How would you like it?"

"I wouldn't mind. I hereby invite you to listen when I'm on. I'll give you something to listen to!"

"Good man. And I don't think he can object. After all, with what we've paid, we're entitled to something while we're waiting. A fore-taste of the fun."

"A nibble of the peel."

"Hush, then." And there was silence in the corridor.

Soon they broke out in titters.

"There's bodily contact going on in there, all right!" They kept listening, occasionally slapping each other and simmering with evil mirth.

It seemed I was going to have to wait in my closet for a while. Most of the space was taken up by a wicker basket, full of bed-linen, but I didn't care to sit on it because some of the sheets were stained with human juices.

"Hell, it sounds like action! He's out of control, spinning her, mixing it with her—that's the way it should go in the first couple of hours. You don't want to settle into any one grip too soon."

"But what's that sound? Isn't that a kiss coming apart and closing up again?"

Hard listening.

"No, already! That rich 'Urgh, Urgh,' I'd know it anywhere. That's full buggury!"

"He's crazy if he's in burgery already." (Or vigory or boggery; I couldn't be sure of the term.)

"Well, he *is* crazy, how couldn't he be? I'll be crazy too, the moment I get in there with her!"

"He's not so young that he can afford it this early in the night. A fork or two near the beginning, if you like, but then plenty of time and save the puckery for the very end."

"I disagree. Bougueraie right off, while you can. He's deep implunged." "If not englushed." "Yes, probably using handfuls of glush to double the frictionpassage." And they were quite quiet as they listened to what they hoped was this voguery or vulgary. (Or bulgery or bauchery or whatever it was. Perhaps they meant burglary.)

"Haven't heard a sound from her, though. Surely he wouldn't gag her? Girl's chirruping is half the fun."

"She may be the scornful firmlipped type. I like that. Pillar of purity. A challenge to get a gurgle out of her."

"This one, no. Surely you remember how the gigglery ran riot when we were tickling her!"

"But now tickling isn't what he's doing."

"Right! He's— What can he be doing that keeps her so serious?"

I took the risk of peeping past the closet curtain. Their ears were actually laid to the door, tall ones on tiptoe to lean over short ones, some kneeling, even lying with their ears between others' shoes. Twenty men, packed in a pyramid against a door hardly larger in area than the sum of their left ears. What surprised me most was that they had all pushed their clothes apart from the waist. I knew that grasshoppers hear with their thighs, but I hadn't known it works that way with humans. Their glushes (or gleitches as I believe the gristlier male versions are called) were interesting but not elegant, so I missed little by prudently reclosing the curtain and merely listening in my turn. After all, I was bare too—and yes, it did seem to alert the senses.

"That *could* be fucking. Pretty pugnacious grunts."

"Too irregular, too sort of struggling."

"Well, it wouldn't be the driving-down-the-straight yet, would it? A stoking stage: weaving thrusts, while persecuting her with prods and pinches to keep her awriggle."

"Yes. Yes, that's good. Let's picture that and listen."

Silence again. One or two traces of sound reached even to my closet. I knew the note in them for fury, but ears without the clue could take it for ecstasy.

"No. It doesn't fit. He's munching her cunt."

"Possibly, but the sound is mainly due to his glory as he rises in her mouth. You can tell by the climbing urgency. He's in a sixtynine under her; he has her hind reared before him to express himself on, but essentially it's a man abandoning himself to having it pulled out of him by a girl's speech-organs."

"I'd like to believe it, but I can't. Think of the girl. Our fighting Applepeel. I don't believe he can have tamed and trained her that quickly."

"You're right. —I have it: he's reaming her! That stifled quality. And it would be just right for about this time, beginning the second hour: down to thorough obscenity but plenty more to come!" ("What's reaming?" asked a beginner. "Tonguecultivating . . .")

"Gorgeous! Let's listen and think of it. *He's reaming Applepeel.*"

Then there followed a long silence while they listened to what they fancied was my owner reaming me. Whatever it was, it was plainly engrossing. Not quite a silence: I heard pumping sounds which I could not interpret.

"Ah!" sighed one of them at last, "he keeps on and on, he inspires me! I shall do as much—this alone I could do for a month! Oh woe that I'll have only an hour of her! And then to have to live for ever after remembering and only remembering Applepeel! A day to remember rimming her, a day—each day for fond reconstitution of one part of her!"

"Yes, for instance her—" And they took turns describing parts of me; or one would apostrophize a part, and there would be a devotional pause filled with those same mysterious chafings and pantings. In the closet just behind them, I had been sitting against the wall, arms around knees, beginning to daydream of other things such as horsemeadows and hotcakes; but cries of "Applepeel's—!" and so on were distracting, and I got up on my knees to feel these parts and wonder. And when they grew blasphemous— "The creamy culmination of creation, the parchment of the most sacred scripture: Applepeel's skin!"—I clicked my tongue.

"Oh boy, listen to that!"—the highest gust yet of strangled expression— "Climax *must* be imminent!" "How can flesh go on so long and hard without?" "Reminds me of the advice the consul gave me when I went on that trip to Algesia: 'You gotta show your satisfaction with the food by belching (you can belch but you mustn't fart, you can get expelled from the whole Middle Beast and the diplamatic corps for that), and then when they give you a bint you gotta do the same: Make plentya noise, so they know you're satisfied with her too—the louder and fiercer your Aahs, the more pleased they'll be—you gotta sound *amazed.*" "Well, he sounds amazed—except that he seems to be keeping his lips shut."

"Yet still she doesn't make a sound. Don't you think a girl who rings so charmingly when merely grazed or prodded would chime at least a little under sterner working?"

"You've got a point. She's the incarnation of response (as well as freshness, shininess . . . spirit). He's using some curious skill if he can touch her waist, let alone her sitch or her clitch, without setting off a single peal."

"A perverted skill. It really spoils the show for us. Just think how we could be sharing the orgy if she were in full squeal. That clear voice, so—so—so *she*; and every wail and trill and 'No, no, no!' telling of some intimate indignity, some in-dig, even in-time—"

"Don't! What we're missing! Yes, when I have her I'll play her like a harp. He must be a clod, he's just boring her."

"Wait, I heard something! Didn't you? A high-pitched bit mixed in with his. It made my balls jump."

"It was just a squeak of him, falsetto."

"No, it was a bit of her. Wait. Something was squeezed out of her. Listen. I believe she's at last going to start mewing. No. No more."

"She really is holding it in. By thunder, when I set about her I'll have her singing her scales, up and up! It's what thrills me to the come! I want you all listening when her shrill and my roar reach heaven!"

"You know what?"

"What?"

"Something's wrong. You've just made such a noise that he must have heard you. But he goes on making the same sounds. And I fear I know what it is he's sucking."

"What?"

"A gag."

They tried the door, discovered that it was unbolted—had been all the time. The slam of it against a wall, a moment's pause, and then there really was a peal: of laughter.

Poor Theopard had to be cut free (with scant respect for Gordian topology). I was rather relieved for his sake. But not for mine.

The moment they loosed his gag, there issued a howl the like of which had not been heard since the eruption of Mount Krakatow in

1883. Everyone in the building must have stood thunderstruck. It burst at the top of the scale, and subsided in three gasps and a moan.

"Man, you hit the ceiling! Talk about frustration! Let her tie you up, did you?" "Fraid so," I heard Theopard mumble. "You fell for that one?— 'Oh darling, that was so exciting, now it's *your* turn to be *my* slave'—what a sucker!" They went on crowing with mirth, till he managed to cut through: "All right, fellows—enough. At least I've had some" (liar). "If you want some, get out after her. Dangerous female loose."

"Right! How many minutes does she have? She can't have got far!" And the footsteps came stampeding back through the door, straight toward me.

Oe

THE FOOTSTEPS went past me like a herd of buffalo—the floorboards of my closet bounced—and then I heard them rattling down the stairs like a ton of coal. I put out a cautious eye; then slipped across the corridor in two strides. I coolly reoccupied the bedroom, quietly bolted the door behind me, and looked around for resources.

Besides my red-black apple with the single white bite, I found three tangerines, a jar of maltesers, a note saying "Blueberry muffins in icebox!" and that little pot of lard, for which I saw no use. Of rope I had plenty of choice. The knife that had cut it might have been useful.

The bed had no bedclothes except one blanket, tucked in tightly all around like an undersheet. I don't know whether to call it sheet or blanket: it was rubberized, as if to repel liquids or be wipable from greases—altogether not the prettiest of blankets. Still, it was just right for a field campaign, in case I got no offers of beds: it would make a rain-proof tent, though a sweaty sleeping-bag. I tried to wrap it around my waist like a sarong, but there was just too much of it. Certainly I wouldn't be able to run in it. So I bundled the other things inside it to sling over my shoulder.

Now, the window. It was covered by shutters made of slanting slats, to admit daylight but prevent anybody peeping in. Onto what did the window open? I set my eye to one of the interstices. I found myself looking into another eye!

It was the cookwife. The window opened onto the gallery around the courtyard. The slats didn't really bar peepers: there were chinks enough if you thought of looking for them, and happened to be on the balcony, and happened to want to look in. If the Bidders had known of that, they could have foregathered there from the start and enjoyed our whole scene. That was what my friend Oe had done.

"Bully for you!" she said. "May I come in?" And she pushed the shutters and hopped nimbly over the sill.

She had a face like an apple: a wrinkled one now, but still fat and bursting with lifejuice.

"It wasn't what I expected to watch, but I had a good time watching it! And I stayed to see if there'd be a sequel. But you won't let them have you till you choose, eh? Well, I dare say you'll love it all the more when the time comes."

"Why do men want to chase me and invade me?" I asked her.

She brought her eye around to rest on me as if just noticing, and chucked me under the chin. "It's like a kitten among children," she said: "you can't be that cute and expect to be left alone." She turned me sideways and looked me over fore and aft, and incanted like a witch: "First it's your air that makes them aware, which draws to your roundels so outward and round, sharp-squeezing your ingangs between them."

She was sitting on the bed and I was standing before her, and I didn't mind letting her glide her hands over my glushes and whatever else as seemed to console her. This was the first time anyone ran a palm so floatingly across my nerve-ends, and I made a mental note to try it myself. I sat on her lap and we had a kiss.

"Child, your hair is a mess," she said.

"It was in a ponytail," I said, "but I suppose the ribbon's gone."

"It has, and not surprising. We'll tie the pony by its own tail, but first we have to comb it. Of course you've no comb, you can have this one when I've finished. Where do you part them?" she said, looking at my breasts, but she meant my hair. And she combed; and combed, and combed.

"Isn't that enough?" I said. (My little sister usually brushes me— hard, but never so long.)

"Your hair is rich—a man would get drunk on it."

"The Mongers didn't think so. They said it should be blond."

"The Mongers have learned better. Blond is corny (if that isn't a pun). Your color is as rare as a ruby."

"What, black?"

"*Black?* Don't you even know the color of your own hair? Your hair is *red*."

I sat, still on her knee, with my mouth agape. And she went on combing and combing, and often pressing her face to my stretched temple.

She combed till hair and comb began to crackle. Sighing all the time at the ruddy glossiness, she tried various overlapping shells, and fixed them with a knot at the base of the ponytail—it felt as if she yanked the mass very tight, and yet the knot was four inches behind my nape—but left one wisp to wander over my left cheek. And as tied by her it all held up through all the rest of my rough adventures.

"Thank you," I said, sliding off her lap and fetching the strange apple. "Do you happen to know what this is?"

"That," she said, "is an Arkansas Black. Remind you of something?"

"Yes, it does now."

"The Mongers come by here at the beginning of summer. They

trade as far as Australia in the east and, I guess, Arkansas in the west. As for their home, some say it's in Dardistan."

"They had a cartload of these."

"It's a fine black one," she said, turning it over in her hands. "It must have been dry in Arkansas last summer. I've never seen more than one or two a year before, and mostly as pale as any other apple. They must have known what was going to happen. After your hair-ribbon, they'll have made the most on that cartload."

"And there was," I said before I could stop myself, "my skirt."

"Immodest person! There was, indeed, your skirt. That represents another citizen bankrupted."

I put the apple away and said, "Do you live in a room here? Can I come and hide in it?"

"No, you can't go down the stairs, so you'd have to run along the way I came. The idlers in the courtyard are used to seeing me up here spying into bedrooms, but if you were to get out of the window and run along the balcony your legs and bottom would surprise them."

"So how can I escape from here? Could I disguise myself as a man?"

She slapped both hands over her popping mouth and cheeks, but still drenched the surroundings with her laughter.

"Well, a boy."

"Some girls," she told me, "can be disguised as boys. But *you burn.*"

Witches and wizards! So if I put on boys' clothes, my body would burn out through them? I'd really better be careful.

"What's left, then?" I said. "An old lady? Another girl?"

"Applepeel with my wrinkles," she said, "would look like baby Applepeel with painted wrinkles. As for another girl, yes, you could make yourself into one, by bleaching your hair. But you'd be just as much of a girl. Multiply Applepeels, multiply hunters."

"I see. That wouldn't help."

"Do you really want to get away? Outside is where they're hunting for you, all across the prairie and along the highway. Here's the only place they won't think of looking."

"But they'll come back. I can't just stay here and wait for them."

"You can't?"

"No! If they were going to do bad things to me before, think what they'd do now!"

"I am thinking!"

"I'd rather even be running across the plain from them than just waiting here. But please, haven't you got a skirt and a clevel you could lend me?"

"I'll go and rummage for what I can find among me drawers."

While she was away, I paced to and fro, holding my hands over my nakednesses, because I was imagining whether it was worse to be run down by men on the plain or converged on by them in this cara-vanserai. This whole place was a girltrap, a machine made of dusty poles and stucco—its courtyard for marketing me, its bedrooms for locking me, its gallery for leerers down over my marketing or in on my using!

I had been carried three days' journey away from my home, and this third day had become a long one. I found myself making a strange gesture of defiance. From someone's radio down at the courtyard gate came a strain of alien music. I found it nasty. (I got over all this in another day or so; a little homesickness, a little culture-shock, is excus-able.) I opened the shutter wide and leaned out and whistled (I have a strong clear whistle):

> As pants the hart for cooling streams
> When heated in the chase,
> So longs, O Lord, my soul for thee
> And thy refreshing grace!

This was because I thought it a tune which in its simplicity would put to shame all the arabesques of eastern and southern decadence. Someone called: "A whistling woman, a crowing hen, are neither good to God nor—" Hastily I shut the window.

Oe returned in her own good time, bringing me a gooseberry and a gourd of ale, a fishline, flint, tampons, and other useful trifles. "And how about these?—a bunch of strong onions—they may be able to keep one or two men at bay."

"No skirt?"

"Well, mine are all years out of fashion."

"But couldn't you at least find me a cleftveil?"

"I picked out several and pictured you in them—I've still got some nice frilly ones. But our figures are so different."

"Granny Oe, you didn't try! Why do you like to think of me fleeing around the world at men's mercy?"

She laughed heartily, and caressed me some more to, as she said, start getting me braced for it. "They mean it the same way, under," she said, "they're just clumsier."

I would have preferred to stay and learn from her, if I'd been sure the men wouldn't come back.

"It seems," I said, "that they are the enjoyers and we are the enjoyed. Is that about right? It's a bit unfair."

"But you can enjoy being enjoyed, at least as much as they can enjoy enjoying. It's equal if not double."

Remembering Theopard's frownful and laborious joy, I thought she might be right.

"Look at it this way, you get most of the caressure. Generally it's only the palm of his hand, versus your breasts and your sides and your everything. And," she said, "I advise you later to become a joyeur, like me, and enjoy the sight of both enjoying. —Do one more thing for me, honey."

"Ngkay."*

"Let me see you running. Run around the room."

So I got up and obliged her. The room was too small to run around: to run as if chased, I had to run from end to end and slam into the wall. We shifted the bed to the middle so that I could hurdle it like a hedge. I rolled and hid behind it, mimed a man landing on top of me and us tussling.

She shut her eyes to fix the image.

"Motion suits you," she said; "it interprets you. The quicker you move the better you look. So the harder you run the harder they'll chase you, so it's a mistake to begin. —But all right, time to set out, since you must. What are you going to do?"

"Going to do? I usually don't know until I do it."

"What is your plan?"

"Should I have one?"

"In the end, you know, it's just a matter of which man or men you

---

* This is the "co-ed okay," or offhand *Okay* often heard from college-age girls, because either chewing gum or caught with the mouth half open. Among variants to be uttered by Applepeel under greater stress is the "Whoohkhay" of which the first part, cognate with "Whew," is phonetically either a bilabial fricative or a prominent example of the kind of "h" that is a vowel with breath instead of voice, or it could be said that the whole is accompanied by a gasp as a suprasegmental phoneme; elicited typically from the female part of a couple just at or after the completion of a strenuous twenty minutes of—mattress-moving, cat-catching, or flooded-basement-bailing. Like *ow* and *pshaw* (and unlike *O.K.* and its Japanese variants *okidoki* and *okeefenokee*) it is what the OED calls a "natural exclamation." In the form "Whkhay" or "Phphkhay," it *precedes* a burst of activity for which the program, the tools, and the will, if not the relish, have just been assembled. The utterance is conventionally regarded as an interjection, but Applepeel herself has been recorded as using it in all parts of speech, including declinable adjective, *Okay, okayer, okayest, oqueísimo!* and preposition, "on me and okay me." See Chen Yen Tao, "From 'Very Well' to 'Brilliant,' a Bifurcated Interjectional Escalator," *Proc. Ling. Soc. Anduv.* xviii: 3.

get under for protection against the others. That's destiny for us women—always has been."

"Is that so? Well, then, I'll tell you what my plan is: to stay free."

"Good luck to you, and I won't take a bet one way or the other. Go however you like, but I suggest you don't hitchhike." She took me across to the hamper in the closet. My bundle and I went in on the mound of laundry, and I curled up and she pressed the lid down over me.

Five minutes later two porters came back with her. As they lifted it she said, "Heavyish load today?" "Nah, bout the same as ever. But hey, better fix the strap." And she couldn't prevent them from setting it down to buckle it. I felt myself again lofted, then shot forward to the basket's end as they trotted down the stairs. Thus I was carried away in state to the cellars, to await wash-day.

Scrubbed

I T WAS now night, and if my hand could just have squeezed through the straphole I could have freed the buckle and raised the lid. As it was, I had to sleep in the basket, like a chick in an egg.

The bedsheets were filthy, but before long my nose forgot the stench, and I bore the copying of grime to my skin by thinking of rivers. Yes, when I was free I would find each morning a sweet river to rush into!—and with that image I went easily to sleep. I can't stay curled one way when I sleep—my old nursemaid Zed, watching me through the night, said she'd never seen such a child for opening and shutting and sprawling and rolling, and kicking all the sheets off or else piling them in a tower on my belly. "Any place you sleep will be a disaster-area," she predicted. "If you ever have a husband, he'll wake with your toes in his face, if you're in the bed at all—or if he is." The basket was large enough to be a tank, and I swam down among the voluted sheets. My shirt and breastlet came off and I lost them somewhere in the depths, and that felt better. I had a pleasant night.

Except for being too hot; but I wouldn't know about the heat-dream if I hadn't been wakened from it. A door opened and boots came grating in. Blackish voices knocked against each other: "What's this place—the jakes?" "It's the laundry." "Anywhere but this, you could catch her by her applepeel scent." "Actually she smells even nicer than that; she smells like orangepeel." This wasn't the dream any more—though it was like it—and I kept very still. I heard one basket kicked and another flung open. "Naw. She's miles away. Give up for tonight." "Give up? The outside party may have her by now; I'm going after them." "All right, me too, but first—I can't wait any longer—this is a good place—turn off that light." A heavy body sat down against my basket. Fingers started to undo the strap, but someone else said "Towels here" and flung them around. My basket began to shudder, went into a quick creaking rhythm. I didn't know what it was, but I let myself sway with it.

"I see nine Applepeels printed on the darkness."

"So do I. Trouble is, none of them will keep still."

It seemed there were at least nine other baskets in the cellar; all were creaking, in a counterpoint of different beats, fast and faster. The climaxing creaks were overtaken by a ragged storm of gasps and invocations. Then there was quiet and the sub-creaks of breathing.

"Damn!" said one. "I got it worse than before."

The boots scrambled, the door shut, perhaps it wasn't midnight yet, and I shrugged (so far as I could) and resumed my sleeping.

Cold light of morning came in onto the dank flagstones. I nestled deeper. But now came in a troop of raw-armed washerwomen. I could hear them unstrapping the lids of baskets and throwing them back. They unstrapped mine and I swam to the very bottom. They hefted armfuls of linen, immersed them in the sink, then spread them on the great stone counter for scrubbing, all the while singing lustily.

"A pretty green blouse!" called one.

"What, among the bedsheets? That's in the wrong lot."

"And here's a sky-blue breastlet, edged wi' white like summer clouds! I fear me there's more wrong than misclassification o' articles. Ah, what a place o' wickedment this is! To think of those guests, or beasts, upstairs, tumbling and winding some innocent maid in these sheets o' ours, and inducing of her to add her stains to theirs, and sending her off of a morning wi' only a skirt and a clevel to her back, in a manner of speaking, leaving her to walk the world bare-tittied, her blouse and her breastlet lost forever in some bed o' sin." They sighed, and washed my garments for me. "I'll have these for my little Til," said the one who had found them. "She's growing so she'll be witchier than that coal-red thing the men went berserk over yestren." And they all sighed again, or was it a hiss?

After some measures of ruminative scrubbing, one said: "I wouldn't so much mind them daydreaming about her, if they'd just not *talk* about her."

"You're right, Mabe," said another. "What they wouldn't let us see, why should we have to hear about?" "They say she was arrested for going around the country in an illegal green shirt just down to *here*, so as to tantalize." "A green—?" "Look, let's get off the subject, shall we? I've heard so much already, I'd have to know her wherever I saw her, perish her. With her coy green shirt and her hair so-red-that-it's-etcetera." "Color of dried blood, I'd call it. You can't even call her That Blonde, like that one as used to hang around your—" "All right, enough of that, Erm." "What was her name?—oh yes, Bet. Remember how you used to say, 'If I catch her I'll pull her blonde hair out by its black roots!' Ha ha!" "Poor old Bet, I wouldn't even mind seeing her back here. Harmless she seems now . . ."

The scrubstrokes kept time with the emotions, vicious or mellow-ing.

"It's a good thing there's really *no such thing* as someone prettier than anyone else."

"You've got to say this for her: she's cured all the lechers in this town."

"*Cured* 'em?"

"Yes, you should have heard the bawdytalk at the bar last night— not quite their usual stuff. Every one o' them used to imagine nothing but sultan-orgies, him and forty women. Now they're all nogamus, or monotonous or whatever it is. Just Let Me Alone With That Applepeel!"

"Yep, them was their words exactly. Mystifying, I should think, to any visitor, such as a hog-farmer from over Itshot way. And then instead of rolling on around to Jemima Tutchett's or Maria Plungeupp's, they all slipped off home to rest up for today's hunting."

To rest up for *what?*

"Well, she should be far away by now, the vixen. They'll have to chase her to China—I hope."

When the basket was nearly empty, they tipped it over to shake out the dregs, and I rolled forth into the gray puddles at their feet.

"My, my!" they said, standing around me, hands on mighty hips. "Speak of the devil!"

"Another misplaced article!"

"This little bolster will be a tough one."

"Yes, the dirt's ingrained."

And they took me by heels and shoulders. Were they drunk? "Hi," I shouted, "I'm not laundry, I'm a gir—!" But they swung me into the tub.

Surfacing after the splash, I opened my mouth to expostulate, but they filled it with soap, then turned me over to rinse it out. While my head was under, they made sure my tail was deeply clean. The water was hot! but soon it felt fine and I wanted to stay in. But they hoisted me into the air again and brought me down on the counter. (I don't think they meant to blunt my spine but, just in case, I did a smart twist at the right moment; I know how to fall, having a cat among my fore-bears.) There was foam crackling in my ear, an angel-wing of foam attached to my left nipple, soapy water ebbing from my navel, a town wall of foam between my legs; this wasn't enough, so they rolled me till I was dressed in froufrous of foam. Two spread me into an X by my wrists and ankles (sometimes I think I'd be better off without wrists and ankles) and the others came at me with scrubbing-brushes.

They scrubbed my fur, and my tongue when I put it out at them; but my breasts they only feinted at. They used enough vim to make me rosy but not sore: they were just jealous of the slut's triumph, as they saw it. They turned me over to give me a light lesson in both the ways that scrubbing-brushes can be used for spanking, the prickly way and the noisy way—amplified by my skin of water—we made the important discovery that spanking through a liquid film stings four times less but sounds four times louder. I was one glossy rainbowy bubble. I sat up and was met by two intersecting bucketfuls of water—cold; "Aaae!" I shrieked appreciatively.

"How's that, Miss Fulvue, are you well bathed and cleansed?—refreshed?"

"I blubblieve I am, thank you, ladies."

"Good, good; all ready again for public show?"

And they carried me out into the kitchen yard and threw me over the line, with my rear to the windows for the merriment of the scullery-maids peeling the carrots for lunch.

The sheets and I gleamed in the sun. Soon nicely dry, I set about getting down—not simple, when the torso hanging one side is balanced by the legs the other. Ignoring catcalls, I threw a heel up over, sat astride the sharp line, whirled around it to hang underneath, dropped off to stand on my hands. (There were some kinder calls of "Good luck, Applepeel!") Springing up, I touched my earlobes: neither night nor scrubbing had dislodged the lightly dangling rings. I took down my two garments and put them on, and if the second wash had been done I could have taken my pick of skirts and clevels. But they had purposely put it off till after lunch. So Miss Fulvue, reluctant stripper, really not hoping for another audience, threw her bundle over her shoulder and opened the iron gate, hoping there was a forest just outside.

Tashartris

N

O SUCH luck—not quite. It was a busy morning street, with shoppers, sightseers, beggars, constables. I might have called out "Taxi!" but it was probably as well I didn't.

There was a vehicle going right past in front of me. It was a shrine-wain, pulled by two sacred asses. The reins were loosely held by an old priest in a yellow robe, sitting bowed in meditation.

By a miracle, no one was at this instant looking in my direction. To the left up the street, all the traffic and pedestrians happened to be going to the left, and likewise to the right, where the street turned the corner of the caravanserai wall, all were going to the right and no one had yet come around the corner—at this instant. But the next instant was imminent, and before it came I would have to find cover, and as there was no other I threw myself into the cart.

So soon, I broke Oe's rule against hitchhiking. And it did cause immediate damage, though not the multiple pile-up she may have pictured.

The space behind the saintly driver's bench contained only the goddess Tashartris. She was returning from her ritual purification in the spring Sang Lakh. This was a monthly event, which was why there was not much ceremonial fuss. The crowds did not line the street showering her with fig-leaves as at her yearly marriage, but those who saw her in her painted cart would stand and make the customary gestures. And I had knocked her down. I was curled beside her, both of us invisible—which was fine for me, but she would be missed. It was necessary for her to rise again into view, and soon.

So why didn't I just set her up? Because by impiously felling her to the floor I had shattered her from her crown down into two pieces and some minor rubble.

Seconds, only, were allotted by fate for my emergence from the gate, my dive into the cart, and the overthrow of Tashartris. And before the next few seconds were out, crouching between her fragments, I had whipped off my shirt and breastlet and wound them on top of my head in a passable replica of Tashartris's aegis-turban, representing the Green Flash from which she was born and the mountain-capping cloud on which she dwells.

The priest must have heard her fall, but only from the remotenesses of his meditation; and only slowly did his hand, a dear old long yellow veiny scholar's hand, come feeling around behind him. It found my chin, and I rose at its gentle lifting. I had to mime the easy rise of a fallen Kelly-doll, for the goddess was light, being hollow.

Thus a goddess fell, a goddess rose. Bare-Breasted Tashartris was in place as soon as the first pencil-vendor on the sidewalk, hearing the cart, looked over his shoulder and then faced me with adoring eyes to make his lucky prayer.

I had to keep my own eyes wide and still and slightly heavenward, like the painted eyes of the statue. That was hard when what I most wanted was to monitor each other pair of eyes along the street, lest ritual adoration should pass into recognition, or, as dangerous, non-ritual adoration. It was good practice for my peripheral vision, and also for my posture. Sitting still in the swaying cart was easy for Tashartris because she had no lower end, only a flat pottery bottom. For me, sitting cross-legged, it was not at all easy. I had to suppress the flexibility of my waist; when the floor tilted to the left I had to pivot stiffly to the left with it instead of bending naturally to the right. The fingers of my right hand, luckily, were pressed to the floor. I was about to lower the other hand surreptitiously when someone threw a poppy into it, and I had to hold it where it was. Thus I sat tense, afraid that a leftward lurch would send me toppling just as I had sent Tashartris, and perhaps from the Virgo Cloud where she really makes her home she would hurl a bolt to split me in pieces as I had split her image.

Yet you may think I now had few real troubles, having nothing to do but be borne passively along toward safety in some sanctuary. On the contrary, it was my severest trial, an ordeal more vexing than any danger or exertion. For I have never in my life been able to hold still. As Zed used to scold, "Have you got sand in your knickers, child?"—or it might be "burrs," "spiders," or something else she liked to fancy. I *cannot* sit still, but now I had to. I can tell you that the life of a statue is not as tranquil as it seems. It's no wonder they sometimes give crotchety responses to our prayers.

Nor did I fully enjoy the comments I overheard, such as: "I'd forgotten how—young the statue looks. Can it be a new one?"

"No, we'd have heard. But it's certainly been cleaned. And given new earrings."

That was true: the earrings that lay on the floor, still threaded through Tashartris's pink clay lobes, were real rings—great circles of silver wire, with the moon's concave face set in one side (young on the left ear, old on the right), smiling across at the little evening or morning star.

By pinching myself sternly with the hand that was at floor-level, I held my frame still. But I am not only frame: I'm also tissue. Of this I was reminded when I heard a lady remark:

"I'd swear the idol's breasts jounce."

"They do seem to," said her husband, considering carefully. "They don't flop but I do believe they tremble, even nicer than real ones—nearly as nicely as yours, my dear. But it's the skill of the sculptor, or the fine art substances they use nowadays, or our rapture that deceives our eyes."

This credulousness made me think I could get away with more, so, when nobody was looking at my eyes, I lowered them. The heavenward gaze had come to be one of the most trying parts. It just wasn't me.

To my consternation, I saw a mosquito drift downward past my chin.

And now the lifelikeness of my breasts was beginning to make the curiosity of bystanders prevail over their piety. Men didn't go so far as to crane their necks, but they stood as tall as they could. They could see me no lower than my waist; below that, they had to look at the sides of the cart (decorated with scenes galactic and calendrical) but, by their expressions, they hoped these were a vision which would dissolve and disclose something about the fundamentals of their cult. Out of the tail of my eye I saw some irreverent small boys fall in behind us, in the gutter, and I knew they would soon be jumping.

At this moment the left-hand ass (the jenny) brayed.

This frightful sound gave me a start, but my start passed unnoticed. When Tashartris's ass brays, it means she is not her usual complaisant self. She has, perhaps, heartburn, or has seen Brayab wink at an earthly milkmaid. To appease her, all must fall on their knees.

(And whatever Tashartris's temper, mine was not of the best. With the mosquito hovering between my breasts, I was itching in anticipation.)

As far as the eye could see, or ears could hear those wrenching lamentations of hoarse despair, kneeling people lined the street. Now they had to look up from below, but none took their eyes off me.

The mosquito was feeling its way down one of the flutings of my stomach, like a rappeller descending the Jungfrau. Now, with its wavy flight that is slow but not quite slow enough, the very handwriting of infuriating indecisiveness, it was exploring the upper borderland of my fur, where belly-down by degrees gives way to combable hairs.

Would the little ghost of a gray devil never choose a site? He did: inside my navel. Have you ever had an itch there?

My skin flickered, and he was in the air again without drinking his fill. He made up for it at a finely selected place lower down. And then another; he found scrubbed flesh pasturable.

We reached another suburb, where only the most far-hearing kneeled. But if Tashartris was grumpy before, she was livid now. The ass (which I later rewarded with a rubdown) brayed again, and again the people paled and got to their knees. And so we came to open country.

A few persistently devoted peasants followed, but the lane turned between oaks, and at last, cautiously glancing back, I saw no one. You can believe that I scratched.

Second came slapping the mosquito—but he too at this moment assessed the situation and took his leave. (Heavily, full of applejuice.) As the only worshipper privileged to touch and even kiss me, he perhaps deserved to live.

Out of suffering into beatitude! Scratching—both-handed, generous, to the end of necessity and beyond—kept me blissful for two miles. One hand began at my navel, the other at a thigh, and they worked—but you can imagine their exhaustive itineraries.

We were passing under aspens, in a light breeze. I watched it shuffle the wisps of white hair on the ancient head before me. A woodpecker paused in profile on a trunk, hesitating to let me see him at work; a thrasher blundered out of the hedge and made a russet flutter at the donkeys' feet. I smiled at them as I finished the scratching of my sides, which had not even been stung.

First to scratch and then to stretch. If I flung my arms wide behind the priest he might see them, and if I flung them forward I would thump him, so I flung them back, and then up. I unrolled my spine, locked my fingers in the air, stretched my arms, meandered my torso, seesawed my shoulders, and tried how far back I could press my shoulderblades and how far forward my nipples without sacrilege to the saffron robe. But most of the need was in my crossed legs and seat.

So, with caution, I stood on my head. I had to wriggle back to make a space, put my head and hands down close behind the driver, and kick off from the rear board. I tried to touch the apple-boughs with my toes, and then I bicycled in the air. The turban made a soft plinth for my scalp. The cart sent medicinal tremors up me as it ambled over the gravel.

In this attitude I might have stayed and traveled, if only, with my head down between the cart-rails, I could have kept a watch for farmers in the fields. What would they see?—donkeys lost in their meditation, priest in his, and third in the row, me, from ribs up to soles, ass forward—and the laughter came up (or down) in my throat and I had to come down quick. There was a boy sitting on a gate. The straw dropped out of his mouth, and as we passed he slowly turned his head, staring after the miracle.

Having finished my exercises, I opened my bundle and ate the gooseberry and the blueberry muffins. Then I drank the ale, wiped my mouth, and wondered whether I should have conserved some. Then stealthily I slipped over the rearboard, relieved myself behind a magnolia (this isn't one of those unnatural stories where the heroine never goes wee-wee), ran after the cart and clambered back aboard.

Only then did it occur to me that I might just hop off and go my own way. But what about the old priest? I had broken his Tashartris; if I just gave him the slip he would be left goddessless. The thought of him arriving at his journey's end, getting painfully down, coming reverently around to tend his holy ark, and finding only the pieces, made me feel like crying.

But then I told myself, You've got to think of yourself. You're no real goddess. This is the only man in the world who won't misuse you; the world is full of others who will—so campaign! On your way!

At this moment we halted. We had come to the Rattlebridge, which crosses the ravine of Sume, a headwater of the Cresfont. The bridge is one of those made with the most vibratory surface yet devised by road-makers: planks set on edge. So Master Yoryo took a rope from under his seat and walked twice around me. I was a statue again; and his eyes were dim from studying sacred scrolls, and they pierced far through the plane of my flesh into Tashartris's world of spirit. I nearly told him that the coils were not tight enough: they lay like a girdle around my hips. He had paid them out by long habit, and Tashartris, though her size and figure were much like mine, was a shade thicker in the waist. Climbing back to his place, he held the rope's end in one hand and resumed the reins with the other.

The oily planks are bolted together, all at slightly different heights, and to go on wheels over them is to have your teeth hammered against your brainpan; *Urrr-a-jah!* Any onlookers here would certainly have distinguished my breasts from ceramic ones. Even my eyelids were shaken open, much against my will—for the bridge was narrow and the tops of the trees that lodged in the descents to the coil of angry water were house-heights below us. The sun, declining on our right, sent an orange glance along the upper cliffs; below, everything was purple. In the middle the priest stopped again. He knew by the feel of the rope that Tashartris was held too loose—and it would be the end of the world if she were to fall off into this gorge, haunted by the goblins Bobsuncle and Kitbusily. He yanked the rope so that it throttled my waist, and if he had tugged an inch more I would have had to speak. Thus lashed in place, I was drawn up between rocks and pines to the gate of my temple.

The Cleft

I ENTERED it at sunset, still seated in my cart. The asses, jack and jenny, take it right to the top of the ramp, and when they disengage themselves from it to retire to their luxurious quarters it becomes the altar. This is where Tashartris lives.

The priest unwinds her bindings and makes a last obeisance to her uplifted eyes and breasts in the failing light as he withdraws through the great bronze doors, but then she comes to life and unfolds her legs. I had the night to myself, but not much to do with it except hide the pieces of Tashartris, feel vainly around the walls for exits, make friends with resident spiders, and curl in my blanket where I could be ready to leap to my place at a sound from the door.

Only when the moon is up but the sun is not is Tashartris present in her image; only then can she be visited. For when the moon is under the sea, there she is in it; and when the sun is in the sky, she either is riding with him, or has quarreled with him. The month was drawing toward its close: the moon rose three hours before dawn. Three hours before dawn, the hinges mewled and I woke and slid to my place as quick as a temple snake. There I had to sit in the chilly dark, which grew barely lighter and no less chilly as the old moon, mouth agape, floated slowly up into the eastern sky on the tide of twilight.

One feature of Tashartris's temple allowed me to get away with my impersonation of her: the Cleft. For reasons of modesty I prefer to call it the Fissure. It is a bottomless slot in the naked rock. Before you imagine some kind of lubricious natural sculpture, I must explain that it is just a straight crack, passing across in front of the altar. Such chasms are found in oracular shrines and caverns of many lands; some-times there arise from them chthonic vapors that send the prophetess into her trance, or smokes that mask priestly conjuring tricks. What comes up out of Tashartris's Fissure is pure heat.

There is a screen of shimmering air between the adorers and the goddess they adore. They feel themselves entranced by her presence, they see her as in a dream—they see her seem to shift and ripple—they see her eyes move and her breast breathe as if she lives—they imagine golden coils that sparkle beside her throat—they see her melt into the likeness of some earthly daughter who has them in her spell.

But however the beyond-woman lures them with her earthly-wom-anlikeness, the mystic fiery Fissure divides them from her, disinclining them to make a leap. After addressing her by some of her sublime titles, such as "Huntress Chased and Unchaste, Slut of Sluts, Lushest Trollop"—or her parts ("Horns of Plenty"— "Holy Twinnity")—they make their pious requests ("O Tashartris, grant that I get under Cindy Prince's frock within the month!" "O Tashartris, nerve me to mention to my Jandy that there are other ways—or, better, make her think of them herself and beg me for them!") and toss their offerings across the Fissure, or if particularly ardent may send a more personal offering siz-zling down into the Fissure itself; and bow themselves out.

When the worshippers had gone I ate the barley and juleps they had cast at my feet; wondered how I could stop them leaving gammon and gizzards. I started on the nut paste, and stopped just in time to get my jaws apart before they were set in rock. It is understandable that households would not make offerings of their freshest food.

There is a latrine for the goddess, but like herself it is a make-believe one, cut short not very far down, so it would serve a live goddess for only a few days.

There are other subterranean features; perhaps there is as much of the temple below the rock as above. Under my altar there was a grating to give air to devotees in the cella attempting to attain Thoroughtouch.

I had all day to myself in the rambling building and the garden, which are surrounded by the same high wall. From the steps descending into the garden there was a glimpse across into the temple library, where the old monk Yoryo under a long steep rain of light pored over his manuscripts in Greek and Japanese.

I was soon hungry for exercise of my attention and of my body. High up in the wall as it ran beside the garden, inaccessible to me, there was a pillared gallery, looking out on the garden and also over the outside world. I kept to the gravel path among the shrubs at the side. I glanced up at the gallery and no one came along it. I kept glancing and no one was there. So I ran out on the lawn and turned cartwheels. I felt brighter and the sun was on my skin. I turned cartwheels all around the lawn one way and somersaults the other, and walked on my hands in figures of eight.

"The goddess! Look!"

Child's voice from the gallery! I ran and dived into the bushes.

"Daddy! I saw the goddess in her garden! I really did! She was running and flying and doing the splits and handsprings and backflips and rolling in the grass and shaking her hair about and laughing!"

"Now don't tell fibs, little one."

"I did see her!"

"Well, well, it was a vision."

"She was bare, like she's supposed to be! Her tummy and everything! It must have been her. She's prettier than people are."

The second morning, to avoid surprise, I got up when it felt coldest and watched out to the east, between the alabaster panthers, for the moon to rise. She rose an hour later than yesterday: when she first betrayed herself she looked like a bed of reeds on fire, then, when she swam up to the horizon, like a spoon, then like two monkeys boxing, but I, having climbed out early many mornings to feel the grass and track snails, was not surprised by the many forms the moon can take.

By the time I saw her turn over and look like a half-breastlet, I had hurried into my place to be worshipped.

The worshippers this morning were surprised to find the previous morning's offerings actually eaten. I hoped they would spread the word, so that the third morning would bring offerings that were actually edible.

Worshipped

O N THE third morning there was less than an hour between moonrise and sunrise, and the moon was not even seen. So no worshippers had troubled to get out of bed—except one.

He stood before me with his eyes shut, looking to me for an answer to his prayer but with his inward vision bent on another, who was the subject of his prayer.

"Goddess of passion," he said, "I am one of those who hunt the maiden Applepeel. As you know, she has deceitfully eluded us, but every day and every night we go out, quartering the country, in our faith that she must be either near or not terribly far, and that she will be ours in the end. We are not alone in desiring her: appetite for Applepeel has spread already from Swanmark to the Violet Hills; every-where men, imagining her, are able afresh to swive their wives. But we are the priests among her lovers. Some of us ride out by day and some by night; we have four shifts, as a matter of fact, marshalled by our founder and leader, and every day more hunters join the sacred hunt. I myself was not there to see her when they worshipped her with feathers in the place of commerce, but I believe I know exactly what she looks like. For, as they say, the sides of the spear can be anywhere, but the point has to be in the middle. My stallock feels so fresh when I think about her—oh to glove it in her! Just to mouth her name—I get no further than *Ap-!* before I feel my frown melting upward. Why, I never used to be able to get out of bed; now I wake—think—am saying *Applp*—and here I am! Although I demur not to the vows of our brotherhood as to how we shall entreat our shining quarry when we have her, it is my private faith—a secret I entrust to you now, goddess, because no other brother has braved the cold of this last morning of your calendar to be with me as I seek you out—that I, alone, am fated to come upon her, and to accept her surrender whether willingly or not; thus I shall have a higher duty than to sound our agreed signal and summon my brothers to the sharing. It is for confirmation of this my faith, lissom goddess, that I come to you; my prayer is that it shall be vouchsafed to me to discover one morning (for I'm in the pack that rides out in the morning) behind a hedge, Applepeel Curtis, no less; and I also crave of you the strength and wits to make sure of my prize if, as some of our more fearful brethren murmur, she is as dangerous as a cornered badger or a mockingbird at nesting-time or has magic under her fingernails. —Tashartris, the moon silvers your breasts: now is the time to grant my prayer!" and he startled me by opening his eyes and staring straight at me. His eyes, though, were glazed by a gleam which I took for madness, till I realized it was the sun about to rise behind me. I had been fighting to hold my laughter, but suddenly it came—I gave way and rocked, chiming like a bell.

It satisfied him; "Tashartris, Laugher-in-Pleasure, I thank you for your sign. I am your slave, Abdi-Tashartris," and he skipped away.

"Hey, where's your offering?" I called after him— "no offering, no Ap-" but the door clanged and I was left breakfastless.

Safe and alone for another long day, the door shut and the sun rising, I went and stood at the balustrade and gazed over the tide of sparkling-yellow light as it flooded past below me.

"What next?" I said. "This can't be the end."

"Little sister," said the priest. He was standing behind me. I jumped in my skin.

Turning and facing him, I felt no need to cover myself.

"So you've known all the time, Master? I'm sorry I broke your goddess."

He shook his head sadly. "Yes, and I know not even where her parts are."

I didn't say anything to that, because I had the parts in a grotto and was trying to figure out how they might be mended.

"Well, come with me," he said, "and have some coffee to warm you."

He led me to his apartment. It was a mere cell in the wall, but because the temple stood high it had a view over great distances to the west. There was one couch, which he never used himself. Its luxury was for guests, though he may never have had one before. I sprawled on it and purred. A couch to burrow into, leathery black, but soft after three nights and two days—is that right, have you kept count?—an eternity, anyway, of the slabs and altars which are temple-builders' idea of comfort for us immortals.

"You could, you know," he said, glancing away from my white sections distributed along the black background, "wear your clothes while you're off duty."

"Oh, I don't really care to, thank you. I've only my topclothes, and they leave my Antarctica feeling breezier."

"All I can offer, I'm afraid, is my spare robe. Here it is."

I laughed and applied it down my front and showed him that it was a handspan too long. "And it would leave me feeling all the colder at night." I hung it back on its peg.

"Besides," I said, "it's such a relief to cut out the most boring parts of the day, putting on clothes, taking off clothes—plus maybe finding clothes to put on, folding clothes after taking them off (if my mother has her way)—five minutes, at least, wasted out of every day! Multiply by all the days in eighteen years—that makes whole weeks when one could be doing something better! This is a perk of the job—the uniform's a turban and I don't have to travel to work so why bother to dress at all? But," I reassured him, "I don't mind you covering up if that's your choice."

He smiled and thanked me. But something more was bothering him. Waiting for him to speak, I sat folded-legged on the couch. After much anxious pacing and scratching of his lined forehead, he took his place on his stool.

"My poor young maid—" he said.

I suddenly decided to run across and kiss him and offer myself to him. "We can do whatever you like or can," I said. "We could just stroke each other all night. I really love you and I'll stay with you till you go to heaven!"

He smiled and I could see that what I'd said was like a child offering a king a lollipop. He wasn't angry, nor did I feel ashamed. I just had to sit back down and listen.

"Please," he said, "do not distress yourself too much over the action—the damage—"

"The sacrilege," I suggested; and then, as his face went from pink to white, told myself to shut up and let him get things out in his own hesitant way.

"The statue was old," he said. "It was already cracked. And of course rather discolored. It's had cleanings, but cleanings couldn't modernize its style. It was made in the last century, and I am informed that beauty has changed. I do not believe that can be so, but the trappings of worship may shift to and fro like seaweed in the tide. At any rate we have intended for more than a decade to replace the image, and in fact it is more than a month since we sent— But that doesn't matter now." He was clasping his knee and gazing at the stone floor, off to my right, and he swung himself and his gaze a little way toward me.

"We are lucky," he said, "Tashartris is lucky, that you became Tashartris."

"Thank you, Master."

"My Tashartris has become a lovelier goddess."

I didn't know what to say. I didn't think "lovely" was a word I deserved.

"But *you* are not lucky."

"Aren't I being patient, Master, sitting still while the worshippers worship me?"

"Yes, and I wonder at it."

"This morning it was less than an hour."

"And tomorrow morning you have a rest, because it is new moon. The moon rides with Brayab all day and all night."

"Ah! No worshippers! I'll sleep in the garden, and wake in the sunshine."

"But then tomorrow evening, the crescent moon will find her way into a new sky, before the sun sets, and most of the people will turn out to see you, though for a short time. But the next evening it will be longer. And then it will be three hours, and four hours, and six hours, until at full moon the goddess must be worshipped all night."

I hadn't thought of that. Eight hours of the summer night I would have to endure on my altar, while the moon crept from the east to the west.

"And this is the way it will be every month."

I was silent.

"And when winter comes—"

"Yes, I know." The coldest nights of the full moon would be fully fifteen hours.

We had a breakfast of fritters—that is, he fried me a pile of fritters but himself picked his customary grains of rice. I'm afraid he cooked with saffron, which made me even more hyperactive.

"You want to get out again into the wide world; or rather, you must. The trouble is, I can think of only one way."

"Well, then," I said with my mouth full, "I must do it."

"I'd have to tell you about it first."

"Well then, tell me about it."

"I don't think I can!" he said, and we laughed.

"Well, tell me in a little while."

"You may not choose to do it."

"But if I must do it, as you said, I must do it."

"No, sometimes it's possible not to do the thing you must do."

He now had either to become philosophical and explain his riddles in yet more riddly terms, or give an example I could understand. Thus he had succeeded in his maneuvers to bring himself to the point where he could steel himself to say what he was going to have to say to me.

"The way is," said, "the way is this. The only way for you to get out of here is, that there is a ritual. A ritual that the goddess, or rather really not the goddess—"

"Oh Master, I think I understand you!"

This is what Master Yoryo was trying to explain to me:

Tashartris is given to marrying. At present she was tired of Brayab, the Sun, who was too set in his ways; she purposed to marry the young god Ritan.

"The wedding of the divinities must be celebrated by human surrogates. And there is no other way than this for you to escape from here: to be chosen as the Tashartris-surrogate.

"But there are aspects of this plan to which grave consideration must be given. The first is that both surrogates must be virginal. So, sadly, I dismissed the plan and held my peace. I did not imagine you likely to qualify."

"Master Yoryo!"

"You appeared to me to fit only too well what I understand to be the requirements of biological nubility, to have been allowed to preserve that status all the way to the age of eighteen."

I said, "We grow up slowly in my part of the world; at any rate I did."

"Yes, though others may have grown up faster around you. —But this morning I heard your devotee call you a maiden, that is to say, a virgin. On the other hand, he may have been using the term in the theological sense in which we find it used in the Astarte and Cybele cults, as well as that of Atergotis."

"Well, a virgin I am—here, have a look. Put your finger in and feel."

"I'll take your word."

"See, there's a lid across this, which is called my cunt."

"I know, I—"

"Isn't it a beautiful word?"

"Do you think so? Some people think it should be—shouldn't be spoken—that it's too English."

"Oh, I like it. It reminds me of things neatly shaped, like a boat. Don't you want to check it?"

"No, your assurance is perfectly enough. And you are not, I suppose, betrothed?"

"Oh . . ." I sent my thoughts quickly back. What a long time ago it seemed! Was I betrothed or wasn't I?

"I guess I was about to be, Master—but then it was all torn up."

"I see. One of those regrettable infant-swapping arrangements, no doubt thought better of by one family or the other for some commercial reason. There is then no obstacle—no cause, reason, or just impediment that might embarrass the gods when the banns are called."

"But I think you said the virginity bit isn't the only thing I've got to be grave about? What else can there be? What are you smiling at?"

"The idea of you being grave about anything. However, here goes, gravely or bravely: the surrogates, starting as virginal, must—become otherwise." As usual, it took some time to get the specifics out of Master Yoryo, but what he meant was that the wedding would be very public, and would not stop at the symbolic level; and after it I would actually have to be the consort of the Ritan-Surrogate and settle down and live with him.

This certainly wasn't the ideal plan. Some youth who would handle me with the clumsiness of inexperience and then take me to his hovel in the backwoods of this province! I hadn't thought of settling down with anyone, and as for the spending of my virginity, I had decided either never to do it, or to select a wise man of at least fifty to be my gentle guide and initiator.

"How long have I got to decide?"

"The wedding will be when the moon is six days old, since each day of the moon's cycle corresponds to three years of human life."

"So what's my deadline?"

He was incapable of giving me a deadline; all he would say was, "Do let me know as soon as possible—I told the selection committee I thought I might have a candidate, so I'll be in trouble if they find I haven't when the moon is five days old. One year we couldn't find a virgin nearer than Spitsbergen."

That night as I lay in the cot he had given me I tried the way the bad girls in our town say they use for deciding whether to marry a fellow or not. (Actually I only heard this from my little brother: he said his fiancée, also aged eight, used it and it said she was to marry him and so they went and married behind the henhouse.) You go to sleep and see whether you wake up with your hand clutching your cunt or your sitch. It seemed a relief to rely on some such sure method of divination, till I was half asleep and realized I wasn't sure which was supposed to mean which. After all, there were various interpretations: a husband would be allowed to do this, but if you were celibate you would have girl-friends instead and do that . . . And then what if I woke up clutching neither? Well, I woke up clutching both.

Anyway I jumped up to see the sun come feeling along the terraces. A temple is almost as fine as forests and mountains in the level-lighted ends of the day.

This new day was my holiday, so I romped in the garden and climbed orange-trees (getting scratched) and was sure I'd be content to stay here. I even forgot to inform Master Yoryo of my decision till he came diffidently inquiring. He bowed and said, "*We* shall be glad you decided to stay. I'll tell the committee to resume the search. Okay?" (This was a modern word I had taught him.) "Okay," I said.

Since it was settled that I was to live in the temple for evermore, he offered to take me on a tour.

"A tour of the sacrum and the perineum and septum and so on? Are you sure it would be safe for me?" I said, walking along with him and trying to take his hand. "You know—I may not be as good a maiden as you think I am. I mean I may be pure but I'm not very holy. And curiosity killed the cat."

"Yes," he said, "but only after nine tries."

"To tell you the truth I've already explored a lot of it, some only in the dark—when I was misguidedly trying to find a way out. And I'd like to learn what the shapes were that I groped over—the ritual objects, yes?"

"Yes, and I could if you wish teach you the correct names of E-Tashartris's parts, such as the sanctum and the naos and the transept. E-Tashartris is the name of this whole holy complex. It means the 'House of Tashartris.'"

"Yes, I must get all that right," I said, "sacrum is part of Tashartris and sanctum is part of her house. It may have been the sanctum where I thought I felt quite a dangerous buzz—in my sacrum, actually."

We peeped through lunettes and crossed the high place called the Threshing-Floor of Onan, and descended a steep wide flight of steps; in the middle, half way down, stood a one-legged table. Among Tashartris's ninety-eight known titles is that of Table-Turner. This is a backgammon table. Like others of its kind it is a box opening into two halves with the spikes painted inside, and like chess tables in the cafés of Asia it stands on a single wooden post. What is unusual is that it rotates on its post. You can open it (slowly, because it's heavy) and you can spin it (slowly). What you couldn't do was both open it and spin it. It would spin when shut; but opening it froze something.

"What's the matter with it, then?" I asked. "Why don't you just call the repairman?"

"Repairperson," said the priest, "may take a century or more."

I laughed scornfully. He said: "Some of the experts" (meaning the alarmingly beautiful theologians we had glimpsed in their cloister across the garden) "are inclined to think that the title belongs to a daughter of Tashartris, yet to come. When Table-Turning Tashartris arrives—Tashartris Mensiversa—it will be found she can both open and turn this table."

Of course I with my meddlesome fingers promptly opened the table and— No. Just *in case*, don't try it, Lady Jane. It certainly wouldn't move for me if it hadn't moved for generations, but just in case—leave well alone. We're in enough of a pickle trying to be Tashartris's statue; let's not find ourself figuring out how to be her daughter too—Tashar-

tris II, Tashartrida. I gave a pretended push, to prove it wasn't me, and
we continued our guided tour.

We ended, by my request, in Yoryo's study. He thought I could not
be interested in the text he was collating, but I was.   It was the
Astrapocrypha of Haamg ibn Auhanda. And as he explained it I edged
tighter against him and at last inserted myself onto his lap, like a snuggling kitten that will not be repulsed. He didn't really mind, though it
took him a while to learn that I could both twine my arms around him
and ask sensible questions about the lore of the nine worlds, the flow-
ingness of life, the secrets of permanence, the sixteen sleeps, and the
meaning of the Thorotouch.

"Surely you're cold," he said—

"No, feel," and I pressed a kiss on him, richer with Tashartris-
knowledge.

"But your shoulder"—he touched it— "You are. Won't you put a
robe on?"

"Oh, all right."

He again fetched it and I stepped into it. It was still a handspan too
long; I made fun by running around and tripping over it. He was a little
pained. I drew it up, tied a string around my loins, and let the linen spill
over in that pouch of female drapery, whose rhyme in nude male sculpture is the downroll of inguinal muscle over the hip and groin. And so
the robe looked like a chiton, though in the pungent yellow of the
orient.

"Now on washdays," I said, "we'll both have to go bare"—to get
him used to domesticity.

Thorotouch

FROM DEEP under my altar, in quiet times, I could make out faint careful voices, naming parts of the body in reverent rhythms.

It is said that there was once a lonely student who, for lack of access to skin, began to list on paper the ways of worshipping: " . . . He worships her shoulders—her arms—her hands . . . with his mouth—his hands—his stalk . . ." and soon found that everything had to be subdivided and multiplied and tabulated in increasing numbers of dimensions. If indeed this legendary founder of the Thorotouch was human, and a student, or perhaps a librarian, and if he persisted even as the goal kept receding ahead, and if the extending quest kept him alive, then he will now be listing the phases of the Thorotouch by computer. But since the Thorotouch is infinite, I think it is more likely that its founder was, or became, a god.

From a listing of naughty things ("She worships his stalk with her lips—her tongue—her mouthinners—her eyelashes . . .") it became relentlessly a classification, a finely graded classification, an even and proportioned classification, and finally the Thorotouch. It was driven to find the most general, all-applicable, primary vocabulary. And, root of all, it was driven on the only verb that could embrace all actions: *worship*.

Actually to try to write down the steps of the Thorotouch drives people mad. Instead, a couple must improvise aloud. In practice, they try it naively for an hour; then, if not yet daunted, they are ready to receive philosophical instruction. Then, if still not daunted, they come to the cell in the temple, no more than one entire night in a month. And I heard their careful voices coming up: "He clasps her left elbow— with his left armcrook—fingergaps—palmcup—fingertipcircle— handgrip—waistside—armpit . . ."

Generally, the man speaks while the woman applies (" . . . his groinchannels with her hair—her ear—her cheek—her chin . . .") and vice versa.

Words with *d* and *sh* in them, carried on the light voice of a girl . . .

What is the object of Thorotouch? In a crude sense it is to make the bodies of lovers touch each other at every point. And the least of the difficulties is defining where "surface" ends. (Hard as it seems, the defining of the ero-surface has been done; the questions of the mouth, the eyeballs, the hair, have with time been tackled. And the Thoroughtouch of course includes the Throughtouch.)

If you take two small cards and slide one accurately over the other from right to left, then from top to bottom, then turn one card over and again slide from right to left and from top to bottom, then turn the second card over and again slide from right to left and from top to bottom, then turn the first card over a second time and again slide it in one direction and then the perpendicular direction over the surface of the second card, then the two cards have—or have they?—touched at all points. That is, *every point has touched every point.* Every *point.* So in principle, two bodies can do it. It's just that they are more complicated than cards.

When a loving couple—a couple so united that they do not understand whether to refer to themselves in the plural or the singular—thinks about it, they cannot bear that there are parts of each other that have never touched. It is relatively very easy to touch every part of your lover. That is, to touch every point of her with one point of you, say, your right palm. If you define "point" more narrowly, as, say, your right index fingertip, then it takes a month or two longer. But that is merely to touch every point (defined as palm, or part of palm, or fingertip . . .) of her with *one* point of you. To do the same with *every point of you* is . . .

Yet they attempt the Thorotouch. But it is safe to say that there has not yet existed a couple who have achieved it, or half achieved it. (The half of infinity is itself infinity.)

The pre-instruction, which Master Yoryo has to give, reading out of the Grammar of Thorotouch, consists entirely of terminology, or of principles of subdivision, which is the same thing.

The actions begin to be divided something like this: "Among the modes of worshipping are seeing and touching. Among the modes of touching are rubbing, digging, clasping, and crowning . . ." (The last of these is what you and I call orgazzing.)

The Commentaries on the Grammar are mostly on the prosaic side. They say things like: "The persons are naked unless otherwise mentioned," or: "It is important to persist through all actions of a cycle. Outbreaks of a sense of comedy are to be expected; just don't act (negatively) on them. Cycles may be reattempted; therefore, the first time, get as near as you can to each action . . ." The cycles themselves (or zonefests, or, if they end in Crowning, lays) read as poems.

If you divide by zero, you get infinity and an error-message; if you multiply infinity, you get what? Having multiplied itself up to infinity because there is not one arm but two, not one side to the hand but two, not only fingers but gaps between them, not one direction or pressure or speed or style to a caress but an infinity (or at least as many as there are colors in the spectrum), not one direction of worship but *three*, the Thorotouch as a whole is all too easily multiplied—by stages of undress, by stages of desire and acceptance, by retreats and advances, by numbers of worshippers and worshipped.

Completely forgotten are such illusions as the "beauty" or "age" of the worshipped. The worshipper (who is also worshipped) worships on, and it is ever further from their minds to question whether what is worshipped is worshipworthy. The passion gently grows so that, if Thorotouch had an end that could be reached, it would be death; since it does not, if persisted in it is perpetual life.

The discipline of the Thorotouch was what my chaotic adventures lacked: they followed no smooth gradient of salacity. They had the mere hint of progression: I had as yet been worshipped only with eyes, thoughts, words, and feathers.

Tiplady

I DON'T THINK that fine old hymn by Augustus Toplady had ever been sung in this temple, but some of the worshippers came in humming it, and then I heard, mingled with laughter and with other sounds of breath and impact:

"Picklady. Hopelady. Runlady. Traplady. Stoplady. Coplady. Copelady.

"Riplady. Striplady.

"Scanlady.

"Touchlady. Shocklady.

"Straplady . . . Hoplady . . . Tiplady . . . Driplady . . . Droplady . . . Ducklady . . . Proplady . . . Patlady . . . Flicklady . . . Fliplady . . . Plucklady . . . Stroplady . . . Clutchlady . . . Smirchlady . . . Slaplady . . . Thumplady . . . Spanklady . . . Whiplady . . . Niplady . . . Tricklady . . . Strokelady . . . Griplady . . .

"Liplady. Siplady. Licklady. Sucklady. Drinklady. Gulplady. Croplady. Rublady. Scrublady.

"(And a little bit of Gripchick; Flipchick; Lipchick . . .)

"Jumplady, Spreadlady, Opelady, Diplady, Humplady, Bumplady, Pumplady, Wringlady! . . . Rocklady . . . Thanklady."

By which time she was a thoroughly wet purring limp lady.

Waxing Month

NEXT EVENING, an hour's duty.

The horn hanging on the west wall gave its nasal wail at the setting of Brayab. (Its note falls away, into a groan that seems to slide beneath the sea; the horn on the east wall splits upward a diminished ninth as the priest sets his lips to it at sunrise.) And I took my place.

Within a minute I was itching to get off my pedestal and rush my change of decision to him. The minutes crept by, the worshippers worshipped me, and all I could think of was that it might be too late. At this moment, the surprised and overjoyed parents of some virgin might be eagerly signing her away.

The moon on this first night of its new life was too thin to be actually visible. Instead the priest would consult his tables before sounding moonset on the great cratered gong. Between horn and gong is the reign of the Infanta moon.

But my eyes, good at any time, and now celestial, were keener than ever as I stared fixedly into the west. And I saw it! In a patch of the melon-colored sky, above the black graph of the horizon, a patch where there had been only sky, the sky subtly opened; opened into a smile, thin-lipped, fine, refined, yet there, present, and not restrained, but broadly gay! I forgot the buzzing worshippers under me and had no hardship staring, my face slowly descending with my eyes which slowly descended with the moon. It reached the black; one mischievous corner of the mouth was left; it set! I sprang off my altar and ran down its back steps.

Behind me the buzzing ceased momentarily, then burst louder, but I didn't even think of it until, as I ran along an aisle, the gong started up. The moon had set behind a northwestern mountain!

"Oh, Master Yoryo, I hope it's not too late! I've—"

His smile was more melancholy than the moon's.

"I'm afraid I put off notifying the committee till tonight." He had known exactly what I would do.

I still had to wait out my time.

As a slim child the moon climbs boldly out from the palace window of the sun; and it is on this second evening that the greatest throngs come up to the temple. I perceived them and they me through the curtain of molten air, each imagining into sight his own ideal of beauty: each saw what he would have fashioned if it had been his to create

Tashartris. Each in turn, stepping to the rocky edge, worshipped me with words, his own peculiar words (from which I omit the "ohs" and "superbs")— "the all-over gentle surplus"— "bathe my eyes in feme"— "the rich fatnesses of the center and the clear facts"— "slendresse and jussufficient plumptitudes"— "the taper outward, delicately delayed at wrist and calf and ankle"—wait a moment, the statue was sitting in her altar, she didn't even have any legs! But one called to me: "Ay-Khatun, Lady Moon, Tashartris, I pray you to stand, show us your standing self," and seemed to see me rise naked, and such was his faith that the rest seemed to see the same; and they praised what they seemed to see.

It was from these worshippers that I did my first fast learning about sex—in words. For two hours, three hours, four, I endured the worshippers, while the moon, each evening more buxom, cruised each evening later to bed.

In the late afternoons I would be in the priest's room, lounging on his couch and bothering him with chatter, or possibly dusting his shelves and cleaning his pens—but then he would say, "No, please don't; please sit down—be easy while you can." The only place to sit was on the couch, and then the lowering sun struck through the window: and if I was wearing his robe the room caught yellow fire, or, if my own shirt, it blanched apple-green. I pulled the garment over my head, to prepare myself for the night, and all the walls changed to glowing skin.

Then I stood and we looked together at the monstrous spark floundering to its death on the western horizon. Then I heard a faint priestly sigh as I went out of his door.

On my chilly altar, the heat from the Fissure sometimes reached my front, leaving my back to feel even colder. Once I sneezed, startling the worshippers, but it came out all right— "Tashoo!" (Some people sneeze "Kyakhkh" and some "Ye-heiy!"; my usual style is "Haa-*bichii*.") I tried to warm myself by thinking of ways the wedding might be. I never came close to imagining it as hot as it really was.

Now it was tomorrow. I finished my worship-duty an hour before midnight, could hardly uncrimp my blue limbs, went to the priest's apartment to jump into the tub he always had ready for me. It was a little hooped half-barrel; the water was as much and as hot as he could manage, and I made rather a splashy mess in the middle of his floor. (But I usually got down on my knees and mopped it up afterwards.) It was the last night of my stay with him. Before, he had watched me with innocent pleasure, or at least had raised his eyes as far as my toes and shins flopping over the side and had listened to my noise as I sat joyously wallowing and hot-scrubbing myself with a loofah. But now he was too uneasy; I must listen, he said, to the lesson he really ought to have begun earlier, as to the nature of what I was about to undergo.

He sat at the front of his stool, clasping and unclasping his hands; he became red in the face, as if it was he who was in hot water. Finally he embarked: "My child, let me begin by apprising you that the curious name—an ancient name, of course—otherwise it would hardly be countenanced—it is always the case that we find ourselves able to countenance something if it is ancient—one has reason to wonder how the ancients themselves were able—either they had ancients still more ancient—or there were none among them at that time not uncouth enough to care—"

"The ancient name of what is what?" I prompted him.

Well, it turned out that the ancient and technical name of this type of sacral wedding was Belly-Wedding. —But just at that moment I thought of something else.

"What will happen when the worshippers come tomorrow and there's no Tashartris on the altar?"

"Oh, they will tear me limb from limb. But they'll get a carver to make another one" (another Tashartris, he meant) "and they'll send for another priest, so all will continue and be well."

I was appalled!

"That shan't be!" I cried. I leaped to my feet (the soap, which I had shelved in the hollow below my throat, landed some distance away and skidded across the flagstones). "I'll make your Tashartris as good as new." "No, stop—" he called, but I ran out, forgetting about toweling myself or waiting for the rest of my pre-Belly-Wedding instructions; went to the grotto where I had the pieces hid, and worked the rest of the night with the nut paste. (Nut paste, I found, is the second best adhesive after the food that gets burned onto cooking pots, which would be strong enough to hold Space Shuttles together.)

Soon I had her back and her front reunited, never again to part. Around three (the Lyre sang overhead) I took a break and played a game of backgammon. Instead of refreshing me it brought on my sleepiness—that's what playing with yourself does—so I stopped; first, since nobody was there to watch the result, I gave the table a push; of course it didn't turn; so I shut it up. But carelessly I had left something lying across the rim: not my finger, luckily, but one of the dice; and when the heavy "Outer" table slammed down on the "Inner" the hinge was wrenched up. I heaved the box open again to see the extent of the damage; disguised it by pushing the screws down, but their holes were boogered. How long would Tashartris and her temple survive a hooligan like me?—wreck her statue, now wreck her gaming-table! I gave it a petulant push, and it turned.

It turned, though open. —I assumed it didn't signify anything, since I had merely broken something. I shut it, leaving the Black end facing up the steps, and hoped that nothing would be noticed, and got back to mending Tashartris.

I couldn't resist scraping a little off her waist. Her exposed substance was a fresher color than her paint, so I slimmed her in a few more places, and nearly went on to skin her. She really needed a thorough renovation.

I finished at her earlobes; one having cracked, both had to be enlarged—she became Indian. I repierced them—the best time for piercing ears is just after the moon begins to wane, Zed once told me, and now it was nearly a week waxing, but that couldn't be helped. I reinserted the lunar rings, to which I had given a polish; and the glint of the sun, coming up far off through a forest of columns, found them.

Master Yoryo looked as if he hadn't slept. "I've got her stuck together, Master! Come and I'll show you," and I pulled him along by his hand.

"There, you see!" I said proudly. "I've only to fit in these chips and dust, and figure out why the colors don't quite match here, and Bob's-your-uncle!"

He put his brow to the ground and remained for a while, sobbing gently with joy. He didn't kiss her, as I thought he might.

"She really is lovely," I said, "now I see her by daylight."

He got to his feet. "Have you never seen yourself by daylight?" He took my arm and began to lead me away as if the goddess should not overhear.

"She will pass," he said, "in the temple, where the people cannot see her clearly, but not in the street. They've seen her springcleaned form"—he lightly squeezed my arm— "she couldn't come so unspringcleaned in less than about a century. So . . . It's lucky she is marrying today."

"What do you mean?"

"Well, she can soon find that she—each month—we will find that we do not need—the spring Sang Lakh, you know . . ."

"Ah, yes, I see what you're driving at. She'll stop what's it called, strewing men. No, men-strewing. I know, I do it myself."

"Yes," muttered Yoryo, struggling with his face. "Tashartris, however, does it only once a month."

I saw that, naturally, he didn't understand feminine matters. "That's what we all do," I explained. "I do it at full moon and she seems to do it in the waning phase. So you're going to pretend that she's stopped, so that she doesn't need purification and you can get out of taking her in the street for a few months. Right?"

"Right," he said, though he didn't much like the talk of "pretending."

"But, you know," I told him, "if she stops, that's supposed to mean she's going to have a baby. Did you know that?"

"Yes."

"But can the statue really have a baby?"

"No, not literally. What will happen is that we shall get our new image."

"Ah—I see. It's just your way of saying that there will be a new statue, which will look all fresh and nice. So then you can pretend that Tashartris has had her baby, *and* that she has started men-strewing again and can go out for her purification each month. Clever doctrine—though a shade complicated: which will this new statue be, Tashartris or her daughter? But anyway, the main thing is it'll be all right, you won't be in trouble."

"Yes," he said. We had arrived at a small door and I sensed that there would be no time for continuing our conversation on the other side of it.

"Wait," I said. "You won't be in trouble for nine months, right?"

"Actually, three. The gods live faster than us as well as longer."

"Only three months. So, have the carver get the statue ready right now, to be on the safe side. Okay?"

Master Yoryo was incapable even of the white lie of a nod, so I detected something was wrong.

"What did you start saying to me before?— 'It's now more than a month since we sent . . .' It was the carver who was sent somewhere, wasn't it? Why? And why hasn't he come back?"

"Probably," in a small strained voice, "because he's fallen in love with her or something. It's happened before."

"With who?"

"With the model that was found."

There was a silence while I thought over this. I'm not always dumb.

"So it's fine because only in three months, when he still hasn't come back, will you be torn in pieces. —That's ridiculous! Why can't you find another carver and another model then? Or now? Get the statue made here and now. How long does it take? Does it have to be that carver and that model?"

"Carvers are two a penny but there can only be one model. We're talking about the incarnation of Tashartris. Things have gone wrong because, as I saw a week ago, the field report was at fault. Our agents missed *you*. But it's too late now."

"No, it isn't. I bet I can carve. See what I've done with her already? Bring me some clay, let me make a whole new Tashartris."

"If there were time to do it, you would be the model, not the carver."

"Just let me try! I don't need a model. I feel I have a knowledge of the body. I'll have her finished in time for sunset!"

"I thank you with tears in my eyes, my most beautiful Tashartris-Surrogate. But we must leave for the Lower Sanctuary *now*."

"Why?"

"Because the people of five provinces, together with the religious establishments of three cults, and the Tashartris-pilgrims of the wide world, are waiting there to see you married. Ritan has arrived."

"Ritan," I said, "can go stuff or suck himself, whichever is easier. He can go home to his uncle's farm and have his aunt, or his aunt's goat. *I'm* going to stay here and either make or be (it's confusing!) your Tashartris for you."

"No, sweetheart. I'll come back here as soon as I see you wedded (or rather as soon as I know you wedded, for when the time comes it may comfort you a little to know that I at least will have my eyes closed) and I'll finish patching her. I've watched you a bit and I think I know how."

I looked at him doubtfully and wanted to make him do some pastework under my inspection so I was sure he could manage. But he said there wasn't time and took my elbow in a surprisingly strong grip.

The Bellywedding

H E UNLOCKED the door; it opened into precincts where I had never been, and he walked me rapidly along galleries and down steps. Ahead I saw a space milling with girls in orange-and-white-and-green pantaloons. I said, "Aren't I going aside somewhere first? To be prepared or something?"

"No, there is no need. We can go straight there."

"No—wedding dress?"

No: my wedding was, for me, a come-as-you-are occasion.

In the last shadows where I could be alone with my priest, I stopped him and held him. I felt his poor ivory body gain warmth from me, like a candle on a sunny windowsill. I tried one more time to persuade him that this should be my mission. But he stroked my head and sent me on to the temple maids.

They were in a bustle because I was late. Though I saw none but females around me, I was bashful and clothed myself with my hands, but they impatiently managed me out of that. They were marshalled by the Priestess, a figure who would have made a statue far more imposing than me. She was taller than most men, her marble face sprang from the auburn amphitheatre of her hair, and her white robe fell sheer from the points of her shoulders and shone inward on her tigrine body. I hadn't seen her before, because while the old priest was the caretaker of the temple and the image, she ruled her girls and the great festivals. The blood of Boleslaw ran in her veins, and her name was Zhanga Starchick.

They wasted no time in sweeping me along. I saw, rising between pillars of the Phallic Order, a tall curtain, immoderate green and orange, with the stitch side of over-lifesize curvaceous devices in black and gold and my name—ZIRTRAHZAT. Before this curtain's rustling foot lay another little vehicle sacred to the goddess: not a cart like that I knew so well, but a flat low float, in shape like a cracked eggshell or the crescent moon—not really; it can't be comprehended till its mate comes into view.

They lifted me and set me on this thing with my feet apart. Someone took my elbows and brought them together behind me. This annoyed me, but the grip was firm and they didn't listen to my protest. So I had to stand with my shoulders jammed back, my hands flapping like chicken-wings, my chest spread, and my eyes looking into the deep folds of the curtain. It swung ponderously open.

What I saw, afire with noonday light from Brayab's Viewhole high
overhead, was the stage. It was the Lower Sanctuary, but in effect it was
a stage, except that the audience was on it, lining it to left and right. As
yet I saw only the toes and beards of the front ranks, and the open
avenue between. This led to the facing curtain, shimmering blue and
tan. Before I had time to make out the soaring silver devices on it,* it
also parted, disclosing the god Ritan.

His swarming attendants were, like mine, temple handmaidens.
When Tashartris marries away from home she is glad enough to let the
local male acolytes do the handling of herself, yet she will never allow
male "bridesmaids" near her opposite number. Ritan rose above the
bevy, not because he was particularly tall but because he like me was
standing on a wheeled float. Of course he was not really the god Ritan:
he was the Ritan Surrogate. He was a youth, as naked as me.

He was an even brown from head to foot, which told me that in his
innocent life as a shepherd he must have gone bare summer and winter.
He was bald; no, not bald: his polished scalp was sprinkled with knots
of hair, like raisins. The uncommon whiteness of his teeth seemed to
foam out between lips that spread back over them. His body was the
most beautiful since Memnon's, but this attribute was only dependent
from the necessary one: that he be virgin. Since a man's virginity can
be tested no more objectively than his veracity, the way the Ritan-surrogate had to be chosen was that he was a fellow who, all the judges
agreed, *had* to be a virgin. And on catching sight of him I gave him my
vote too. He had the most bewildered face I had ever seen.

For this I fell for him, and felt I might consent inwardly as well as
outwardly to become his consort.

---

* They were no doubt ithyphallic. Or rather, Ritan being not a goat-god as
Applepeel seems to think but a fish-god, *ichthyphallic*. If you don't believe in
the occurrence of this spectacular word, see Nancy Luomala, "Matrilineal Rein-
terpretation of Some Egyptian Sacred Cows," in *Feminism and Art History*,
edited by Norma Broude and Mary Garrard, 1982, page 28. There are solecisms
whose gift of hilarity is tempered by the sad reflection that the less erudite
majority will derive from them no mirth at all, as when entering a bar you see
a chalkboard offering *Liebfraumulch*, or when a Russian Internet gang offers
pictures of little Alices who *simulate* each other (they must be in a Looking-
Glass world), or a secretary asks you by e-mail to "bare with me for a couple of
days," or a spammer entices you with "Would you like to meet girls who like to
be tied up? What do you have to loose?" or when you call the Nashbar bicycle
company to inquire about their Flashing Belt Beacon and the girl reads from her
catalogue: " . . . it has a solid-state osculator." You start giggling—but how, in
our intellectually stratified and specialized society, can interlegjewel jokes be
shared?

He appeared to fall for me too: at any rate when he saw me his stalk rose. —But he contradicted himself by shutting his eyes, and turning his head convulsively aside. Not a pleasing omen! His attendants admonished him in undertones and he agreed to reopen his eyes and direct them forward along the axis pointed out by his lower sensor. This he clearly wished to cover; but he too had his arms pinioned behind him. (His elbows may not have met; not everyone is as flexible as me.)

The uplifting of the elect stalk was the signal to begin. We each started wedward.

Now, about these holy floats. Make an elliptical board, about six feet by three; then saw it across the middle, not with a straight line, but with two straight cuts meeting at a right-angle. What you have is two half ovals, of curious shape, one male, one female. If the point of the male is rammed back into the angle in the front of the female, they reunite as the original oval. They are nothing but maleness and female-ness: a positive and a negative angle. —Put little wheels underneath them, and, in the case of the female float, machinery for raising it.

It was because I stood on the female shape that I had to stand with my legs apart: my feet were on the two forward points, with only gap between them. Ritan's heels were hard together on his single forward point. His toes nervously gripped the two meeting edges; sometimes they turned up and I noticed they were yellow underneath.

I used to think that the gods and goddesses push us mortals around; well, after experience on both sides, I find it's mainly us divinities that get wheeled around by mortals. But wait till you hear the manner in which we were now transported. It would have taken Master Yoryo a century of circumlocution before he could have brought himself to say it:

I was pulled by my nipples, and Ritan was pulled by his stalk. On either side of me walked a maiden attendant precisely holding a nipple between thumb and two fingers. My breasts elastically pouted and then I began to follow them. Likewise two of his maiden attendants (yes, two: innocence was not the only qualification for Ritan-surrogacy) wrapped each a petite fist around his stalk as if it was a leading-pole, and drew him along. The little wheels under us were well trued and oiled, so we traveled without force, though with feeling.

Such is the ritual method prescribed in the Book of Zgan for the first stage of the approach. One of my companions played a pipe, another made low patterings on a drum, and there was pomp and liturgy, which I omit because, though I found it absorbing, you may not.

And I was borne out through the rent hymen of the portal into the cylinder of brilliant light.

A shiver of sound sprang from the front of the audience:

"It's—it's Applepeel!" "Applepeel!" "Why, I do believe—" "You're right, it's Applepeel!"

Only gasps and whispers, but they piled to a wave, which rolled to the outer walls: *"Applepeel!" "Oh heaven, Applepeel!"* . . .

My attendants glanced up at me quizzically. Perhaps they expected the smile on my face to have more of simper and less of nosewrinkle. But what was amusing me was the sound's *plplpl*-ness and how different it would seem if the citizenry were whispering *"Felicity!" "Isn't this Felicity?" "Yes, it is it is" "So listen, Licity, complicit in soliciting illicity"* . . . (I remembered a time when I was a little girl and a kind lady asked me my name and I teethingly answered "Thoothey" and then watched her expression as I said "So sorry, must scoot soon.") Whether lapping or susurrating, the sound washed about me like a refinement of tickling; my body felt an all-over frisson, and flowed in the grip of those who were holding it apart and drawing it forward.

My nudity, in the eye of a crowd seven times larger than that of the caravanserai, was twice as utter, but half as lonely; which should have made me feel even more imperilled.

"Aplplpl" said the play of multiple lips . . . Sibilant undertones there were: I heard a furtive *"Should we rush them?"*— *"This is our chance"*— *"Sacrilege, but"*— *"What do they expect, secrete her from us so many days and then suddenly* THIS— *"* The girls behind me heard too; "The crowd seems to know this Surrogate," they muttered anxiously— "Things are getting a shade dangerous"— "They shouldn't have chosen such a looker, Tashartris may be jealous, something awful's going to happen" . . . I felt I might need my arms. Our avenue was narrowing, a charge was shaping up. But such was the force of the Priestess that she quelled it with a glare.

Ritan and I reached a mutual distance of a dozen bodylengths and halted for the Alignment. The pipes fell silent, the kettledrums (one on my side, one on his) fell into a slow fixed *d, d, d* . . . An attendant behind me took sightings through my crotch with an oracular tripod and called out the readings to the others, who cranked the floor of my float until I was on exactly the level to receive my bridegroom. He was only a little on the tall side, I am on the small side, my legs were straddled apart, but are on the long side, so I didn't have to be cranked up very far.

Meanwhile on my left, shoved into view by the priestess, a clerk holding a ledger muttered in a rapid peevish singsong: "I publish the banns of marriage between Ritan, aegagogue and choropomp, hieralph, henchgod, capricorn, and maniarch, 'bachelor,' of this parish and of the little hills and oceans, and Tashartris, 'spinster,' of the lightning, the galaxies, and cosmic love; semicolon; sthis is for the first and only time of asking; semicolon; if any of you know cause or just imbediment why these two principles may not be joined together in holey Belly-wedlock you'd better keep quiet as it's far too late to stop it now." Nobody else uttered a sound except impatient ones.

As we were about to resume forward motion, I gave Ritan an encouraging smile. But at this his nerves again got the better of him. This time in his desperation he managed to free his arms; and he covered—his eyes! There was a murmur of scandal. The handmaids regained control of him, whispering fiercely. "A blindfold!" he moaned. "Whatsa matter with you, boy?" said one, exasperatedly (and not help-fully) slapping his rump. But another, more sympathetic, said "She's too beautiful, is that it?" *"Too secussy,"* he gasped. He submitted uneasily, as if he wouldn't be responsible for the consequences. If his eyes revulsed from me, his stalk disagreed. His bridesmaids had to use strength in depressing it to the required horizontal.

One of them called across to our group: "Don't let Tashartris smile! It's too much for him!"

"Oh, okay," I said. But it was easier said than done. I had to strive to keep my face down to its customary ground-grin.

And we moved into the next and ultimate walk, which was managed in a different way. Behind each divinity, on the floats, an attendant knelt. The one behind me put both hands around to my front and held open my concentric sets of lips. All ten fingertips had their calculated places. The air came cold on my inner slipway—as if it was moist. As soon as I had got partly used to this, I looked to see whether some corresponding arrangement was being made with Ritan, and it was. The two maidens who had been drawing him along by his shaft released it—whereupon the holy instrument sprang erect, came for the first time in full profile view of the crowds on either side, and for the first time drew some eyes off me. (It appeared to have a slipcase of something shiny; soap?) Now the kneeler behind him put both arms around him and with both fists forced the prodigious shaft back to the horizontal and firmly held it out like a rifle. She didn't just pillow her face on his glushes, but peered intently over the gunsight, that is, his right hip. She was the senior and most skilful temple maiden, for it was she who had to do the aiming.

The elbow-holders also had to ride on the floats, standing astride the kneeling weapon- and target-holders. The rest of each team pushed, and we started off with a slight jerk. The language of the Book of Zgan prescribes a quickening pace to end in a shock of defloration. In former times this was attempted, but experience suggested that it might be better to bend the translation (for *accelerando* read *rallentando*, but in either case *crescendo*) so we start on the slow side and bear toward the climax ever slower.

It is exciting, and I was getting as excited as anyone. After all, a girl couldn't ask for a more sensational wedding.

The nakers (that's what the two kettledrums are called) fell slower with the steps of the drummers; tenser. They could have throbbed tenser and quieter if people had been drawing in their breath; but they had to throb tenser-louder because the hum was rising around us. Soon of each drumbeat there could be heard only the foundation grunt.

Hum and drums were such that the only person I could chat with was the strapping handmaiden, or handle-maiden, who stood close behind me holding my elbows. "Pleased to know you, Polly," she said; "I'm Marily." "Applepeel," I said. "What?" "My name's Applepeel." "What a flaky name. Mind if I call you Polly?" "No, that's near enough." "That's what it sounds like—what they're all saying. You do seem to have lots of friends. We never go outside the temple, you know. This is something new, I've never seen a congregation so involved. They seem to have mixed feelings, though." "How d'you mean, mixed feelings?" "They act as if they'd like to be *more* involved. It's making even Fanged Zhanga lose her cool.

"Just listen to them, Polly!" she went on. "Actually what it sounds like is *'Lipple lipple lipple.'* You know what lipple means?" "No, I don't think I know the word." "It means kiss, of course—only the inter-lip-playing kind of kissing. You can speak of lippling other things too, like a nipple or a dickle. It's one of those *handle-fondle-rumple* words like *breastle* and *hipple* and *gluzzle* and *cundle*, and there's somethink you do to a man called *teasetickle*; they're all parsley on *snuggle* or (I believe the extreme) *couple*. We had to learn them last week. Like 'Ogle not, orgle not,' and if a dimple is the opposite of a pimple, what's opposta a nipple? Perhaps that *is* what they're saying, your friends— that they'd all like to lipple you—d'you think?"

"I'nt know," I said. "Are you all really maidens?"

"Yes," she told me, "in my class. We're still on our man-sturbating lessons—they used to start that at furteen, but there's been a reform. Next semester we'll be up to sweedling."

"I see."

"Of course, nobody needs to teach us cliftrotting—" "Clifftrotting?" "Lipfrogging, you may call it. If my friend Uncommonly down there were to shift a finger centerward, she could in less than two seconds—"

"If you're maidens, why couldn't the Surrogate have been one of you?"

"Oh, no, we're all reserved for the Bounty of Tashartris, that's the nine-night open orgy every third or fourth midsummer. You'll have to come back for that, Polly, if your hubby will let you, I mean you won't strictly qualify, by then, but you're so cute," she said, prodding the hollow of my back, "I'm sure you'd be welcome into the team. And after that, why not stay on?—you could live with us as Happily, ever after. Some of the girls'll be jealous, they won't like slipping down a place, but the way I see it, it'd do us all good to have our beauty-average raised."

"Thank you," I said. Out of the tail of my eye I could see a pleased-with-herself face, belonging to a young lady walking in step with us. "Who's she?" I asked. "Who?" I tried to point backward with my chin, then whispered "In the flimsy-looking shift with handles each side." "Oh, in the offwhiskable; that's your understudy, Bewley or Beaulieu or Bellew I believe her name is, the Hon. Miss Belinda Bellew. If you ask me, she's a virginoid—an Honorary Virgin. She's in case you catch cold or something, but I can see she's going to be disappointed. If she's waiting for you to faint or go silly, she'll have to wait till shrimps learn to whistle." "Thank you," I said again. "And does Ritan have an understudy?" "Why, no. I mean, they just wouldn't consider the possibility of a *male* fainting, would they? or doing anything at all to lose his chance." "But he might— don't they have something like a period?" "I suppose so; I'm not sure; we haven't covered that yet. I think there *is* some ancient rule on the book, about the whole crowd—quite an idea, eh?" and she gave me a wicked pinch. "The audience as understudy!" But I was feeling an augmented interest in Ritan and his continued health.

"Look, Marily," I said, "how about letting go of my elbows? I *am* doublejointed, but I do like to change position. I'm not going to make any trouble. I just might want to hug the man, when we get within range."

"No, no!" she said. "The Book doesn't allow that. Every detail of the Bellywedding has to be in unobstructed public view. That's also why—excuse me," and she flexed me sharply backward from the middle, so that my pubes propruded—I mean to say, jutted, assuming the lead from my breasts; I was arched like a bow. Ritan's handler did the same to him, so that he too was a bow (plus, in his case, an arrow); we now approached each other as if one should clap with the wrists instead of the palms.

"It'll be all right, Polly," she said, "you'll get your chance later. They didn't tell you what happens?" "No, they were going to, but—" "You should have been catechized. Well, I'll give you a quick run-down. You should also, normally, have been lightly Creamed, but Uncommonly reports that you're ready enough without it. (*Readily*—that could be your name if you became one of us!) But, oh yes, to the procedure. After the inburst (which is known for mythological reasons as the Breaking of the Ma'rib Dam) Verily—that's the Aimer—must be quick and angle him up into you, and after that we've only got glushes to shove on if you have to be helped home. You will remain joined right to the hilt, but nowhere else, while the Zigzig is pronounced, and you are then considered truly and very well Bellywed. Then Ritan withdraws two thirds of his length so that the families can file past, witnessing The Point of Fusion and censing it. The third that's still in keeps zigging, which you'll probably find the best part. Any couple that's watching at the moment of the Fountaining will have a child within the year, or any little girl that's watching will get a little brother, and if you Fountain, or I should say Quake, at the same time you must say so (you'll have to say it—'*E O O!*' is the formula—because your hands aren't free to pinch him) and this will get us plenty of twin lambs born next spring. Got that?" "Yes," I said, "I think so. E O O." "Yiy, not yet! someone may think you're jumping the gun—don't want to get Uncommonly into trouble, do you?" "Sorry." "Yes, well, steadily does it. Where was I?—oh yes, he's just Fountained in you and you've Quaked, if you're lucky (if not, don't worry, you should be able to get nine more for every one of his), and the Bridge of Union is still thrumming between you. So then the heads of households lay their garlands across it until all movement is smothered. That's the end of the ceremony, but we carry the two of you away, without taking you apart, to the Lowest Theatre, which is mattressed from wall to wall and over the ledges and up the walls and beams too, and there you can romp all afternoon while the people watch you from the galleries and then wander around as they wish (it's Open Day in the temple) and maybe get an ice cream and come by to watch some more." "And my lunch break?" "Hush now," she said, "we're getting close."

So we were. "Concentrate!" breathed my pal over my shoulder, rather needlessly. I didn't want to miss anything: his face, which now looked like that of someone falling off a cliff or opening by mistake a tiger's cage; or his stalktip, which wore a similar expression; but as they got farther apart in my field of view I had to choose one. And as I looked down at it more steeply between my breasts, the Aiming Maiden pulled her hands back to its base, to keep it braced and aimed while leaving a working length. (In retrospect, it may be that she should have loosened her hands before sliding them back.) The tip crept into spitting distance of my cunt; which fizzed in anticipation. The whole temple hushed, the hair on *everyone's* scalp had turned to cornrows, Ritan in a silent shriek had ceased to breathe, I involuntarily shut my eyes, and—

Counter-Tashartris

O UCH!
What was it?
Perhaps you have had the experience of being touched by an icicle when you expected a red hot poker, and not knowing whether you were frozen or scalded.

I was scalded, by a powerful jet which stuck all my thatch together.

I opened wide my eyes, and saw the hands of the Aiming Maiden blown apart by the surge that had passed between them. The gob clung on my mound like a stranded jellyfish; it is called jism, Arabic for "the body." Instead of having the presence of mind to poke at least some of it into me, before it rolled off down my thighs, the cunt-holding attendant whipped her hands away and madly shook them, sprinkling her colleagues. And the Aiming Maiden, too, should not have let her hands desert their post, that is, the stalk: it sprang up, and a second salvo flew out, and plastered me on the forehead!

Everyone stared, still paralysed with astonishment, while the stalk sank, paused with a slight up-bob to shoot again, sank, shot, and so silvered me with declining splashes from breasts to toes. Having discharged, if not its duty, the first and greatest viscous product of its life, it hung its head in repose. Then the temple found its breath and roared.

Something had gone mightily wrong with the Bellywedding. And whose fault was it? Mine, of course.

High Priestess Zhanga Starcica came striding past the dithering handmaidens, and her voice (which was much like a krummhorn) overtopped the voice of the crowd.

"I know you who you are!" she shouted. "You are the Adversary, the Dark Lady of Denial, Counter-Tashartris, penetrating her sanctum and stealing her form to foil her joy and wither her followers and abort her marriage by casting a crafty spell of impotence on her bridegroom—not impotence—incontinence—any weapon for you! What ills and plagues, if I had not unmasked you—a thousand years of chastity, I should think! Ha, demiurge though you are, you have no power over me when I ban you with this sign," and she gave me the finger, and with the other hand, just to be sure, the two fingers, in case I was of the British rite. For a priestess of love she was on the intimidating side and I wondered how many men she had eaten. "Don't think you can hide from me," she bellowed, staring me up and down my runny front, "however thick the disguise that muffles you! You dare to think it amusing?—" (I did, somewhat, as did a few other irresponsibles) "—that mocking smirk alone would betray you! Wipe it off! speak! do I not know you, are you not the skittish spirit of coyness, Thwart Janet, Cross-Leggèd Hegarty, Shy Anne, Kitty Tease-Tail! Answer me!"

Difficult to do, because the stuff had dripped from my eyebrow and run down to my mouth, nor could I wipe it because the handmaidens were still too petrified to let go of my elbows; I had to slap at it with my tongue. It tasted okay, a bit like Bleu Cheese.

"If you b-lb-lb—pwh," I said, bubbling.

She flung out her arm; with one finger (the forefinger this time) she pointed imperiously west. They finally got the cue and released me, and I was glad enough to step off my float and get on my way. The carts kept gently rolling by themselves and the male angle socketed into the female angle with a jolt, and Ritan, paler and shrunken, rocked but was held on his feet by his maidens. I remembered to turn and blow him a kiss (perhaps I should say, blow *back* some of his kiss), but he didn't see me, his eyes still crossed on the space where I had been. And so in shame, totally naked, lustcustard flowing down my chin and navel and knees, I fled through the avenue that opened in the congregation.

Actually I didn't bother to run, because nobody was likely to chase me—yet. As long as they were in her furious presence they had to act as if they believed they'd catch the clap by touching me. I passed the Hon. Miss Belinda Bellew, whose face now wore a notable mixture of expressions. (One eye "No not that!" the other "Yes oh yes!") At the back of the transept, a well of eight or nine semicircular steps led down to a postern door. Just before the door was a small foyer for coatpegs and hymnal-rack. There in the shadows my priestly friend waited for me to pass. He had with him to give me, as if he had known what was going to happen, the bundle of my only possessions. He even had a sponge, ready dipped in the font.

I held up my arms for him to give my front a swabdown, but after only dabbing my bangs (stuck to my brow) and gently wiping my cheeks he put the sponge in my hand and I gladly splashed mouth and cunt and thighs and the rosy stone of the floor.

As he watched me he gave me his blessing: "May you never come to harm. And," he added in an undertone, *"keep turning the tables."* I kissed him and stood to chat, but he hurried me on, because there was a growing movement to sidle away from the priestess, and disreputable fellows at the back of the crowd were already slipping down the steps after me. Saying "'Tis all I have, it may serve thee in some dire necessity," old Master Yoryo gave me a gold coin. My hand carried it to my hip pocket—hip, but no pocket, so for safe keeping I tucked it into the only pocket I had, my sitch (having read of that trick in, I think, Voltaire's *Candide*).

The comers-behind quickened their pace, but he took from under his robe a key about a foot and a half long. For a moment I thought he was going to use it as a quarter-staff and defend me against the mob. But he opened the door and urged me through, and I heard him locking it behind me and some of them arguing with him, but most of them tumbling back up the steps, to get around at me another way. But long before that I had to face worse.

What Yoryo didn't know of was the crowd outside. Inside the temple, it was standing-room-only; yet the largest part hadn't even been able to get in. They were encamped in the country round about, a large fraction of that fraction of the world's population that had succeeded in getting out of bed that day: families sitting on blankets with picnics, groups of young men shuffling their cowboy boots and nudging each other, ladies' clubs, school classes on social-studies trips, here and there a detachment of Hunters on horseback. But mostly, just men; drifts and stag-nations of them. They covered the bare hillside below the great western temple wall. And out of the little door in the middle of this wall I had to step before them, Harry-starkers. Hardly a fair start.

The Bloons

TIMIDLY I edged out, bumped by the door as it shut behind me, and I shrank back against it. The unaccustomed sunshine dazzled my face and picked me out, a white slip cowering against the locked door. The expanse of the wall towered above me, and the Applepeel-avid multitude seethed before me.

Yet my appearance caused not a ripple. *They didn't notice me!*

I broke slowly into a grin.

There was the forest of people on the grassy hillside—but there was a kind of second layer: wobbly people standing in the air on the heads of the first layer. And higher again, smudging the sky, gigantic translucent figures swayed and swooped. That was my impression. Then I saw what it was.

Vendors were selling Applepeel balloons. You bought a little dollop of rubber and they gave you a squirt from their helium bottle and pfrrt! you had a life-size Applepeel. Her hair was flesh-colored and her flesh the same color though somehow not flesh-colored; her shape was so-so. The grooves and cleavages were the trouble: where they should have gone swallowing inward, technology required them to stop short and come a little way back out in the form of seams (as does happen in one part of the flesh body). But the convex surfaces were tight and plump, and their texture even more glabrous than life. And you could put your eye to them and see dimly inside.

A balloon has advantages but its limbs, unlike those of some other kinds of effigy, cannot be repositioned, at least not without danger of a sudden loud death for the whole figure. There has to be a separate balloon-Applepeel for each attitude desired. So far there was only Applepeel (position I); after all, the manufacturers had done well to rush into production in time for the occasion. Other models would be forthcoming. The posture was a vulgar one which I won't specify. All the Applepeels crouched at the ends of their strings above the heads of their new owners, gently swinging, a few spinning; the way they happened to face was their only variation, and even that became uniform when the breeze freshened and they all turned with it, like aerial sheep. At home each owner, alone with his private Applepeel, might remember why he had bought her and find a way to use her, but as just one in the fleet she had lost some of the excitement she promised on first swelling to life. Some happy purchasers still lay on their backs looking up at their very own tethered Applepeels and jiggling them, but the reason why most were shading their eyes and staring at the sky was the mating of Tashartris and Ritan.

These two balloons were forty feet tall, the correct size for the deities, as opposed to their usual reduced images, incarnations, surrogates, and impersonators. And of course their volume was correspondingly vast but their density small, as is true of all supernaturals. The larger balloon was a generalized male shape, that is, a rough assemblage of parts with no attempt at harmony (or at likeness to the particular Ritan I had seen). The big female balloon bore a strong resemblance to the little female balloons below, but I supposed that was another production constraint: they were little Applepeels and she was almighty Tashartris.

You will see why I couldn't just say that on coming out of the postern door I saw the crowd and some sex-balloons. If sex-balloons were everyday objects I would be understood, and saying "I came out the door and saw a lot a folks and sex-balloons" would take no longer than the action took. As it is, the description has been longer than the action. It unfolded *immen'chenonsidice*, as the Italians say, in less time than it takes to fail to tell itself. The people seeking another route to get out after me had not yet emerged, nor even had the news of the mishap inside the temple. The crowd out here still thought that in the sanctuary, at this moment, Tashartris in the form of a human virgin of their acquaintance was being popped by Ritan in the form of a shy young man. They didn't have tickets to get in and witness this main event, but out here for them Tashartris in the shape of a balloon lay spreadeagled in the sky, looking down, and up toward her came the perpendicular stalk of Ritan.

The gods used the inverse of the Missionary Position, perhaps because in the religion of desire Tashartris was the missionary.

I was inclined to join the crowd and watch, but I really couldn't spare the time. I slipped along the foot of the wall behind people's backs. I was safe enough; no one, it seemed, had peripheral vision when an Applepeel was in their focus. But I was not quite the only one not gazing skyward. For now I had to pass the balloon entrepreneurs. Two of them, operating the gods' strings, were down in the middle of the crowd looking up, but the others were at their portable stall near the wall, and kept their sharp commercial eyes darting around all parts of the earthly scene, including me. They were my old friends and hosts, the Mongers.

I stopped in dismay. Would they repossess me and put me on sale a second time? (And my earrings at least a third?) The Mother Monger considered it, as we stood looking at each other. Even if they could maintain control of me against this crowd, they'd be subject to legal action by the purchaser they had already sold me to. Legal action was nothing to Mongers, since borders were nothing to them. But the purchaser was reputed now to have a militia, with which he might come in pursuit. Better not to jeopardize the run of sales they were already making at this fairground. These were Applepeel-related sales and flourished on the unavailability of the actual Applepeel. The Mother issued her decision. (Expressed as a small fat fart; you will remember about Old Vulgarian, the secret language of the Mongers.)

So her followers made no move on me, nor did they call the crowd's attention to me. The Younger Monger went on hawking the wares, addressing me, as if he didn't know who I was:

"Bloons, ladies and gen'lmen, Applepeel bloons, as nice as life, take 'em home to bed! Washable, they float in the bath too, can be parked on the ceiling and admired when not in direct use. Just remember to keep 'em indoors and away from sharp objects; use only as directed. Applepeel repair kits also available—twenty-four hour service in case of emergency—*nine month* limited warranty. Personalized on either cheek for only six ackers extra. Here you are, darling, pfrrt!—ain't she lovely! Add her up, you'll like her, you can tuck a hand around her positives and into her negatives. But careful now, first tie her leash to your apron-strings or your coat-tails if you have any—don't let her get away and go to heaven! Decorate your own Applepeel, intimate julery, changes of earrings, paints in several ethnic colors; Applepeel novelties of all kinds, ingenious foreign products, imported from Hong Kong, Applepeel Hearthstoppers"—and here I saw that these were the familiar iconic collages, but coiffed with apple rinds instead of wood shavings—not too practical an idea. The salestalk pattered on, though nobody but me was paying attention: " . . . naughty gloves and thighribbons signed by Applepeel, trick chastity-belts, paste-on vulva-fluff, crotchthongs and cuntabs and titlifters (specify small-medium-large black-white-nude), Arkansassy (TM) hair-rinse (gives you *almost* that genuine mystique), bedroom-radiation-seeking telescopes from the Deep Sly Observing Society; howsabout an Applepeel swimsuit, reel peely one, half ounce plus packaging, if you don't dare to wear it you can try it on her, and pull it sharp through *here* to point out her punctuation, she's a well-formed sentence, ain't she? Applepeel giggling dolls, Applepeel wriggling dolls, Applepeel ovulating dolls, pairs of Applepeel wrestling dolls, tickets to the big fight (revenge match, Mighty Zhanga vows 'That little escape artist shan't escape me this time'), Applepeel coloring books (together with Applepeel's confessions in her own silly words), roll up, special prices for a special day."

"How much the coloring books?" I asked cautiously. (I wanted to use discreet Monger, but my fluency hadn't kept up with my comprehension.)

"How much you got, lady?"

I wasn't sure. I reached for the coin in my sitch. The Mongers ironically watched my contortions.

Now I want you to promise that you will never follow my ill-advised example. This method is for trained smugglers only. You've read of the cases of self-abusing young men who had to be taken to hospital to have bottles and corncobs extracted . . . The Mongers offered the assistance of the two Urchin Mongers, who had small wiry hands, but I preferred to manage myself. I braced myself against the wall and eventually succeeded. I showed the coin to the Mongers and they grabbed it and rubbed it in the grass and found it to be a gold head-of-state—that is, a sovereign—which was the exact price of the coloring book.

"So I've nothing left for an Applepeel swimsuit?"

"You'd have to shave to wear that."

"I will, I will."

"Sorry. Not for sale to minors."

"Couldn't you throw in just a crotchthong?"

"Worse. It would barely hide your uscle, let alone your glushes."

"Better than nothing!"

He drew one from his bag but wickedly flicked me with it.

I clutched my book and hurried on.

The crowd was more intent than ever. Ritan, steered from below, was rising toward the stretched-rubber socket in Tashartris.

The center of the crowd, the hundred or so worshippers directly below the god-sized couple, could look up only at Ritan's narrow (relatively) glushes. And yet transparent lovers may offer some solution to the voyeur's eternal dilemma.

The rest of us, looking from our stations around the hillside, saw the stalk (a tree-sized sausage-balloon itself) lazily bump a wrong place, buckle, then spring straight, propelling Ritan downward. But calmly he rose again. I wished him eventual success but meanwhile a dozen further tries. A thousand eyes gazed spellbound. I wanted to congratulate the Mongers. As a crowd-gathering gimmick, this had skywriting and hot-air balloons beat hollow.

It had been unwonted Monger generosity to give me my own free Applepeel (they must have saturated the market and had a surplus). She was useful camouflage as I moved along the edge of the crowd, but on sidling away I carefully pulled out her nipple (*pthththth*...) and rolled her up (*uh-ththth; thth; thth; dhdh*...) and stowed her in my bundle along with the coloring book.

In the lower meadow I passed the Society for Creative Anachronism, who had earlier been entertaining the crowd with innocent jousts and morris-dances; still dressed in their pied jerkins or chain mail, they were packing up their wooden swords. Queen Eleanor, in spire headdress and liripipe, spied me and waved, taking me for a hamadryad.

As I reached the cover of some gorse-bushes, I heard a communal sigh with a few claps, followed by a rhythmic murmuring. I looked back and saw that Ritan was sedately bobbing, as fast as his vast air-resistant form allowed. He curved slightly at each rise and fall, his distant head and feet following his middle. The huge stalk rose and fell in the tunnel, not without sticking (so that from deep in Tashartris's perineum issued the squawking noise that balloons make when rubbed together), because the ground team had forgotten to pour a bucket of oil over it before launch. But the people below might not have stood for that; they were already wondering whether to expect a rain of heavenly semen. The operators released two of Ritan's three strings and at his will he slowly rotated wheel-like about his pivot in his bride.

I lengthened my stride and crossed a stream, two fields, and a low ridge before again glancing back. The god-balloons were still above the horizon, serenely mating against a background of light cirrus. The temple was lost to view, and all the crowd.

Acorned

EXCEPT FOR two: those infernal brats, the Mongerkins.
They had been sent to trail me, just in case I could still in some way help the Mongers' bank-account.

When I realized that they were going to keep a fixed distance, speeding if I did and slowing if I did, and cooperating with me in keeping out of the rest of the world's sight, I just walked grimly on. We kept to fields, slunk across lanes, and kept on.

At this season there were wooly-bear caterpillars trotting foolishly across the earthen paths. I avoided stepping on them; the urchins stepped on them all, except for those they popped in their mouths.

We walked through the middle of the day—a day in which I had had nothing to eat. They pulled out sandwiches wrapped in grimy news-paper, and ate them on the march. I turned and held out my hand. They merely stood and munched. They tossed me a caterpillar. Perhaps this was well intentioned, but I said "Mneeagh!" to them and walked on hungry. I had also missed the preceding night of sleep. Sleep to me is always the more important—really I eat just to calm down. The sun started horizonward, and I thought of camping early. I even thought of having them snuggle up with me for warmth, before we continued our game next day.

These mellow thoughts were dispersed by a sharp sting to my right glush. They had a slingshot and had winged me with an acorn.

All right, sons of Mongers.

The next acorn lodged in my cleft. I disdained to remove it. Just as well: the third ricocheted off it.

They took turns with the slingshot, vying in marksmanship. (One was left-handed like the slingers of the tribe of Benjamin.) The object was to drive the puck acorn deeper in. Their aim was phenomenal; unluckily, not perfect. If they were archers one would have said they had had long practice at the butts.

Stepping-stones over a brook. I appeared to slip and twist my ankle. Now I was pained as well as peppered and persecuted. It was some-thing even I couldn't laugh at. Far enough from laughing, I moaned and sobbed as I limped desperately on. The stony-faced imps had no mercy. Imagine them relenting or offering help! They merely reduced the gap.

Thank Tashartris they were out of acorns. But now the path skirted an oak-wood; they rebuilt their supply. I slowed a shade more. Past a bend, I saw a handful of acorns and oak-apples within the wood, stepped in and helpfully tossed them on the path, but did not follow them. Coming around the curve, the two stooped, and I was out and on them.

We were well matched and the bout was long and interesting. Actually they had the better of it almost all the time: my muscles added up to theirs, but theirs could be tactically divided. One would have me by the hair or arms while the other scored with steely little fingers— which to them was the object. I won't tell you the kinds of scoring, there wasn't just one. (One of them might have been called a-coring, being an improvement on the slingshot.) It was very subversive of a lady's decorum to be intimately pestered by little delinquents, and at first I sharply told them so; then I had to shut up and work; but we granted each other yelps, grunts and other admonishments in the vocabulary that is common to Human and Monger. Sometimes I got them both under my arms, but more often I only had a lock on one, so the other could have run away (neither would have cared in the least about leaving his brother to my mercy), or in the frequent times when they were both on top of me they could both have scampered away, and mockingly stayed out of reach as before. They didn't because they were little scrappers and greedy for yet higher scores. I got annoyed enough to be interested in scoring back on them. But one of their advantages was that they were clothed, if you could call it that: being street-arabs, they wore djellabas, patched and filthy gowns. (The Mongers were richer than kings—at least since their sale of me—but didn't waste money on clothes for their offspring.) These sacks obstructed between-the-legs grips such as they used on me.

Their surest weapon was my ticklishness. Time and again I had them beat but they unfairly bored in and I became a gigglinh jelly. As for them, leather-skinned little bastards, they were as ticklish as fossils. If I could have remembered which was the left-hander, it would often have helped me to know which hand was going to grip and which drive—but their poker faces and mats of hair and thin hard limbs were identical.

At least I realized the cuddling-up-at-night-for-warmth idea was no loss. It is I who have the hot skin of children; their skin was so unchild-like cold that I wondered if Mongers are old from birth, or are part lizard.

I tried to fight clean—but that meant I wasn't even in the same fight. So I moved inside the djellabas, and found a tiny stalk. It was no more to grasp than an ear-lobe or a nipple; but within seconds, not really age-qualified to do so, it pushed to the size and boniness of a pinkie. This Mongerkin, when I bent, had to prostrate himself and kiss the ground, his djellaba falling to his shoulders, and it would have been all over bar the victory score, but for the distractions inflicted by his twin. There was no way but to gain control of the other stalk too, but I couldn't seem to find it, and then the first one actually became slippery and spat itself out of my fingers. And then they came in chuckling "If that's the way you want it!" and got me upended on my head and kept me there, one of them in front of me and one behind, for one of my less autonomous times.

But if they were wrestling for fun and spite, I was wrestling for peace and freedom. Far behind on points, I at last won with a knockout, doing to them what they had once done to me: I got their djellabas up around their heads and knotted them together with their upraised arms inside. Only then did I discover that one of the Mongerkins was female.

I sank back, breathing *"Ayhi..."* and rested on my bundle as a pillow. They struggled to their feet and stood, white little facing bodies with one large muffled head, on the woodside path. If I had to wrestle naked with two half-naked manikins, there could have been worse wrestling-mats than this corky one, made of equal parts dust and acorn-meal. Boots or hooves must have done the crushing, though none came along while we were at work.

"What's your name?" I demanded.

"Which of us?" they piped.

"You—the one with the plain belly" or rather the little bald slit.

"Squirrel," she said.

"And yours—Acornkin?"

"No," said the one with the pipette (which, remembering itself in my fingers, restrengthened itself under my eyes), "I'm Cornwallis."

Squirrel and Cornwallis. Not bad. Still better would have been Gristle and Corkscrew.

They were standing expectant of my revenge, or "forfeit" as they called it. But since it was impossible to tickle them I couldn't think of any. They were disappointed. "Couldn't you massage our bladders until we have to pee on each other?" "Ree-volting little scamps!" I said—"Just start on home, go on," and I gave them a switch on their bottoms, "you should manage it by supper-time, if you're careful to keep in step." They rocked away, dancing both leading feet forward, scraping the rear ones along; I saw them stumble once or twice in the path as it threaded the cornfield, but they were already dextrous at this odd locomotion. And I went on in the opposite direction, enjoying a fine clear sunset.

The sky shone grainless, a scooped-out muskmelon, with the one seed of the sun on its rim. As this sank, a single crepuscular ray shot upward, sent through some cleft of clouds a hundred miles below the horizon. Overhead, washing across the moon, the ray was lost in vague width, but I turned to see if it could be traced descending in the east. Back there stood a population of thunderheads, salmon pink but with their feet already drying to gray. And in one of the canyons among them floated something smaller caught by the orange sparkle: a kind of double star. It slightly breathed. It was the gods, still hovering in their nuptial. —The light went out as the sun-floor lifted.

Since E-Tashartris stood on a crag, I was already in the spreading lake of evening air when I heard faintly the horn. I meant to listen later and know whether my statue had passed and Master Yoryo had survived to touch the gong.

On high the nearly-seven-day moon, filling to the erect line of her spine, a nymph of twenty, slipped her blue gauzes and took over with her dazzling nudity the night.

Now to test the waterproof blanket as a sleeping-bag. It was clammy-hot, as I feared. I wanted to *separate* myself—didn't want anything touching. In the middle hours I woke thinking I had heard a distant bang. I was as stewed as if in a crock-pot. I threw the blanket off and tried heaping leaves over me. That was fine. The moon had just set, her light following her. Just before dropping to sleep for the rest of the night, lying on my back and looking at the black slab of the sky, I saw Tashartris fly slowly over, high above me. Stars shone through her.

Across country

I OPENED my eyes and saw cloud-wisps that one by one, as if lit by a match, took fire. There broke on the world, preceded by his million courtiers, the vast placid smile of Brayab: no mystery about him.

I found that priest Yoryo had stored my bundle with holy seed-cakes, so sustaining that I really didn't need to look for other food. Still, I boiled pokeweed shoots and daylily petals, milked the agreeable cows, and usually around breakfast-time raided farm hedgerows for eggs, swallowing some of them raw from sheer laziness. I used a slate for a skillet, and cleaned it by scrubbing it with horsetails or plunging it in brook gravel. I had no meat, except the gnats I'm always collecting because of leaving my mouth open. The Arkansas apple I kept as a jewel. Even the bite out of it did not brown. Thus I lived for nearly a fortnight. When my belly had filled from flat to the roundness of the eight-day moon, I would sit back against a hay-rick or the bank of a quiet path to enjoy my Applepeel coloring-book.

My mind wandered from it to my own body spread before me. It had been refreshed by rains like a plant. How neat a kit for living! No wonder I hardly needed to carry anything else. All of it was beams and cables and engines and pumps and pipes and storage, and yet they fitted together as wastelessly as soap-bubbles and were wrapped roundly by the rubbery skin. What could be left over without other purpose than to be just person?—in the mind, is it, or the female fatblanket that smooths the cusps between muscles? And where is the mary, the essence-of-gender?—the shehood, the hership?

The state to which I had been assigned was half-nakedness, but the top half, too, went bare in rainy weather, to keep my two clothes dry inside the bundle. And when the sun shone. And of course in bed. At remaining times (there was a last bit of what my mother calls gloveweather) I assumed my half-modest state.

None of me was bothered by the sun except my ears, and I remembered my mother saying: "Itching ears, that means people are talking abouchyer." The over-felicitous green of my shirt faded in the weather till its milk became straw; all of me went moderate gold. This, the Mongers would have thought, decreased my value: for even more salable than blond hair is the *virtual clevel* left by the proper worship of Brayab—the white triangles concisely defining the delectabilia.

I dangled old Oe's fishline in streams but never caught anything; her onions were stronger than ever so I rubbed them over me at nightfall as mosquito-repellent; I got ticks and chiggers, but that was all right: I found someone's bottle of Arthropoff with the doctor's scribbled directions "Apply all over body wash off after 12 yrs" so I made a note to have a good shower at my twenty-ninth birthday. I had a fathom of Theopard's rope and used it one Tuesday to let myself down a rocky step into a new country. The full moon came and went, taking the tampons with her; around that time I was inclined to stay up all night, and got moonburn.

The brooks I crossed were disappearing under early summer leafage. The woods were as varicolored as they would not be again till October, even the evergreens were rinsed with lightgreen newgrowth. I slept less than usual: I lay out on hilltops, Naked-I stargazing, but also I loved to walk at night in the quiet under massed trees and hear the wide river of wind flowing in their tops. Then too I could walk on roads, where the dark print of rain shed a mist, and the fragments of the moonlight swam to my ankles like white sharks.

The coloring-book was, on the whole, a bomb. It did arouse thoughts in me, and I studied my stomach and glushes with my hands—questioned them—as I had done while kneeling in the closet and listening to the extravagances about myself. But only because of my interest in sculpture. —As for the bloon, I blew into it one evening till I was blue in the face, but achieved only a half-turgid rubber doll who folded limply in the middle. I was not so full of breath as I thought, and Applepeel must be full of sap to be Applepeel.

Discreetly at the bottom of the bundle lay a one-volume *Digest* of Haamg Ibn Auhanda. But I did not need it to remember the teaching of the sixteen sleeps, or waves, or deeps. For now that whenever in the night I woke and opened my eyes I saw the constellations, I saw a clock, that had turned not an hour, but an hour and a half. The turning earth lulls us to the deeply duple rhythm of a gamelan, halves of its turn, and halves of halves of halves—no triplicity, and so no twelfths or twenty-fourths or thirds or eights. Sixteen times in an earth-turning a baby wakes and cries; as it grows, the valleys of the night deepen and merge, and the peaks of the day rise and merge, but the wave-form goes rippling on for ever, and still each hour-and-a-half through the night we climb up through the dream—the four dreams lost and the fifth brought to light; each hour-and-a-half we climb into dreaming and perhaps wetting our straw and rising from the dreamths into bleak waking and needing a drink, and each hour-and-a-half through the day we sink into passivity or a secret moment of unconsciousness. "If," says Haamg, "you watch a pair of bodies through the night of their first passion, each hour and a half it is that they stir and reinvolve." Sixteen times we dip and sixteen times soar, at each bearing-point as the earth whirls us like a merry-go-round, tilted to the nightward.

Nor does the moon really divide her circle into twenty-fourths, rising an hour later each night. She compromises between twenty-four and thirty-two, and moves by only a moon-hour.

If you learn to observe the peaks and valleys—your own and others'—you can achieve great things, outsmart anybody, and dodge some catastrophes. For they are not the same each day, but have some stretch; I stretch them if I wake too hot in the night, or doze too hard in the day; they only average the sixteenth of an earth-revolution, just as my period only averages one moon-revolution. But for the time being I had no one to conflict with and no material to work on.

Sometimes I loped down slopes, but then a counter-traveling bumblebee would hit me—whit-dzoing!—too hard on the cheekbone. But the more I ran the more I couldn't help running. The unrebukable air drew its tepid fingers around me, denoting the lion's-paw muscles between my sideribs, reminding me of the structures that throbbed in my groin. Some girls can't run naked because their breasts won't stay with them; mine are too firm to flap. I paused to watch cows kissing— you know how often they do that? In the afternoons when the birds drowzed, the dominant sound was my breathing. My senses told me of woodsmoke on the other side of a coppice, and windchimes in a porch far to the north. Those juniper bushes that have a smell of male cat; and a skunk, which at six miles is a fine spice to the quiet odor of the country. Near wet banks I could hear the soft earth growing.

I saw every dawn. That alone makes life magnificent. The sun roaring up, the moon queening it over the morning sky, the rain had fallen, I had slept, I had eaten a little—I felt so good I could hardly bear it! Nakedness had led me to solitude, and it was adventure enough.

Detour

I SENT a postcard to Fortesant. No, I didn't do that, since I hadn't got a stamp or a pencil, but I thought about him—in particular, about how he had arrived before anyone else at our party, assuming it as his right to get in the way and bore us and require entertaining. He only had to come from the big house across the street. Looking smug, he said to my mother: "What do you think I should give her for her birthday?" "A lesson," she suggested.

And when we had finished laying the table, I decided to take a shot at dissuading him. I took him by the elbow and steered him into another room, and he looked interested until he saw that I had brought a chaperone along—Zed—pulling her by the other hand.

"What's the matter?" he said. "Have you got something to tell me?"

"Yes, I have," I said. "I feel like telling you about myself, since I really don't think you've noticed. You've no idea what I'm like. I'm irresponsible, lazy, and immature."

"Huh! Immature, are you, at sixteen?"

"Yes. I'm as bad as a kid. I forget to do things. I get muddy. Isn't that right, Zed?" She backed me up.

"Well, so the hell what?"

"And that reminds me, I swear too. (I didn't know you did, though.)"

"So—the hell—what?"

"I don't think you really want to go through with this, that's what."

He seemed unpersuaded, and tried to take my hand between his.

"Look, Fortesant, I'm serious. I really am a deplorable match for you. I laugh at you, which I know you don't like."

"Anything else?" he said bravely.

"Oh yes, plenty. You can ask my mother. Just because I'm a girl doesn't mean I know how to behave like one. I go to sleep at the wrong moments. I forget to look in the mirror, and when I do I just pull faces. I say what's on top of my head." "Yes," contributed Zed, "and she goes around with her mouth open. I'm always telling her." "That's right. And I dress in too much of a hurry. And don't like to waste time changing my clothes. I chew my nails and suck my tongue. (That's all the meat I'll eat.) I can't sit still." "Sit!" said Zed, "she doesn't sit at all—she sprawls on the floor. Or somewhere down the garden, she's generally in the bushes or up the creek and you have to go calling for her. Mind you, she might grow out of it one day." "Oh, yes!" I said, "I could start a good habit, any day! but I keep forgetting. Imagine, the day comes when Fristy age ninety definitively stops picking her nose! Fristy age ninety-two starts remembering to think before she speaks!" ("Fristy might sometimes consider sleeping on it before she speaks.") "Fristy at the ripe age of nineteen learns to squeeze tubes from the tail end. Listen," I said, warming to the subject, "I tell fibs and I pick my nose (oh, I mentioned that already) and bolt my food and talk with my mouth full and put my elbows on the table and rile on chairs and swing on door-lintels and break things. I'm tactless, I'm hyperactive." "I thought you said you were lazy?" "I'm hyper or lazy, depending which is more annoying at the time. One of the exceptions that improve the rule. I'm inconsistent, I'm even ungrammatical, I'm not a lady, in spite of all Zed's efforts. I'm a nuisance. I outrun boys. I break taboos. I read books."

He looked perceptibly shaken, but folded his arms and took it like a man.

"So let's call off this betrothal business, okay?"

After a moment he unfolded his arms and, to my surprise, tried to take me by my shoulders and kiss me. I couldn't help sniggering, while I shook him off and dodged behind Zed.

"That's my answer," he said.

"Well, it isn't exactly an answer."

"Yes, it is. I'm in love with you. I don't care whether you miss church or steal cookies or wet your pants, or laugh so that the whole town can hear you. I'm in love with you, you silly infant."

"You could be just saying that."

He exploded. "Are you telling me I'm lying? Are you daring to contradict what I said? You know that of all things in the world that *must* be true, because—because—"

"Because what?"

"Because *everyone* is in love with you."

"Bull," I said, carefully, as it was a word whose use I had only recently learnt. ("Eyewash" might have been safer.)

"Name four people who aren't! Ha, I have you there, don't I? You can only think of three." (I took it he meant my mother, sister, and brother.)

"It's nonsense, what he says, isn't it, Zed?" I asked her.

"No," she said and turned away. Which worried me.

"Look, I don't know many people at all," I said. "I've never been anywhere and my acquaintance isn't wide; I'm sure that as time goes on I'll meet plenty of people who take no notice of me. I really hope so.

Perhaps—I tell you what—let's just wait till I've had a chance to travel and see the world a bit."

When I made this proposal I could see that it only scared him. He pretended he would let me travel and see the world and widen my acquaintance, but he still was adamant that we get betrothed first. Others were arriving and I needed to check the house for mistletoe, and we broke off the conversation.

Fortesant. And another thing that annoyed him about me was that I would keep calling him that instead of Peter.

Across More Country

I WASN'T going anywhere in particular, but I had started west and so I kept west by the sun and the Twins. I liked the wind in my face and the morning sun on my back. I didn't mind having no contact with society for a few days, knowing that when it resumed life would kick off as eventful as ever. A slim dog fell in with me. I called him Spot, though he was white from head to tail. It was good to have someone to talk with. As it happened, that day we encountered a yokel and later a big farmer with a riding-crop—perhaps in my new protector's company I had been incautious. He scared the yokel off with a low growl, and sank his teeth into the farmer's gaiters.

But we were overtaken next by a knight, no less.

We were going along a trail between woods edged with dense honseysuckle, and it would have been easy to run in where the huge shirehorse couldn't follow. But Spot, though I tried to call him off, did his gallant best to get even with the horse's fetlocks, till the knight leaned down and scooped him up in one mailed fist (quite a feat of horsemanship) and tied him across the pommel, where he kept up a paroxysm of yapping. The knight then tapped me on the shoulder with his lance and directed me to stand with my back to a tree while he dismounted and doffed his armor.

This took him twenty minutes. In such a situation one is not sure whether to hope that others will come along—or not. I told him he should be saving damsels in distress, but he said he had done enough of that and earned a break, and besides I didn't appear to be in distress, yet, unless I thought him some kind of dragon? "Nor," he added, "is it clear that you're a damsel."

"It's not? I should have thought it was." "You're a wench. Why otherwise are you wandering the byroads cuntbare, seducing the wind?" "Why aren't you? This state has advantages," I told him; "the secret of living in the open is to wear almost nothing, then getting wet doesn't matter. I imagine in the present weather you're rusting on the inside. People shouldn't wear too much—it's unhealthy. But don't judge by appearances: you would think differently of me if you knew what has brought me to this pass." And I prepared to waste as much as possible of his time with my whole history, just as I have wasted yours:

"Of course I wasn't born naked: I lived well if modestly clothed until my eighteenth birthday feast, which was also to be the occasion of my betrothal—"

"Excuse the interruption, but don't try to be cute with me, Lady Judy—Lady Lackwear. I don't think you were born dumb, either. I'll hear the beguiling tale later, thank you—the Thousand and One Steps to Nakedness," he said, struggling to disengage his right pauldron and vambrace; "I may well, if I decide to linger with you in this bosky dell for a second joust, be in the mood for a thousand and one such delays. For the present what excites my courtly interest is your present state."

"Well, as to that," I ventured, "I'm enchanted." "Thank you. I too." "You know what I mean, surely? I'm only a vision. The enchanter Deepdevil has bemused your eyes. I'm actually a ugly wench. I'm thirty-four. No, fifty-one. I'm not really naked. I'm not even here. You'll find yourself attempting union with a slab of air, or worse, a thorn-thicket, a wild wood-lobster, a burning fiery combine harvester—*another knight*. A big hairy one, with a bad pong and a worse temper." He wouldn't buy it. An ill-read errant. From time to time I had to help him with a hard-to-reach zipper or point out that he was using a metric wrench on an English nut. "Dab thiggs," he said (he was getting a slight cold), "damp godfounded nuisance. Alexad-der," he told me when I inquired his knightly name. "Where's your squire, anyway?" I asked. "Well, just as I sighted you," he explained, "I resolved to send him back and pay a bill we had overlooked at last night's inn. —Ah, shut up!" he barked, distracted by the comments of his hostage, the dog, who was tied just where I once had been but not gagged; trying to apply one of his socks, the knight snatched his hand away with some loss of blood.

"You wish you lived in an earlier age, don't you?" I said to him— "but I don't. Think of all the things that have happened for the first time, and the things that exist that never existed before."

"Yes, such as you," he replied, "and that's why I don't wish it any more."

Finally he stood before me free of all ironmongery. (Also of string vest and long johns.) He rolled his shoulders and swelled his seigneurial person to show me how honored I was, touched himself to reappoint his erection (or perhaps there hadn't been room for such a luxury inside the armor), and strode toward me with fingers atwitch, commanding me to brace my shoulders against the tree, set my legs a shield's width apart, and keep my hands behind me and my eyes meekly lowered upon the blue-blooded member by which I was about to become the mother of a race of heroes.

I obeyed him absolutely. Not till I could see the whites of his foreskin did I produce the slingshot from behind my back and inflict him with it. (Rubber band only; at that range ammunition was needless.)

The immediate collapse of ardor and manhood almost displeased me.

With my slingshot threatening at his rear, or a little below, he unbound Spot, and had to vault with alacrity to the saddle and pull his legs up after him if he didn't want to shed some of his mediaevil haemogoblin.

As his vanquisher, I bade him return to his lady and give her an exact account of his exploit. The laws of knight-errantry compelled him to carry out my command to the letter. I turned the horse's head for him, and they wended one way, Spot and I the other, while the suit of armor remained sitting reflectively.

But wait: armor is clothing, of a sort. I stopped and contemplated it. Not clothing: sculpture. It has to acknowledge anatomy, enrich it. The greaves swelled more ornate than the calves they had encased, the tasses overlapped more flexibly than the hips. Too large for me, unfortunately. I picked out his iron cropguard and tried it around me; then his long johns, but they made me look like the roots of a tooth. I ran after the poor bare champion (who was desperately plucking sprays from the branches) and tossed the garment up to him. He said humbly, "Gramercy, milady, for your magnanimy."

"You bet, knight. I'm thinking of the feelings of your pure lady."

"There is precedent," he said, "for a knight submitting to conquest by an Amazon, and taking service under her—" I slapped the horse's croup to start him homeward.

But before we got out of the forest, having been tempted to bring down a quail for supper, I threw the Mongerkins' wicked slingshot away.

That evening we came to the beginning of a range of chalk hills, each hill a round down like a pudding, perfectly mantled with short grass. The country was getting ever more open. Surely it was about time to find a little town and shops; with my practice in filching lettuces and honeycombs, I ought to be able to steal myself some nether clothes. By now they might tickle me.

When I say I talked with the dog, I don't mean we exchanged sentences. I am given, when alone, to bursting out with utterances like "Yankton!" and "Hunkpapa!" which mean nothing except that I feel full of spunk and ready for anything. He understood me perfectly, and answered in a dialect of Mongrel—running circles around me, crouching on his elbows, and flapping his cheeks.

Spot and I slept, like a little spiral galaxy, on top of the first round hill. Each time I reversed my curl he reversed his, giving my nose another lick. I slept cool those nights on the moors, no dreams at all, or if there were they slunk humbly away because it was life that seemed the dream since that—spectacular event. Early next morning we were bowling along, crossing the third hill, traveling in high skips, not because I was in any hurry but because a thunderstorm was forming: the wind was arriving, the electric air overhead was light, lifting. And this was the most unusual thing that ever happened to me, since thunderstorms never form in the morning. It was still a little chilly and I was wearing my two topclothes. I happened to be giving one of my few fleeting thoughts to that chief hunter of mine—what was his name?— Theopard—and thinking, now, did he say "Put you in the stocks" or "Put you in the pillory"? and what exactly is the difference? or had he only been splutter-hissing at me? On the way down from a leap I turned to look behind me for no reason that I knew of, and there on the second hill of the row was a party of men on horses. They had a telescope and had seen us.

I told the dog to go home; I didn't want him hurt. He argued with me but at last obeyed. I ran down the hill, off to the right into more covered country. Just as the shower began I found my way barred by a deep river.

Bibliographical Interlude

A T THIS point, breathless reader, we'll allow you a rest from your pursuit of Applepeel and see if we can interest you in stocking your bookshelf with some of the other learned works we hope to issue, mentioning only *Lovemaking in a Warm Climate* (romping on hillsides), *Ways to Make Love in a Cold Climate* (overcoming the limitations of being *in* bed), *Bed, Have a Question Ready for Girls Who Smile, Much Lusher, Outloved, Suppressed Portions of Brit. Mus. Ms. Copt. 2393QZ, Oral-Anal-Genital Manual, Saltantii Antici Lex. Porn. Libri Tres, History of the Publishing House of Poor Nog, The Pornucopia* (attributed to Gallust, ed. Von Titzenasz), *Xes* (Reports of the Papyrological Society on the texts unearthed at Xes in Inner Egypt, together with still older texts unearthed in the temples of Karnal and Uxor) tome XVII: *Nudellae Pericula ("Avventure d'una Ragazza Nuda"*, trans. Nucchi and Burleschoni), *Blonda Nuda, Estoy Lista, Recline and Fall (A Backward Look at the Roman Empire), Equatorial Countercurrent, Orgy and Fesse, The Strumpet-Majorette, Dristan and Icecolde, And* (distillation of all "and" tales from *Jack and Jill* and *Tristan and Isolde* and *Heloise and Abelard* to *Leila wa Majnoon), Heteromeo, Mister Ioso and Miss Conception, Old Swive Tale, Rosy Cranny and Gilded Stern* (a play in three scenes—Proscene, Obscene, and Epicene), *Sex Exposed, Next to Naked, Just Barely Possible, Almost a Maiden, Near Miss, Skivvy in a Skivvy, Alice in Underpants, The Pushinto Religion, The Breast of Her, Guide to the Fingerpaths, Wild Oats and Wild Goats, Too True to Be Good, Take Kate* (by Denka Boyd), *The Night with the Won Girl, Field Guide to the Vulva (With Key), Tutoyé par la Reine, Prehistoric Women* (a bawdlerized portrait of the amorist as a young man), *Still Wife With Willies, Worship with Words, Say After Me, It's Nice I Like It, Thy Thigh* (a study of minimal phonemic contrasts), *I Sigh For Thy Thigh, Pipe: Masculine or Feminine? Designs on Her* (bodypainting), *Ifshy, Whoizhshe? I She, But If, On, In, Serenade in Jill Sharp Minor, What Cindy Saves for Telling Me at Bedtime, She of the Two Pillows, The Damp Patch, Third Finger, Sinpulse, At Their Mercy, Tit for Pat and Ass for Izzy, Leg, International Rules of Grunting, Sale Catalogue of Stills and Loops Made at the Trisulci Club, Suggestions for the Hostess at an Orgy* (described in a curious understatement as "the book that has raised the most erections"), *Increase and Multiply* (a Roman fertility festival beginning with the night of the One Plus Two and culminating in the night of the Many Plus Many), *Median Maiden*, *I Saw I Conquered I Came*, *Via Gracialis* (a Roman byway), *The Hole in the Golden Rule* (a study of von Sacher-Masoch), *La Elle* (not a French paean to *das ewige Weiblich* but a soap opera about Columbus LePonce Johnson and his sisters La-Elle, Lay-Ette, LaWhore, LaBore, Lousy-Ann, Ae Mae, Yae Nae, Dezzie-Rae, Straecee, Sherree-Brandee, Tirramy-Sue, Syndi-Kate, A'MaryKay, and the twins Maybee and Junebug, a standard subdivision family), *Coin-Operated Ladies* (history of the so-called Oldest Profession, tracing it from Danae, whom Zeus possessed after descending on her in a shower of gold), *Once Upon a Time They Lived Happily Ever After* (fairy story), *Who's Whose* (snob directory), *The Daily Maid* (illustrated magazine and working directory), *Embarrass* (newsrag of the named-and-shamed), *The Daily Lady*, *Cheaper to Keep Her* (film), *Twould Be Fun to Fuck Her* (popular song), *Who Needs a Virgin?* (by the aggressive pamphleteer of *Will There Always Be Right Wing People?*), *The Urchin Virgin or the Urgent Verger or The Persian Perversion* (handbook for catamites; a version has been long known in prep schools as *The Persian Race By I. Ran*), *How to Hug* (vol. eleven of the encyclopaedia), *How Not to Win a Mate and Whether It Matters*, *Heat-Dream of a Would-Be Naked Girl*, *They Wouldn't* (seminal piece of pornological detection by Elland Harmer, one of those sexologists with a curiously sexless or even angelic name. He (she?) realized that no pronographer—pornographer (we mustn't forget the supinographers)—is likely to use for his female lead—or indeed any of the multitude of females he may show in situations they mightn't like to be shown in—the name of his own wife, mother, sister, aunt, current or past mistress, or especially past wife (but is moderately likely to use the names of close acquaintances). Most pornography is anonymous or pseudonymous, but, armed with this powerful tool, Harmer subjected the pornographers of all languages and centuries to biographical study, and succeeding in exposing the identities of *every one*. All, therefore, who have an underground income from shoddily produced little fuck-books must now tremble, and all who intend to give birth to yet another bawdy classic should think better of it. There is one exception: Harmer overlooked the fact that not too many wives, mothers, sisters, aunts, or even girlfriends are called Applepeel, though that may change), *Wouldn't You?* (counterblast to Harmer, argues that Harmer's method can lead to false exclusion of the culprit, that is, pornographer, because he, having fantasized a Marie, is likely to seek out some real Marie in the future. Again, may not yet be applicable to an Applepeel. And if he has in adolescence fantasized or idolized some Yolande or Helen, he may be

cauterized by the size, age, and frequency of the Yolandes and Helens
he discovers), *I Wouldn't* (another counterblast, contends that no
respectable pornographer would want to spoil a pretty name, especially a saintsname, for future generations of innocent girls. The only result
of this research is to identify the few respectable pornographers), *Alf
Lay Wa-Lay* (The Thousand and One Lays, or the Arabian Nights' Tails—
amplification of an earlier work* in which a cobbler, a stone-grinder, a
brick-layer, a horse-tamer and other specialists describe their wedding
nights in the language of their trades; includes *Kiz Kichi* ("The Lass's
Ass"), *Kiz Kaynaki* ("The Springline Where the Lass's Glushes Join"),
Kss Ummak (never mind), *The History of Princess Kuntalbint and
the Forty Calenders*, and *Ladayki* ("For Thy (Feminine) Sake")); *Sulth*
(palace slut, "Her name's Shayth bint Sultâan but she's such an imp we
call her Sulth bint Shaytaan—devilsdaughter"); *Aversa Venus, or, Venus
At Midnight.*

　　Venus our sister in the sky can never be seen at midnight, not even
with averted vision, for she stays on the sunward side of life—but the
Venus who brings down heaven with her often can, never averse
though sometimes averted . . .   Yet more has been exhumed from the
abounding soil of Xes, but too much is excess, and some recessive.
How easy it is to conceive; how easy, while the biochemistry lasts, to
heat the fever of an erotic fable, at any rate a serious one; how disqui-
eting to think that none of it would mean anything to a literate crow or
angel or cockroach, or to one of our descendants, the rational species
of the far future! But we must hurry back to Applepeel's authentic nar-
rative, dictated by her to her little sister of a winter evening, and catch
up with her as she flees through the tamarisks and is confronted by the
rustling waters of the Cressfont:

* A real one.

Treed

I WAS GLAD to see the river: I ran in till the cold water belled at my waist. There I paused to pull off my topclothes and thrust them into my bundle, and slid into the main current. I should have just crossed to the other bank, but the hunt hadn't yet come close enough to be exciting; besides, nobody fights in wet weather. Downstream I went on my back, holding clothes and bundle above me. Then I thought, how waterproof is this blanket? Working with it on my chest, I loosened the knot to ease more air in, then pulled it tight and let it into the water. It bobbed like a bladder. I twisted around and embraced it, and forged along, frog-kicking my legs behind me. "You can't push a blanket," says the proverb—or in my mother's version "Managing you is like trying to herd cats or push a blanket"—but that only applies to making a bed. It occurred to me to patent this thing as a rainproof bike pannier. I was glad to get rid of the sweat of running (though experts say you sweat underwater too) and I took a drink long enough to lower the level.

The rain was heaviering, it made the river warm on me. Away from my eye along the surface stood the little chalices it raised or, as I now saw them to be, Tashartris turbans. The lightning walked beside me on the hills, and once I saw it silhouette a party of routed figures, and I was pleased to think that only the horses didn't mind.

If, as looked quite likely, I was going to be caught, I preferred to be nice and clean; and in the uplands of the last few days I had found only springs to splash at. So I welcomed the river between my limbs, and freed a hand to run back along myself and help it.

The sun came out and the flags shook out their yellow. I went under a bridge, from which a tourist in a felt hat was leaning. He made a vain grab for his dropping pipe, moved quickly to the lower side to watch me emerge, and called after me, "Wait, wait!"

I held onto a rock and asked him what he wanted.

"Could you come back and swim in place for a while?"

"No way. I'm late already. What for, anyhow?"

"I'm painting a picture, you see, and if suddenly a water-nymph—"

"You're wasting my time!" I shouted and swam quickly back to give him five minutes. He tried to get up on the parapet and crouch with his back to the water, must have found it an awkward way to paint, and said "Could I trouble you to turn around?" "What the hell, you can't swim in place facing downstream!" "Then could you move back to the upstream side of the bridge?" Give me patience!—I did, and so did he, and studied in quiet, and I suppose painted. My thighs had to thresh hard, since my arms were clasped around the bundle and the current was fast through the arch. After I had given fifteen kicks, drops of Titanium White splattered around me, and I was about to tell him to paint less wildly when a blob fell on my back, and it was hot. —Enough; I stopped and shot back under the bridge (a cry from him like a bittern's) and away; to make up time I changed from breaststroke to Butterfly, bunting my bundle before me like a beachball, and rocking the margins of the stately river with my splash.

But there came in sight another bridge. It was about time I started fleeing in more serious style. They could get to either bank as easily as I could, and I might find myself floating along between two lines of trotting horsemen. (Besides, I'd been too long in the water and my fingertips looked like brains.) I'd better get out while I could and look for somewhere to hide.

I scrambled out on the northern bank. North of this river begins the healthful country where they call boys lads and girls lasses.

Just below the bridge was the corner of a wood, its trees overhanging river and road. The wood was an obvious hiding-place. The most obvious part of it was the great horse-chestnut at the corner. I told myself cheerfully that they wouldn't expect me to hide in the most obvious place. The rail of the bridge ended within a spring of the lowest limb. I looped the bundle to my wrist, leaped and hung for a minute kicking, then hauled myself in among the canopy of seven-fingered leaves.

I mounted a spiral stair of five branches, stepped through a door of the divided trunk, and came out on a powerful limb, broad, gray, smooth, rising only gently, then curving up in the way of horse chestnuts to its sky-end. Below was a clear drop to the river, but in every other direction—bridge, road, opposite bank, depths of the wood behind—the tree was like a castle: halls lit by a thousand tall white pink-touched candles, for this was the time of full bloom; walls mazily chambered with sills and peepholes. Here was my nest to wait out the passage of the riders.

When they came in sight along the road I felt less sure I was right in choosing the citadel of the wood. Leading them was Theopard. He now looked three quarters mad, and was accoutered in what I at first took to be ropes, but only some of them were: the rest were his clothes, much neglected. The Applepeel-spotting telescope was slung over his shoulder. His followers, streaked with days of dust and now steaming from the rain, didn't look much better. Their faces were agitated, and the one riding at the rear grasped something before him on the saddle—a banana?—no, a candle, for luck.

On the hump of the bridge, they reined in, and shaded their eyes and turned them up toward me!

But their eyes went on into the tower of foliage above me: just appraising, it seemed, the tree itself. How reassuring to think that in the minds of such men, bent fiercely on their small fellow being, there still was space for a moment of response to the formosity of an alien and grander being for which they could not lust. They seemed to watch the tree's crown shifting in the wind, then made a gesture of acknowledgment and dropped their eyes to the world below. After a short conference, they rode off the bridge and most went ahead on the lane into the farmland. Two turned up along the right bank, and two down along it into the wood.

But their muzzles soon got stuck in the undergrowth below me, and they backed out to the bridgehead.

"Best stay here," said one. "If she went this way she may double back this way, like cunning vixens often do. And," in a lower voice, "I don't believe that lad's to be trusted." (What lad?)

They dismounted and hitched their steeds to the rail; then sat down at the foot of my tree. Right under me.

I lay like moss along the branch, with one arm straight to my side and the other straight ahead balancing my bundle. There was silence below, and I peeped over. I saw their faces upside down, or in reflection, either of which improved them. They were taking it easy in the throne-like spaces between the great roots that descended into deep water. And they were each peeling an apple, one of the green-yellow kind, one red. They peeled with close attention, as if it was a ritual.

The result was two unbroken spirals of peel. They shaped them back together into apparently whole apples, and set them down reverently, side by side, slightly pressing together. Then they closed their eyes and ate the flesh.

I had sometimes thought it silly that I had come to be called Applepeel, since I never leave anything of an apple but the stalk. (I draw the limit at eating stalk. But I do use it for a toothpick.) The pips are said to be poisonous, and they may be, like coffee, but they are nicely nutty. These two were wasting the peel and I supposed I'd have to see them chuck the cores to the fishes. —No: they gobbled them.

What I should do was move to a position over the bridge and drop onto one of their horses. I'd never ridden but I bet I could cling on by

thighs and mane. I surveyed the branches to my left and began to draw
in my limbs for a leap.

They licked their lips, and one said: "The sun's come out, she must
be smiling. You've seen her, haven't you, Clixter?"

Clixter nodded.

"Hain't you got another pair in your saddlebag?"

"Nope. None left," said Clixter.

"I don't even like apples. They're for the horses. The red ones go
bready, the green are for cooking, the yellow stay sweet and bland. And
we never get to try the real Arkansaws."

"You know they're not for eating; they're sacred. The boss has only
got one himself."

"What is it about her, anyway? Is she really stacked?"

Clixter just drew his shoulders up and darted a glance.

I decided to keep my limbs where they were for a while. Who isn't
tempted to eavesdrop on a critique of herself?

"Well, what shape is she? Willowy? Majestically tall?"

"Boy, you really don't have the vision, do you? What are you doing
in this Hunt?"

"Isn't she even big or little?"

"No. Well, she may be a little on the—that is, a shade on the little
side, by average. But the point is, she's *just right.*"

"Oh. I see. Is that all?"

"Is that all?"

"Well, it's not so easy for us who haven't been so lucky. I mean, you
could imagine flaming hair or strawberry lips or swinging gallons or
wasp waist or great long creamy thighs or churning hips or sopping sea-
weedy cunth—"

"Will you choke it?"

"She doesn't have any of those?"

"Horror, no."

"But then how can she be visible two miles off?"

"Look, I don't blame you, really. The world is divided into three
parts: those who have seen her and those who've only heard about
her—the Gloaters and the Gleaners, like me and you—and those
who've only Glimpsed a bit of her, perhaps a blade of thigh as she was
vanishing over a wall; and those poor devils of Glimpsers are the ones
who are the most fever-crazy. I pity you if we glimpse her today and
nothing more. It's only the Comma that jumps out at two miles. You
know what that means?" "No." "The thigh-glush assemblage—sometimes known as the Greater Thigh. That and her earrings. The rest

moves into focus at about one point seven. (With the telescope you can multiply by four. Depending on atmospheric conditions.)"

"But still! At those distances you just can't recognize things her size, unless perhaps they're luminous."

"Which she is."

"You mean she actually burns? Gives off light?"

"No, not quite. I mean she's just right, like the sun."

"Oh. I understand."

"I don't think you do, but you will once you see. She'll be printed on your mind. If she were suddenly to appear before your eyes, it would be as if someone threw a splash of water in your face—you'd be several times wider awake. Colors would be that much brighter. She'd change your character at a glance. But you don't have to wait for that. She's so vivid you'd *feel* her two miles off. I tell you, I'd tingle if she was anywhere near—hiding in this tree for instance."

"Oh? Well, I'm tingling!"

"Yes, but that's because you're masturbating your mind by talking about her. Look, let me try to explain: let's take her halves—her glushes—her children, I call them. They're what everyone takes. They're the capital of her body; the seat of government, you might say; they stand for her. The world's glyptic summit."

"Luscious, are they?—juicy? Glooshy?"

"*No*, man, I'm trying to tell you. They're not too much *this*, nor too much *that*, nor extremely *this*, nor a great deal *that*: they're *exactly right*. How else could glushes be sweetly perfect? And now please a silence."

The other man respectfully observed the silence, only rubbing his tummy hungrily.

"Aah," said Clixter at length, to indicate that the apprentice could speak again if he really wished. He did.

"Perfect average, is that all she is?"

"No! The angles, the proportions, the textures—they're only hers, there's never been any just like them. Her body and her face. But how can I tell you? I'd have to draw her. Which is rather easy to do, I've seen all kinds of men do it. But I'm not going to draw her in the dust."

"All I really know about her is the notorious red-so-red-that-it's-black. And even that I can't actually picture. How can something be intensely black and intensely red?—it's a mystery. Are you sure it isn't just brown?"

"You have to explore deeper and deeper into the idea of redness until it's black. She has too much of pigment as she has too much of everything. It's like—let's see—whatever color it is outside the limit of your vision, the color inside your head. No, not that, because that has no gloss. The gloss is what makes men move around her trying to catch the best angles—even when she's naked."

"Well, I'll try. Color's usually the only thing you can't not know about a woman."

"You do understand, don't you, that it's the color of her hair, not her skin?—or eyes?"

"Yes! Though come to think of it . . . But you know what I mean. They're so often called just 'blondes.' Or some, of course, brunettes or redheads."

"Her voice, now, that *is* blonde. Her skin is so smooth, so *recent*, it's hardly there. As for her face: high cheeks with a fine sprinkle of orange freckles, lemon eyes with long upcurved lashes and flat flesh around, as if filled out with merriment. And her armpits are like that, too—filled out almost flush, no caverns, almost no hair. But the hair down on her *matter* is thick and short and impudent. Burnt turf."

"Does she have any dimples?"

"Yes. Not on her face, though. —Fingers a little pudgy and finely tapering, with dirty nails; nose long and shallow, makes everyone else's face look like an eroded ape, mouth never shut, so it's a matter of debate what shape it is. Chin outsailing, like, what was it, that Egyptian queen, Queen Graffititi. You asked about the color of the eyes (didn't you?): they're very pale greentinged grey; the pupils look like floating dots, the light splashes madly through behind them; they're as shiny as—as that nut."

"That nut, by the way, is a chestnut! They're lying all around. Let's build a fire and roast some."

I couldn't believe it! They didn't know the difference between chestnuts and horse chestnuts. Hadn't they played conkers in school?

"You know the vow," said Clixter reprovingly. "Only apples. Nothing else, till she serves it to us."

I reached out for an old conker that was still hanging on the tree, shelled it, passed it back to my toes, and accurately dropped it on the balder head, which was the novice's. They decided to accept the heavenly sign.

It took them a quarter of an hour, striking a bushel of matches on their belts, to get a smoky fire going, by which time the wood was much clearer of underbrush and I owed some coughs. I looked forward to seeing them bite conker and, if possible, taste it—last October's, too.

"Could I ask you something else?" said the chestnut man diffidently. "When we catch her, what'll happen? I mean after we've all had her. Will that be all? We can't all marry her. Aren't we going to find ourselves fighting over her?"

"Marrying her is not what you'll want to do to her," said Clixter. "We'll all live in a castle with her, our leader promises, so I suppose we *could* all marry her, but marrying is not what you'll want to do. Even 'having' her may not be what you'll want to do. You'll want to enslave her. You'll want to play with her. You'll want to use her. You'll want to stretch her. You'll want to shock her. You'll want more of it all done to her than you can ever do alone."

The chestnut man was plainly shocked himself.

"Understand this," said Clixter, "the words *suffer* and *fun* will come to you. It isn't in her glushes, it might be in her whole body, perhaps her dear waist, perhaps her breasts (which *are* on the small side); it's in her face, which is a blindingly vivid one, though again only because it's *just right*; it's really in her whole air. You have an instinct to make her suffer, but only in ways that make her a heroine. Why? Because she gets fun out of it. That's what's so damned tempting about her: she gets foaming fun out of everything. It isn't your own fun you care about, you even forget that. You can let yourself tease her to suffer because you know her fun will absorb any harm from it; and because she'll treat it as fun (whatever she pretends) you can't disappoint her by making it serious suffering. Our leader is going to rename her Adame—what a nut of a name!—and have her dressed always in nothing but great green boots. (And her everlasting earrings, of course.) We'll shame her; we'll never come close to—never even go in the same direction as—hurting her. Do I make sense?"

"Yes," said the chestnut man, who I'm sure wanted to say "No." "But," he objected, "if she gets fun out of it, why the hell does she keep running away from us?"

"Why, to increase our fun and hers! To screw it up to the ultimate. Have you never heard of foreplay? This whole Hunt is nothing but an Applepeel-scale variety of foreplay."

"I think you're right," I called down from the tree. But I made it sound like a bird-call. (Then I thought: Watch out, Lady Jane. Your enemy's getting close: laughter. She's what coughs and sneezes are to other people. (Laughter is a girl. Not an enemy, really, but a little terror.) I don't know whether it's more dangerous to forget about her creeping up or remember. One way she gets you more suddenly, the other way more remorselessly. Anyway, once you've remembered, there's no choice: you can't say "*Don't* think about how you *must not laugh*.")

Clixter was concluding his description of the final scene of the hunt. It was on the awe-inspiring side, yet delivered in a monotone, in which he then added: "Aren't those things ready?"

"Yes, just let them cool a minute. Time for one more question: what about when she becomes old?"

"That girl isn't ever going to be old. She won't ever even grow up. She's going to be almost but not quite rescued by a hero as a villain throws her off a cliff, or she's going to save the world by giving herself to the lightning, or she's going to fall into a block of ice and be preserved—laugh and all—or she's going to die of a lifetime's orgasms one afternoon in the Roman Forum, or she'll be never heard of again in the desert somewhere south of Harar."

Listening to all this, I wondered how I was ever going to climb back down to the real world. I didn't feel like laughing any more.

"But those are all dying ways of getting out of growing old. Couldn't there be some other way?"

"If there is, she'll be the one to find it."

"I think," said the chestnut man, to whom I was warming as quite a domestic type, "I think she'll grow old as a jolly grandmother with always at least fifteen kids sleeping in her bed and kicking and tickling her."

"Pass me a chestnut."

I'd have warned them if I'd known they were going to bite with such gusto. They hadn't even taken the iron skins off. Clixter cracked a tooth, the other fellow actually lost one in the conker and didn't realize till he'd thrown the thing into the river. They were well punished for not sticking to apples.

They sprang up holding their jaws, threw themselves on their horses, and galloped back over the bridge and the horizon in search of a dentist.

Safe again! And behind enemy lines.

But it was prudent to rest in my lofty haven a while longer.

I undid my bundle and stowed the contents in a crotch just above me. Then I folded the blanket the long way a couple of times so its skirts wouldn't hang down in view, and laid it along my bough. And on it I stretched luxuriously. My ankles were crossed, my knees and elbows hung easy on either side, my cheek lay where the bough's downward bevel began, and I gazed dreamily at the sun-shafts and shadow-masses standing side by side, like brown glades and blue forests, in the depths of the stream. On the dark leafmould of the bank, the two little globes of applepeel fell open. Their insides had gone yellowish brown, though it seemed to me that the green glowed through one of them and the red through the other.

A patch of sun found its way through the foliage onto my saddle—my middle—just the place where warmth is most acceptable—where you let a hot-water bottle ride you on a winter night, or pull the corner of the only sheet across you on a summer one. I smiled to think how my glushes, softly blazing in this selective beam, would combust the eyes of those lechers if they could have been in the tree above me. (If that painter had been up there, he could have made me a not-bad jacket picture.) There came a rustle, though I felt no breeze, and I thought of exploring higher in my leafy castle and scanning the country—but put it off for later. My mind meandered, thinking of better names I might have given my dog—Dogamus, Floppidog, Floppidisk, Sir Gelert, Alexikak—and my eyelids slacked and there was no little danger that I would doze and lapse from my perch like treacle from a spoon. But that was why it was delightful that only the cool river drifted beneath.

Warning, too late, a rustle closer: then whooph! my breath was thumped out of me by a crash-landing body.

The Lad

A SNORTING in my ear, a digging of chin into my neck, a sack of ribs and shirtbuttons grinding my ribs into the tree, and a slapping of skin all along the skin of my lower back and legs!

This lad had been above me all the time; in fact when I climbed into the tree he may have had his station on this very bough and moved higher to make way for me. He was one of the Beaters, sent out in the morning to watch at posts such as the bridge and give signals to the hunters. So I should have been caught between them below and him above; but he was older than they thought, and he gave them a false signal. When they departed, he lowered himself stealthily from bough to bough, watching me as I lay sprawled along my lofty mattress silhouetted against the lights and shades of the gliding water, till he could drop on me. He had prepared his dropping body to match mine: half shirted, half bare.

Like me he had been almost smoked out, and our bodily smokiness was a bond between us. It failed to cancel his other smell: he was one of those people who go around in the center of an acrid, slightly sugary cloud emanating from their own armpits, of which only their own nose is oblivious. It should have warned me of his approach, but I had taken it for the beginning of a dream about the caravanserai.

He wrapped his arms around me and the bough. I couldn't move, or even get back the breath I had puffed out; I couldn't wriggle out to left or right, clamped by my own breasts athwart the bough; I couldn't turn my head, and had to receive his messy kiss on my left cheek, close to my startled eye. Worse was the proximity of his armpit, but what was seriously worse was that my thighs were caught apart, straddling the bough, and I felt something wagging and prodding in the space between them. Not long ago I would have said it felt like a trout or a broomhandle, but now I suspected it was a stalk—a specimen smallish, sharp and slender.

It lost a little time blundering among creases and wishing it had eyes, or at least the accurate nerves of a finger. Here and there I could feel it losing some of the lubricant it was going to need. But once on its mark it gathered weight and popped in.

To think that my virginity, after fending off the god Ritan, should be conquered by a peasant lad! That instead of being wedded in a temple I should be first bedded in a tree!

But the stalk in its haste had found the wrong hollow. I almost sang out, "Hey, watch it, that's not right, you're in my sitch—a tad lower," but why should I tell him? Virginity saved again! I'd better just keep quiet.

That's what I thought when he was only a thimble's-length in. He had his feet braced against the trunk; he gave a push, frowned and said a sort of "Ay-nhihh!" in his tinny new-broken voice (I could see his black-lashed eye and hear his breath up close). But he gritted his teeth and came on again manfully. The feeling, which I ought to try to describe since, through his mistake, I may be the only one ever to have felt it, was not totally strange: it was like feelings everyone has had at this point, but reversed and much stoutened. I decided I'd had enough of it. But again he tightened his grip around the pair of us at shoulder-level, pedalled against the tree, and overcame the constriction. We both winced, but from then on it was if I sucked him into me by uscular reaction.

There were only two courses open to me. One was to lie and learn to like this. (And I did consider it.) The other was to give a sharp outward tug with my left hand to one of the edges of the blanket under me. Even a beginning student of topology will readily see that if this tug is given to the upper exposed edge, in the case that the two open edges are below the fold, or the lower exposed edge, in the case that the two exposed edges are above—in general, the more centerward of the two exposed edges—then, in the case of a blanket with a reasonably slippery surface, the two central layers, in other words half of the blanket, will come flying out. This happened smoothly. The mass that his arms were encircling—girl, blanket, bough—shrank; not by much, but enough to start it slipping. The mass consisting of lad, lass, and blanket loosened, slipped, gathered speed, plunged. And there we were, suspended under the bough.

As he was not expecting this, his hands lost their grip, or rather had already abandoned it because he had, in a remarkably quick apprenticeship, transferred them to the sides of my glushes, in order to palp those and, by squeezing them inward, to lengthen the frigpath for his stalk. My hands held; and meanwhile I had uncrossed my ankles, thrown them around the bough, and crossed them again. On me alone depended both of us; but not for long. The last of him to part from me was his stalk: it came out with a sort of de-squelching plop. A silence long enough to say "Must you go?"—then the smack of his back on the river.

You were hoping next, I know, for a splashy battle in the water, but I was determined to disappoint you. Hanging from locked fingers, with the blanket draped across my stomach, I got one knee up over the bough. In several efforts my hips followed it and at last my shoulders. I hauled in my breath, then looked below. He wasn't there, not even his ripples, which had slid downstream; I scanned downstream after them. What if he couldn't swim? I'd have to dive from the tree and rescue him.

But up he came, still on his back, spitting and sneezing, his black hair parted in the wrong place. He looked quite a nice boy, a bit on the stupid side, wearing a red plaid shirt (its color deepened by the water) and a whistle on a string around his neck.

He was sailing seaward head first, and I sat up to wish him a long safe voyage. If he came back, it would be easy to stop him rejoining me in the tree. I had almost forgiven him, when one more thing happened: plaf! yet another body fell on me.

Goddammit, what now? But it fell on my head and slapped my face, so I recognized that it was not another lecher: it was this lecher's britch-es. He had hung them on a twig, from which they were shaken by our activity. I tore them off my head and flung them after him, out of sheer bad temper. Legs flying wide, they could hardly miss: they caught him around *his* face, and he again sank spluttering out of sight, his nose involved in a struggle with his own fly.

Then I thought, "Why did I do that?" It might be true that a boy's britches couldn't disguise me, but at least they could cover me. And if he was the one public from the waist down, he might slink into hiding instead of stalking me again.

There was no time to lose. I dropped my loose properties into the blanket and then to the foot of the tree, slithered down after them, left them there (but gave the two coils of applepeel a kick that sent them into midstream); then I picked my way through the wood until I came out on a meadow. He had disappeared around a bend, and I ran on along the bank.

There he was!—making like a croquet-hoop, with his fingers in the mud and his white rear toward me—oh, I see, he's getting to his feet, now he's wading marshily ashore—on the far side! Of course, for I was on the outer curve of the meander, where the current undercut a high bank; naturally it was easier to get out on the shelving inner shore. In my disappointment I nearly yelled, "Hey, turkey! You give those pants back to me!"

I didn't need to yell: he saw me through the back of his head, and turned around. His stalk, which the cold water had shrunk to the like-ness of an icicle, flipped up, flinging drops of spray.

He gulped and lost control of his face. Instantly forgetting any thought of pulling his wet britches on, he ran at top speed, clattering through the black sedgy mudbed, into the river. He didn't waste breath shouting. The dog that comes at you without barking means business. I turned and ran too.

But I too had changed my plan. I glanced behind me, and as soon as his head disappeared below the level of the bank I turned about and ran stooping back. I threw myself flat, slithered to the brim, and peered out through a clump of groundsel. There he was, a bit down-stream, much slowed in the middle of the current because the only way he knew to swim with his pants held aloft was to tread water and paddle with his other hand. (I'd have told him to turban them on his head.)

When he reached my bank, I was ready for him. Not too hasty: any moment would do for pushing him back in, but it was his britches I wanted. His feet jabbed for a hold below the waterline, but the steep gray clay was slick; he fell forward on his face, slid back feet first, and was carried another few yards downstream. Keeping out of sight, I kept level with him, lifting myself off the grass and running crabwise on palms and toes. He got to the bank again, found a foothold, rose, grabbed at a tuft of dusty-miller. It tore away, and down he went, this time on his back. He circled out, beating the water, and thus address-ing himself: "Oh fuck, hurry, you clown, she's getting away—holy crocus, when I catch her I'm going to *split* her! splmphuuy," this last expletive interjected by the river as much as by the speaker.

I just rolled along in the grass a couple of rolls to stay level with him, then lay on my chin to look down on his third attempt. It was a little better, and he clung precariously above the waterline. But he still had to claw his way up the bank, so he did the thing he might have thought of earlier: to have both hands free, he lobbed his britches up ahead. The cartwheel of blue legs, scattering drips in the sunlight, flew over my head onto the meadow.

I raised my head from his grassy skyline with a shout of laughter. Back he went, and that bewildered expression I so love!—it nearly made me relent and help him ashore. (He now smelt better, too.) But that would have spoiled the felicity of my stratagem. Yet once more his crashing body annoyed the green calm of the noble Cressfont.

Never again did he get both feet out on this shore, though I played with him for a full furlong. Never have a boy naked below the waist and a girl naked below the waist fought a running battle with such consis-tent worsting for the boy. Once he rose like a walrus and grabbed me by one wrist, and you might have got that water-wrestle, but I pulled out everything—yelled *"Baa-heee!,"* placed a scoop of mud in his mouth, set his stalk twanging like a metronome—and he moaned and explored the bottom by himself. The river had only two thighs to play with.

At last he kicked off and floated gasping in the middle, nearly crying while he pleaded: "Just ma durn britches, for peessake! Just toss me them britches and I'll go home, promise! Haa-*bikhii*," he continued as if for emphasis (he snoze in about the same words as me, except for adding "Hubscuse be"—a well-mannered lad).

I walked along beside him, considering his case. But I had lived bottomless long enough; if I could, he could.

"No, I can't! You're used to it, I'm not!"

"There's something in what you say. But you've got a home to go to. Hide in a bush till after dark," I advised him, "and then try to slip in the pantry window without your daddy seeing."

"He'll catch me and paddle me!"

"That should warm you up, you look chilly. And tomorrow you can put on your other britches, and then we'll both be decent."

"Aha: ain't got no other britches. We're poor folks!"

"Why then, give me your address and I'll send you a pair of my mother's bloomers, and that will be better than nothing. Now that's my last word."

I folded my arms and studied the buttercups and the clouds as I kept walking and he kept feebly kicking and talking. He gave up on persuasion and started saying bitter things like "Ha ha, I can see your cunny and you can't see my johnny, your cunny looks like the town dump," and so on, sentences that lost some force because divided into breath-groups between mouthfuls of water. I looked down and patted the parts he referred to and said, "Yes, they are, aren't they" or "So it is, how kyorous," and he found he was only giving himself a Theopard effect.

Unlike him, I could see ahead to where the high bank on my side sloped down as the counter-meander began. My topographical advantage wouldn't last much longer.

"Think I can't see your privates, huh?" I remarked sardonically. He looked uneasy. "What's that yellow stain in the water near you?" His face went a different color and he raised it clearer. "And by the way, I see a bubble burst every now and then. Brown. (Girls can see it, you know.)"

I soon had the bumpkin fearing he was more exposed in the water than out.

"Okay, missy," he said cunningly. "You win. You're not so damn cute anyway" (at which he swallowed a bobbet of floating parrotfeather. Or it may have been a shred of applepeel or some such garbage). "I'll go."

"On *that* side." And I kept walking with him till he really did give in and go ashore on the far bank.

Then I ran, hard, picked up his britches on the run, ran again, picked up my other belongings on the run, and kept running.

Clad. And Well

THE ONLY reason I ever stopped running was that scenes from the Battle of the Britches kept popping into my head and making me whoop with laughter, so that I got a stitch. I sat down crosslegged in the middle of a bridle-track and heaved on my breath.

Another scene appeared, and I rolled on the ground and retched with laughter as if I was being tickled. A limousine came along the bridle-track, which was actually the driveway to someone's mansion. But all I did was lay the pants over my lap and wave and get back to my laughing. The limousine had to drive around me, and the chauffeur put his nose in the air and pulled the curtains tight. I remembered my situation and smacked my face to straighten it, picked and swallowed a stitchwort, and ran into a grove of pine trees to put the britches on.

Now the Floating Lad, as I liked to think of him, was bonier than me in the hips. Secondly, he was, as he said, poor folks, and hadn't had new britches in three years. Thirdly, though the britches had never in their longish life had a chance to shrink from being washed, they had shrunk a bit each time they got dunked in the river. Fourthly, they were still heavy with water through and through, and it was rash to put them on before they seized their chance to shrink yet more.

They fit *too soon*, as poor folks say; in fact, they fit immediately; which is to say, anybody could immediately see that my body had zero chance of fitting into them at all, even with zero space to spare. They told me so themselves (in a mean linty little voice): "Just try to get your ass into *us*, baby. Uh-*uhh*." Even my green shirt after rainshowers and river-dunkings had never formclung me as tight as this. But once the Second Battle of the Britches was joined, my blood was up and I was not about to give in. After some minutes a truce was called; I flung the britches aside. —But treacherously sprang on them and disarmed them a bit by emptying his oddments out of the pockets: four farthings, a fly spinner, a veteran conker, a marble, a lingerie ad torn from "Mellow Mail" (model modeling lonjeray on a shayze lounge), and an Easter card from Cousin Bel. I memorized his address so that I could write and tell him on which branch I had left them drying in the sunshine.

The britches and I eyed one another. They were old pale blue, with plenty of oil stains and moss bruises. With their places rubbed almost threadbare, places slightly different from those I would be rubbing, they didn't look as strong as I now knew them to be. They were marked EUGENES in large sewn letters on the seat pocket. That can't have meant that the Dropping or Floating Lad's name was Eugene, for then it would have said EUGENE'S. As for them, they measured my various plumpnesses with their cold blue gaze and deemed me a fit adversary.

I wrung them out with a twist, and then we got to grips again and wrestled in silence while the sun sidled around us like a referee.

I conquered this cloth python in the way Hercules managed to strangle the earth-born giant Antaeus: by holding him aloft where he could not draw new strength from touching his mother Earth. I lay on my back on the pine-needles with my legs in the air and dragged those britches down over heel, over calf, over thigh. They had some stretch—not enough to help forward over a bulge, only enough to shrink back in a grip on it. But slowly each bulge passed on each bit to the next bulge and faced the next bit. The next-to-final bulge: the woman-bulge, or skirt-bulge as it is sometimes called, that is level with the legjoin (or a shade below) and unlike any bulge of man. For the reluctance these britches showed to touch me higher than that, they must have been male themselves. I dragged them onto mid glush and my strength gave out and I had to collapse and lie panting. I considered leaving it at that and wearing them as legsheaths, with my fur spilling over the top. But again I reared in the air and hauled. I wriggled as I had never wriggled and have seldom wriggled since. They gave way, they crept, slid, shot on to my waist—well, to just past my hipsockets; their loins with a gasp of defeat yielded—sank—clamped—into place around my loins.

I sucked in my breath, my ribs, my diaphragm, shrank my glushes to quivering hard balls, and thus for a few tense seconds opened a ditch of operational space in front of my belly: drove the buttons, or brass rivets as they actually were, into their slots in the fly—having to yelp when hairs got involved. The lowest and tightest, the superclitoral, was almost impossible, but no, one should not be open here, and at last it snuggled into its place. Now the britches were down and out, vanquished and manacled, dead and buried.

But they had me in their death-grip! I couldn't move!

Grappling now with panic, I told myself step by step how to get to my feet, how to set one foot in front of another. I moved off; gradually attained a pace which minimized the creaking. —Damn! I had forgotten to pick up my bundle. I creaked back to it, and set about bending.

The creases at the front cut through thighmeat like sacrificial knives; the strained cloth at the back compressed my glushes to sheets. —Bppp! three stitches of the back-seam burst—hastily I straightened. I tried straddling my legs apart like a giraffe at a water-hole—worse! there went another stitch under the lateral stress. I managed at last by flexing everywhere, nowhere too much.

When that effort was over, I felt better. If I could achieve that, I could achieve anything. I walked. I walked with natural ease. Surely? My glushes, thighs, and calves worked together like segments of an artist's dummy, strung on strings too tight—but no one else would notice. My subsection *felt* different, but to the indifferent observer it would not *look* so different. I was decent at last. I could venture to walk along roads.

As each thigh folded forward and then back, squeezed water welled in the front crease, and then in the underglush crease, springs which renewed the dark blue of these valleys while the uplands they bounded dried paler.

The lowest cold rivet made me giggle. For, you understand, each rivet nestled through both layers of cloth, and this one through the fur-cleft also.

Ahead, a family of tinkers. I waddled nonchalantly on—or rather strode, a free spirit, my bundle over my shoulder. They stopped. They watched hard as I passed, each member from patriarch to tot taking responsibility for memorizing a different level of my figure.

I began to feel more naked in the breeches than without them.

I met a clergyman, out for a stroll while composing his sermon (book in one hand, drumming a tune on his collarbone with the other). He looked and then quickly shut his book and raised his eyes to the foliage and pursued his thought about Ecclesiastes, and after we had passed he drew a small mirror from his breast pocket and raised it just above his shoulder, circumspectly slowing his pace.

Perhaps they thought I was a boy a trifle on the strange side.

I met a hayseed, who grinned and simply fell in behind me. I ignored him, till he had caught up with me so close that he was giving me flats with his toes—fetching my shoes off, supposing I had had any. Regularly he dipped his hand and felt my glushes, I swatted him away, he came back like a fly. I walked faster; the only result was that he got two glush-taps for the price of one. I pushed him into a holly hedge. You may think that cruel, but it wasn't even effective: a holly hedge in May is fleshed with soft waxy new leaves, smiling-green; he just bounced out. I broke into a run—thought better of it. Without the britches I could have left him far behind. He was marginally retarded, and the first light-hearted person I had met since Granny Oe. It was good to be in company I had so much in common with, so I bore with his goosing for at least half a mile. And once you've started bearing something there's no one moment better than another to stop—that's how records are set. But a procession consisting of a girl in skintight boypants walking in lockstep with a peasant who has apparently lost his plow hand between her overhangs is too absurd: nobody could see us, we weren't marching along a city street, but the very birds were laughing. There was nothing for it, I had to turn and take him by the ears, and sit him firmly down among the thistles.

He grinned good-naturedly and I felt a little sorry but had to continue on my way. But which way?—there was a gate across the road, and a stile to the right. I had to ask him, and he grinned and pointed to the stile.

To hurry along—let's skip my getting over the stile and whether I had to accept his help.

When he started over the stile after me, I pushed him sharply back. Grinning up from the ground, he said, "Bye then, Sis!"

So it seemed he had guessed I was a girl.

What was it, anyway, that made my form so distinguishable? A bulge here, not a bulge there, was it really important? —Moss on a tree-root: here's an idea. I gathered a roll and stuffed it down my front to simulate the lacking bulge. Or at least, after another insucking struggle, I did get a little of it in past the waistband. It may have been all I achieved was some crumbs of soil between the labia and a draggle of green among my gold. I wasn't confident that it constituted such a bulge as the examples I had seen—certainly not that of my Bound Suitor at the height of his emotion, nor even the Floating Lad's at his most discouraged. But I walked masculinely on.

Something that must have been the case for some time reached my consciousness: it felt good.

Yes, I'm afraid I mean that being tightly and a little coarsely held all through the slideway (sometimes coarsely known as the sply, or crotch) *felt good.* It made me wonder about being held that way by something that moved; that didn't just grip, but shifted its grip. I became inclined to put some dance and rumble into my walk, and to be not averse to the idea of spectators. But I was crossing pastureland where the spectators were toadstools, cowpats, and felty-leaved mulleins.

By this time the pants were nearly dry. In fact they were baking warm.

I had been sloping across the flat moist fields of the river's flood-plain. Where it met the more crumpled country there was a tempting bank, and I eased myself down—legs on the plain, back reclining on the hilly chairback—and put one hand onto the grass to see if it was damp and the other into my bundle to fetch out something to eat or read. But both hands went languid as my eyes did. There in front of me lay my thighs, narrower than themselves despite their added cladding; feeling as if they had been packed into iron pipes; hot and uncomfortable, and I wished that at least while resting I could be freed to my accustomed

freshness, but knew the effort would be superhuman. And I slept stick-
ily, and while I slept the early afternoon sun filled my eyelids and
poured onto the four brass rivets.

I woke with a sharp burning pain. A four-point pain. But I couldn't
count the separate stabs. All I knew was that intimate parts of my epi-
dermis shrilled a warning.

As I sprang up, I remembered what my mentor, old Oe, had said
about me *burning through*.

I glanced down. Was that steam or smoke?

I clapped my hands to my focus, and howled because I had pressed
the spark into my flesh.

Help!

I must get these things off!

Hercules and Deianeira!

The reverse of the wrestle with the britches, or the double-python I
now saw them truly to be. They had only feigned reluctance to swallow
me; never would they disgorge me!

"Holy Chronicle!" I thought, "don't say these things have got glue in
them! They'll have to be *steamed* off?"

Standing wrestle; then floundering wrestle on the mat (a field with
daisies and tansies); then I leaped to my feet and howled again. "Dear
Dog! On fire! Somebody to help me strip!" I didn't even remember
dropping my bundle. I ran around in a circle and took off at a tangent.

Over the fields I saw a church spire. That meant a village. I
stretched my legs (wouldn't the things split!), hurdled a five-bar gate,
did a burning turn in the lane, passed a DANGER GANDER sign, came thundering out into the village street. No thought now of avoiding people,
people I needed! An old lady with a walking-stick, a little girl with a
skip-rope, I flew by them, I needed able-bodied hands—able-handed
bodies—men, or at least large boys, and soon, where were they? I ran
around the bend of the street, between thatched cottages and the
village well, and there ahead, coming along the sidewalk, was a crocodile.

The Uncasing

A CROCODILE, in case you've forgotten, is a column of school-children marching two and two, from Point A to Point B. Just as a crocodile of the horny kind is either male or female, so a Croc-odile of the scholastic kind is either male or female in every cell, not a mixture. Each vertebra is a pair of boys, or else a pair of girls (even so, they may hold hands, for greater internal rigidity). This Crocodile con-sisted of boys.

I ran toward them, shouting "Help! Take my pants off! Please!"

The Crocodile halted and stood on its forty feet, gaping at me. But not for long.

It exploded. Its parts flew through the air like projectiles and reassembled as a tight ring around me: a ring of panting pimply faces and clawing hands.

At first they must have thought they could just pop the fastenings of my britches and whisk them off, that if I couldn't it was because of the fumbling haste of my craving. Fingers sought the fly, from cunt up to navel, wriggled behind it, found that the brass rivets were not to be prised out of their lodgment in the stiff cloth. Other fingers, squads of them, went for my waistband like besiegers at a castle wall, grappled over, dived in, prodded my waistflesh, tried to tunnel down. Nails scratched my textured glushes. Hands queued to occupy my crotch and yank on the meridian seam that ran over clit and cunt and sitch—no, not *over* clit, cunt, sitch, but *through* clit-cunt-sitch. "Wow, she's hot!"—withdrawing fingers to shake and lick them before returning them to the fray. Even the little boys who, not yet thirteen, had boasted "Girls? Never!" crawled in at ground-level and set their teeth to my ankles, that is, to the ankles of the pants, though they did nick my ankles too in their eagerness to help. The scrimmage flattened like a dropped jelly and I was on my back on the cobbles, and some who couldn't fight their way in to places at the trousered end of me took their chance to have at my face with tongues and run hands under my shirt, but the serious central workers barked "Stop that, time for that later, we need you here"— "How did the bitch ever get these things *on?*"— "She was born in them!"— "It's no good, too tight here, try turning her over," and feet and knees on one side of me clattered forward and on the other side stumbled back and I was rolled on my front and one of them went crazy and slobbered "Glush-glush-glush! And glush-glush-glush!" "Shut up and get peeling! Don't just flap at them! anybody got a penknife? try to slit the seam in her seat"— "No need! there's a way in, and look where it is!" and a finger entered the puncture where the threads had parted. "Don't dig now! hook your finger and pull!" and the finger multiplied to at least eleven in the lengthening breach, and at last there was a kiss which grew into the angry-baby-crocodile sound made by tearing denim, and a whole flap came free and my flesh pressed up flush with the fringes and two of them shrieked and had to take a minute's medical leave.

"We can't have her out here on the street!—drag her into this alley!"

"Don't waste time!" I yelled, "do it here!"

"My GOD!" breathed the biggest boy in awe, "I never knew it took women like this!"

Some dragged, some snatched at the corners of the white rectangles to rip them larger, the little boys still hung like terriers by their teeth to the leg-ends—one had chewed as far as my calf, as if out to liberate Italy. I suggested (but they didn't hear) "Just drag'm off!" (Once my little precocious sister bought some jeans so tight I don't know how she got into them, I had to drag them off this way, couldn't even get the hem over her heel, told her she'd have to wait while I ran out and assembled a tug-of-war team, then thought of starting from the waist instead, they came off that way, but inside out, I told her she needed to return them to their maker but first turn them back outside-in—no, the opposite of inside-out isn't outside-in, it's inside-in—or outside-out—topology, you know.) I snapped over again so that they could free my front, where the real fire was, when:

"What's all this!"

It was the teacher, who should have been leading the Crocodile, but had stopped off for his shag in the pipe-shop.

"Animal on heat, sir!"

"Diz-gustin'! Not for young eyes! Stand aside!"

The scrum burst apart, for the teacher, thinking there was a pair of mating cats to be separated before they demonstrated the facts of life, had a bucket of water from the well. The waterglobe flew through the gap, catching a few of the slower backs as they scattered, and drenched me except my brow and toes. *Eichi*... A subsiding sizzle, and I was out of danger. Relatively.

"My trousers! it's a"—he took a step forward— "it *is* a girl, but in a boy's breeches! How did she get into those?"

"That's exactly what we were wondering, sir," they said with feeling.

"Shocking and unnatural!"

"We thought so too, sir, that's why we were trying to help her out of them."

"I see they're in disarray—you weren't attempting to rob her of anything?"

"No, sir, feel for yourself, you couldn't even get a penny into these pockets."

"Stand her up." Willing hands did so, the ones concealed behind me supporting me at unnecessary points. Then with a final kiss-click the whole upper mass, the abdomen of the breeches, fell apart. Weighted by the rivets still embedded in the fly, the blue shield guarding my belly and its lower borderlands toppled and hung like a slipped apron; the two shells behind, each vacuum-fitted to its hemiglobe, yielded their suction with reluctant gasp, then hung in tatters.

From the whole semicircle behind me arose a low but irrepressible hiss-whisper of *"Asssss!"* and from the whole arc in front a hot gritty growl of *"Cunnnnn . . .*

". . . NNNnnNNNnnNNNnn . . ."

(It had a low throbbing tune, like a swarm of bees.)

". . . nnnnnnnnT!"

More than coal-red, the ember smouldered. A few of the wires slowly writhed, like ash snakes.

The teacher covered his eyes with his hand, and the boys obeyed his example. One and all, they opened a pair of fingers to peep through, and I winked at them.

Forced to glare, the teacher glared. *"What*, young madam, may be the meaning of this?"

"Bust ma durn britches, mister."

"Borrocks," he screamed, "give her your trousers—no, not your trousers, your sweater, it should reach down to below her Plimsoll Line." Borrocks, a big lad, unwillingly peeled, revealing a tattooed pansy-chain across his boobs. "Will I get it back, sir?" he whined; "my dad bought it from a little girl in Puno." It was very roomy and fluffy, being of alpaca, oatmeal-color mixed with long black hairs which continually worked their way out and pricked the skin, whether you were wearing a shirt under or not (Borrocks who, against the rules, wasn't, must have been a penitent); a yoke (a procession of white alpacas on a black road) dipped from shoulder to shoulder, without which Borrocks looked less broad and with which I looked more busty. From nearly the architraves of my breasts, the sweater billowed out and came back in to mingle the lowest of its fringe hairs with almost the lowest of my intercrural hairs; it needed only a modest thumb to stretch it down each hipside.

But first, the ruin around my ankles being now worse than useless—ridiculous—I bent to pull it off. "No, no! stand straight!" came the last wheeze of the teacher's voice before it sublimated through the top of his skull, and he directed by gesticulation: two took my elbows and propelled me up in the air, two others fetched the thing off with a clean jerk past my heels. (The rest stood with breath and eyelids suspended; no sound, except for the thumps of those who fainted.) Then they rather slowly set me back on my feet; *then* I stretched the sweater down.

I was a girl no more, but a teddy-bear. With trifling exceptions (neck, legs) all of my femininity was for the first time in weeks retired, muffled up, in purdah, and I could go about in peace, ignored, a private citizen.

The crocodile swallowed the teddy-bear and marched to the school. Thus the Third Battle of the Britches ended in my capture and subjugation.

Sunnymead

THIS SCHOOL was a peculiar one. It was divided into two parts, for boys and girls, divided so sharply that they were really two schools. They were on either side of the village. As a barrier between them the village was more effective than deserts or glaciers. In the unthinkable event that a boy and a girl should steal out to meet each other, they would meet in the village and *be seen*.

The crocodile of boys had certainly not been marched into the village to meet any female crocodile, let alone a vagrant girl to strip. It had been circumspectly marched in on a non girl day, so that the boys could spend their pocket-money if they dared. Marching on into unknown territory, to escort me to the girls' school, was a risky venture. But their general, the male teacher, brought it off. He pushed me in at the front door, and quickly retired with his troops, leaving me to march by myself up to a wide glassy desk behind which sat a burly woman, with brown shoes and a borkish beard.

All the boys' teachers were men, nervous grave excitable bald ones, and all the girls' teachers were women, burly whiskery ones. All the teachers had to be called "Sir." I'm not kidding. You had to call the men "sir" and the women "Sir."

"Well, who are you?" demanded this teacher.

"I'm a waif," I said.

"Sir," said the teacher.

"Ma'm?"

"*Sir*. Say *Sir* when you speak to me."

"*Sir?*" I said.

"I said," she repeated, "say *Sir* when you speak to me."

"Sir," I said.

"I *said*, say *Sir* when you speak to me!"

"Yes'm."

This could have gone on for some while. Or, I could have chosen not to speak to her.

But I began again brightly, telling her what the male teacher had told me to tell her.

"Sir," I said, "I'm a waif, Sir. I am, Sir, a wicked runaway girl making a vain and immoral attempt to disguise myself as a boy, with an immoral and now vain object of insinuating myself among boys and corrupting them. How do you like that, Sir?"

"You—I—indeed—," she stammered.

"I need a chance of reform, Sir, a life of Men sana and Corporal Sano, clean living and mental thinking and sound discipline such as Sunnymead can uniquely provide, Sir. It will be a bearing of a burden which should be a public charge, but we'll damn well do it, Sir. You'll damn well do it, Sir, that is."

I had her on the run for a while but she rallied and beat me down. She said I would get to know the ways here soon enough, and asked me if I was trying to be funny, to which I gave the correct answer "Yes, Sir!" and hung my head. She had an assortment of rulers on her desk but couldn't lay her hands on a pen; while she was searching in her drawers I helped myself to a peppermint from her jar.

"Your name?"

"Applepeel."

"What-appeal?"

I took her pen and spelt it for her, upside down to make it easier:

733d37ddV

"Oh, uhah. And first name?"

A shade late, I remembered why I was consenting to hide here, and said, "Actually, Sir, scratch that." I reached over (at some risk to my coverage by the sweater) and scratched it out well for her. "That's just a nickname, and not my first—No Sir. Not even mine, Sir. I'm afraid I was still trying to be funny, Sir. My real name is, Sir, Felicity Jane Pepper." She wrote it down, Sir Felicity Jane Pepper, hurriedly completed a few other imaginary details, and closed the ledger.

She sat back in her mahogany chair, playing with the longest ruler, and told me to come right up to the desk, so that the bottom of Borrocks's sweater pressed against it.

"This is a traditional school, Miss Pepper," she said. "We neglect neither mind nor body . . . There is no rowdyism here, certainly no degeneracy, and very seldom are our rules broken. We rarely have to employ Corporal Punishment."

"Oh, good," I said, feeling I had to fill the pause with some foolish response. "I suppose that saves expense—having to send for him and so on."

"Hold out your hand," she said and gave me a whack for forgetting to say Sir. After this scarcely noticed check to the stream of her thought, she went on: "And the marvelous thing, Miss Pepper, is that this tranquility, this harmony if you will, is self-enforced. Our gels and our boys exercise this restraint upon *each other*; they police *each other*. Do I make myself clear?"

"Oh yes, Sir, I think so."

"So you already understand?"

"Well, I heard what you said, Sir. The girls and boys police themselves."

"That's *not* quite what I said, Pepper. But anyway, time enough and so forth. Do you think you will like it here?"

"It sounds peaceful, Sir. I'll give it a try."

She got up to shake hands with me, but missed, so felt around for her glasses. And put them on.

First she stared at my earrings. Then my hair. Then at my face. I swear that she only caught sight of Borrocks's sweater fourth, my breast-tops fifth, and more of Borrocks's sweater sixth.

Mastering her rage, she roared: "What's that you're wearing? Lift it up! My God! Turn around!" The ruler snapped in pieces. "Put it down, you shameless! Where are your own clothes? That! Did you tear it up yourself, or did you have help? Must we suffer such an ugly gel here! Go to the Wardrobe Mistress and be issued with a uniform! What's that you said?" "I said 'Brother!'" "Your bath-night is Tuesday," she rejoined, "now get out of my sight." "Cool it, Man," I told her, and she rang for the Matron.

They sent home for my transcript, and meanwhile put me in a low class where I could at least begin to learn manners and how to tie shoelaces. About a week later the postman brought a parcel for me containing a mass of old rags with pink spots, rather puzzling, and next day I got a letter from home.

Letter from home

❦ FELICITY JANE! So there you are. What do you mean by waltzing off like that, without so much as a goodbye or a postcard from the beaches where I suppose you've been lazing if not flirting or worse! You know very well that if I had been invited to sit in on your party as I offered there would have been no licker snuck in and you would have stayed within bounds of decency and not got drunk or hysterical I suppose I should call it and made an exhibition of yourself and had to be put under restraint by Officer (now Superintendent) Gottany, who of course called on us in great concern the next morning and dropped all charges and would have delivered you back safe and sound after you had had your little lesson and sobered up (calmed down). You ran away I'll be bound to the Mongers like your fool greataunt Evergreen didn't you like you were always talking about, you're lucky you were ever heard of again and got off I hope with nothing worse than a sound scrubbing and disinfecting. And now they tell me you're at some liberal school where you'll learn to give cheek and lip to your elders. Your Pop and I have been so worried, and your rabbit is moping, he just sits all the time, or perhaps he's glad to be left in peace by you, you were always such a fidget and tumblepuppy. We've been surprised by all the offers to look for you (Sir Muchtoby even said something about joining a search-party he'd heard of) and when you come back, as I suppose you'll soon have to, there are several old family friends who have expressed themselves willing to take you in as a companion, single persons mainly but some couples, I expect you to consider their kind offer, they have good houses out in the country, such respectable employ would begin to make a lady of you. No doubt you're got up as scruffily as usual so I'm sending you by separate post a pair of my own bloomers, a sacrifice for me but these type articles which you may consider "out of date" you'll find practical around the house, and for plain girls like you there's no sense trying to look "glamorous" all the time or any of the time for that matter, it just makes the luckier ones laugh at you behind their sleeve. Come what may, Fristy, your mother sees your good points if no one else does and will be glad to have you back, where we can keep an eye on you, in fact I've been thinking we should give you Uncle Berooney's flat in the attic when married, you can be a help sometimes when you try. (The other upstairs room's empty now too, that good for nothing lodger who couldn't seem to find a job left the day after you did, but we need to get another good for nothing lodger I suppose.) Young Fortesant still considers himself engaged to you, I think he's barmy, he could do so much better, but anyway you should think yourself lucky and be quick about it and come home to your loving family and start thinking about your trousseau and bedlinen and such and baby-clothes, though I praps oughtn't to refer to ~~such~~ that side of life to you but you've got to start learning some day. —MA PEPPER

❛ MOTHER DEAR, Thanks for your note which I was so glad to get, wish you were here, the weather stays fine. Nothing much has been happening, just messed around mainly.

It don't seem long since I've been away, do it? But I must have been ready for a growing phase, you'd be surprised how I've developed, the boys take quite a bit of notice! I've outgrown my breastlets and ~~shr~~ cleftveils, please send me some more, in fact all of every kind of clothes you can, I seem to keep losing mine. Oh, thanks for the bloomers, ~~Mrs. Baquard was~~ I'm sure they'll come in handy. I don't need money.

Give ~~Shaluke~~ Fortesant a kiss for me (just kidding) and tell him I'm trying as best I can to be a good girl. In closing—

Love to all—

~~Ap~~ FRISTY

PS Don't mind the picture on the other side, I can't get out to the shops so I had to cadge this from someone, the French words look to me like "For immediate consumption" but he says they mean "You too could get a tan like this."

The Poorlouis

I BEGAN rather suddenly, didn't I, on this atrocious and tremendous story. You may have noticed that I have changed in the course of it. That's because the me at the beginning, the little princess, was not really me. Back then I pretended more.

We aren't one of the better families, we're only an ordinary family. My father used to work for J. Coldwin & Sons Lamented; he is now a government clerk. My mother is older and larger. They both have dark hair, so no one knows where the blondeur of my siblings came from. But they all have in common with each other, as distinct from me, the quality of being not light-hearted. Donaldine is nearly fourteen, a little sobersides. I can make her smile, but it requires effort, whereas none is required to make her deride. She wants us to be at least as respectable as we once were, if we can't be as respectable as we looked like becoming. There may be hope—not that we shall become respectable, but that she will grow out of wanting us to be. My little brother of nine sometimes has fun, but he is showing a determination which will become unpleasant as it enlarges with him. We have to call him Clarence; you may well point out that there never is such a thing as an old Alan or David or a young Claude or Clarence, so we should use his middle name, but unfortunately that's Cantacuzenus.

A winter, a summer, a winter, and another summer ago, my father took the Mandarin exam. He had tried for three years to get up his courage to do this. But, as you're aware, the Mandarin exam consists of being shut up in a house for three days with pen and paper and writing *all you know*.

I was now old enough to prepare my father for this exam. We sat opposite to each other with a table in between, because I thought he might want to take notes. But he just stared at me, slightly dribbling, as if what I was telling him was beginning to run back out. I told him things I knew, and we went on for a month. You may wonder how I know so much. Well, I do quite well, but I'm not like the lady who was such a Desperate Scholar that she scared off all her suitors, the country squires for miles around. Somehow I always had one book to read, and then I'd find another, from a church jumblesale, from a Gypsy, from the Mongers, from a trashcan, from an elderly neighbor. I had already read so much that I scarcely knew what century I was living in. I have a vivid (I didn't say a perfect) memory and no aptitude for classification, otherwise I'd have spent the month wondering where to begin.

Everyone knows as much as everyone else, but most of what everyone knows is that that leaf sticks out above that leaf, those grains of dust are down there by the wall, Aunt Slory died last week, or, on the historic level, the Rev. Stillion Templeton was the next vicar after the Rev. Ortho Ryjust. My father said to me, "How am I to know which is knowledge and which isn't?"

> How d'ye do? My name is Jowett.
> There's no knowledge but I know it.
> I'm the Master of this College.
> What I don't know isn't knowledge.

But we couldn't find the works of Jowett, so we knew no more, except which way to pronounce his name.

My poor dad, who was very classificatory, suffered more than I can ever know, but he passed the Mandarin exam; I had managed to mix enough beads into the sand in his head.

He was promised a State Mandarinship, and on the strength of the salary he would start drawing we left the apartment in the concrete tenement and bought our house. It is in the north-eastern angle which is becoming rather empty, but it has a garden, one of the few of any size inside the town, and this was why he had longed for it for fifteen years. The garden, overgrown and too steep to do much with, goes rapidly down to the stream called the Poorlouis.

So I did not spend my childhood in the garden and down by the Poorlouis, except in imagination, only the last two summers and two winters.

Where it came in, it was a brown glistening surface spooling into eddies and scratched by traveling fragments of leaves. It went on to become, in the middle of the town, a bed of white rocks among greasy channels, haunted by storks, joining the greater sewer of the Yessage.

My father was content to sit hunched on his back step looking down over his garden and me as long as I remained in sight. I was content with more parts of the garden and the stream. To my amazement, I discovered that the stream came in under the city wall. It had to, as anyone could have told me. But what they couldn't have told me was that it was possible to dive through the tunnel and come up on the other side. I kept this weakness in the city's defences to myself.

(Later I learned that it wasn't a wall: it was a high motorway. But it cut city from country and to me it remained a wall.)

You could reach the back country this way, but you couldn't take your clothes with you. And so I was not quite ingenuous when, for the sake of a sudden start, I said I'd never been used to nakedness before that birthday.

The stream, like a story told backward, led me up into the moors. It was a pathway, or a tunnel, beneath the level of the surroundings, umber-floored and green-roofed, within which the water swung from side to side between benches of rock. After half a mile it opened out, and here was my island, just below where another stream flowed in— the island that shaped me, perhaps even literally; that fashioned me into both a Desperate Scholar and a tomboy.

Just above it was a confluence, two branches of the stream meeting as they came out of woods. The rising woods closed the view, but over them was a skyline pale with distance and altitude, and a knot in it which must be the hill called White Daughter. I had heard my father say it was a beacon. What was a beacon? Nobody went there any more; warning fires were lit there back in the times when there were wars and invasions.

It was my father who called me Fristy from the cradle and never called me anything less affectionate. My little sister (whom I sometimes call Miss Primnoise) doesn't like it, she says it's baby, she tried to institute Filly or Lissie until my mother explained to her that those might be too—unbaby. My mother and my sister often called me other things— "Lady Jane" when I came back from the wild or lay late in bed; sometimes Hilarity Jane when they had to fend off my noisy spirits. "Would you care to descend and partake of breakfast, Lady Jane?" "Do you think you might condescend to sew your own button, Lady J.?" "Would you kindly stand still, Lady Asticle?" Donaldine was good at knowing all the programs of work that a house makes possible and I was glad to take instructions from her. I could be safely left to polish the spoons, and straighten them out (my mother was so strong she sometimes bent them by merely picking them up. And could clap under water and push sheets instead of pulling them).).

It's also by no means true that I was untouched before that gaoler hand ran up my leg. I was the center of touch in our family—the touch-exchange. My father and my tiny brother were always tussling with me; my father just hugged me, and if my brother couldn't think of anything better he would trip me up and pretend to fall on me, or get angry and come pummeling me. And my huge mother, my little sister, and Zed were forever washing me, brushing me, blowing my nose, washing my ears, correcting my clothes, flicking things off my cheeks, steering me in directions, saving me from collisions, pressing me into chairs, pulling me out of chairs, frisking me for lost gloves, or spanking me for idleness. They rarely touched each other, but they touched me all the time I was inside the house; if no excuse presented itself, they just— touched me. Usually below the shoulders and above the knees. Mostly maintaining their serious faces. It is usually little kids in bedrooms and playgrounds who are all over each other, pulling each other's hair, scratching each other's rashes, torturing each other's pimples, rolling up together in blankets. I was apparently a perpetual kid of about five. And so my family and my schoolmates all had ticks and chiggers and lice and occasionally a leech, picked up by me in the undergrowth and along the Poorlouis.

Mostly maintaining their serious faces. It is usually little kids in bed-rooms and playgrounds who are all over each other, pulling each other's hair, scratching each other's rashes, torturing each other's pimples, rolling up together in blankets. I was apparently a perpetual kid of about five. And so my family and my schoolmates all had ticks and chiggers and lice and occasionally a leech, picked up by me in the undergrowth and along the Poorlouis.

For I had to go to school, lest I read too much. In the streets, people, even those who know you well, will simply look at you all the time you are in sight, often lengthening this time by turning to walk in sight of you, and some of them will actually give voice to their thoughts, enouncing *"A shapely person"* or *"Refreshing"* or *"Sheeee"* or *"Oh, saintly!"* or *"Up her, up her . . ."*

They said nothing about my hair, so I think the red in it must have reached a threshold at my birthday.

Once I turned in surprise on hearing the noise of a bubble erupting from an unblocked drain. There was no drain, just a throat from which the most perilous of words had gurgitated through a plug of emotion: *"dgkq'URL!"*

Sometimes I felt like telling them: *"Tagueule!"* I don't know when this *remarking* began, because it may have been long before the moment when I realized it was only me they did it to. Nobody would explain it to me, until at last I asked one of the vocalizing strangers himself. It turned out he did not even know he had said *"Twinkle twinkle"* aloud, and he had trouble elaborating on it. But he did try to give enlightenment: he said, "It's because you have a flawless body."

That certainly was not correct. My body always had several cuts and green-purple bruises and swellings and broken nails, not only because of my ramblings in the garden and the Poorlouis and the back country and my treading on a bee in clover at least once every May but because in the house I was frequently kicked by the corners of furni-

ture. As for the abstract quality about my body that they must have
meant, I could not isolate it, when I looked in a mirror. And I could not
see how it derived from anything else about me. (Except possibly from
my not eating corpse. I wasn't the only one in the world refusing to do
that, but I didn't know it.) Is that all it is, just something additional? It
seems a logical shame, it makes you feel helpless, to live a story determined by something which, like a large nose, could just as well have
been stuck onto somebody else.

The house also has a cobbled forecourt, opening onto the long
broken street which, not much farther on, dead-ends into the old fort
at the northeast corner. The house doesn't belong to us any more. My
dad lost his job before receiving his first quarter's salary—he didn't do
anything bad, he was simply found inadequate, and they moved him
down to a desk by the door of the corn exchange, where he does all day
something that doesn't need to be done at all, logging in the names of
those who go in and out. Fortesant's father took over the mortgage and
lets us rent the house cheap. (And even then we have to sublet the
upstairs.)

Debate between Helen of Troy and Mr. Right

I spent my days sitting at a tiny desk in a class of tiny girls. Sometimes I was put at the front so that I could be kept an eye on, and sometimes I was put at the back so as not be a ringleader or bad example.

My earrings had been stripped off me. I had to accept a chit in place of them: "Ornaments Ear Gilt Crude 2, Impounded." I was issued, first, with hoofs—that is, shoes, about which the less said the better. And bootblack to polish them (I rubbed it in my hair).

And short white socks, rolled down to the ankles; regulation grey wool skirt; virginal white blouse. The regulation blouses were nearly diaphanous. This was to make it inspectably clear that we were wearing our regulation black breastlets. If they had extended the same policy to the lower garments, making the skirt filmy white and the clevel black, clevel would have gleamed through skirt and I wouldn't have got away with my disobedience—for I could not, after all this time, tolerate the imprisonment of my loins. The clevel was made of regulation itchy muslin, with SUNNYMEAD sewn into the crotchpiece and PEPPER F stamped on one cheek. Nobody except Saxie, my friend, knew that within my skirt I was shredless. In fact she was wearing mine, under her own, because she felt draughts, and because it wouldn't have been safe to leave it in our inspectable lockers.

(The other cheek, the left, bore traces which could be read as KLEI-DEBERGER S. "That was Sylvia," Saxie told me. "She was a great blond maid from Hamburg or somewhere—she had weird swearwords, something like Shikes or Shyson or Scheissberg. She left last term to be the mistress of a silk-baron." "What's a silk-baron?" "I've no idea." "Sounds like a manufacturer, or a peer of the realm, or a Chinese magnate, or a judge?—they 'take the silk,' you know." "Whatever kind of a nob he was," said Saxie, "he wouldn't have taken her if he could have seen you." She already worried me with her loyalty.)

As for *bed*clothes, you can imagine what I thought about sleeping inside two sheets, three blankets, and a nightshirt. I'm as impatient with bedclothes as I am with clothes. I dumped all of them on the floor, but then, while standing and picking one blanket to roll in, I was aware of a commotion. So the second night I tried to lie swaddled as by regulation. I sweated and steamed until toward morning I came tunneling, whimpering out of one of those horrible or at any rate rich dreams I call heat-dreams and height-dreams (and others call nightmares) in which—

but I don't yet dare to tell you; I can't believe such depravity boiled up in my head. Are we sure that "dying in your sleep" is a peaceful death?

From then on I waited till lights-out before wriggling free of the garment and kicking through the sheets and shedding the blankets. Then I tested my woodcraft, sneaking unseen under the others' beds to open one of the windows at least a crack and bring the room's air alive; later, when I was bolder, to ease them all open wide.

One morning I found myself alone on the bed with a handkerchief. My fingers had it by a corner and it did happen to be covering one of the three or four most necessary points. I held it there while I ran to my clothes.

"Practical joke," Saxie explained to me. "Thank you, Saxie. I think I realized that." "They found you'd opened the windows again, and they said you must be first cousin to Eskimo Nell, and how many covers did you have on anyway? 'One, and most of her is outside it, and it's only to hide the fact that she has nothing else on.' — 'If it was a *hand-kerchief* she wouldn't notice the difference!' — 'Let's try and see!' And so they gave it to you, after teasing the sheet away."

"Right after, I hope?"

"Almost."

I also hoped Saxie, who was always defending me, hadn't laid her life on the line trying to save my decency; it seemed she hadn't.

A school isn't the place for me. I tend to be either in motion or asleep. Not only was this a school, with classes all day, but it was a boarding school, with an even longer class in the evening called Home-work. Either I would sit dozing, and giving predictably disastrous answers when questions came my way, or I would become restless and lead furtive mountaineering expeditions, railway operations, murders and book-burnings in the jungle—the mass of cupboards and rafters and secret passages that, between the wainscots and the eaves, made up most of the old building, surrounding the huddled clearings of the rooms. —Even the playground-times weren't much of a relief, because I didn't want to draw attention to myself by winning the world skipping championship over again (at thirteen I had raised the double-under record to infinity, that is, had to be stopped after three days), nor the sports afternoons, I didn't want to show I could jump twice the height of the bar.

My transcript got lost in the mail. But one day they asked me some-thing, I think it was about the Treaty of Unkiar Skelessi, and I absent-mindedly gave the answer, and went on to tell them about the War of Jenkin's Ear, and Crazy Sultan Ibrahim and how he made his wives pretend to be mares. (It must have been on some worse ground that he was called Crazy.) They realized they'd better move me up a class. By a series of such accidents I was moved up until one teacher said to another, "I'm afraid we'll have to move Miss Felicity to a higher class," and the other replied, "That would mean moving her to a university."

On each of these moves I brought Saxie along, by coaching her and secretly prompting her too with occasional smart answers. It went against her nature, but she did it to stay with me. More ignorant than me, she was wiser (in the melancholy way).

We were now sitting at tiny desks in a class of women (as I thought of them), larger than us. Sometimes I would gaze around curiously at them. They were all pretty, but they no longer seemed to believe it. There were enough snowy cheeks and red lips and clear chins and gesturing lashes to set any male on edge with hope, but the sparkle in the eyes had narrowed to a glitter.

Each classroom, I noticed, had its scent: one of Cayenne pepper, one of chlorine—ingredients in the hair-oil used by the inhabiting teacher. The teachers' common-room, to which we were sent for trials or interrogations, made me instantly think of Lad Eugene: it was distended—larger and fainter—but unmistakably an armpit.

When a teacher wanted to go for an assignation with the parachute instructor, or when she simply wanted to go home and lie on her bed, she would say, "Miss Pepper will lead the class while I am away." And she would leave me lecturing on Clovis and Childeric, or on the theory of phlogiston (which could have accounted for my burning through clothes), and I would still be lecturing when she came back, though in between I would lead yoga exercises or tell stories from the Arabian classics, or even worse stories that I made up myself, about King Ladislass, the Transvestite. But none of this made me popular.

At night the girls would talk for several hours. After one hour I said, "People! Could you turn it off now? I want to sleep, and I'd rather think about—fields or something."

"It's your fault," they said. "We didn't talk like this before you were around."

Here's what "like this" was:

One of them re-started it for the night by remarking: "When I grow up, I'll be a dancer and my stage name will be Crazy Joy."

Quite an opening! They pictured the lashing lasskivvioius legs, the sequined waist, the billowing feathers, the flashing painted face, the reeling auditorium.

"Crazy Joy! And off the stage, too, she'll be just buried in lovers, won't she?"

"Maybe," said the girl, whose present name was Betty Claypuddle. "She'll let it be whispered, certainly."

"Well, that's just fantasy," said another. "*I* think of being so beautiful, so record-breaking beautiful, that men will do anything I want. Not just men, everyone. You know, change my wheel when I have a flat—anything."

"That *would* be useful. —Is that what actually happens, Fristy?" This was let out by mistake, and without waiting for my reply (which would have been "Not quite: they mainly do what you *don't* want") they hurtled on:

"Pooh, that's easy, we can almost all of us have that."

"Get me right, I mean I'll be so beautiful they'll do anything I want even *without* thought of sex."

"Really? Ha! They might, too. But that won't be how it is for me. I'll be so smashing they won't have any *other* thought than sex. In fact they'll often come the moment they *see* me."

"Come? You mean like dogs?"

Derision from those who knew Anglo-Saxon. (One explained: "It means they have a period, on the spot." "Oh, I see." "You read that in the school manual, didn't you?" "I did not. I actually saw it last year when we had to Punish that boy who—" "Hush! Gross!")

"Me," said Betty "Crazy Joy" Claypuddle, "they'll come when they merely picture me. When they *remember* me. My leg waving up there."

"OoOoOo." (A tremolo sound made by somebody.)

"Gives you the shivers, doesn't it?" said the gratified Claypuddle.

"Actually I'm shivering because I'm a shade on the cold side, I don't know why."

"Like a wand. Waving the wand of my leg . . ."

"Do you know," said a girl whose nose suggested her origin (she was a Jebusite), "there's a tradition of the elders that Queen Esther was so beautiful, men came when they *heard her name!* They could have been at home listening to the radio, or even in some other country, in the Land of Nob, and somebody said 'Queen Esther,' and—choowoosh! (They came.) Queen Esther, that's who I'm going to be. She was the most beautiful ever."

"Queen Vashti was more beautiful than her. She didn't even bother to come," said the confused one. "I'd rather be Queen Vashti. Besides, her name is so much more ravishing. That's what I'm going to call myself from now on. Vashti Jones."

"Almost as good as Crazy Joy—Watson," said Crazy Joy Betty Claypuddle, who should have recognized that Crazy Joy was name enough. — "Say, that sonofabitch window isn't open again, is it?"

I heard my friend Saxie slipping in a humble word. "Beauty isn't everything," she said. "To be attractive you've got to be something else; boisterous—"

"Don't you mean girlsterous?"

"Yes, perhaps—boisterous in a higher key. Like Fristy when she's awake."

But plain beauty was easier to quantify.

"Here's the tops," said a final contributor. "Wouldn't it be boss to be so beautiful that all the men in the world *come at once?*"

"And keep on coming," said one contributor more.

"The ones that are old enough, of course . . ."

There was a moment of golden silence.

It was broken by the first of the realist party. "Hey," she said, "doesn't anybody believe in Mr. Right any more? All you Helens-of-Troy! Doesn't anybody just want to find a nice boy and maybe feel totally romantic about him for a month and then be off-and-on for a while and play around with a few others but eventually get back together and decide you really like each other best and settle down steady, and, you know, when you're old get married, and feel sentimental for ever, like?"

"Drear-ee! Boor-joy!"

But it turned out that the Crazy Joys, or Helen-of-Troys, were only three and a half, and they found themselves surrounded by Mr. Right's groupies. Dreamers of beauty past compare were in a minority among mainline homemakers. But they fought back with seductive word-pictures, and turned a few converts. Thus encouraged, they used every weapon—Mata Hari, the Isle of Capri, serenades by moonlight, whiffs of orgy, airs that hint of shameful mystery—and one homemaker after another was tempted to let Mr. Right wait.

"You're just as bad," said a realist, "as the goofy males, the superstitious clods around here, who are supposed to be saying that the goddess Tashartris has come to earth in the shape of a maiden called Applepeel."

"She has!" said a lyrist. "*Someone* has made them believe it. Helen-of-Troy's record can be broken: beauty can go on, up and up."

"I have a suggestion," I said, and they were startled enough to listen.

"Well?"

"Bring it to a vote, while there's some of the night left."

They did, and the two parties were dead level. Mr. Right eleven, Helen of Troy eleven.

All eyes turned to me for the casting vote. At least I suppose they did; my eyes were the only eyes shut.

"Well, Miss Frosty? What's your vote? What do you think?"

"About what?" I said. "Is it time to get up?"

"Which are you waiting for, when you lie there like that with your hands on your cunt?—Mr. Right, or gangs of demon lovers?" (They weren't on my cunt, they were over my eyes.) "Come on, what do you dream of?"

"I don't know, I haven't had any dreams yet." (To be honest, I *was* idly turning over the thought of Mr. Right-Tan.)

"You know what we mean: which are you going to be when you grow up?—a happy wholesome girl (or woman) with a good sound boyfriend, or the body most desired since time began? We haven't got all night—what do you want to be?"

"I thought maybe a bicycle mechanic."

"She's dreaming—forget her; you have to treat her like a kid. Give her to Mr. Right. —The windows *are* open, all of 'em, we've got gremlins!—make Lady Freesia get up and shut 'em, bare or not," but their voices were at last crumbling into nothingness.

Saxie had been one of the quiet and firm Mr. Right defenders. "I've been wondering," she said to me next day, "do you think one of us could be Applepeel?"

"What do you mean?" I answered. "It sounds rather mystical."

"You've heard of her, have you?"

"Of who?"

"This Applepeel. She's been, you know, in the news."

"Mmm . . ."

"And there are so many Miss Universes here, aren't there? You heard them saying so, last night. If they're so beautiful, one of them might actually be the Applepeel. After all, she might well want to hide out somewhere, to get away from the attentions of men, and this would be just the place."

"Yes, I see," I said. "You could be right. I wonder which of them it would be?"

"Not any of the blondes."

"No, unless they have darker roots. Hmm."

"Well, I was thinking it might be my best friend."

"Oh." I couldn't help being disappointed. "Who is that?"

"I was thinking it might be my only friend."

"Go on."

"I was thinking it might be the one I suffer draughts for." I just raised my eyebrows and held down my blush. "I was thinking it might be my friend Fristy."

I tried to look as if I was considering her theory.

She moved a little nearer and looked a little harder.

"I'm afraid you may have a bit of a crush on that Felicity," I said, "but I'm not so blinded. She's an ordinary enough lass and I don't think the color of her hair matches up. It's supposed to be reddish, isn't it, and hers is blackish."

She came nearer still and sifted some of my hair between her fingers (getting bootblack on them).

"Am I *your* best friend?" she asked. She had an honest face with snub nose (which I wish I had) and beechbark-colored hair and wide brown eyes; I really loved her.

"Yes, Saxie," I said at length. "You are, because I trust you with this secret which you *must* keep."

"I knew it," she said. "Only you could be that beautiful."

"I'm not."

"Of course you are! I've heard these fantastic stories of them making you into a goddess and printing dirty books about you and forming clubs to hunt you and armies to capture you."

"I'm no more beautiful than you," I explained. "It just came about because they saw me undressed and saw me tormented, all by myself. I mean, alone. Somehow that stretches men's randiness. I've had unwanted publicity, that's all. And look, I want *you* to treat me as a human being." I had a sudden doubt. "*You* don't want to fondle me and so on, do you, Saxie?"

She slowly nodded.

"Oh, all right," I said descendingly. "Come along, then."

The Rules of the School

S AXIE ASKED, while she was buttoning me up, "You are really Felicity Jane Pepper, aren't you?"

"What d'you mean *now?* Of course I am. —Well, actually, I could have been Pippa or Cora; Cora was what my dad hankered after, but my mother thought it was too short, and somehow vulgar, and like the name of a place, and possibly the name of his old flame, and so for the first two weeks of my life while they argued about it I was just Baby Pepper, but then they had to put something on my birth certificate and so they put Philippa, but soon they realized I'd be called Pippa Pepper, or perhaps Flippa Pepper; and as I was born with a lot of hair somebody suggested Rubra-Nigra—no, Nigella—but in the end they realized I'd be happier as plain Felicity."

"Anyway—"

"And Jane, I suppose, for added femininity. Boy, if names were clothes I'd have plenty to wear!"

"*Anyway*, that's what they call you at home?"

"Yes. Especially if I don't come the first time I'm called. 'Felicity *Jane!*'"

"Then why don't you just go back there?"

"Oh! Well, you see, I do want to lead a quiet life. At least some of the time. But not at home—not just yet."

Saxie's blunt little face cleared, she looked happy.

"Come for a walk around the hockey field," she said, "and tell me everything."

"Everything?"

She didn't mean everything, she meant the much lesser subject of me and what had brought me here. I couldn't get her off it, and had bit by bit to tell her what seemed like half of everything—most of the idiot things I've told you. I left out the beginning, since I myself didn't understand it—but when I had told her everything else she made me come back to it.

"How *did* you get into this career of nakedness?" she said.

"Only halfnakedness. Which does the optimist say, half naked or half dressed? I don't think it's right to be all naked, all the time, reduces the value of nakedness." — "How *did* you get into it?"

So first of all I told her that there was a magician brought to my birthday party; he did the usual tricks such as pulling rabbits out of each other and guessing what was on the guesseds' minds, and then he used me as stooge, levitated me, sawed me in half, finally did a fast sleight of hand and—presto!—my clevel vanished into thin air.

Saxie grimaced patiently and said: "Yes. Now what really happened?"

"Well," I said, "I know that isn't possible. He wasn't a magician, he was a hypnotist—"

"Don't go on with that. It's a sore topic around here, as you'll learn at the end of the term. Next story?"

I told her several more: that I had lost a game of strip poker; that I had been stripped by a tornado; that my pants had been on their last legs; that I had been persuaded it's the custom to give my clevel to my fiancé and let him carry it around in his pocket; that I had suggested to my fiancé that we write some pornography together, and he had kicked me out on the streets; that I just wanted to have an adventure; that my aunt's present was a shift made of Tractex (opposite of Spandex), it shrank a half inch each week— "Hey, what an idea! The Storymonger should have thought of this. It shrank up my thigh; up past my navel . . ."

"Ah'mm. And your grandmother's?"

"That was—a belt, a valuable one; it was so heavy with silver buckles that it sank slowly over my hips. What do you think of that!"— I was pleased at my inventions— "as a solution to the problem of gradual stripping."

Saxie merely said: "What are you trying to cover up?" Which gave me a chance to laugh at her, but my laugh had to terminate, and there she still was with her plodding insistence on the truth.

"I don't *know* the truth," I said. "I'll tell you what seemed to happen, and then perhaps you can help me explain it." I told her how out of the blue I had been accused of parading on the roof, and thus was caught up into the whirlwind.

"What theories have you had about it?" she asked.

"None, really. That they really did play me an April Fool trick—but then they'd all have had to be in the conspiracy, the police and half the town. Or that it was a trick of the light, or the moon rising, or the goddess Tashartris, or something done with mirrors, or a fireworks display. Or that I really did do it and forgot about it. Can you think of anything, Saxie?"

"I could think," she said, "that if someone told them you were going to appear up there, they would all so much want to believe they saw you that they did."

"Oh, Saxie! A kind of 'The Empress *Has* Clothes' and no one will believe it!"

I was disappointed in Saxie, but soon I saw that she could be generally wise without being a detective of particular things.

I said: "Saxie, let's change the subject to something more at hand. The Disciplinary System at this school." (I saw her face closing up.) "I've heard the hints about it, I suspect I need to learn more before I fall afoul of it."

"You should know it well enough. You've already been caned every day for refusing to 'eat corpse'."

"Oh, I don't count that, I'm used to it. Because I don't eat corpse my bottom can take it. You know there are all these hints and winks about a System."

But on this subject Saxie would not talk to me. But it didn't take many more days of hint-gathering for me to grasp the outlines of it.

There were three degrees of crime: Invisible, Disobedience, and Horror. For instance, what Saxie did to me was Invisible, and not merely because it was done in a mop closet. The teachers could no more conceive of girls worshipping girls physically—or spiritually, for that matter—than they could believe in trees flying. And this despite the fact, obvious to all but themselves, that they all lusted desperately for at least some of the adolescents in their charge.

At any rate this type of behavior was Invisible as a crime, however visible it might be. And elsewhere too the line zigzagged with some perversity between Invisible non-crimes and punishable acts of Disobedience. Thus you could talk all night, keeping others awake; but if you talked by day in the classroom, keeping others awake, Something Had To Be Done.

I have to admit that the line was mainly based on whether you were caught, a criterion reasonable enough, even predictable enough. Another factor was whether, when caught, you had the Right Attitude. Right attitude was expressed in a reverential "Sir"; by application of it you could get away with a surprising amount, and lay up insurance against future trouble, and so girls tended to interleave their words with "Sir"— "Sir" as universal modifier and particle, much like "fucking" in the conversation of a British road-crew; a susurration of "Sirs" hung over the areas where girls' and teachers' paths crossed. Flagrant evidence of wrong attitude was laughing. Indeed, laughing about anything came close to being itself a misdemeanor, since it could lead to unconscionable disorder and successful rebellion.

Even more remarkable was the line on the other side, between all this mere Disobedience (otherwise termed Dratted Nuisance) and Horrors. If you were caught in the former, you were punished, but with a kind of sigh. You had forced them to go to the bother of punishing you. You could smuggle; you could smoke; you could blackmail; you could set hair on fire; you could make your juniors drink out of inkwells; you could extort protection-money; you could burgle Sir Mandeville Parker's mansion (burgling the villagers' cottages was almost Invisible); you could lay waste the school rhubarb garden under the pretence of searching for tennis balls; you could festoon toilet paper around the chimney; you could reassemble a car on the chimney; you could risk your life (and the chimney's) by performing the dare-drop from it with a rope two inches short enough; you could smear pine-resin on the teachers' doorknobs; you could blow doors down the hallways with cordite; you could put tadpoles in the lemonade, pollywogs in the porridge, and capsules of lighter-fluid in the soup. For those peccadilloes you merely went without food, or took a cold shower, or maybe you had to polish fifty pairs of shoes before dawn, or mow the lawn with scissors, or sniff salt water through your nostrils, or copy out the 119th Psalm on a postage stamp. You could even release adders or thistledown or laughing gas in the classroom of a weak teacher destined for extinction; for this you merely were manacled to the chalkboard or had to run around the playground holding a rifle above your head. You were just slapped on the wrist; just punished.

For an act of Horror—a Grave Transgression—if such really had to be admitted to have occurred—you had to be Punished. Nay, you had to be *Shamed*.

You had to be sent over to the boys' school.

And after you returned, your blush (and possibly your glush) still burning, the most you could bring yourself to say, if anybody got up courage to ask you, was that you had undergone Corporal Punishment.

("*Undergone* him?")

What kind of sin deserved this?

It was never very clear, because it was never mentioned. But it seemed to be anything that had a connection with normal lechery. And a few matters that somehow had become attached to lechery, such as blasphemy.

To give an example: anyone caught with a pin-up picture, or saying a dirty word like *trouser* or *nostril*— No, let's take a once-and-for-all example: anyone caught reading or writing this book would deserve it. Probably round-the-clock for a week.

Not every year did a Horror happen. But it cast the shadow of fear over succeeding generations.

The rationale for this kind of punishment-suiting-the-crime was to give it strong negative vibrations, to forge an association of It with Horror and Shame. The culprit, and through her example the rest, would thenceforth shy away from It as from something carrying an electric shock. Punishment was properly distinguished from mere punishment by being called Chastisement, because it drove back to the fold of chastity.

But since It (the punishment) was suspiciously akin to It (the crime), the actual result was not so simple. Indeed it was complex and contradictory to the point of tanglement; it was a deformed psychology. The girls were morbidly fascinated with, and preternaturally afraid of, *It*. The thought of the punishment led to the thought of It; but if the thought led to talk or to action directed toward It, it led to the punishment; so swelling thought strained against shrinking expression; there was a mighty tension between restrained behavior and what was building underneath. Even when there was no reason to be thinking about It, indeed every reason to be worried about anything else, they wore curious fevered expressions and slunk guiltily around corners.

Their mothers had brought them up like mine, to feel that pussy and whatever-boys-have-in-place-of-pussy are opposite poles of the universe; for pudicy—that is, Pussy, to be even thought about is bad, talked about, worse; seen, worse still; touched—well, worse and worse with the strangeness of the toucher, and the extreme would be that other shameful pole.

Great shame curves to meet great glory, as madness meets with inspiration. Heloises and Abelards of the past lived on in a murmur as much of envy as of pity; a girl singled out by scandal would hang her head in pride.

There was one a few years before I came. Her name was Rider. Or so it had become in legend. I never found out what she did, or who it was who loved her. It seems she endured her fall for only a few days, and then was taken away on a white horse.

As for me, I wasn't playing with any risk of crossing this line, but I was always cruising close to the other one. I was the leading Dratted Nuisance, without intending to be or to let myself be conspicuous in any way. Actually I'm not sure any of these petty crimes had ever been committed before I arrived. And yet I didn't commit them—well, not most of them. I'm afraid they were mostly committed to catch my attention. At any rate, it was expected that where I was, there would be some scene of tumult. I was responsible for it, whether I had wanted it or not. Yet I was never quite punishably caught. The teachers never quite had excuse to lay their hands or rulers on me, and there were times when this gave them the shaking ague.

The nights were hot, so I really had to find my way out along window ledges and fence-tops to the pond, which meant that I became the guide for nightly break-outs. But still I was not popular, even after I set up a matchbox telephone that broadcast conversations from the teachers' quarters into our dormitory.

They merely said, "Who cares what those cows gossip about? From the *other school*, now, that would be something." So, working by night from back yard to back yard through the village, and getting into the boys' school through the coal hole without being seen by a soul, I set up a string telephone all the way from the *male* teachers' quarters. But it appeared that even that was not what was wanted.

"The *boys*, yuffool! We want to hear what *the boys* are saying!"

"What they're saying about *us!*"

"I want to hear if they say things about *me!*"

"How can they, when they've never seen you except on the other side of the hall at Joint Assembly?"

"Yes, they don't have a chance to know us by name, poor things. —But all boys talk about *girl*."

"Or when they're not talking about *girl*, they're talking about *cunt*."

"Ooh, don't, how wicked!"

"Or even about *stalk*." "Ee-eek!" "They talk about each other's stalks!" "No, really?" "Think of that whole building bristling with little stalks!" "Hurry, Fristy!" (I was packing my string and thumbtacks into a matchbox.)

"I think I'd really rather hear them say my name. Or even anybody's name. Don't you think they know some of us by reputation?"

Here there was a silence. I was out on the landing, raising the window sash.

"Felicity . . ."

"What?"

"Too risky. Don't bother."

Between the Tables

I HAD been at the school just short of a week when I nearly got fired from it like a rocket. Tuesday came, which was crocodile-day. Pocket-money had been given out on Wednesday, just before I arrived. The idea of dispensing it on Wednesdays was that there was maximum chance it would be lost by Tuesday, so that girls would find themselves unable to buy anything and would be saved from rotting their teeth. Generally this worked, and many of the coins had been stolen or gambled or lost between floorboards; but this time everyone managed to have something in their pocket, except of course me.

The she-crocodile set out for the village. We wore our usual drab garb, with the addition of huge straw hats. These were meant to protect our complexions from the sun, or from the eyes of villagers, but they were floppy and voluptuous in form, and the sun pricked through them and gave us sun-freckles and the yokels peered beneath.

I slipped to the crocodile's tail where the teacher was not watching me, and tore my hat off to drink the sky. After a week of indoors I was starved for it.

We entered Closeover—that was the village's name—and were allowed into several untempting shops. You'd think it would have been nice to finish with crumpets and cream at the teashop beside the green, but instead we were steered out of the village, to the carsick highway that went by on the north edge, where there was a tawdry truck-stop— once it was The Gooder 'N Good, but some called it The Better 'N Noth'n, so it was reborn as The Clock, but still was more often referred to as The Clock That's Always Wrong, more often as just Bertha's. (Her name was really Gudrun.) It was one of those places boldly fronted by a yellow plastic sign with red spring-on letters that drop off and nobody fixes them, so that whatever it once said it now fascinates you by saying

HO TNE A

DAYS

A UU E

On the other side it said

LIVE

AND

TONI

so that I was almost jealous of Toni, until I realized that what it meant to say was LIVE BAND TONITE. It was also a place of the kind that watches out for such as me with "PLEASE WAIT TO BE SEATED" and "NO SHIRT NO SHOES NO ENTRY." But here we were let in for ice creams (what I call snow creams), while the teacher stood guard outside.

Having no money, I could no more order an ice cream than I could buy a gobstopper or a comic, and as the wallpaper was not pleasing to look at I sat and practiced my art of sleeping with my eyes open. But my friends were in an obliging mood: "Give her one too," they said. I said that was all right, I didn't need anything, but they insisted on me choosing a variety. Well, okay then, since it was apparently on the house—I asked for a banana split and a butter pecan milkshake. "Is that all?" said Bertha. Choosing not to take this as formality or sarcasm, I agreed to have a slurpy and a pineapple flurry and a strawberry daiquiri. I'd rather have had a Small Mega-Bar or a Country Pride Double Quarter-Pounder, but she said "No, for that you'd have to go to the other place down the street, where Contradiction in Terms is playing. Or there's Belt Busters" (or was it Belly Busters?) "if you want an Obeseburger or a Hot Hog, or the Cantonment if you like Fake Lam Chop or Lock Jaw Suey . . ." Still hungry, I fired at Saxie: "D'you want the rest of your scone?"— "No."— "Are you sure?"— "No," and knowing she meant "Yes" I scarfed or scoffed it.

The others had finished and I was still dissolving sherbet in my mouth when we heard a factory siren, and then blue-overalled workers from the tire-shop next door trooped in, wearing Bubba-caps and rubbing Go-Jo off their hands, and sat down for their supper. The teacher hastened in to fetch us, and the girls queued to pay. I just started for the door. Well, you can guess what happened.

"This girl," shouted Bertha at the teacher, "bogged into a jam roll and two helpings of nougat-praline softserve with marshmallows and hot fudge and caramel and a chocolate continent, not to mention several sodas and stummy cakes and a Dike Coke" (diarrhea cola, I think she meant) "and more else than I can remember—may it all come out in a boil at the tip of her nose!—and now she says she can't pay!"

"But my friends—" I began and looked around for them, but they were gone.

The workers reached into their overall pockets, but Bertha said sharply: "She'll have to work it off for me. She'll wait tables here till closing time."

The gallant workers nodded, changing their minds about paying for me, though keeping their hands in their pockets.

"Don't be ridiculous," I said. "I'm a schoolchild. I've got to get back and do my homework. It's my bath-night." (Mentioning that was a kindova misstep.) I appealed to the teacher, who said feebly, "Yes, after all. Come, come. Only a trifle."

"Don't you feed her at school?" demanded Bertha. "My good woman—" said the teacher. Bertha raised a coffeepot with one hand, and with the other fingered the billspike—the needle-like weapon beside the cash register, on which fat-stained tickets were impaled. And to my disgust the teacher withdrew, after merely requesting that I be dismissed by bedtime.

"We'll give her breakfast," said Al (they all had names like Al or Frank stitched above their shirt pockets).

"I didn't hear that," said Bertha. "You come into the back with me, Miss Mustard, and get your uniform. If you work out well at this job, I'll call you Becky." "Why?" "I've always dreamed of having two good waitresses, called Becky and Callie, so you'd be a start." "Don't let her wear her sweater like that," called one of the men—I had it tied by its sleeves around my waist— "it hides her fanny."

I followed her to the kitchen, where the cook paused with his ladle in the air. "What's with you?" she barked at him, "when's that corn coming?" "Right'm, M's Boitha," he said, "I've got it on a rolling goil" (oil he meant). "She my new assistant? Can you cook?" he asked me, and answered his own question: "Of course not, always had men to cook for ya." Ignoring him, Bertha handed me a sort of cap, consisting only of a beak and a band, which encircled my hair to hold up the masses at front and back; and a sort of bolero vest, not too different in color from my hair; and thin white pants. I could see the case against wearing school clothes, but I baulked at pulling these things on. They were not clean, and they reminded me of the physical or at least moral discomfort I had felt in the late pants of Eugene.

"I don't have to wear these," I said.

"Sanitary regulations," answered Bertha.

"I don't believe you. What I've got on is perfectly sanitary."

"Our waitresses always wear these."

"What, the same ones? Is that sanitary?"

"Stop arguing, miss. The customers expect these, and"—she snatched my skirt off in a single sweep, with the decisiveness of one who twirls pizzas and bounces troublemakers— "if you don't have them on pronto I'll get Pete to spank you. With his fishslice."

"Perhaps you'd like me to come out just like this?" I said— "-wouldn't that be still better for sales?"

"No, we're not selling that kind of meat. We don't need a riot."

The cook (all short-order cooks are called Pete, just as all grease-monkeys are called Nick) wiped his hands and came forward, but Bertha said, "Your pot's boiling over, get back to it; give her two minutes." He retired to his stove, reaching for his bottle of EXTRA VIRGIN Olive Oil and stirring empty air while I got into the pants. They reminded me now of the bloons, rather than the bluejeans: their mass was almost small enough to scrunch up in the palm of the hand, but they had so much stretch that they could have been inflated around the haunches of the bulkiest waitress, perhaps even of Bertha, who I suspected was the only other.

At any rate I had the first experience of what is called panty-line anxiety. Pete said: "There's a mirror in there," and I went into the closet. Fortunately the school clevel was almost the same off-white, so I believed it didn't really show through. Reassured, I turned around, and found my way obstructed by the cook. He had lifted his apron and brought forth something that put me off link sausages.

I raised my eyes from it and looked him in the face with displeasure.

"Isn't it beautiful?" he said.

"What?"

"This!" he said, bouncing it, "my log, my pripe, my cunplug, my womprobe, my tap, my greasegun, my Lord of the Forest—magnificent, isn't it! Isn't it?"

"Hardly," I said. "Useful, maybe."

"Gid Lloyd!" he screamed, "you're supposed to woyship it! YOU'RE SUPPOSTA ENVY IT! Go down on your knees to it, bitch!"

"I've seen more than one of these by now," I remarked, "and I guess I'm getting used to them." (Main use, I thought, exclamation-marks— they always point upward.) "But still basically they're a shade—I have to say it—absurd, an affront to harmonious outline."

(I do indeed think stalk is, as a device, a shade piffling. Wouldn't something like a broad soft flap be better, mating into a broad soft fold?—more contact?)

His face fell, and he had to drop his apron in time to cover his crest-fallenness. "Oh, really? One might argue" (glancing, not for the first time, at my lower belly) "that it's the more interesting formation. What I need," he sniveled, "is a dishwasher, not a wishdasher," and he went back to his corn, which was spitting all over the stove. "Sorry to dis-uppoint you," I said, and crossed to the door and heard a newcomer saying "Where is she, then?" "She rode her hips away into the kitchen." "Just so she didn't row 'm down the river!" "She's a neat craft, I'd like to ram her amidhips" . . .

The café was fuller now. But, for a moment, silent. I heard

murmurs mainly as yet from behind me: "Take a look at those *facts*"—
"Territory worth exploring"— "Those pants looks good. Take 'em
off . . ."

Bertha gave me some hasty training and I stepped out among the
tables, holding my little green order-pad and pencil. The menu was
hand-written each day by Pete in elaborate copperplate, rendered illeg-
ible by large flourishes and circles over the *i*'s; faint purple copies, made
with a duplicating machine, were propped on each table between the
ketchup, the plastic flowers, the ashtray, and the Texas Joe banana
peppers. The offerings appeared to be Spoiled Cauliflour, Weak-Eyed
Peas, Botched Eggs, Fried Trash, Cursed Ham, Bronto Bears, Horse
Salad, Cork Slaw, Shattered Beets, Onion Breath, Savage Biscuit,
Chicken Forest, Scream of Broccolic, Hasbeens, French Fires, Mice &
Gravy, Walrus Loaf, Alice Antelope, Clown Chowder, Bearded Chop,
Bald Pnuts, Comedy Pie, Snakes On Toast, Potatoes Smashed or Over-
Burned, Ped Xing (a Cantonese dish), Sir Lion, and Scruffy Fumbled
Legs, but at least everybody could make out that honest old favorite,
Candid Yams. The men puzzled over their menu, and made me lean
over and help them with it. They would have done better if they hadn't
been trying with one eye to read the crescent of my orogenous zones.
And the vest, I felt, was somewhat short in the back. It goes without
saying that they placed their toes where I was likeliest to step on them,
and their coffee cups where I had to stretch the farthest to refill them.
As I won my way from table to table I had to hear "She walks like a
brung-up lady" and less cultivated comments on my ars ambulandi; felt
the eyes that kept a level watch on my *jagana* as it traveled around the
room; and had to pretend I didn't know what they meant when they
asked which fruits I served for the sweet course and whether I gave
second helpings.

I could take only half an hour of it at a time, and then asked Bertha
to let me have a change, wash dishes or run an errand. "Okay," she said.
"You could bus that table," pointing to the only empty one, where a
family with small appetites had departed leaving their meal half eaten
(and leaving me and Bertha as the only female element—though I didn't
have time to sex the cockroaches). The table was sordid with salt and
crumbs and ash, and I hardly wanted to kiss it, which was what "buss"
meant to me, but she explained that I was to clear it. So I swept away
the bones and cornbread, and then as I leaned forward, heartily wiping
with a damp gray rag, there was a heavy stop to all sound in the room.

The vest must have ridden up and exposed flesh along my spine—
Bertha hurried over and plucked me away by it. "For fluff's sake," she

muttered, taking me behind the counter, "want us to have a worse mess to clear up?" "I was doing my best," I said. "You were wagging your tail; you were making the table look like a bed. My carpet's bad enough without people having passion on it. Take a smoke-break." "I don't smoke—" "Go on," she said, "come back in ten minutes when they've cooled down."

The only place to go was the kitchen, but I had Pete under control. "Stand this side of the range," I told him; "the moment you turn around I go. I'm taking an eye-break." "An eye-break?" "A smoke-break, but I don't want any eyes on me for a while." "Fair enough. —You hungry again yet?" I admitted I was; "What are you working on?" "Leftovers Supreme, the usual, whatever you call it; help yourself to a spud," and I admitted I already had. "Don't kiss with your mouth full." "I wasn't going to." "Just a proverb.

"Can I talk to you?" he said. "Yes," I said between mouthfuls. "Will you talk back?" "Well, I won't be rude." "So I can hear your verse anyway." "My verse?—the most I'll do is answer in prose, thank you!" "Your *voice*.

"Place is doing well." "Uhuh." "The woid's spread: 'Hoid about the pretty waitress they got down Boitha's? Let's go harass her.' Ah, men!" "Careful," I said.

"Aren't you pleased when people like you?"

"Not so much."

"How can you not enjoy being pretty?"

"But my prettiness isn't me," I said. "When they flatter it, I feel it's not me they're looking at but something standing beside me."

"That's just where you're wrong," said the cook. (He was kneading something vigorously at spigot-level, while looking contemplatively up at his shelves and hanging pans.) "Your prettiness *is* you. It's really your poysonality more than your poyson—that's what makes you so pretty."

A pretty theory, I thought, intended to get in under my guard. But still I quite enjoyed this, him talking to me and not looking at me. I retorted: "Why didn't such a smarty stay in New Yoik?" "Ah, so you know where I'm from," he said, and started telling me his life—he had had a fine situation as a ship's cook but somehow got into trouble on a voyage in. "But you mustn't put me down as a materialist," he said, returning to his elevated theme. "Yes, I want your body, but it's your spirit that makes me want it. A delusion if you like. At any rate it's more the way you move than the way you're shaped. Yes, it's the way those parts, relatively, move."

The way they move?—was he sneaking a look at me? No, he was still obediently facing away.

"May I ask *you* something?" I said.

"Please do."

"What you did is called 'flashing,' isn't it?"

"I don't like to hear a lady say that. Call it 'exhibitionism.'"

"Is there such a thing as a female flasher—exhibitionist?"

"Not in this village, but you could become the foist."

I realized he was watching my image in the polished bottom of a pressure cooker, so I said "Time's up" and hurried back to work.

The door was now just left ajar, and I heard trucks pulling into the parking lot. And there came patrons of other kinds—all kinds, you might say (except women)—executive-age men driving young-man cars—sometimes there was a godawful noise, a car in bad need of a tune-up, but when it shut off you realized it was music; nowadays you can't tell music from engine-trouble. They piled in, though Bertha tried to slow them— "Can't you read?—STAY TO BE WEIGHTED—I mean WAY TO BE SATED"—the café was filled with low hubbub but, oddly, no radio, though this was the type of place where you usually get rasping music to digest by and twelve-minute-long high-pressure ranting used-car or waterbed commercials to prevent you from meditating. But I saw a radio on a high shelf, and thought it might be a diversion, so I walked over and tried to switch it on. They let me stand on tiptoe, twiddling, till the knob came off in my hand.

They laughed. "Broke!" said Hud. "Don't need it," said Gurney. "I'll fix it," said the man from Tolly's Autronic, "if you'll dance with me." I took up my pad and returned to work, trying to get some sense out of the customers at yet another table. "A bun, you said?" "No, two. Or more. Abundance." "I beg your pardon?" "A bundance. Or a cundance . . ." It was approvable, in a way, that lubricity brought out the powers of punning latent in the people.

Some of them had finished eating but they didn't leave, except for a few that had to hurry out for some urgent reason. One of these was up in a half-crouch over his table as I passed and he said pleadingly: "What's your name?—just your name so I can . . ." "Gertrude," I replied. (Why shouldn't "Gertrude" have her turn to be murmured to by fantasizing wankers?) He absorbed it with a gulp and leapt for the door.

Then behind me I heard Joe say to Bill: "Whatchu studyin', boy? You posta be studyin' yore menu." "Leamy alone," said Bill, "I'm studying the map of heaven!"

And I realized that paradise, though white like its approaches, had a visible border, a slight ridge: for I felt a finger tracing it.

Bath-Night

I FLUNG down my pad and walked to the counter. Confronting Bertha, I said, "You'd better find something else for me to do."

"You'll do what you're told to do," she said, at her most menacing. "There's nothing else to do," she went on as I didn't budge, "but waiting; and bussing the tables, but—there aren't any to bus. You're doing fine, and I know best how to mind the register."

"On the contrary," I said, "my brain is as good as yours, so I can mind the register, and your body is superior to mine, so you can go deal with your drecky customers."

She shot out her beam-shaped arm, but mine got to the billspike
first.

"It's either that," I said, "or go home."

She considered. "Well," she said, "it's been a good evening, but I
don't like the way they're just sitting around." (Indeed there wasn't
much eating going on any more—which was okay with me because it
meant that the restaurant's concentration of digestive or, shall we say,
savory air began to level off.) "It's fine to have all this company, but it
doesn't do us any good unless they finish and pay and go. Here I've
been standing and no one's coming and paying and leaving. You can
stand here and I'll change places with you and we'll see if I can persuade a few of them it's time to drink their coffee and get home to their
wives."

"Smart idea," I said.

But when I saw her trying to stoop for the pad, I hurried back to
pick it up for her and said, "Look, I'll go on if you like."

"No, you do as I say," she said, sighing. — "It's a hell of a life for
waitresses."

"Then let me do it, it's only this evening."

"I've had four before you," she said. "Three of them wore out; the
last one, she was young and strong, so she hooked a husband— 'I didn't
hear that,' that was the line she used for flirting, every goddam day."
And she straightened up and marched into the combat zone.

I stood at the cash-register, and a few ambled up to me, and I began
ringing the till and counting change. But still most of them remained
content to lounge in their chairs, gazing at what they could see of me.
Bertha then had the better idea of shifting the register to the end of the
counter, where I had to stand in profile. I went along with it, if it would
get the evening over. A longer line formed, or rather a fan. It looked as
if Bertha's might break even and close for the night.

But all did not go smoothly. First eight or ten were standing up and
shuffling toward the counter, and then half were standing while the rest
were still at the tables. "A-hmm, Harvey," ventured Scott. "What?"
"Would you mind?" "Would I mind what?" *"Don't block our view of
the girl!"*

Harvey stood firm, and others had to climb on their chairs and
tables, and there were calls of "Move over, fellas!"— "Form the line to
the side, couldn't you?"— "Who are you telling to move over?"— "Who
are you shoving?"— "You, d'ya think it's your ass we want to see?" In a
minute two were fighting, and then like a match lighting a pile of news-
papers they were all fighting.

I've had to see about an equal number of real fights and fights in movies, and I'm always amazed by the difference. In movies every punch sounds like a cap-gun (which it probably is), drives squarely to the middle of the bony sinuses, and sends someone over a chair and through two brick walls (though he gets up and comes back and helps the other fellow through three brick walls). Real fights, on the other hand, are conducted as if by incompetent drunkards; no fist ever connects, except accidentally with a hat or a watchstrap; if anyone falls down, it's because he's lost his balance or tripped over his shoelace. What can they expect when they don't look at one another?

But there was some violence to tablecloths and pepperpots, so Bertha hissed at me: "Get out. Go home." I offered to stay and help separate the combatants, but she said it would be easy once they'd tired, and anyway they'd stop as soon as they saw I'd gone. "So just scram! and don't try to go past that mob—slip out through the larder, and run."

Thus ended my short career in the catering trade.

I found there was no way out of the larder but a window. It was dark by now—and moonless—and I had to jump on trust, fearing broken crocks or a nettlebed, but I fell through a haze of fruitflies and sweet-rancid stench into a soggy midden of grapefruit peels and cabbage stalks and melon gougings and coffeegrounds, laced with dental floss and layered with wads of bills (or tickets or tabs or orders or reckonings or *additions* or Guest Checks or whatever those prolific pages of gravy-sodden literature are called—not often Invoices, I think). I landed sittingly and slithered down the heap and crawled out through a slough that had already rotted to the squeezytawny stage of compost—*ayy-hyuk!* There were nettles too—my mother used to warn us "Men are like nettles, stroke them and they sting you, you gotta grasp them by the short hairs," but I found it hard to apply her advice. — Hearing thumps behind me (brawlers ejected by Bertha through doors and windows) I picked up my pace.

The restaurant had made me feel greasy enough before daubing me with its garbage. It was a soiled and stinking Applepeel that slunk back along the lane.

I might have quit the school at this point—if it hadn't been my bath-night. Assigning me, when I arrived on a Wednesday, Tuesday as bath-night was of a piece with handing out pocket-money on Wednesday to be spent on Tuesday. Already I hadn't bathed for a week, and I certainly couldn't go another week like this. Lights were blinking out in the cottages and probably, by now, in the school, and I might have missed my bath-time, but I didn't intend to be done out of it.

In fact it had to come first: I didn't want to pass through the dormitory in my grungy state. Looking from the fringe of trees, I made sure that the light was off in the bathroom window, high under the third-story eave; so I determined to climb in that way. It was a technical challenge—and the start was delayed because Caiaphas, the watchdog, who was fourteen years old, could for once smell me, and I had to spend some minutes quieting him. But at last I dropped from a branch onto the roof and swung down over the gutter to the sill and got a filthy foot through the window and into the tub.

There was no bolt on the bathroom door. I hoped this really was my bath-hour, or else it was late enough for everyone to be asleep. The tub stood on four griffon-legs and was large enough to float two of me. I ran the water down my arm to keep it quiet.

I lay and the grease and tealeaves drifted off me. At least I hoped so, but did I really need to lie in the dark hoping? I got out and switched the light on. It was a bare bulb up in the far corner of the little blue-painted room. I got back in and reached for the soap, but it escaped from my fingers. Actually we weren't allowed soap, a consumable; what I found on the soap-dish was a loofah and a piece of pumice, rather fun to play with, but I was already too drowsy. "Been in the mud again!" I seemed to hear Saxie say—or Zed— "this kid could get muddy if you locked her in an icebox. Well, maybe it's what gives her her complexion . . ." If there's one thing I like even more than cold water on my skin it's hot water. I lay folding first one leg and then the other, to submerge them and raise the level around my middle. The light glanced down along my thigh and splashed up from my belly. And I noticed how beautiful bodies are. That is, when (by sinking a thigh, or scooping with a hand) I sent a wave lapping over me, suddenly the forms were clear, the regions and the meetings between them—the quadriceps-mass and the adductor-mass, or the fading end of a dome and the stretched tenderness of a sheet; a difference of gleam distinguished them, or a thread of shine lay along the valley of their precise though shifting boundary. But the skin of water lasted only an eye-blink after each splash; it slipped away; the planes and joins and pressures were still there, but without their glaze, above water or under, you had to search for them.

Between my rib and my hip-bone there was a slanting surface which the sheen showed to be really two: two shoals, each wearing its slipcase of fluid. And the moment it drained away you could not see them *at all*: just a plain, on it a satiny damp which was subtle but drew out the form hardly more than dryness did. (But now I recollected what it might have been that I admired in the dark mirror skin of Ritan.) I'm not so simple (I thought) as my lechers and venerers think—for often it seems that all they worship in me is simplicity, the lack of deviations. But they ignore not only the wrinkles that are to come, but the structures that are within.

But if I had to say which is the single most beautiful part of me, I would choose the triangle that supports the thumb—stock, strings, dell, lobe, shore.

I nudged the tap with my foot and let in some more hot water, down my leg. A carpet of fine bubbles had formed on the cold enamel, and they came feeling up my sides and traced an outline of me on the surface. I pressed my body to the left, then right, and the water sluicing over made me a belly-plate of armor rushing under a rim-wave now at this hip, now at that. I let my head sink back, so that my body rose; sole touch to solid was afar at my soles; I grasped my ankles, and my body floated to the left, bumped that shore, and set off slowly for the right. I crossed my paws on my chest like a sea-otter. My head sank back, and my evemound rose, groved and grooved, shedding rivulets, like the world from the flood.

And it was then, just before I shut my eyes, that I noticed a small hole in the ceiling. Nobody could have been looking through; there was no space for an attic under the roof. But the solution of my mystery came to me, at any rate the first step. And the second step too, for I remember thinking that I would say nothing about it to Saxie. It would embarrass me; it would imply that I was the incarnation of the goddess.

My head sank back, sank back, till my hair floated around me; till the last bubbles broke from my ears; till the water crept over my brow, and trickled into the hollow around my eyes, and—why not?—I let it rise to inundate my eyes. (Outside behind the wood the old moon was rising.) The island of me—chin and lips and nostrils—shrank to a coast, slightly tickling, on the ridge of my nose.

Under the silver ceiling of water and the crimson cupolas of my eyelids I was gazing back, and back, and back. Now I could hear all the sounds of the house—not of anything that whispered or snored in the air of the rooms, but of those that lived in the pipes and walls and rafters and furnace and foundations, mice, worms, spirits. And I began to see that I was in another world, another planet, a planet of truly beautiful beings. Every gasping wonder of their forms shone steady to be studied: for they were sheathed in gelatin.

I slept like a yolk in the warm darkness.

The darkness! My face came crashing up out of the water. Who had switched the light off?

It would be one of my enemies, or several of them. Jones and Claypuddle. I must have lain on into someone else's bath-time, and now they were going to duck me, or shave my hair, or empty the toilet bowl on me.

"Sh!" whispered Saxie. She slipped into the bathtub at my feet, and found the melting soap and began slowly with my toes.

Breakout

JUNE FAINTED into July, but school continued. I protested, "Where I come from, school stops in the summer!" "Ah, we've heard of that. That's a relic of the old times, when children were needed on the farm. Most of us are from families that— Well, holidays will come with Christmas."

Most mornings I find myself on my feet before even knowing I'm awake—the world seems that good—and it was so even here, which did not help my popularity. Yet living all through the longest days of the year in an institution, indoors, under wan lightbulbs, poetryless, my skin paled, the lustre of my hair went into hiding, and I had lost touch with the moon—I thought. I didn't notice her by day, and couldn't have said where she was. And yet it was as if the habit of the temple persisted. Whenever, led by me, we climbed out, I found that the moon was up; and when a panic came over me to get safely back to bed, I saw that she had gone. When she did not rise till midnight there was a neap tide in my blood, and when the moonage was, say, twenty-seven and the tashage eighty-one, I ran up stairs no more than two at a time. (By the way, the reason for the bend you may have noticed in my nose was coming *down* stairs more than one at a time—not a good plan; I learned to confine myself to taking off from the fifth or sixth step from the bottom.)

Many people are cheerful only with sunshine on their skin, and I groan with pleasure as the sun blesses me, but what starts the current in me is the touch of the moon.

Constance ("Vashti") Jones and Betty ("Crazy Joy") Claypuddle disappeared from the school. I asked Saxie what had become of them— had they been carried away on white horses? "They're behind you," she said. I turned, and so they were, though retreating through a doorway. "They've been behind you for several days." And I found that they had taken desks just behind mine, and stood behind me in cafeteria lines. Once I felt (without her thinking I did) Crazy Joy pick a hair off my collar, and heard (without her thinking I did) Vashti whisper "What did you gain by that?"

Next afternoon it was Saxie who had disappeared—I afterwards found she was in the sick bay with a cracked wrist, having tripped over an outstretched toe. Then Crazy Joy and Vashti got me into a corner between the chapel and the air raid shelter.

"This is it," I thought. "This is where they tear me to shreds with their nails" (which were long, but not sterilized with scarlet polish because that would have been a noticeable Horror).

But Vashti hissed: "Felicity, listen. How about an expedition into town to pick up a man?"

I was dumbfounded.

"*Fristy*," said Crazy Joy, lowering herself to friendly wheedling.

"It almost sounds," I said, "as if you were suggesting something against the rules."

"Look, it's not serious." (A drip of perspiration fell off Claypuddle's chin.) "We just thought we'd like to see how it's done and what happens and how good we are at it, sort of thing. We'd pick up a Man each and then of course we'd drop him straight away—maybe we'll try it a few more times, maybe a hundred or so, just to get an idea of what kind of things they say and how irresistible we are—and of course you needn't be in on all this part; you could be just having a sundae in Fortes while you wait for us, and then we'll catch the last bus back."

"So why do I need to be along at all?"

"Oh, we thought we'd let you in on it," said Vashti with hollow airiness. "Check our technique. You may need some education."

It took them a while to admit they thought I could get away with anything and they wouldn't dare their hides on such an undertaking unless I were along as pilot.

But I felt a torpid reluctance, not at the outrageousness of their proposal but at the very idea that I could ever climb out of the school. I suspected the reason why. But if I had told them they would have thought I was just choosing an eccentric way of saying "It's the wrong time of the month." I said: "Could we wait till—about three in the morning?"

"What!" said Crazy Joy, daisy eyes widening to starbursts—I had a close view of spikes of mascara— "*get up* at a time like that?"

"Certainly not!" said Vashti. "No *men* would be around. We've got to go while there's plenty of the night left. We need to be *back* by three. Not scared, are you?"

Vashti, in contrast with her flabbily pleasure-loving friend, was an intense person of the definitely brown-eyed kind with thrusting face and rat-brown hair. Naive when she arrived, not long before me, from her Welsh sheep-farm, she had set herself to *learn*. (By the time she finished at school, she had learnt so much that she decided her sexual instar was at an end and she became a missionary. Crazy Joy, who never learnt anything much, and who was one of those hippobottomous young women—pyramidal—with pin face above and substantial architecture below (not easy to wave in the air), went on to Hollywood, though her nom de guerre was disallowed and she is famous under Hedony Backlier. She is famous for not speaking; they won't let her; she was the first of the new silent stars.)

"Not scared," I said, "just a bit tired and my head is aching."

"Tired and your head's aching! So Fristy Pepper is human after all!"

"I went out for a walk about two last night."

"Liar!" they burst out. "Stop making excuses; will you come or won't you?" "Well, no, thanks a lot, but I think for now—" Whereupon Crazy Joy smothered me from the front in an ample bearhug while Vashti stepped behind me and got me in a hammerlock—turned my left arm behind my back; Crazy Joy prepared to slap, poke, tweak or possibly fork me while Vashti kept on forcing my arm higher. "All right, plan B. We know you'd rather have Girl than Man, so we're going to do you like Saxie does." "Oh, tickle me?" "Is that all she does with you?" "That's bad enough, isn't it?" "Well, you're going to learn badder. Sure you've got her, Vashti?" Vashti hoisted tighter, and I convincingly evinced pain. But it happened that about that time I noticed an itch at my left ear (perhaps it felt the loss of the earring) and so, after using my heel to tap Vashti's fingers away, I raised my hand further between my shoulders to scratch my earlobe. This was all it took to convince them I was made of rubber and could probably use martial arts to dissect and redistribute them. (I did add a few stylized gestures, sort of corkscrewing the air.) They backed off, saying "Look, sorry, we were just disappointed . . ."

"You are disappointed, really?"

"Really really."

Well, I can't really disappoint anyone.

So I overcame my lassitude and climbed out into the long twilight of the first night of August. There was of course no moon. I waited below for them, but they couldn't get their hips through the bars of the stairway window, let alone swing along the lightning rod to the second gable, so I just let them out by dropping a couple of storeys and opening the boot room door, which the teachers bolted from the outside to keep us in.

Their feet made a noise like marching Goliasauruses on the gravel driveway, but we got out onto the howling highway and hitched a ride to town with a trucker who was blind on dope (Vashti did the thumbing and selecting, having first hidden me off the road so as not, she said, to get the wrong kind of ride); my two friends occupied themselves

* In which the object is to check not the King but the Black King's Rook's Pawn (Applepeel). Applepeel sometimes does not move at all, and is said to be "asleep." But then again, spying a line of three pieces, she jumps clear over them. There is no resignation, and the game doesn't stop at checkmate: Applepeel is not removed, and the mating piece (whether king, knight, pawn, or queen—even the bishop does not stand aloof) joins her on her square. The pieces fit together in several ways.

** The game of changing one letter at a time—most lines start with *Applepeek* or *Applefeel*—the record so far is said to be *moongoose* in 39 moves.

applying facepaste, while I watched the wheel, sometimes snatching it to save us from hitting a goat or flying off a bridge, and now we were strolling—much as you stroll across Antarctica—along a street among lighted signs and raincoats and faces that we didn't dare to look at.

I was thinking of what would happen to us if we were caught. "How did the system come about?" I asked. I had once asked Saxie this, but she wouldn't talk. "Can't hear you—wait till we get past that dustbin into the carshadow. What did you say?" "How did the system come about?" I asked again. Crazy Joy knew what I meant—because she was worrying too—and readily held forth. "It was the biology teachers that started it, they say. (Two out of three of the teachers are biology teachers.) They would send one of us over to the other school to be stood on a table and have her construction explained . . . Naturally no one went willingly, so it started happening that those who misbehaved had to go."

"Terrible!"

"Yes, it is, for the subjects. The rest have come to rather—hope for it."

"But," I said, "the *parents!*"

"Oh, we don't remember to tell our parents."

"Don't *remember* to tell them?"

"No, there's the Debriefing, you see. A hypnotist is brought in at the end of each term to erase part of everyone's memories for the duration of the vacation."

"I don't believe it!" I said.

"No. Neither will your parents."

I was in my school uniform. They had skilfully slipped out of theirs and concealed them in their handbags: Crazy Joy had an outfit of several independent parts topped by a crimson feather half as large as herself (clashing with her scarlet nails) and Vashti did look quite like a Babylonian duchess. We passed some good graffiti, and signs with interesting information such as LARGE VEHICLES DO NOT ENTER HERE and OUTSIZE MEN SWEAR and GET THE BODY YOU WANT IN 14 DAYS ("Twon't take me that long to get 'im" muttered Crazy Joy) and people at a sidewalk table playing Applepeel chess* or Applepeel Consequences,** and a shop called Beauty Supplies—I thought they'd go in, but they doubted they could buy any more beauty. We made a wake, the crowd parting and filling in at our heels in a churning sort of way. But Vashti and Crazy Joy, arm in arm, fell back a pace, kindly protecting my rear since I was the youngest. We were, I understood, first just walking in search of the café where I could be parked. I was licking a chocolate popsicle, and I clutched in the other hand (since I had no handbag and no pocket) half a pound of loose change, the rest of ten weeks' unspent pocket-money. We heard penetrating *reemääks*, as Vashti and Crazy Joy called them, applying them to themselves. We passed such haunts as Perver City and the Nighty Club and had to stop at a crossing for the traffic, and over the shoulder of someone in front of me I saw that he was reading the *Applepeel Weekly*. ("Applepeel Weekly!" said his neighbor (who was reading *OUCH* magazine); "hey, I'd want her hourly!") A few other women punctuated the crowd, mainly along its edges. Some I didn't at once parse as women because they were wearing, apparently without duress, britches. They had red hair, blue trunk, white britches; or blue hair, yellow trunk, pink britches; like the insect, woman is often sharply divided into three unequal segments, hair, thorax, abdolegs. Some had hair not too far from mine; marmalade hair or marmite hair.

"Aren't you glad not to be male?" said Vashti with anticipation, though in an undertone. "How shattering to be *dropped!*"

"Yes," said Crazy Joy, but she whispered, and gripped her friend's arm, "thank goodness to be a girl and gorgeous, we never have to be *scared!*"

I realized there might be something sexy always denied me. Could I never, supposing I wanted to, woo a human person (short of Master Yoryo) and risk rejection? Terror is the sinew of thrill.

Ahead, past a raincoat, I saw a person of almost certainly the same gender as me turn into an alley, but pause on the corner and, before disappearing, glance behind her with an alarming smile and cock her hip. The ears above the raincoat went red.

"See, that must be the way," said Vashti; "We'll all do that," said Crazy Joy. "You first, Fristy." "Think she can do it?—the hiptilt?" "Oh, she might; she's got a tip-tilt nose and a lilt to her syllables. Give it a try." So as we reached the corner, I led around it, doing what I could to imitate the lift of hip and the glance back over.

Hard behind me was the requisite man, in fact several—but Vashti and Crazy Joy, whose nerve had cracked, were in the middle distance, running to catch the bus.

High-Speed Chase

THE ALLEY faced me, a black slit, with a glimmer of yellow sky above and grimy pavingstones below and lights only at the far end.

"How much?-ch?-ch?"—a chorus of calls behind me— "How much, Popsie?"— "How much, Sheila?"— "How much for an hour?"— "How much for your ass?"— "How much for all night?"— "How much for up against the wall?"— "May I worship you?" Propelled as by a puff of bad air, I set off like a bullet, or like a stag. "How much—hey, wait!" and they started after me. The first weapon I flung back at them, Parthian style, was the chocolate popsicle, for which I selected a well whiskered face. Next, my shoes, which were slowing me: I snatched them off, bowled one underarm, spun the other backhand. Two of my admirers went down, losing their footing and perhaps their admiration, and two more fought over each shoovenir, so that the pursuit was thinned by six. Barefoot would have been better still, but I didn't have time to pull off my white socks; they skeltered over puddles and dogpiles and orangepeels. The wolf-pack bayed behind me: "Throw us your skivvie next!" I got out into the next street.

It was the same kind of street or even worse, and the pursuit increased by twenty. I collided them neatly against a line outside a cinema, like a horse brushing a rider off on a branch, but myself got nabbed by the doorman; he said "`Ere, no queue-jumping, go to the back, missy!" "I'm trying to start an argument," I said, "for sociological research," to puzzle him, and ducked under his arm and got through, and the pursuit got around and came on *ir*regardless. It was the obligatory high-speed chase, though without cars—yes, bygolly, cars could have helped me by getting in the way but there were'nt any cars in the streets any more, cars aren't interested in girls. I noticed a few interesting sights, such as a sign pointing to places called Noston, Mud Chute, and Alarm, also tinkerbell reflections caused by sunlight reflected off watches and cellphones. I was out of condition after a couple of months of confinement—damn 'm, why did they run so fast, they were running faster than most boys I'd run races with, how fast would they go if my clothes did drop off, would they grow wings?—what I wished I could discard was my hair: the heavy *plokamos* flopped from side to side behind me like a sack; it unstreamlined me, overfemaled me, and I was afraid they would grab it. They were gaining on me, one stretched out his fingertip and established a claim by touching my coccyx, or the folds of my blouse (I'm sway-backed, so that clothing gathers on top of my rump, even when I'm running); he was the winner by a photo-finish and when they caught me, which was going to be the next instant, he would be the first haver and the others the first holders; but I turned and flung at him my left hand. It still clutched that bunch of coins, and I opened it at the instant of impact; the silver fistful burst in air. Everyone halted around him, appalled, as he grabbed his jaw which seemed to have disintegrated in slivers. That was the best thing I ever did with money. By the time he found he wasn't hurt I had ducked into another alley.

This was no dream (unless it was a dream inside a dream) and yet glancing back I saw them inevitably appear at the alley's mouth and come thundering in. They wanted to return my cash to me with interest. It might have been better to keep out of alleys, but they seemed my kind of setting. This was a long alley and I was tiring and again they were about to catch me; I leaped and grabbed a warehouse hoist and stood on my head in the air, while they all passed under, carried by their own impetus; before they managed to clatter into reverse I had dropped to my feet and started back the other way. But it wasn't the way I wanted to go, so I dodged into a dark entrance and let them pass again, and thought I was safe, but an arm stole around me and a breath scraped my ear, "Hulluuww, darling! Doing anything tonight?"

I killed a scream and replied, "No, minding my business," but he insisted on trying to do business with me; I writhed, punching his hip with mine, so that a bottle in the pocket of his raincoat shattered, but he only felt for my hollows and murmured "Nice time, yes?" I pulled his cap down over his face, and while his right hand went up to dislodge it I spun, unwinding myself from his left; he came after me whining "Nice time!" and the others heard and about-turned. "Seen a girl?" they shouted to him; he tried to stall: "Girl, what sort of a girl?"— "An ideal girl"— "That was her" he admitted, and on they came. It wasn't quite fair, they had relays of leaders, and they were again on the point of catching me (How would relays of leaders help, Fristy? This isn't a bicycle race. Stop and think before you speak. Okay. But how about "Think before you cough," don't some people need that said to them? The thought is worth pursuing. "Think before you scratch." "Think before you breathe"), and this time, rising in a skip, I seized a fire-escape ladder that ended eight feet above the ground. I scrambled up onto it as if a bear was after me, and was able to relax awhile, looking down on them and making them a short speech, and stamping on the fingers of the few who had energy for the leap. Then I ascended toward an open fourth-floor window, but decided not to disturb the yoga class inside, because I could hear a pouring of feet up the stairs. I started to slide back down, but saw I was trapped because a section waited below, in fact were giving each other a shoulder up to the bottom rung. On a ladder!—I tried to picture it (more interesting even than a tree; they'd have to swarm over my back one by one like ants as they took their turns) but to hesitate was to lose nerve for what I had to do: across the alley was another open window. I hung out from one hand and foot, then sprang, successfully spurning the sill and ducking the sash—and finding myself in the arms of a salesman in slippers and a bathrobe, which he had opened in enthusiasm while watching my motions on the ladder. The expression on this man's face when I came flying in through his window—it lifted his toupee clean off his brow. After a short dance around his rented room he backheeled me and felled me onto the bed. "Okay," I said, caught at last. (Amazing: on my back, I immediately felt closer to yielding.) "But I'm a professional. Thirty bucks, which ought to be forty for my travel expenses, but I'll make it twenty for you, or twenty-one if you want all the trimmings. Let's make it fifteen, because once I start moving you're liable for Value Added Tax." He was only too pleased. "Cash first—oh well, put it on account if you like, just shake on it." Readily he stuck out his hand, and I grabbed his thumb and, twisting, laid him on the linoleum, and got out, but he followed, one arm in his bathrobe and one leg in his pants and one toe still in each of his slippers, bawling something about "britch of promise" as he harried me along the hallways. I tore open fire-doors and laundry-room doors and stairhead doors and a door that said PLEASE CLOSE THIS DOOR AS IT CREATES A DRAFT THAT CAN BE FELT ON THE THIRD of what month I didn't have time to read and even a door that said PLEASE USE ANOTHER DOOR and slammed them behind me, but like any salesman he breezed through doors as if they weren't there. I tore open the door marked

legs-icon skirt-icon

and inside it the door marked

legs-icon

thinking he wouldn't chase me in there, but I heard him coming and nipped into a stall and as he nipped into it after me I vaulted over into the next stall and out and into the door marked

skirt-icon

but so did he—those icons, by the way, would be clearer (not all females wear skirts nor all males pants) if they just showed profile figures with their respective protuberances—and we did the same stall-jump there and I ran out but forgot which way I'd come and took several wrong turns within this submaze that all public buildings have (while he mistakenly sometimes took the right turns) until we both at last—I only slightly before him—found the back of the door marked

legs-icon skirt-icon

and were out into the fresh air, or at least the main corridor. We bolted down the stairs, his slippers spanking the steps, and through a department store ("ALL UPLIFTERS WILL BE VERSECUTED") where we got mixed up with the swastikas and spun around them several times (I'm talking about the swastikas that clothes hang on) and an all-night diner, where the only eaters I noticed—and the only ones who never noticed me— were a young orange-haired mother and a little homely blond girl of three, the two of them talking into each other's blue eyes with such tender smiling love that I thought: "There are worlds and worlds." But I had to canter through a glass door into yet another street.

I was trying to circle to the right and get back to where I had parted from my treacherous friends. But my plan was bollixed—nixed, I mean—because here came a bloody nother posse, which had gone around a block to head me off. I was on a collision course with the middle one of the row; thought of lowering my head and ramming him amidribs, but had a better idea: laughed gaily and pointed at his fly. (It *was* open, but I didn't necessarily blame him for that—the little tabs by which you pull zippers up not only are in danger—if you're not wearing a clevel—of tangling with your personal hairs, but have a habit of getting stuck in the seam if you leave them pointing down, so that you can't get hold of them in a hurry—in fact you sometimes need pliers or the tip of a screwdriver. MAN, 22, CIRCUMCISES SELF WHILE TRYING TO FREE FLY.) His eyes and hands went down; I placed my hands on his bowed head and leapfrogged over it (the skirt barely opened wide enough) and was off. The others hooted with glee, and I noticed again that the laughter even of lummoxes is a girl, or at least its voice hasn't broken. "All right, Nimblenina—but we'll get you." Another corner, a street of more respectable air, but heedless behind me came my would-be clients. "Here, you can't rape schoolgirls in this neighborhood!" shouted a pensioner, but they answered "She's a hooker, she's leading us on!"— "See that hip, that's what she hooked us with"— "You should've seen her hook us with that hip!" Well, I was beginning to think, this is too much effort, why don't I just let myself be caught?— but I was running more easily now, I'd remembered that the trick is not to burp, then you don't get that breathlessness-in-the-legs (but an occasional yawn is okay, it boosts your oxygen. As for sending packets of wind in the other direction, it might add propulsion and stun the pursuit, but I haven't yet learned the art of it). I am long of leg (we are the running apes, aren't we?) and sound in wind (as they say of horses, and sometimes I blow my lips scofflingly like a horse—looks awful, shows the teeth), and if there'd been an uphill stretch I could have left them far behind—they were still wasting their breath laughing and shouting things like "Just Say Yes!" I felt one of the reasons I like running: it makes the glushes bounce, so you can feel where they begin and end. Most girls turn their glushes out as they run, so their knees knock together. Could we run if we didn't have glushes? —But enough of run-theory: just run! One more corner and I was back at the bus stop. No bus, one charlady standing, as I passed I called "When's the next bus?"— "Last bus twelve-ten"— "Hold me a place!"—it seemed I was going to have to sprint round and round the district (an exactly integral number of times) till ten past midnight. Again the corner—Hiptilt Corner—it must be the same corner, for still standing there bargaining with her customer was the tart who had set the lurid example. With the pack at my heels, once more I whipped (controlling my hips this time) around the corner into the alley.

But it was not the same alley. It was a blind alley, seven or eight running-paces long.

Picked Up

I SURVEYED it in a split second; I had to.

Its only features, other than trashcans and drainpipes and another custard tart—I mean another tart-customer pair—were three doorways. The one on the left was down three steps and over it hung a rusty sign:

RUBY EL'S GLUSHBROTHEL
buy one get one free
UNLIMITED FREE REAMING
while choosing

Its brown paint was peeling and it had a look of desperation; perhaps it appealed to too limited a clientele, or perhaps it had recently been eclipsed by the wide glass doors in the middle. Over these stretched HOUSE OF APPLEPEEL, and stuck to them or standing outside or in the brightly lighted foyer other signs abounded—LATEST APPLEPEEL NEWSREEL, BE WITH APPLEPEEL THROUGH HYPNOSIS, MEET FRIENDS OF FRIENDS OF APPLEPEEL, HAND SATISFACTION BY APPLEPEEL NARRATORS . . . I found myself at the back of a small crowd pressing in at these doors, blocking me even if I had wanted to go that way. Since the crowd pressing into the alley behind me was faster-moving, I had no time to decide what to do, but it was automatic: I ran up the step on the right and burst open the third and only respectable door, the one with a discreet brass plaque STATE INSPECT-ED. Already there were several hands at my tail; if they had settled for grabbing the tail of my shirt I wouldn't have got through the door, but I did and slammed it behind me, and luckily there was a chair just inside, which I tipped and placed under the doorhandle. Ayy-*hee!*

The porter who had been sitting on the chair dusted himself off and said stiffly to me, "You know, young lady, this is outrageous."

"Outrageous!" I said, and I leaned my head on the chest of his blue uniform and burst into sobs.

I was only sobbing to get my breath back, but it did the trick, and he escorted me up the narrow stairs to an office where a gentleman in a white labcoat sat slumped behind a desk. This doctor listlessly motioned me toward him and selected a purple fountain pen from his pocket (he was one of those technical men who have a substantial left breast composed of serried pens and pencils, together with a sliderule, a calculator, a thermometer, a flashlight, a battery-lighted magnifying glass, a toothpick, a spectacle-case, a nail-file, a tire pressure gauge, a cell phone, and three cigars in their wrappers; plus a platinum label pinned to the front, with the legend "HICKET" (his name?) and a U.S. eagle).

"Well, who are you?"

"Adame."

"I know you're a dame. What's your name?"

"Adame," I said, pronouncing it differently. "De Mont d'Eve."

"I didn't quite catch the surname, but never mind; better to be without. Not your true name, I take it?—would you like me to suggest another?"

"Oh no, please don't!"

"All right, just answer a few basics: are you prepared to go down?—to go around the world?" and a string of other abstract questions; I soon found it went quicker if I answered "Yes," otherwise he would stop and demand "Why not?" He jotted checks in a long line of boxes, then had me touch my toes and stand between his knees while he applied a stethoscope. He took my temperature orally and, while I was silenced, a back-up way.

"Not in very good shape, are you? Even I can climb the stairs without quite so much puffing. Lead an inactive life, don't you, vege-tate in front of the tee vee like so many kids these days. What you need is some regular bumpy exercise to shake up these—lungs—and pelv-muscles, we'll see if we can find you some. You've got no Virtual Clevel, I see, or Virtual Breastlet; same color all over; did you never get any sun? A man might fail to locate your bestparts." But he managed to locate them, and reaching the last detail of my medical inspection he exclaimed "Strike me dead with a feather, you really are a virgin!"

That was a relief: I hadn't been sure what he would find. I felt all the better about Saxie and the several other people who had by now handled me. I felt that if ever I could get safely out of here I'd just live happily with Saxie—and Spot and Master Yoryo, also Granny Oe and my old nursemaid Zed, and old Him, our gardener, all together in some quiet place. Even the Mongertwins if they'd behave, and maybe let Ritan the Innocent come visiting and Eugene Bluejean and that poor salesman (who's probably still tearing around that hotel tearing doors open) and even Mr. Theopard Justings—no, no!—

While I stood thus meditating, Doctor Hicket suddenly made a violent and successful attack. He shoved me so that I crashed down into a corner which was arranged like a small alcove, piled with white cush-ions and half screened with plastic curtains; and there was an ultravio-lent flash and a reptilian buzz as an automatic camera took a picture, which it then extruded from its jaw like a tongue. "Album photo," said this egregious official, as he detached it and looked it over. "The skirt flew up quite well, but I wouldn't call the face horrified enough—you even look amused, that won't do." I had, after a moment of sprawling in astonishment and rebounding into a defensive posture, got up to look at the photo with him, but when I saw he was about to ram me again I held up my hand: "Please," I said, and this time I threw my own self down. The doctor took the camera from its bracket and aimed it manually, and I had to hold my panicky face and flared legs while he chose an angle. "Much better," he said— "you're quite a ham. Remind me to take a few more later when you're wearing less, and I guess we need a saycheezy face shot." (I never did remind him and he forgot all about it.)

"Have some puréed spinach, Adame," he said, resuming his place behind his desk and serving me a saucer of it from a little office hot-ring on which he kept it simmering. I got up a shade reluctantly from the nest of cushions. "If you have any questions please feel free to answer them" (handing me a leaflet entitled "Patient Information," as if I might tire it out). "I expect you're wondering how come I'm pasting this photo in beside the list of all the things you're Willing to do; well, you'd be amazed at the power of men to believe clashing things at the same time. Anxious to begin, are you?" "To begin?" "Yes, of course you are, but I'm afraid we're rather quiet here. You will have noticed our competition," and he made a shrug toward the bright light and raving noise (the Sex Objects' "Ahlavva Piece a' Appupeel") that came in through the window overlooking the alley. "But you are newly arrived from France, non?" he said. "Hein?"

"Ah oui m'sieu," I faltered. "Hélas."

"A visiteuse from the land of the enchantante forerunner, Gamine Boiredeau. So you cannot know."

"Who is zis Apilpil?" I enquired— "some gross estar?" ("Grand estar" was what I meant.)

"Applepeel! No. She's a girl. That's all she needs to be."

"She doesn't sing or dance?"

"Sing? or dance? For Applepeel," he said to me with slow emphasis, "it's enough to *be*. If she were to sing, people would—people would have to lie down; would have to go climb mountains. Would melt and become pure. If Applepeel were to *dance*," and he began to faint, "we would all die."

Here was final proof to me of the disconnection of legends from life. He was talking like this, piling Applepeel on Applepeel to overtop heaven, while indifferently staring the living Applepeel in the face.

(Well, he was staring slightly over my shoulder. And his glasses were primrose-tinted, which could have quenched my color scheme.)

A thought occurred to me: had it perhaps reached the point where I would no longer be able to prove that I was Applepeel? There was hope that it had.

I meditatively set my hands on my hips and tried a quiet jolt and pirouette or two, and ended with my knee stuck out.

He brought his eyes all the way back to mundane reality. "Keep still, lassie," he said. "I like the schoolgirl getup. You've done your homework on our country. But this is a government institution, we aren't allowed to use minors."

"But taking my uniform off wouldn't change my age," I said.

"I think you'll find it will," he said, without asking my age. "Let's find you some nudewear," and he peered into a closet where things were hanging. "How about this—white boots and a short white cloak. Let's try the test."

He handed the outfit to me. Still sitting slumped in his chair, which was on casters, he scooted it out from behind his desk by paddling with his feet. I dropped my demure clothes, except that he now noticed the white socks, and I had to stand hopping with one sock half off.

"Those spectacular splashes of mud—an artful touch, suggestive of schoolgirl misadventure. Another time, them only, but now off," and I finished stripping my feet. Then I picked up the boots. "I think it's coming," he said as I pulled them on. Then I straightened up and took the cloak or cape, which was of stiffish mock leather, white with black buttonholes and a black lining silky to the skin. It went over my shoulders, with a collar upstanding to my earlobes, and was fixed with just a large brooch at the throat, from which it opened out to show the inner breastsides and ended not far offshore of my elbows.

"Yes, you see," he said, indicating for me the snail-like bulge in his trousers. "I do get a kick out of those boots. Ahem. Better not think about being witty or I'll lose it. Turn. Now turn just your face back; and, you know, gleam at me." (He didn't seem to like to say a word as strong as *smile*.) So I had another shot at the glance-back-over, left shoulder this time; I made a gleam, or glisten, with my cheek and eye. His shoulders jolted forward as if he had been struck in the middle and

---

* This paragraph has had to be compressed. Each raiment minimally mentioned by the doctor deserves lengthy description.

he said: "What did I tell you? I wouldn't promote you to *woman* even now, but anybody would bet you've left the age of consent some distance behind. Turn some more, let it swing out—that's enough, definitely will do. *Adame*," he intoned, associating Adame and costume.

"We match each other, don't we?" I said.

"What d'you mean, girl?"

"Well, white and white."

He looked at me curiously, then made an *"oh dear"* hand-wave: "I'd like to oblige you," he said wearily, *"pet,"* he added effortfully, "but I have to operate in the mornings (can't live on a government whoremaster's salary) and it puts one off. I might be able to do it in the dark?" he suggested wanly.

I realized what he was talking about, and said "No, that's all right," and he was glad to let the snail ooze away.

"Ah," he said. "That wasn't too bad. I'm not one of those with a permanent hard, but I do, like everyone in this Age of Applepeel, this Applepeel Age, have to be careful to be pointing up when I pull my clothes on, in case the thought of her crosses my mind at some awkward moment. But," he confided, "even if you were Applepeel, I might not be able to Achieve—you know. That's the trouble with dealing in fantasies and strangers. Everyone who comes here wants a stranger or (which is the same thing) a fantasy, so I've had to take on their way of thinking. Within seconds, I'd be in danger of feeling you no longer a stranger, so I'd have to start over with you as another kind of stranger—a slave, say, a captive, a dancer or a kitchen slut or a royal daughter served to me at a court (ancient or oriental); and still I'd have to race before again you were no stranger, and my mind would have to hammer you into some other stranger . . . Do you see? Even if you were Applepeel, who is the perpetual stranger, the perpetually new." "I do see."

So that was that, but what was next? Nothing. We settled back. He seemed to have time on his hands for talking.

"We have to rely on the costumes nowadays—would you like to see some others? This is the thing Benice wears when we send her out to parties, a sort of farthingale, it'll only stay up while she holds it up. If someone offers her a cocktail and a handshake—it becomes a great *ankleskirt*." "And that hanging next to it," I asked, "it looks like a skirt too, or is it pants?" "It's both, it's what she calls a calfskirt: it's got such wide bottoms—excuse me, the part from the knees downward—it looks like a skirt swishing along, but that's to set off how tight it is knee-up; you've never really seen thighs till you've seen them in these. And

this is Miss Anita Parvue's window suit.* She's got another with magnifying glasses instead. Or she likes to wear a negative bikini, or a
transparent figleaf, or three picture frames, or a strap wound 8-shape
around her crotch, or a star on the tip of each nipple 'n glush, or a suit
of adhesive bits (takes an hour to strip even if they don't dice for turns),
or a huge bustle with man-chambers inside it, or a loose nightgown
tucked into her clefts, or a Belt and Tail, or a Puss-in-Boots (just big
black waders and rabbit-fur gloves), or painted zones or arrows or
target-circles, or lightbulbs inside her dress, or a Chinese clevel-box
(that's a series of them, one inside another, each smaller than the last,
you keep thinking you've got to the smallest but there's a smaller yet),
or a plain suit with a large *F* on it. Quite a wardrobe she has, that one.
I almost forgot her Trikini, with the arrangement of threads so that each
of the erozones is covered independently (and uncovered independently)—and the Quadrikini version, and the Monokini—well, the Monokini is actually only remnant kini, Trikini or Quadrikini in a late stage of
reduction; the Badge (we call it) when it's reduced to this triangle. And
there's the Triple Revelation: pop the snap that's at the navel and it flies
off all three zones simultaneously. I remember hearing someone
exclaim, at seeing her come on stage in one of her more conventionally queeny outfits, 'What a magnificent setting for a cunt!' She's got
talent too—she was Versa in *Vice and Versa*, but the bottom's dropped
out of porn flicks now, no one wants to see anything that hasn't got
applecore in it. Our other girl who's on now, Smyle, is wearing two
ostrich feathers planted in her, or was, when she and her customer
closed that door."

The door, which I had taken for that of a safe, must have been
soundproof. Nothing had come from behind it to give variety to our
duologue. (The faint sounds that I did distinguish, and fortunately he
did not, were raps on the locked door downstairs and the porter stolid-
ly refusing them. Once a face appeared at the window—someone had
struggled up a drainpipe—but fell away before the doctor noticed it.)

"Excuse me, Doctor, what are we waiting for?"

"For the telephone to ring."

"I see. No storefront traffic?"

"Hardly; we've almost given up on it. You know, very few people
are fucking any more. They're waiting for Applepeel, and meanwhile
just talking or dreaming or masturbating about her. Natural orgasm is
out. You didn't realize that?"

No, nor did I believe it.

"To make any sales at all these days," he said, "you've got to stock the somewhat Applepeelish types: Approxapeels, as they're called—the ones with at least a touch of the killing look. (The Appleal, as it's called.) That's why I didn't turn you away."

"I have a little of it, do I?"

"Yes, you have the eyes. *Tu as um'p'tit j'n'sais-quoi d'la Pomm'p'lure"*—he held up the phrasebook he was studying: *How to Say 'You Look a Bit Like Applepeel' in 36 Languages.* "For my Whitsun vacation," he said with a thin smile.

"'A Bit'! That seems on the modest side. Girls don't usually want to be told they're a bit or a shade anything."

"Well, exaggeration spoils believability," he said. "And maybe—tuck your leg up under you again, would you, the way you were doing, sit on your heel?—yes, maybe other components. A necklace or something would do a lot for you, you know—earrings, have you ever thought of earrings? . . . Anyway, it's either that or work harder than ever on the old tricks, the ridiculous clothes and the specialty promises. We have relatively few—but special—patrons. Patrons who like to have—special experiences, you know; extended—experimental—experiences . . . That's why we're waiting for the phone to ring."

I decided I'd give the phone another hour. I didn't know how it would offer a way out, but at least it would be a development. If not, I'd risk the street door. It was coming up on one in the morning.

"If you like, you can wait in your bower," he said, indicating a white-washed archway with blue curtains set open.

And he went back to reading Applepeel magazines while I wandered in there and tried the couches. It was something of an equipment bay. Variously shaped blocks of carved foam stood on the blue carpet, and by them were pictures demonstrating their use. I liked the girl in the pictures. "Yes, her name was Elvet," the doctor told me. "She was double-jointed—don't you try all that." Also on the wall hung an embroidered sampler that said:

NSNEEE

What was it?—an eye test?—a geographical direction? I asked the doctor and he said sharply without looking up: "No Sadism No Excrement Everything Else." "No Say . . . Could you put that in shorter words for me?" "How about four-letter ones," he answered impatiently, "would they do?—No Shit No Pain Thee Rest Okay. House rules. —Actually," he added after several moments of reflection (how long is several moments?), "you could add No Pregnancy. P plus P equal negative P: Pornography and Prostitution admit no Procreation. Sex makes no babies here. Babes yes, babies no" he trailed away, and I felt sorry for him. I nodded and looked around some more and next I wondered about the curtains: "Do you watch?" "*I* don't," he said, "but we sometimes invite a small civic audience." Eventually I just stretched out on one of the altars and idly flipped my cloak and dug dirt out of my toenails and hummed hymnbits that came back to me— "When all was sin and shame, A second Adam to the fight And to the something came"— and listened to the noise still raving along outside the window (*shi . . . shi . . . shi . . .* —it still takes me a while to realize that that intermittent rustling *shi* is me) and I may have dozed. This was the eye of the hurricane of the night.

("May have dozed!" I hear you say—or Saxie or my mother; "you know darn well you'll have slept like a baby." Not like a baby, for babies stay in one place, whereas I found I had swarmed over several structures and was wedged in a kind of stocks, with side-slots for other bodies.) When I opened my eyes, the doctor was still at his desk, and the clock above him had only just crept past one; it was on slow time, to make you think the night was in its teen-age. But all this was jangled from my mind by what had woken me.

The telephone rang.

"Yes, Mr. Parolong. As it happens we have a new one right now, who'll do anything. Literally. Checked every box. Yes, I can't remember another instance. No, on the contrary, an absolute beginner—a youngle but useful—useful though youthful—usefully youthful—no more than a-teen—a teenyer, maybe an eighteenyer (you like?) or younger than teams of teens—younger, she looks, than the rest of us put together. In fact, hmm! a Spica"—(dropping his voice, and imagining I couldn't guess his codeword)— "can you handle that? Adame; might well be called Supplepeel, I'd say; never even heard of Applepeel; that fresh. And French, into the bargain; Frenchwench. Oh no, she'll understand as much as you need her to. You'll charge it, won't you?—and arrive in the usual way?"

I sat up. "What's his usual way?" I asked. It sounded a shade alarming, as if he would materialize, or be delivered in a box. "On a iggle!" said the doctor; he too was sitting up brightly, busying himself with data entry; he giggled. "You have maybe less than a minute. Get yourself mateready—could you use cuntlube? a tot of rum?"

"No, that's all right. What's Supplepeel mean?"

"Supplepeel—some will tell you it's short for Super-Applepeel, but that of course is impossible, a heresy." (A deep thrum became audible.) "It really stands for Sub-Applepeel, Substitute Applepeel" (his voice rose as the sound magnified and became bumpy; where was it? I felt vibration, glanced down and snatched my feet off the floor. Never mind explaining Supplepeel, tell me what's happening—they're removing the wall that holds this room up!)— "Successor to Applepeel, somebody who, if we give up hope that Applepeel herself—"

It swelled to a throbbing roar: it was in the ceiling! I jumped up and ran as far as the archway and looked back. The noise grew worse, worse, the ceiling opened, and down out of the black sky came a noose.

Picked Up Higher

IT CAME bobbing and swinging through the hole, and having penetrated the room in many wavering thrusts it flopped onto the floor. "Put your foot in it!" called the doctor gaily.

"Oh yes! Sure! Why not my head?"

"No, your foot, he's not into ess-em. Go on—hee hee, you're scared, aren't you!"

"I am not," I said, and I strode forward and put my foot through the noose. It started to lift off the floor.

"Not through it, you idgit, put your foot *on* it, on the bottom!—Phew" (the doctor's sobriety returned for a moment), "now grab the rope—ah. I should have done a bit of explaining, but he didn't give us time, he called from his heli-phone. He just wants you to go up with him and commit"—and I lost the doctor's voice, together with his white coat and the other incongruous and illuminated sights of the interior, and found myself above the city, suspended in a ferocious downdraft of the impure city air.

I gave a little scream, not because I was frightened but because, like many females, I can't help doing this when my body is transferred either upward or downward faster than my stomach. My scream was lost in the blast.

My cloak protected me from the worst of it. Then the roar of the wings above me grew even more strident, we shot upward faster, I screamed higher, the city (now staggering into its ill-earned dawnward sleep) shrank to a nest of spider-eye lights—and a rasping noise began at my throat. The brooch tore out: the cloak suddenly whipped down me and was nothing but a handkerchief swallowed in the vortex.

"Hold out your foot," said a voice above, "let's see if it can do *that*."

I was curious too, and with another roar the downdraft unzippered my left white boot and fired it at the planet like a meteor. This effort put us near the stratosphere.

"Now change foots," came the call.

"No, Mr. Parolong," I called back, trying to look up, but my eyelids got sealed, "I'm damn cold, no more fun till you pull me up."

"No naked out in public view, eh?"

"That's right, sir. Too shocking for the town." (Or rather the province, at this height.)

"Tell me exactly what you desire," he insisted.

"I refuse to finish stripping myself to heretofoot nakedness until I can be shut up alone with Mr. Parolong in some inaccessible private place of his and hug his whole body with my whole body so I can get some heat back into me," I chattered. He was pleased and hauled me up.

I emerged (with an earnest sigh of *"Ayhi"*) into a dial-illuminated bubble in the sky. My host first backed away from me, then: "Henry Parolong, attorney," he said, offering me his card (which said something like "Smith, Brown, Jones, Parolong, Black, Reed, Sims, Swagg, Whag, White, Green, Damyer & Fockutt"). I ignored it and seized his small tight-coated figure in a long embrace that transferred to him most of my breathlessness and shivering. I thought he expected it, but he disengaged himself as soon as he could, which was when I noticed that he was struggling to. I did not seem to have an awful lot to fear from him.

Muttering, he grabbed his controls and put us back on an even keel—not before I had had to let out a couple more screams. They were almost perfunctory by now, but he found them charming. Realizing the cause, he elicited some more by bouncing the helicopter up and down. "A pretty shower!" he said. His pleasure was not hearty—he merely cocked an ear toward me for each scream, grimaced during it, and gave a dry laugh after it—but since he wouldn't stop I lurched across the floor, seized his head, and positioned my mouth by his ear.

"All right," he said. "We're not up here to enjoy ourselves." "We're not?"—I staggered back as we took off for open country. Through the hatchway I saw the rope snatch itself horizontal; I was glad not to be out there trying to hold on.

This place looked like being a shade harder to get safe away from. I wondered how many of my nine lives I had left.

Having set a steady course, he turned his back on his controls and stood inspecting me. My air legs, which I had to keep wide apart, weren't so steady. He seemed warmed but not especially cheered by the sight of them. Some people do find it more difficult to live than others. "Vegetarian, please, for my in-flight snack," I requested, and gave him a smile. He tottered back and fell to a sitting position against a window.

"Don't do that again," he said, getting to his feet and dusting off his black coat.

"Don't do what?"

"Grin at me. I've got a weak heart, you know."

"Oh, all right." So I had to try to keep my face straight as well. I dropped my eyes and stood smoothing my pussyhair. "But I do—fit, do I?"

"Fit," he said; "fit . . ." He began to sway and blink. Mastering himself and getting his heels together, he said: "Would you kindly not use such suggestive words? In fact, would you kindly just keep still? I can hardly bear to look at you as it is. But take your hands away from there." I braced them on the struts of the wall. "And don't look back at me." I turned my head aside. "Oh no no! the suffering grace of the throat! as transfixing as the interrogative eyes! Face this way but keep your eyelids down. I just want to take in your appleasing applearance without being stabbed prematurely." Finally my passive image was settled to his satisfaction, and he glanced at his wristwatch and gave himself seven seconds of it. "The melting of thigh into mound," he said, "endlessly subtle. And dressed in one white boot. One, White, Boot. A felicitous fortuity. Don't take it off."

I wasn't going to—it might be needed as a weapon. But its high heel put unintended cockiness into my stance. I thought I'd sit down, and looked around for the bed or bunk, but there wasn't one.

"Do you know the country below us?" he asked.

A funny question in the middle of the night. "I know it," I felt like saying, "like the back of my hand, as the gloved lady said." But when I looked down I found that the moon had risen; thin, wrinkled, but she sent out fingers to trace for me some clues—a hook of river, the glitter of a roof. The time must be getting on for four.

"Yes, I think I may."

"What manner of land is it, what are its names, its associations?—is it a gentle land or a bleak?"

Was he expecting answers or should these questions stay where they were in his corny rhetoric?

"One of the names is Closeover," I said. "And another is Sunnymead."

"In me," he said, "you see the Public Prosecutor. I have passed my whole life in that city, which is as black as my garb is black and as my spirit is black. Oh, I have flown on my ruthless errands to other cities as black or blacker, passing over the fleshlike innocence of the countryside but never touching down on it. Sunnymead—let this be our destination."

The helicopter slowed, leaned, and began to circle by itself. He unfixed his bow tie.

"What about your joystick, Henry? Shall I grab it?"

(I won't mention the screams any more, they would make you think I wasn't calm.)

"What does it matter, during this our ultimate act?"

"You bring girls up here and mate with them in flight, do you?"

"Mate with them in flight!—like heedless moths!" He laughed lugubriously.

"I suppose," I said as the helicopter's sideslips amplified, "you've done it so often you know you can right us in time." It looked like being quite a thrill.

He wore a mournful smile (and nothing else) and stepped toward me.

"Watch out, the hatch!" I said—it was between us. "Better close it before you forget."

"Lean toward me over it," he said, "let us grasp each other, and unite as we pass through."

"What! Not likely! Where's my parachute?"

"How poignant, even to the exquisite asymmetry of your one white boot, which stands for the one foot I suspect you are still ever so slightly reluctant to withdraw from this world of evil."

"*Both* feet," I yelled, "I plan to set *both* of my feet back on this wicked world!"

"Don't say I have to force you to the deed?"

"That's what I do say!" (or scream).

We fought a skirmish around the gaping view of poplars and church steeples and fields of yellow rape reeling in the moonlight. "Drattyer," he gasped— "ruining it—I should have demanded a less lively—may be impossible to do away with any two of whom you're one—" Out of his radio came a garble of crosswired avio chatter ("radial one two eight decimal nine-ah" "tracking the Western Macks via Gosse's Bluff" "leaving four thousand for two thousand" "Bravo Uniform Tango, where are you?" "No additional" "The captain has turned off the Fasten Seatbelts sign" "Je vous souhaite un équable vol" "Caution! you are approaching the end of the moving walkway" "a range of duty-free Gifts, Gadgets and Fragrances" "seatback-jiggling war broken out between rows 44 and 45" "Do not leave the baggage unattended" "return to the upright position and breathe normally" "**MIND THE GAP** between the plane and the planet" "passengers Carrera, Izaaksen and Wong. Will passengers Carrera, Izaaksen and Wong kindly get their ass over to Gate Nineteen") mixed somehow with flight physics ("At what speed would a loofah in orbit have the same impact as a baseball thrown by Sandy Koufax?") and plain cellphone ("It's worth every penny of the money we wasted on it," "That's self-confidence for you, ditching your man before you're sure of another," *"Siamo a Lodi"*) Whirling past, I flicked a switch and screamed "Calling all stations: Applepeel in danger!" Before I could even add "Over," out crackled an answer: "Yippee! Where? Over." "High over Closeover; over. Well, not so high any more, rather too close over, over!" "Ten four—film crew on way, over! Airborne Applepickers scrambling!" *"Danger*, you nitwits, Applepeel in grip of murderous monster" (I was hanging onto Henry's wrists), "Applepeel about to be lost to world; reward reserved for rescuer, ov—" Henry broke from me and tore the radio off the wall. We crouched again, facing each other across infinity.

"You're *not* Applepeel," he instructed me.

"Well, I am, in so far as it matters. —But not if you say so," I added concessively.

"I know you are—that was already obvious—but for the purpose of this act you're not. I didn't ask for luck and I don't care for my end to be famous." —Distracting me with a jab to the breast, he got me by my hair and brought me forward over the hole, but released me as my exquisite asymmetry connected with his shin. I had to leap to his side; distracting him with a tenor C when he expected a scream, I swung him around, and he had to leap to where I had been on the other side and I taunted him, "Go on, jump, you're the one who wants to!"

"Only with you and in you, Adame!" he pleaded. "You promised that you'd come with me on the journey into oblivion!"

"I did not!"

"Not in so many words, but you promised to do *anything!*"

"Oh, I see! Well, I didn't check any suicide box!"

"You checked the box that said *Anything else.* The first in history, the doctor told me, to dare to go to that excream! (Extreme.) Do not forsake your sublime excremism!"

"But it might hurt, and that would be against the house rules."

"We're outside the house now," he countered. (These lawyers!)

"Well, I'm ready to do *anything else* than this," I said illogically and licentiously. "I'll tickle your goolies—"

"Stop—"

"Oh, that's right, some men can't stand that" (Crazy Joy had told me); "well, I'll use my t—"

"You'll jump with me," he interrupted, "or I'll crash this thing anyway."

"You mean it?"

"Yes. So reflect, Adame: falling could be your last and best experience. You'll see your whole life before you—"

"What, all seventeen years of it? Hey, there could be a novel about that: she sees her whole life—"

"Eighteen, I trust you mean. In any case you have to die in two minutes, so which would be better: amid—mated to—a mass of twisted metal, or snatching a last bliss in the arms of—"

"A mass of twisted lawyer!"

He winced. "You may sneer at one whom life has used longer and worse than you—" He wiped his eye.

I began to relent. But no: "Henry," I screamed, or rather urged, "dear Henry Parolong, you've got to try and take a more cheerful view! Wouldn't it be better still to snatch that bliss in a parachute?—and maybe we'd land in a haystack and go on with the bliss there!"

He considered me for a moment, though moments were running out as our craft spiralled drunkenly down the last thousands of feet. (Bothered by a pressure in the ears, I tried a yawn, but couldn't consummate it.) I pursued what seemed to be my advantage: "Why, it's a fine idea of yours, Henry, love in free fall—weightless!—like the flying gods!—so many more possibilities than, say, being tied up. Why spoil it with such a sudden end?—why not parolong it (so to speak)?—I bet you're Mr. Prolong himself! Parachute, Henry—otherwise we'll have, what, ten seconds?—is that long enough for you to ejaculate?—or five, because stuck together we'll fall twice as fast!" "If you believe that," he interjected scientifically, "you *deserve* to die." "Better yet," I pursued, "how about a soft landing in the helicopter, and *then* bliss in the haystack?—otherwise we might miss it and find ourselves in a gas tower or a goat paddock—"

"Do you know how to use this?" he interrupted, offering me a bundle.

"What is it?"

"A parachute."

"What do I pull—"

"I'll show you—hold it tight!" He jerked the bundle back so that I toppled toward him, and he tried to twist it aside and meet me. I should have dived to the floor, but the instinct to fight for uprightness served me badly and with a peach of a scream I plummeted through the hole. Instead it was he who got the horizontal impetus and, momentarily stuck across the hole, lost the bundle and me; the last I heard of him was a cry of "Wait!"—how was I supposed to wait?—and I was alone in space with the parachute, and then not even with that: I snatched at it, but it fell away from me upward, opening out against the pit of the sky, a purple-and-yellow-petalled flower that hid Parolong and helicopter and zenith.

Dropped in It

A ND LOOKING down I saw the village pond multiplying in size, and I fell into it, thus offering only a poor challenge to the record of Vesna Vulovic, airline stewardess, who on the 26th of January, 1972, without a parachute, fell thirty-three thousand three hundred and thirty feet (six miles and a bit) and lived. The disemboweling by antic-ipation—sensation horrific enough on roller-skates before a curb, and this was *down*—lower belly gripped by absence, getting absenter, hanging back, into the ribs, above the head, screeching at the rest of me to stop!—after this the watersmash itself was a relief, though it would have been worse if I hadn't remembered to hold my nose and other apertures. The pond as I split it felt like ice—harder than water, I mean, though a tad warmer than the sky; I was shot-stripped of air from toes to scalp; my boot ran into goosh that was chiefly composed of duckshit and reached a tenth of the way to the center of the earth. A green bubble of marsh gas the size of a television scream rose past my eyes and for what seemed like five minutes I thought this was the last gas I would ever breathe.

But I fought a mighty squelchwrestle with the mud, and at last up became up and my head broke the surface, with a drake standing on it and a curtain of slime showering off it, through which I saw that Henry, despite efforts to dodge my parachute, had found himself floundering at its midpoint, surrounded by hills of billow that mocked all determi-nation to crawl back to danger. It caught between two elms and turned slowly over, tipping him out onto the village green with such sardonic gentleness that he arrived on his feet. (It was the helicopter, mean-while, that enjoyed itself in a haystack, setting it on fire.)

He was surprised to see me rise from the pond—or was he? no, he gave a curt glance as he picked his way out of the tangle of cordage.

"Lucky, eh?" I called.

"Luck nothing. Vitality," he grumbled; "I should have known; you've got enough to keep any *ten* alive. And now what am I to do?" His concern about his own predicament was a healthy sign.

"Tear it up into something you can wrap around you"—I meant the parachute— "and get walking quickly; the villagers are up before dawn. I've got to hurry myself. Oh, temporary refuge: there's an insane asylum just over the hill where they'll disbelieve your story till

* More likely *Vasa Vasa!* (Sicilian), "kiss kiss!"

you can think of something better. Hey, that was quite a sensation, wasn't it?—passion at terminal velocity might have its points. Goodbye, Henry—please cheer up, I love you, we'll meet again some day if you promise to stay alive. Become a Public Defender." Was that a twinge of joy? "Oh, Public Defender!" he said, "and I've got a job suggestion for *you.*" "What?" "Stuntman—stuntgirl, I mean!" and he actually grinned; I saw the fall had killed a melancholic. He studied the dripping of my beard as I came clambering out, and he did, for form's sake, invite me to tumble back in and co-drown with him; I dodged and declined. I was sorry to leave him, but the sky was turning pale. (I noticed that those fields of yellow rape made the moonlight look like sunlight.) The rush of fright through my system had done it so much good that I wanted to go sky-diving again, though curling up on a pillow was appealing too. *Ayhhi!* I suctioned my one boot off and left it sole-up on the school gatepost to drain; climbed back in with an hour of the night left, crept into the dormitory, tore back the bedclothes—

Wrong school!—more tired than I had realized. The boy opened his eyes on what he took for a wet-dream. "Vava Vava Vava!"* he said (his name for me?—I had heard that some of them called me Viva) with lips but not teeth open; hastily I dropped the covers back over him, but he fountained through them. I backed away, gazing in fascination as the stout column, a shade sluggish after welling through pajamas, sheet and three blankets, subsided to a black stain; with a beatific smile he closed his eyes, and I retreated by door, window, and drainpipe, streaked through the village—an early-rising cowhand saw a ghost—climbed into the right school with an hour left, crossed the floorboards with a minimum of creaking (the trick is diagonality), and slid into my bed—

"Very funny!" I shouted. The bed had been converted to an "apple pie," the kind where one sheet is folded back to look like two and you find yourself in a sack only long enough for a Tashartris bust to lie in. Actually I kept my shout to myself because waking my dear friends wouldn't have helped me. I leapt up and tore it all off and remade it so hastily that it was more like that new version of the trick (called for some reason an Apple Peel bed), left open at the foot for creepers-in (or, just possibly, for sleepers with hot feet); then at last I slumped down; my body began to dissolve to a drift of sand. You know how sometimes an arm or a leg goes to sleep?—I think there had been times in that night when my head went to sleep while the rest of me kept running. To raise me ever again from this bed was going to take an act of will, if not of Congress. But the dormitory was quieter than my senses expected.

So I lifted my head and saw that all the other beds were empty. I was too weary to wonder about it. My head dropped back and I slept for half an hour—which is just half an hour too much and an hour too little. Sometimes when time for resting is short you want to rest *hard*, but there's no way to rest *harder* (except perhaps by someone sitting on you). I was woken—if you could call it waking—I felt like a Sogdian—by them tramping back in.

"Boy, Felicity, you're in trouble for missing the fire drill!"

I pulled the sheet over my head and rediscovered sleep for another minute, and then my summons arrived and I was shaken out (before I scarcely had time to mutter "Okay I bess I getta bet up") to be frog-marched to my trial.

"Saxie," I said desperately, "can I borrow your second clothes?" (We all had two sets, but I had already lost my spares during an earlier exploit.)

Shaking her head sadly, she tried with pins to make them look reasonable on me. We had to give up on the breastlet. "Fristy, Fristy," she said, "what *have* you been doing, you've got mud in your hair"—gently she combed it out— "and a minnow . . . What's the matter?" "Nothing"; it was just one of the shudders of after-panic about the fall, mixed with a well-deserved yawn. "Stick a pin in my shoulder, please do—I need a dozen guardian angels standing on it, to advise against each kind of mistake I make—social, theological, financial . . ." The frogmarching squad snatched me away (Saxie nearly coming to blows with them for gripping me too tight) and off we went to the teachers' quarters.

We knocked, but they didn't hear us because someone was perking coffee; instead we heard them:

"Even this is not an occasion for a real Discipline," one was saying. "How come the gels are so demure this term? They seem even to have lost the interest they used to show in, ah, each other." "That too, I suspect, is the fault of this One Gel. One can see that, frankly, if one can't have her one doesn't want anyone." I was pushed in and caught sight of the head teacher picking her nose—no, she was powdering it. "Knock before entering!" she said furiously.

There they all sat in their armchairs, having thought this worth a rise before breakfast.

"Lying in sloth while others were out at the call of duty," she said; "for this, Pepper, what would you think a meet penalty?"

"To be sent to bed early, Sir?"

"An egregious response, Pepper—a *viciously stupid* onc. You need a lesson in natural consequences as well as in wakefulness and discipline. You will spend the whole of the coming night *up*. Each of us will invigilate you for an hour (pass around this sign-up sheet, ladies), imposing any activity of her choosing—such as calisthenics, polishing the floor, climbing ropes, playing poker . . . Any disobedience will merit instant corporal sanctions. That's all. Report here at ten tonight, and now go to morning roll-call, unless you have anything else to say."

I said "Oh, shit."

There was what I presently identified as a shocked silence. (My mother had only ever made shocked clamors.)

"Sir," I added, but it didn't do a whole lot of good.

Incident in Block L West

❝ WHAT DID you say, Pepper?"

"Shoot, Sir."

"We do not go quite to those lengths, Pepper. However, you are only too right in regarding this as a serious matter. It is one that cannot be allowed to pass. It is something that has to be stamped on."

"Can I point out, Sir, that I've just spent all night in a brothel, so that I'm rather pooped? Would that count as a mitigating circumstance?" I asked, inside my head. She was perorating: " . . . It is a Failure of Character."

"Yes, I can see it is. I'm sorry, Sir."

They sat back and allowed me to grovel. When I thought I had given them enough of this satisfaction, I got up from the floor and they dismissed the smiles from their faces and said: "You may get up now. It's no use saying you're sorry in order to get out of *being* sorry." Then, to their dismay, I broke down.

"*Stop* that lawfing, Pepper!" I couldn't. The guns of sarcasm had to be brought to bear— "You sound like a rooster laying an egg"—heavy and not always accurate. That set me off again. I was just too tired to resist. At length I sobered up and wiped away the tears. "Do I go straight over to the boys' school, Sir?"

"No, you go to your classes now, so that we can let it be known and they can all look on you with shuddering and pity. We will arrange for tomorrow the, ah—"

"The ordeal, Sir?"

"You could call it that, and it should be none the lighter for this display of attitude. But I can only suppose that your narves are exhaasted."

"Yes, Sar, that's it. And do I have to say goodbye to my friend?"

"Not unless you meditate an escape attempt. Which, I must say, we might wink at—*after* your chastisement."

"Ahem," put in Crussh, the Vice Principal, "don't forget the Debriefing."

"Right—the Debriefing. You will be returning here, Pepper, to serve as an example for a long time to come. But you have a friend, do you? Perhaps we ought to know who that is, so as to separate you from her influence or vice versa."

"No, Sir, not one. Well, if that's all for now, ta-ta, Cock," I said, thinking I might as well be spanked for a ram as a lamb, and started for the door, but collided with it as it was opened by none other than the head teacher from the boys' school.

How could they have sent the message that quick? But he hurried into the room, wearing a worried frown and unknowingly pushing me into the corner, and before they could say "We were just going to call you!" he burst out: "Ladies, I'm afraid I have news for you of great badness."

"Ah! A boy has to be sent over here?"

"Not just a boy! The whole school!"

"What do you mean? You can't mean this literally—an overtaxing of the Sunnymead disciplinary system—calm yourself, Mr. Quitetwice—sit down—have a cup of tea—explain yourself."

"The boys," he said, when he had sipped his tea and the women were all looking expectantly at him, their whiskers quivering, "on a geological excursion, found something in a field."

"A— A—?"

"A book," he said, and their color came back a shade. "A coloring book."

"A coloring book—is that all?"

"And a rubber article; and an evil sort of red-black fruit, and another book, a heretical one without pictures, and some other things of less consequence, all done up in a blanket, a rather obscene sort of blanket, which had preserved them only too well from the weather. I see you don't comprehend the magnitude—how could you? The nature of this book— But I don't propose to describe it— One day you shall— But it's not for the eyes of ladies. And all this time our boys, even the littler ones," and his head descended weavingly into his hands and there was a moment of sympathy with his tears. But the ladies guessed more than he thought they did.

"How long ago was this discovery made?"

"Only last night—"

"Ah, so the poison cannot have spread far?"

"Only last night, when a loud report drew our attention to the demise of the overused balloon. But its warranty must have expired and it had spawned—"

"We mean, when was the discovery by the *boys* made?"

"Weeks ago! All this time they have been poring over this filth, while keeping the knowledge of it from me. And so this is the situation I have come to tell you of, since under our Sunnymead system it concerns us all."

They contemplated it, and so did I, as it concerned us all.

"So you'll have to send them all over," said a young teacher, remov-ing her glasses and lifting her eyes as if beholding a vision.

"Not all at once!" said the boss teacher, "unless you want us over-thrown and rept, and our gels along with us. I'm sorry to speak so bluntly, but never far from us, I have to tell you, is It, and what do I mean by It?—I mean the Mating Urge: I am not afraid to name it. We must keep in mind that these are seck-shew-ally miscreant boys, being sent for a seck-shew-ally appropriate lesson at the hands of young females who may themselves be less seck-shew-ally oblivious than we like to give them credit for. It is clear that the culprits must be deliv-ered to us one by one, and this can be staggered over a number of months. (The cloakroom at the rear of the gymn can be set aside for the remainder of the school year.) It will be a new and extended challenge for the Sunnymead system, but we shall rise to it and quite possibly reach new heights through the experience. It will certainly advance our biology syllabus. Is that satisfactory to everyone? And now, Mr. Quitetwice, we have to tell you that this program cannot begin till tomorrow at the earliest: for we too have a disciplinary problem," and her eyes swung to the prior disciplinary problem.

The other eyes followed; the man's, catching sight of me for the first time, grimaced in discomfort and he had to delve his hand under his belt and rearrange something.

"Don't go, Miss Pepper." (I wasn't trying to; I was still standing peaceably behind the door, on which hung an African batik. In fact I was sniffing the wax in it, to which I had traced that armpit smell. So I had been wronging the teachers.) "You see it's convenient, Mr. Quitetwice, that you happened to come when you did, because you can take her back with you."

They explained my offence to him, in general terms, and we adjourned for breakfast; I was to report back at the second bell. I walked a gauntlet of murmured speculations— " . . . the teachers'll toss for her, and she'll be sent to one of their apartments for the night"— "All night?—so she'll have to take her p.j.s?"— "Does it really take all night to spank her?" . . . "Be sure to tell us all about it afterwards!" called Claypuddle.

"Did you plan this?" I asked her.

"Oh, yes. The boys got an urgent message to us, begging us to get you—begging us to get a victim sent over; they're awfully restive, we've been good too long."

Miss Dopter, to whom belonged the first period, was far too agitat-ed by events, and retired to take a shower, leaving me as often before to teach about geochemistry or Manichaeism. I stood there, the podium and I holding each other up like marathon dancers, and my friends glittered at me and said: "Tell us a story, Fristy."

"About last night," said Vashti.

Crazy Joy, who had less chutzpah, blanched and tried to hush her.

"Once upon a time," I groaned—

"Great Once-upon-a-time! Once Upon a Time They Lived Happily Ever Dafter . . . See if you can tell us a story that *doesn't* have a happy ending, go on, try!"

"The Shirt of a Happy Man—"

"We know that one, he doesn't have a shirt, go on, tell us another"—I'd been going to tell them a variant, the skirt of a happy girl; but I turned sideways to them so that I could shut at least one eye, and babbled: "Once upon a time there were three nogoods called Nogamus, Pligamus, and Olly Gogamus. Nogamus was really agamous, and even Pligamus was only oligogamous, but Olly Gogamus was actively shredophilous. He wallow-swallowed off with Polly Offalous—"

"Oh, *crap!* Make sense! Last night! Story, story!"

I staggered to the chalkboard and sketched them a family tree (King Paramount, his aunt the Dowager Duchess Tantamount, Queen Catamount, Lady Paramour, Bishop Marabout, Captain Blackamoor, Princess Gadabout, Prince Layabout, Cousin Vagabound—oh and howabout their bicycle Tandemount and their cat Catamong, which shall be the name for my cat that walks amoung my legs as I sprawl on bed) and said "Please make up the stories yourselves, free frigments of your imaginations, I have work to catch up on," and I sat down at Miss Dopter's desk and knew a half hour of black peace in the crook of my own elbow.

The bell rang, and my friends propped me on my feet. They didn't need to, I was recovered and much brighter, with just a slight whistling in my ears. But they helped me all the way to the teachers' office and pushed me in. The male teacher took my arm and, because I might be too turbulent for him to manage, all the female teachers came along as a bodyguard, leaving a skeleton staff consisting of the youngest teacher. Another convenient thing was that I could take Master Borrocks's sweater back with me. Such was the lack of contact between the two schools that in all this time there had never been a chance to return it. I laid it over my arm.

"You could put it on."

"That's all right, thank you, Sir. Too warm today."

"Take your blouse off and put it on."

Oh, well, if they wanted a scope of my breasts, why not? The blouse was Saxie's anyway—I began to see my life as a long dive through a discontinuous tunnel of borrowed garments—a Borrock here, a borofrock there . . .   It occurred to me that my own school outfit was now part of the state brothel's novelty wardrobe. "Let's have a general exchange of borrowed properties," I said, handing them the blouse; "I could get back my coloring book, couldn't I, and my Arkansas Black apple, and my blanket (well, Theopard's)," as I pulled on the sweater, thus muffling my words and missing the expressions their faces would have worn if they had heard me. I had been using it on night swimming excursions. Either it had shrunk a bit or I had grown a bit: it didn't come down so far.

Too late, I realized I'd have to come back without it.

"We'll bring the blouse over for you. We may let you wear it on the way back, depending on your frame of mind." In other words, whether I still seemed in need of humiliation. "Why, Pepper, are you wearing no breastlet?"

"You got me up in a hurry this morning, Sir."

"And also you think any little rule of ours is better broken, don't you?"

"Frankly, Sir, yes."

All veils were removed from our hostility. Perhaps not the best diplomatic position to put oneself in when about to be subjected to open-ended punishment.

Yet, the next moment, the Boss was nice to me. Her real name was Bombook—just like that: the heaviest teachers had mono lithic names, Brict, Souns, Claish, Drasmery, Rimian, Bombook, and Phlogamus, without any Miss or Sir. —She opened her wall safe and handed me my earrings.

"Why, thank you," I said. It seemed an odd moment for such a concession. I had to sign a receipt for Ornaments Facial 2 Restored To Child. "Yes, put them on," she said; and as I did so the man looked as if he saw the point, and smiled. And both my arms were grasped, and off we went, by a circuitous route around the village.

One of the pillars at the foot of the driveway had the appearance of a brick leg sticking from the ground and topped by a white boot. Khaki slime had emptied itself over the letters of "FUNNYMEAD (BLOCK L WEFT)."

(The *S*'s were of a fancy sort. And I forgot to mention that, though the school consisted of just two widely separated houses of the Edwardian period, they were called Marycleft and Block L West.)

I knew the layout of Block L West better than they supposed (because of my operation with the string telephone), but the room I was ushered into was a strange one in the middle. It had no windows, only doors in the two shorter walls and, in the other two, large dark mirrors, slightly recessed like windows; and a circle of chairs.

"Now," I was told, "you will take off your lower clothes."

"No I won't."

I didn't care whether I called her Sir or not. If she wanted to slap me she'd have a fight of it.

But there's not much you can do against a man and a dozen large women. After a scuffle in which the only real contest was between themselves, they all withdrew through the door on my right, taking my skirt and clevel with them, also my shoes. They left me my regulation calf-length white hose.

And then in through the door on the left came a dozen boys.

The Overlapping

I PULLED the Borrocksweater down fore and aft. When stretched, it just covered enough.

The boys took their places on the circle of chairs. The largest was Borrocks himself, but he was a softie; the most formidable was a narrower concentrated type called Huntus. And they ranged down through several sorts and sizes to some that were quite small and puzzled. I had thought they might be just the senior class, but the idea was that a cross-section of masculine ages would expose me to more shadings of ignominy.

"My Inca sweater!" said Borrocks. "Give it back!"

"Wait," said Huntus. "Let that be for Part Two." And Borrocks capitulated.

Some were staring at me in a kind of horror, wondering what foreign substance I was made of.

"Have we got to spank her?" asked a smaller one, with a trace of nausea.

"Yes," said Huntus, "but I've an idea a little more is expected. It was *blasphemy*, remember. *Detailed* spanking, shall we say? I'll try to show what I mean. But first, let's let her stand for a bit."

And this they did.

Standing there could soon have become boring for me, and disappointing for them, so I decided to play along. I found it quite easy (especially as I could check my performance in the mirrors) to ham it up as the dreadfully apprehensive maiden in the midst of a ring of itchy-fingered lechers, just managing to stretch her hairy sweater to cover cunt and glushes, or at least midslit and midsplit, and panting and blushing when they began to make jokes about my precarious decency and disconcerting remarks on how much glush they could already see. The panting and the wide eyes were simple; as for blushing, at first it would only come when I didn't intend, but I discovered a way to make it come on cue: by looking at the situation with a sort of intended panic. (Had I blushed in mid air as the pond rushed to rape me?) And when one of them said "Boo!" and feinted at my cunt, I let the hem on the other side fly out of my fingers (an almost impossibly stupid thing to do) and then I got it back down but let it spring away from me at the front. At this they swung into the spirit, whistling and cheering. Those who were in front called across me to those behind, "What's the bottom like?" "Oh, wow!" said those behind, stirred to eloquence and signalling the rest;

"and what's the cunt like?" To which one of the replies was: "It's covered with hair. Is it supposed to be?"

This was not sarcasm: there existed a genuine doubt: was I a sound example or was I ill? I was prepared to say, "Yes, you little willies, yes! That *is* the way it's supposed to be! Underneath the stuff, I *am* all very much in order!" But Huntus had seen pictures (or perhaps Hearth-stoppers southern-style), and Howerel Minor had seen his sister, and Borrocks had seen *me*, so after some debate all were reassured.

"All right," said Huntus, "enough dallying and sparing. Time to begin." He shifted his chair slightly inward toward me. And so did all the others.

"Come here and lay yourself over my lap."

I shook my head.

His face took a turn for the worse. "We were going to chastise you light . . ." The chairs shifted another two inches inward.

I had been hoping for a prolongation of the play-acting till my usual unexpected luck should somehow supervene. But my luck intimated to me that it was going to tease me by waiting awhile. I moved slowly over, holding the sweater down.

I managed to lower myself onto my knees on the right side of the bony knees without bending at the waist. But next I was going to have to lean forward.

While I was steeling myself to do this, some of the others left their chairs and strolled to positions behind me.

I started to bend, and felt the hem scraping up my glushes to the pop-over point. I had to let the cunt-covering hand release the front hem and dive through to help grasp at the back. And I had to lay my face on the fellow's thighs.

"Shift forward."

I shuffled a bit forward, so that my chin hung over the far side.

"Hands on the floor, this side."

Now this was the juncture. This was where a decision had to be made. I wondered why I had been playing along. Presumably because, if I cooperated with them in making these harmless early phases seem exciting enough, we would never get as far as any unspeakable ones. But there was another way of looking at it. If I got them too excited, they might, rather than exhausting themselves with excitement early, ride an avalanche of excitement to phases even beyond the authorized. But it was also debatable which was going to excite them more: the sight of me myself *doing* it, removing my own hands and letting my own covering fly away from my own glushes; or them tearing my hands away—

A clamor of threats made me aware that it was my move: I was going to have to postpone the thinking.

What was I supposed to be doing? Oh yes: getting my knuckles over and down to the floor. —The hem flew clean up to the middle of my back.

I remembered to give a sob of mortification; it was drowned in other noise, including guffaws: some of them were young enough to think that the bare glushes of a girl laying herself across a boy's knees were merely funny. My breasts were between the bastard's skinny thighs and he laid his hand patronizingly on my head.

Huntus, quite an artist, allowed another pause for comment and relish and the sort of audible stage-business that people make with their lips and tongues and cheeks and swallowing-mechanisms, usually to fill more reflective moments. Then he growled, between stage-sinister tight lips (I could imagine the stage-ruthless glittering eyes), "Forward. More."

I had to shuffle my knees forward again, pushing my body over the tops of his thighs. "More." My breasts fell beyond his thighs. "More." Now my thighs came against his. I could kneel no nearer.

"More."

How could I get myself more forward? Only one way: I had to raise my knees off the floor, push forward.

"That's it. *Pour* yourself."

There was some consolation in working for such a ringmaster. If he hadn't used that expression, I'd have had to contribute it ("You mean I must, sort of, *pour* myself?"). I poured myself like a shaped stream of flesh over his lap, till my whole trunk hung one side, my legs the other, and my bottom at the top.

"A shade more, a wriggle more." My cunt passed the midline. "Stop. That's exactly how I want you. Almost exactly. One thing more. Legs apart. Not a lot, just a little. Go on. Open them!"

"No!" I said, "I can't! Obscene!"

I hadn't meant to contribute this, but I really had to. It really was. Especially when I really did it and felt my sitch kiss open. I felt, needless to say, self-conscious—well, not just self-conscious: sitch-conscious.

I felt him lay his left hand on my back, to take my measure, or to confirm the clothing out of the way, or hold me down if I started bucking, or just to get a first touch of my skin and let me feel a first touch of his hand. And then . . .

He did it. He brought his hand down. He didn't spank. No: worse. Far worse. His hand drew near until I could feel its presence, its heat. And:

He touched the inner side of one of my glushes.

There was a great sighing out of collective breath which had been suspended. The daredevil threw himself back in his chair, so did they all, their mouths sank open, their eyes turned up, the fever slowly ungripped their faces—I saw, for I raised my head in amazement and looked around. Something which they considered the extreme, beyond the extreme, had been dared.

Playing along was certainly the way.

Getting to my feet, I covered my face with my hands and actually ran, as if to get it over with, to the next devil and laid myself across his lap. And so to the next and the next, one ordeal after another (the ordeals on the little boys' laps were the most uncomfortable), not putting my hands to the floor but keeping them over my face to cover my shame and my sobs, and in fact running faster and faster and pressing my cheeks harder and harder, because it was becoming doubtful that I would manage to hold my laughter till I got out of the room.

The Throne

I FINISHED with the last of the circle (Huntus, that leading devil, took a second turn, daring to touch my other slope) and scrambled out through the door just in time and slammed it behind me and doubled over, exploding (why aren't there stronger words for laughing, and more *voicy* ones?—has no one ever really laughed before me?) even though I was already aware that my arms, which I would have liked to use for at least a bit of soundmuffling, were in two furious and painful grips.

"You—you—you *cheat!*" the she-teacher was hissing. "Those little *ninnies!*" the he-teacher was nittering— "don't think you'll get off with that, if that's what you imagine you've got another imagine coming!" More was in store for me, apparently communal—they were debating whether to Partition me with the Screens or stand me up for spitball target practice—but the headmaster overruled them; he said it was a job for a specialist. "See what an *adult* does," he nittered on.

"Hey," I said, "play fair! That's the end of my punishment! I fought fair!"

"You didn't fight, you tricked—and this isn't a game," breathed my Boss, failing to stand up for me.

"Oh, isn't it?" I was getting my dander up. "That would have been your only excuse, and you've blown it!" "Shut up, Pepper, shut up, Pepper! And say Sir!" "Sir—Bollocks!" I shouted (and methought I heard, from somewhere within, the plaintive answering call of a poor youth still mourning his possessions). "My, Sunnymead has enlarged our knowledge of modern languages!" she sneered, hoping to suppress me with sarcasm. ("Look out," murmured a frailer teacher, "she's arching her nostrils—a danger-sign.") "You bleeding pooves and per-verts!" I yelled— "trying to train the kids up into little twisted copies of you, and mad because you've only half succeeded! Why don't you stop fluttering around my ass and screw my cunt like men, hey?" and I made a pretty spectacular (considering how tight they were holding me) bow-legged high flaunt of it in their faces—unfortunately in the direction of the wrong crowd, but I didn't withdraw the gesture because it had its fine irony that way too. "*You—you*"—my teacher, blushing hot for me, was beyond her powers of rebuke; spinning away from me, she only urged her he-colleague to do his *upmost*.

And I found myself being dragged past a wide window, which was the other side of one of the mirrors in the observation room, into another special room. At least, it was specially arranged today: alone in the middle of it was placed one great heavy armless antique wooden chair, facing to the right.

We were a substantial crowd as we funneled into this room: all the teachers male and female of the twin schools excepting the skeleton staff (one) of each, and me in the midst, centrally indecent.

The man was already in place on his throne; the throne-room was his study. They had my wrists in front of me and had fixed around them the school bell-rope (cut from its tower and pressed into special service) and they gave the other end into his hands. It was a heavy rope sewn into a covering of blue velvet.

"Shall we stay and witness, Tarquin?" they asked. "No," he said, "I think I shall be more"— "more free," he meant, but "more effective," he said. They filed out, sorry to miss it, but amenable also not to inhibit it. I looked around: I didn't see anything like a two-way mirror in this room, but you never know about chinks and skylights.

And so they left us, and we glided into a pocket of quiet time, him and me. I understood the mechanics at a glance. I was by the door, he was twenty feet off and sideways to me, turning to look at me, dandling his end of the wristrope. "Where did you get this idea?" I asked— "Pompeian fresco?" "It was an Achaemenid palace, I believe," he told me.

All I had to do to defeat the mechanics of it was to walk forward of my own volition, circling out either way around him. His helpers could have defeated that if they had stayed in the room, by forming lines and hemming me in. And then all I'd have had to do was fall on the floor.

But I thought, really, if this is the worst they want to do, investigate my sitch, why not just let them? Let's get it over with. My offer of cunt had been a mite rash—let's be thankful it passed unnoticed. If they want to tie *themselves* up too, so that my virginity is about as unendangered as it's ever been, why should I force it otherwise? Anyway, it might not be so bad: all those niminy-piminy cleftpats had left me so *expectant* that if somebody didn't scratch me soon I'd have to—and I couldn't, because my hands were tied in front just when I needed them in back. And so I hovered at the limit of my tether, and began another playing-along. It was as easy to playalong the professor as the kids.

He took up the slack. He passed his end over his lap, down on his left side, under the seat, and up out on his right side. All he had to do was haul upward. He began to winch me in. I came, slow pitter-patter steps, the terrified slavemaiden—

"Am I a slavemaiden," I shyly asked, "or a captive from one of your wars of conquest?"

"You're, hm!"—he straightened his shoulders and in the act his baggy tweed suit became an Assyrian robe—I'm not sure what my Peruvian sweater and white school socks became. "You're the princess of, ah—" "Susa," I suggested. His lip merely lifted, showing a gleaming white tooth (and a gold one) among the raven curls of the vast square beard, and he added an imperial flourish to his tug.

I pleaded, I bowed over, my captive arms stretched before me, I tried to hang back, but inch by inch he made me totter forward. Oh how unwillingly I drew near (Appiluliuma—no, that's a Hittite sort of a name—Nikillagab, princess of Susa), oh with what trepidation and what a tale of shuffling I had to cross the expanse of the floor until at last I came up against him, right to the hated royal thigh of my conqueror; and there, lest I fall prone, I had to straighten, there I had to stand, hard by him, raising moist supplicant eyes to the far-off gods of my Susian home, raising them in vain, succeeding only (exquisite Elamite) in showing the sheerness of my upraised throat in addition to those profounder profiles over which his eyes were closely coursing. To my song-cured Susian gods I strove to uplift my bound wrists, but with a cruel tug he brought them down; I could cover neither my burning face nor body; "Oh spare my glushes!" I begged, but he was in no mood to be deflected by puns. Another tug, and my wrists wavered forward across him (at which point a two-fisted slam to the regal jaw would have been easy, but unprincessly). My balance was nearly at its edge, and again I had to bow myself over and dip my arms until now they actually rested on his further thigh-side; I struggled to keep my feet under me, jutting my glushes back, but it was in vain, on he tugged, and on down my wrists followed the rope, and only one more tuglet was needed, and yes, merciless tyrant, he gave it, and my balance broke, and my knees went back from under me, and faster I fell, and down across his lap I crashed and lay heaped!

And at once, my ruthless overlord, he pulled the rope tight, brought it up between my thighs, passed it over the nearer one and down again. The Achaemenid throne probably had a special hitching-knob, but he had to make do. He just gave the rope a couple of turns around his own thigh. And there we finished, knitted together, thigh to thigh: it was brought off neatly. (Art conceals art: without my careful balletics it could have been anything but neat, but he hadn't had to notice.) I was not just over his lap, I was wrapped around his lap, my arms bound to my left leg and both down out of the way. My right leg, the sole free quarter of my body, I could lift and kick and wave in treble protest, which served only to proclaim my helplessness and flex my attractions. My face was near the floor and my hair, which poured loose around it, shrouded me into a little dark chamber. In short, I was fixed easily by one soft thong (this thing's the Thong of Tholomon) into the most vulnerable and inescapable posture I had ever been in, not excluding Theopard's multi-rope contraption; and now my glushes on my master's lap awaited his pleasure. (He, I divined, was the kind who after passing something nice on the street glances back at a certain level, hoping for his glance to be taken for curiosity about something odd in her gait or garb.) He himself was also tied to his chair, his stalk was safely out of the way, and his clothes were unremovable, but he didn't think of that. (I soon had reason to think, by the rosiness of his groaning, that he could find auto gasm through his fingers.) Everything's in the mind. I knew that by now. I really knew it: I had only just taken more steps in my command of it. All I had to do to get through the next five minutes, or half hour or however long un-variety takes to do its work, was to switch my mind, waking or dreaming, to some of its favorite scenes—which were to do with anything but male schoolteachers—and I knew I could do it.

Before thus departing from him, I did tarry a little to listen to his beatific sigh. If such a man is ever happy, this was the moment, and I felt quite proud to be a part of it. He then brought a simple fingertip to the point of the nearer glush (*Sylvia*); withdrew it.

Inhaled. (To steady himself.)

Brushed a fingerpad, then three, all down the horizon of the glush; withdrew them.

("A Syrian Caress," I think he named it, tracing with barely fuller touch the whole almost-semicircular contour studied by an envying if imaginary audience. The honeyed stroke, the glide of syrup, even though he had not yet reached for his jar of lovecream. ("*Ass*Syrian Caress, sir?")

Fitted now a whole palm to the glush. Refitted it, very slightly less lightly . . . withdrew it.

Lightly slapped the glush to set it trembling.

—Drew in his breath sharply over his teeth.

Grouped the glushes twain tight together; trailed the other hand across the seal (*bil-lipp*); let it spring back open.

—Paused and asked me, "Was last night your bath-night, by any chance?" "No, sir. That'll be tomorrow. —But I did take a dip in a duck-pond." He sighed at the little liar, and proceeded.—

Proceeded to what was supposed to be the order of business, a spank; a first tepid shy one, and then a floating, lingering, smirking spank that visited every quarter.

Dipped lingeringly into the little springhead dell from which my tail, if I had had a tail, would have sprung. A sweet and decent spot.

Landed one fingertip on the mobile side of the deeper vale, and began to trace a slow inward spiral. —Suddenly sensing my spiritual departure, drew back a furious hand and woke my glushes with a stinger. But only them; and as the breathing and the tempo thickened I went away to a cove in the woods beside the Poorlouis, and so it took me longer than it took the warlord of Assyria to understand what it was that someone was insistently saying at the door:

"Parents, sir."

—yanked one glush aside and—

"Parents, sir."

—and— "What? I'll be out in an hour."

"Parents, sir. Want to see their offspring."

"Well, so, parents! Just send to the relevant classroom and fetch out the relevant monsterkin! Which parents, anyway?"

"Mr. and Mrs. Pepper, sir."

The Bell-Rope

M R. TARQUIN Quitetwice, Litt. D., Dip. Ed., (PC, CD, AI, PVC, TGV, NAACP, FAQ, CCTV, QWERTYUIOP) was uncertain what to do. (Felicity Jane, how *can* you perpetrate these unholy understatements!) He started to snatch my binding off me; then, reflecting that I could walk straight out, he pulled it back, tighter. He would have liked to leave me tied and run out himself to fetch me my clothes, or out another way to flush the toilet and thus explain delay; but he was tied *under* me.

He would very much have liked to take quickly, with headlong fingers, as much as he could of all that was about to be denied to him for ever. But that would have been a minute against his life.

And so I still lay on his lap helpless—physically. But in point of power it was I who had him trussed and on the end of my spoon. I shook a window through my hair and cocked a merry eye up to watch him calculating his various futures.

The only endurable ones all started with negotiation.

"Felicity," he croaked, "what can I promise you if you will keep silent about—about—"

"What can *you* promise *me?*" I tried to keep out any note of contempt—it was just that I couldn't imagine anything that such a person could have to give to me.

He started to mention that he was not well paid but he could— I asked him to fgodsake shut up. Would I be interested in a holiday in— a scholarship to— a set of antique— I turned my head away.

"Please try to think of something, Felicity."

What a crumb! He couldn't conceive that I might forgive him free!

"All right," I said. "I'm your obedient student, and friend. Untie me, please."

He was scared. "Could we possibly—complete our agreement first?"

"No," I said, because my idea required being safe off his lap. "You'll have to take the risk, sir."

He unwound the rope from his thigh and then from mine, as if he might be springing a panther's trap. I stood up, and held my wrists out for him to untie. Then to his pitiable relief I didn't yet stride to the door.

"*Anything*, Felicity?"

"Fristy, they call me when they want to be nice to me, sir."

"Oh I didn't know that! Fristy!"

I had decided to claim one more victim. I really am a wicked girl.

I sidled close to him. No, that's not quite the way. I *blushed*, hung on my heel, squeezed shy hands before my cunt, swung shy shoulders.

"Sir," I said, "could I ask you a question"—his nerves were ready to leap either way— "an etymoglogical question?"

"Hm, yes, I suppose, Fristy," suspecting a trick to tempt him into schoolmaster mode.

"Where does 'clevel' come from, sir, what is its origin?"

"Well, interesting question, my dear. It is playfully said to come from 'cleftveil'—the little veil to veil the, you know, the cleft or clefts— but is more likely a by-form of 'clout,' cognate to 'Kleid,' unless it is some kind of classical handmedown—cliptica, clascula—"

"Thank you, sir. —And 'glush'?"

"Ah! Gl—cl— 'Clutch,' I've always supposed; a softish ablaut-form of 'clutch.' With influence from 'cushion.' As the pillows above, so cushions below. All object (soft) of cl-gl-Clutch." And on the brink of glushglut gulch, where glust doth gush (gushed-lust) at such a glut of cushy glush to clutch—ah, bliss to gliss such glush!—his glad confusion made him gulpengargle—he was, he gan to glom, the gargoyle to sejuisce a jewessy goyule—

"'Clutch'!" I said, "I see. I—sir—well"—oh, to hell with the bashful hesitations. "Sir, will you promise me this: to have a glush-orgy with me?"

He choked on a pickle, regurgitated it and struggled to get his eyes open.

"Oh an all-night one, sir!—Tarquin! I crave it, now that you've touched me, I don't know how it is, there must be magic in your fingers!"

Nourished by rising blood, new hair grew out of the Gobi of his scalp before my eyes.

Kitty Tease-Tail—that is, I—went around behind his throne and gripped the back of it and stooped and whispered huskily in his papery ear:

"An orgy, a fest, a dulge, please let's! First a general wild laughing screaming cartwheeling toptotoe walltowall bumpertobumper allends-on limbcrossing sexgrabbing facescandalizing noholesbarred sexfeast, settling into serious wholenightlong utter mutual engloyment of glush-andofcoursesitchorgy . . ."

I had already thought of a lot more, but he was about to reach capacity.

"Well?"—I came around in front, pretending to wait timorously for the answer which he couldn't yet utter; sank on my knees and begged prettily. Just as he almost got his voice together, I rechoked it by turning around and begging that way. —A strangled cry, he launched himself from his throne; I jumped up and dodged just in time.

"No, don't touch me now, my darling—let's save it all for tonight!" (When I would be gone with my parents.)

And I led the way toward the door.

Wait a minute. What had the poor crustacean really done to me to deserve so much?

I had condemned him to long hollow savage years. There was no going back, no saving him any fraction of that. The least I could do was to give him seconds to remember, more important, to transform it all into something sad but softer.

I turned and he was doggishly following my glushes. I held up my arms and let him slide home. He let his left hand straight down to clutch, though the middle finger no more than rested on its spot; with his other hand he touched my earring; and he drank at my mouth.

I was prepared to stand up to the awful stubbly mouthparts and the tobacco breath. To my surprise—though I shouldn't have been surprised at myself by now—I found that I did love him.

"Why, you're crying, Fristy!"

I nodded. It was well done, it would help him a lot, yet I hadn't done it on purpose.

He wiped my face and I smiled.

"Wait here and I'll fetch you your clothes," he said with happy mastery, and out he went.

While waiting I picked up the long blue bell-rope and whirled it around my head, picking off a few pictures from the walls.

He slipped back in with my clevel and skirt and shoes (actually, Saxie's) and delightedly watched me pulling them on, as if I was packing him his sandwich lunch. I put on the shoes first, one stoopingly, one hoppingly, allowing him time to walk around me choosing viewpoints. Then the skirt; only at the last moment, letting him hold up the skirt and watch, the cleftveil. Then we went out together to his front office to deal with my visiting parents.

There they stood, with their backs to the light of the window:

Mad Theopard.

And an old old woman: my nursemaid, Zed.

The Parents

I SCREAMED—almost. It takes a lot to make me scream for fright.
But Zed winked at me her offside eye.
Could anybody think these were my parents?

Zed was old enough to be my grandmother, in fact she had suckled
my great-grandmother. (However, she looked a mere sixty or seventy.)
As for Theopard the corder, his age was hard to say. He might have
been a yuppie who had come into his fortune young and been distort-
ed by recent stress, or he might have been a veteran rejuvenated by
recent libido. What he was wearing could just possibly have passed for
a rich man's cowboy affectation: denim pants badly in need of patching, leather jacket ending in fringelike strips and with no shirt under it.

There wasn't time for hesitation. I either had to hug them or not. I
hurried to Zed and sheltered in her hug. But the more I prolonged this
the more noticeable it was going to be if I merely gave Theopard a peck
on the cheek. But he had enough wit to foresee this, and by the time I
broke from Zed and put one arm loosely around his chest he was
engaged in manly conversation with headmaster and secretary, and
could affect to be distracted from our filial embrace.

"Well, Mr. Pepper," said Tarquin shakily, "this is an unlooked-for
pleasure. You'll stay for lunch, of course, so that we can give you the
school tour?"

"No, really, thank you," said Theopard, "we'd love to, but I have to
get back to my business; we have a long ride in front of us. We just
came to take Fritzi away." (My daddy got my name a little wrong.)

"To take Fristy away?"

Theopard made no immediate response, and I felt that both of them
knew what was going on behind the façade.

"My dear Mr. Pepper," said Tarquin, "our school contract does
mention, you know, that a month's notice is customary, should there be
any *unusual* and *necessary* occasion of premature withdrawal—withdrawal, that is, in mid term; of course this *fixed school policy* is just for
the protection of all parties, and most of all the child. We do, in all
cases, try to cushion against academic and emotional discontinuities,
and in Felicity's case it would seem an especial shame since she *has*
been making *exceptional* recent progress."

Again Theopard in his dangerous way did not hasten to reply. Then
he said: "She has?"

"Yes, indeed. She's a"—meditatively— "quick learner. She's already in our top ninety percent" (I hoped he meant our top ten percent) "if not our top hundred percent. I suppose she hasn't mentioned it in her letters? Children do mention and unmention such unexpected things."

"Well, tough shit," said Theopard.

"Excuse me?"

"Excused," said Theopard, sniffing loudly. "I merely said it can't be helped." He was complacently taciturn in his position of strength, until I managed to remove my arm (he had taken possession of it with a hand on my wrist and another at my elbow) and he then blew his nose and became more negotiand.

"She has made great strides. Would you like to see some of her work?" said Tarquin with desperate idiocy. He looked around for his secretary, who had however withdrawn.

"It would be most interesting, but, thank you, we can't wait," said Theopard, but Tarquin sat down and began pulling exercise books out of drawers and piling them on his desk. They were boys' exercise books, since we were in the boys' school. But: "Why, yes, here's one of hers!" he said, holding it up, with a hectic smile. And it was: it was my poems, sculpture designs, wiring diagrams, and teacher caricatures (I'd been wondering what had become of it).

"Well, I'd like to see it," said Theopard. He took it and appeared to become engrossed, sitting down in the chair in front of the desk. Tarquin was not sure what to make of this temporary reprieve, but had no wish to interrupt it. I talked in undertones with Zed; didn't get much out of her; Tarquin turned pleading eyes to me. He was desperate because I had been debagged but not Debriefed.

All too soon Theopard stood up and replaced the exercise book among the piles of others as if he had finished with it—then took it up again and said, "Quite interesting. May Fristy bring it with her?"

"You may take it, Mr. Pepper. However, I don't think the question has been resolved, as to whether—"

"It has been resolved, Mr. Quitetwice. As her legal owners—her natural parents, we have the only say in the matter. (*Burupp*—Pardon.) I don't quite know why you're making this fuss. Kisty took it—Fristy, excuse me, took it into her own head to come here; she did not have our permission, but we have been compliant about it up to now, and we do indeed thank you for taking care of her and, I hope, teaching her obedience and how to mind her p's and q's. (Send your bill—you have the Popper Propper, that is the proper Pepper address.) But now we want her back, so having corresponded with her—you did get our letter, did you, Fristykins?—she is no doubt as eager to be home in her own little bedroom as we are to have her there. And so now we really must be going." A slight tremble had begun in Theopard's sinewy brown forearm.

Tarquin grew smaller in his chair, but he looked up at me and said: "What about her own feeling? Do you want to leave, Fristy?"

"That doesn't enter into the matter; why, what nonsense, to ask the child where she wants to be"—Theopard blustered, but he knew that power lay with me.

But what was my position? I was between two men ravening for me, two father-aged men, both of them strange, neither of them savory; both of them calling me Fristy (or by an occasional slip Kisty or Friggsie) when they should have been calling me at least Felicity; one of them pretending to be my father, but not; the other pretending to be my disinterestedly well-intentioned *in-loco-parentis*, but not; both of them somewhat loco, to tell the truth; sticking themselves into these crazy poses out of pure ravenous lust, undisguisable, unbecoming, and, some would say, pretty detailedly unnatural. The sweat in their crotches, as it were, was showing. Of the two I would rather have stayed with Tarquin. He wasn't fearsome, his arms were thinner, his clothes though dowdy were presentable—and it would have been nights only for sexual duty. A shade peculiar (the species of sexual duty) but I expected I'd be able to diversify him. But—why Zed?

A wink has several meanings in Monger, which distracted me.

"*Are* these your parents?" said Tarquin in a small voice.

"My dear sir!"—Theopard blustered over him, laughed mirthlessly, attempted to clap his hand around my shoulders. But Tarquin sat frozen, aware that he had brought the critical moment.

Zed winked at me again. I nodded (which has several meanings in Burushaski). —And immediately, before he died, I said, "I want to say goodbye to my friend."

Theopard tried a lot of time-chafing but I wouldn't be shaken. I had to stay here, Saxie had to be sent for—it gave Tarquin something to do. When she came I insisted on my parents waiting outside, and then I beckoned Tarquin to come back in through the other door.

"What's the matter?" said Saxie. "Am I in trouble too?"—hopefully.

I told her I had to go home because my parents had come for me, and then I hugged her till she had stopped her soundless crying.

Then I asked her to sit down beside him, and I said, "Saxie, Mr. Quitetwice is sort of in love with me."

"So am I," she said.

"I wish," I said, "that the two of you would—"

Mr. Quitetwice tried to conceive a slight hope.

"D'you think it's possible?" I said.

"No," said Saxie.

"But, Saxie, I may never be able to come back."

"No. You won't."

"Yes, I will, then! I'll come back as soon as I can, and we'll all be happy!"

"No, Fristy. You'll just go on and on."

I stared at her, and then I dropped my eyes.

Slowly we all three stood up again, and I gave Saxie a long hug, and then Mr. Quitetwice, and then I was going to give Saxie another one, but she had gone. —When he too realized that, Mr. Quitetwice broke and went insane, and bolted the door and took his trousers off; but attempted those two things in the wrong order (Order is so important, as my mother used to say. Don't butter the bread before putting it in the toaster. No use wiping the smudge if it's on the other side of the glass.) so that I just escaped.

And in front of the school stood the coach, with a palomino in the traces, and Zed up on the driver's seat. The coach was shiny black, narrow. On the left was only a small window, above a gold-painted device: a double-peaked mountain, splitting the sun that set behind it— the Mount of Eve. I went around and climbed in through the door on the right, and Theopard came in behind me, and we rolled.

In the Coach

O N THE floor was lying the old mess of Theopard's ropes. As he climbed in he glanced down at them; glanced dubiously at me; and heeled them out onto the road. Not going to risk that again!

The telescope, too—it went with them.

He sat down, or was sat down, as the coach jerked into motion. In any case he had to sit down, whatever he was going to do, the space being so confined—I could just stand, he could just not. He pulled the door; it closed with a click. He was carrying that school exercise book of mine, which he slung into a corner. It was the only loose object in the coach with us.

His parental expression, never well acted, was wiped away.

"Bye, Daddy," I said. "Hello again, old friend."

"Don't think you can turn me off by calling me old friend."

"Okay then. So, we meet again, my Long-Lost Enemy."

That was indubitably what he was—my longest, worst, and most persistent enemy.

But he paused, and looked at me, and passed his hand across his eyes. "I can't really believe it," he said. *"Applepeel."*

"No, well, it isn't really true. I'm Fristy."

"Applepeel," he intoned (like one of those street-commentators). "The girl of girls. She herself. And *I*, shut up alone with her."

"With me," I corrected. "'With you,' that is."

"At last," he said, still talking as if to himself and to this third super-real person, and leaving me out of it.

"Not for the first time," I reminded him.

"This time is the only time that ever has been or will be; this time is *now*."

He said my legend-name a few more times, trying various tunes, and then he wasted no more of this universal point of time; "Well, we both know what this is about," he said, and sailed in, stripping me.

"I had been led to believe," I wanted to say, "that the first step might be a polite request for a kiss. At most." ("A kiss . . .   What I want is your cunt. Let me at it, please?" "It's twirly," I might have replied.)

I shouted to Zed to stop the coach. But the coach was sound-proofed: she didn't hear me. I snatched at the door, but couldn't get it open.

We fought over every inch. It was stern silent stripping.

Stripwrestling is usually (I take it) a matter of getting garments off over the head and the other four extremities; but this topology did not permit. Or rather I did not permit it. I did not permit my arms to be held while anything was pulled off elsewhere. It wasn't a matter of tricking whole garments off. He had to tear them steadily to bits; he had to nake me strip by strip. First the great sweater.

"Not quite so easy as when you had me tied, eh?" I spat at him. Trying to fix both my hands with one of his (there wasn't room for the recommended wrestle-method of pinning her upper end between your thighs so that both hands are free to go about her lower end), he didn't answer. Though after a while he had breath to observe: "How even much—how more even interesting—how much even more—do you realize?—your *gradual* nakedness?"

After a few minutes we were hot. He stopped, tore off his own tattery leather jacket, and pushed it out through the window.

"You have something against clothes?" I inquired.

"Yes, we human apes are not supposed to live so far north. We're supposed to live in say Sudan, where we could live the natural clothe-less ape way, and maybe migrate up into Ethiopia in the cool season. But we rashly kept adventuring until we found ourselves cold, and chose to make things called clothes instead of migrating back like the birds."

"Hey," I said, "you tossed your— Hey! You'd better not do that, had you?"—there went his pants. "What about your keys, your identity card?" But it was deliberate: his boots followed. "My god, what about life after the—after this coach? We're not moths, you know!"—I was thinking of those creatures that cannot feed, that reach brief adulthood to mate and only mate; but I didn't have leisure to clarify my analogy; he was back to the assault.

He was girded for action in his one surviving garment. It was a male shred into whose creation he must have put some care. It was of the usual economical shape and off-white color, but instead of cotton it was plaster-of-paris, or possibly papier-maché. Monolithic; no loose topology that I might exploit; fixed allowance of room for the apparatus (a sort of buttress or drainpipe up the front); unassailable—in fact I didn't see how he was going to take it off or, for that matter, how he had put it on. It must have been *built* on, wet, then dried on—and only just before he got to the school. Inflexible, it cut into him as the exigencies of the wrestle forced him to bend, and gave an angularity to movements that involved his midsection. Yet I rather admired the look of the thing, a shell set tightly in sculptured curves between brown stomach and thighs. It looked better than the stuff it was hiding.

I made a counterattack on it to distract or scare him, but my fingers only scraped as on rock. The subject of the struggle returned to my sweater. Bit by bit it crumbled from my breasts.

"Aa—ish, your skin," he breathed as his palm first came to it, "so cool!"

"Really? I thought it was hot."

"Maybe it is, but to us it's cool, a drink."

"Us—?"

"Girlaholics!"

At the end of an hour the alpaca wool lay in drifts around the floor. Spiral tatters still adhered to the four gristly edges, around my waist and neck and wrists. These remains, now widely separated by revealed flesh, seemed piquant to me, bearing testimony to the rage and devastation of our combat. But he was methodical, tidy-minded: he yanked on each in turn until it snapped. So much for the Borrocks. *Ayhi!*

"'I-he!'" he echoed, "that's always what you utter in the closing stages of a struggle, isn't it!—but this struggle isn't over." I resolved to utter it no more.

Methodically he turned next to my shoes. They couldn't be torn to pieces. As he got one off, he chucked it out the window.

Only then did it dawn on me that the coach was *not* soundproof. The windows were small, and black blinds hung slapping across them, but there were no panes.

"Zed!" I cried urgently.

No answer; the coach rumbled on.

I went red and moist in shame for Zed. So he really had suborned her.

Zed, who had scolded me up through my childhood, whom I loved and trusted more than myself!

For a while after that I fought weakly, and he grimly took advantage. The other shoe; the socks, almost whole; and a good beginning on the skirt. I remilitarized my mind, clearing Zed from it, and the conquest slowed.

There was a tap of the whip on the window—Zed's signal that we were passing someone on the road—and he switched from stripfighting to clamping his hand over my mouth. Then back to the long battle of the skirt. (Saxie's skirt.)

"Oh stoppit-aah!" I let out. "Are you going to quit this? Yes or no?"

"Mnyao." "I am certifiably mad at you. Is there no redress?" (Yes, I did say this to weaken him into giggles, but he didn't get it.) "What in hell d'you think you're doing anyway?"

"What am I doing?"

"Yes, what! In hell!"

"Destroying your skirt."

"Not even mine," I countered, hoping to gain a stroke by curiosity. Would have been better to conserve breath. Yet a bit later I gasped "Why, why?"

"Why?"

"Yes, why!"

"The Mating *Urgh*-ge!" he said in a deep close chuckle.

The last two pieces to come off were quite large, and these too he tossed through the window.

It was lunchtime. We both sank exhausted. We were down to our shreds, mine silky-flimsy, his bulky-rocky, and you'd think I wouldn't have slid down, my chin on my chest, my palms open at my sides, my legs (not even together) flopped before me as far as the coach would let them stretch. But he was in similar state.

(You don't call them clevels, or clovels, when they're all that's left. When their earthy sacredness is all there is about them.)

"There's something," Theopard moaned, "I've been meaning to ask you: how did you manage to escape from that rig of mine and tie me up in it?"

"Well, I have a knack for topology."

"I suppose you took a course in it?"

"Yes, my mother sent me on one. She was fed up with me putting my shirts on back to front. That happens because I don't unbutton them, I hate wasting time putting clothes on—whenowhen are they going to invent permanent clothes?—I've heard that Beau Brummel liked taking five hours to dress, I'd rather take five seconds—I have better things to do—I hold the world record for getting dressed— fastest and fewest (fewest I can get away with)—so I leave 'em buttoned and pull 'em over my head, there's a method that gets 'em the right way round—usually—you put your arm in first, down the neck; wish I could show you. And clevels inside out because of not looking to see where the label is. There are four ways of putting a clevel on: inside-out, back-to-front, inside-out and back-to-front—" "And how many ways of not putting it on?" "Do you know that if you put it on inside out it's also back-to-front?—I didn't. When I came back from that Intermediate Topology weekend, I could pass the inverted-garment test—can you?"

"And what may that be?"

"Haven't you noticed that if you snatch a clevel (which used to be called a panty) from the drawer to put it on, and it's the right way around—the label's at the back—but inside out—the label's facing toward you—so you flip it to turn it right way out, without taking your hands off, you just never know whether it's going to end up facing away from you, so you can step into it, or toward you, so that you have to turn around?—I mean turn it around. Well, now I know, but I'm not going to demonstrate. I tried to teach my sister—she's always going at it without thinking and getting it the wrong way round and swearing 'Where's the cunt of this thing?'—" "Don't tell me about sisters and mothers of yours, I'd rather imagine you without. So, you hold the world record for dressing fastest; what about undressing?"

"That too; I have other tips on that, such as the role of the thumb in the shirt collar."

"Should you," said Theopard, "be talking to me so . . ."

"So much?"

"So prosaically, at this" (his stalk, which had lost a p.p.s.i. of pressure, regained it at something suggested by the word) "juncture."

"You don't like it?"

"It isn't fitting. Perhaps that's your idea."

"Sorry. I know I should just shriek."

The coach halted. We were on a lonely moor, and we jolted some way off the road to make sure. Zed clambered down and passed us our food through the windows. For a while it just sat in its bowls on our chests, and then we tipped it into our mouths, helping it with our fingers, hardly knowing what it was. It was a very tasty pulse stew with strips of mushroom and rabbit and thyme, and it improved my outlook.

Theopard had been known in school as The Arab's Armpit because of his short tough black scalp. From it my bowl rebounded as I brought it whirling down. But this was only a dream as I slipped into unconsciousness myself; Zed had already reached in and taken our empties.

It was lucky for me that Theopard too was a good dozer. But he woke first, and his fingers were at my shred-edge, and I woke and jack-knifed my body, but his fingers dripped away; he was asleep again.

I cranked myself up off the seat and investigated the window. It was just wide enough for my shoulders to get through. So I was exactly half way out, torso cantilevered over the ground below, when I discovered that it was a millimeter too narrow for my hips. A frantic moment of wriggle and then a very hasty retreat indeed—to get stuck like that (legs alone and nether sexflesh) would have been neither pretty nor defensible. Luckily he was still napping, just stirring. I stepped over him to check the door, which had an even smaller window in it, and was of course locked.

While I was at this, he came at me, and thus for the first round of the shredfight he had me from behind. But I had eaten, so now I felt braver. And he wasted his advantage dipping his hands inside.

Still you'd have to say that round went to him. But there were more rounds. Both of us found more energy than ever before—he out of impatience to nake me, I out of desperation not to be naked, and both of us out of nutrition from the pulse stew—and the shrednake lasted longer than the rest of the nake together. In fact we could have skipped the rest and gone straight to it. I mentioned that thought, in one of the pauses between rounds. He nodded, catching me with an eye-twinkle. It was no use trying to keep a long face: I was enjoying it, if only because I had to.

And his face, though not exactly merry, appeared oddly serene as he went about his insanely steady work. "You don't have your mad look!" I said.

"No," he said. "It's because nothing can stop me now. —Expect to see me gnash my teeth again? Nay, kid. Sorry. You put me through that hoop once; not any more. Straight naking down to the finish."

A shred is next to nothing—the last nod at clothing—that's what "shred" means—it should be snatchable-off. (Some models are, with two bows. Some are snatchable-off-disposable: just two weak places. All you have left is a piece of silk shaped like an hourglass.) The time Theopard took to separate me from it, was it because of his rising enjoyment of anticipation? No, he was too serious a luster for that. And he wasn't a bad amateur naker. It was because of my rising resistance; *my* stiffening enjoyment of anticipation. And I realized the comparative paltriness of him, indeed of all men. I could, when I wished, control him, with my mind or my mood. Though twice or thrice my age and sex, he was a rudimentary organism. I noticed that he was ticklish like me, but in an opposite way; whereas I bathed in it, let it flower, he did his best to hide it. He didn't use it on me for fear of starting the idea.

I began to think he wasn't all bad for me: he was beautiful in a ravaged or eroded way, and it was his unqualified desire that had taught itself in less monomaniac form to the rest of the world. He had created me.

Or—another thought—had the *earrings?* A sort of Venus girdle. The only times I had been without them (one: my childhood up to the betrothal party, and two: in the school) people had treated me as pretty, but they hadn't treated me as *Applepeel.*

As yet I couldn't spare my hands to try the experiment.

Once we went through a small town, so that he had to keep his hand over my mouth all the time Zed halted to buy provisions. She passed a newspaper in to us. The headlines were boring, LATEST APPLEPEEL SIGHTING, APPLEPEEL ACT REPEALED, TOWN CLOSED NEXT WEDNESDAY FOR APPLEPEEL CARNIVAL, APPLEPEEL SHARES JOKE WITH POPE, SCIENTISTS CLONE APPLEPEEL IN TEST-TUBE, "I KNEW APPLEPEEL IN FORMER LIFE," APPLEPEEL MANIA REACHES HUNGARY, AVERAGE MALE PICTURES HER 22.5 TIMES A MINUTE (STUDIES SHOW), APPLEPEEL IMAGE DISCOVERED ON MARS (IT HAS BEEN WIDELY REPORTED), APPLEPEEL LEARNS TO SING—SOCIAL AND CLIMATIC CONSEQUENCES . . . As we left the place I tore the paper up and threw it out the window and he smacked me for littering and we got back to shred-shredding, or stripplepeeling.

His beard was scratching in the hammock between my neck and shoulder and he was sometimes giving me inadvertent thrills by ahead-raids, but on the whole he could only concentrate on one thing at a time and so he didn't think of grabbing my breasts to divert my defences (I almost suggested it). He wasn't so controlled now: as the shred dwindled his lust boiled up, enfevering his tongue, eyes, fingers. Our wrestle tossed me up over him, plied me around and dragged me under him, as the shred strove to get away from his fingers and his fingers kept after it; I tried to settle on his right for a change, but he always got me back to my usual position so as to have swinge for his right arm; and we were back side by side, scrabbling together in my lap. The wrestle ground slower as we spent our energy; it slopped from side to side of the lurching coach. "I'm getting motion-sickness," I said.

"Me too." But he didn't stop; far from it; he got down between me and the theatre of attack.

"Oh! Oh! More!" he cried.

"More what?"

"More of your topography! Not to mention bottomography, let's not forget that."

"You have quite a way with words," I conceded.

"Yes, Away with Words!"

"Look, Theopard," I argued to the back of his head, "you've been REJECTED! That's supposed to crush a man, isn't it, easily including any of your sort that can persuade themselves they're marginally handsome. Give up! How dare you go on even flirting with me? When Woman Say No She Mean NO!"

"When woman is serious about turning me off, she don't call me Theopard."

"Mr. Justings, or whatever your name is, I hate you!"

"You think I'm going to stop now?" he said into my midriff.

"You bet I do. What you're about is illegal."

"I hope a few nice things always will be."

"Ow!—do you MIND? Thou shalt not commit adultery!"

"You're not an adult."

"Well—Thou shalt not commit infantry, as the private said to the general. Listen," I offered— "Which General is that," he interrupted, "General Headquarters or General Hindquarters?" "Listen," I persisted, "I'll give you a way out: we'll make believe it's back to the beginning. You make a cautious pass at me, I give you an easily identifiable snub— and that's that. That way we can still be friends, sort of. Let me out, please."

"It wouldn't work. Not with you. Has any male *ever* treated you that way?"

"With common courtesy, you mean? Yes, a few."

"You don't even know: you've never seen people acting normally. With the ordinarily desirable," he said, "a man can accept a rejection, or even fail to dare to make a pass. It's a fearsome moment, making a pass: it admits that one has a stalk . . . (Sex would be a fairly unembarrassing subject, wouldn't it, if it wasn't for the implication in it of *stallock?*) But with you, there's no choice. One *has* to risk it. One cannot do otherwise. One can do no other, it's the least one can do, etcetera," and he improved his grip on the disputed bit of shred. How the deuce could I slow him down? "You're in real trouble," I began, and was going to quote him another proverb— "When you're in a hole, stop digging"—but thought better of it. Or how about "Pull gently if you'd have me by my roots. —By the way," I said aloud . . . "What, what?" "Could you explain to me, what's the difference between adultery and fornication? I'd been wondering." "Same as the difference between mistress and lover." "That doesn't help me—" "Same as this and this!" and he gave me a horrid grasp and then a horrid soft one.

By the last round but five of this longest strip in the history of tease the poor tortured shred was nothing but a twisted string, wedged tight through my slideway and glushfolds. (Sometimes he used it to shake a glush up and down or squash a lip from side to side, or sawed it to and fro to make me giggle, or pulled it out to let it snap back in on me; I was surprised that he wasted strip-time. He snatched it outward and, peering down inside, gave a wild double whistle— "Whee-*Wheeyew!*"—that disconcerted me into yielding him two more seconds of cunview; "There, you see, you've never even heard a wolf-whistle, because men's mouths drop open when they catch sight of you.") In the last round but four, the shred was not only twisted but soaked, perhaps with sweat; in the last but three, it was fraying in six places, like the sun by the mountains of the moon; in the last but two, it parted over my right hipjoint (Wheee! open skin ran down me from neck to heel, like a lightning-strip down a tree); in the last but one, the thing shattered off me; in the last, its last fragments were grubbed out from inside my crevices. (Which wrung from me the first squeal.)

Neckid.

Or at any rate, down to earrings. And he looked at them, the last external topology, wondering whether I might be capable of tying him up with *them*. But he risked it.

"Let me see," I murmured, "which shall I wear today, my clothes or my earrings? Decisions . . . I'll ask my friends, with luck they'll have an opinion: Theopard, which would you prefer to see me in this evening, my clothes or my earrings?"

He opened his mouth, but couldn't think of anything worth the effort of saying.

His eyes were open even wider; he was running them up and down me like a lawnmower, and then as if some spectator had shouted "Man, at last you've got her NAKED!—aren't you going to do anything about it?" he tried to rouse himself—heaved up over me, toppled toward me to run his tongue up and down the same way—but I pushed him off.

We sank on our shoulderblades, side by side, panting, I in my earrings, Theopard in his china swimsuit.

"Inside this," he said, tapping it, "I've got an erection so hard it hurts." I had to commiserate.

The coach had come to a halt in the heat of the late afternoon at a shady spot in the woods. Zed came to the window and said "Are you Firsty?" "No, I'm Fristy," I said, "and I'm dry as a—well, as a facecloth," and she gave us sumac tea, and then goose eggs, good-king-henry salad, sedge bread, and apple-rings. I felt a shade cool around my latest-bared latitude, but I had to take my hands away to eat with.

Now there was surely to be another rest. Surely I was to be allowed to start catching up on my lost night. I tried to keep my eyes slightly open, watching through my lashes the frizzy horizon of my *matter* (sometimes called my *distinctiveness*) offered upward on the edge of the seat. For next, surely, in his program was the fucking of it, preceded perhaps by the fingeropening of it. So I kept a closed or a close eye on him, a languid lookout for the approaching stalk or, as it might be, preparatory finger, or whole handful, and here it came, swimming into view: five stalks; jointed, flexed, with stalknails; calmly through closed eye I observed . . .

His movement jarred me awake—but he didn't stir craftily, he jumped up, and banged his hip sharply on the doorpost. Was this some signal to Zed? He banged again, nothing happened, he swore, pressed his hands to the erection-cave, banged again (the hollow component in the noise came from the erection-cave), swore again, banged again— and at last the plaster clevel shattered. And I found him guilty of being male.

"Ayhh!" he said in relief, "excuse me," and turned to the window; there followed a moment of heroic struggle (he afterwards explained to me that it is impossible to pee through an erection, but since the erec- tion could not be forced down, he had to accomplish the impossible). He peed upward, though he was high enough not to have to, a long arc into the glade, declining into a deplorable splash on the windowsill. Afterwards he stooped to collect the major pieces of plaster and tip them out; then turned to face me, crouching because of the ceiling, and staggering as Zed prodded the horse and moved us on a few paces.

I said, "I'd been wondering how long—"

"How long!" he said, grinning and still grasping it. (It was, I noticed, salivating.) "Yes, and how long—oh, how long—it's been waiting to get into you! Think of how many wasted inch-hours!"

"—how long," I continued, "one could go. I'd prefer to step outside. (I would also have preferred for you to step outside.)"

"Sorry. We can't get out."

"What d'you mean? Kindly unlock the door for me. My need is as urgent as yours was. I promise I'll return."

"I can't. We're locked in for the whole journey. Zed has the key, and instructions not to bring it near us till we get there, whatever we say."

He really had taken every precaution against his wildcat captive.

"Change the instructions!" I said. "Tell her I'm flooding the coach! Tell her I'm murdering you and she's got to let you out!"

"No good. I already tried that, while you were dozing. She won't. She's one of the old school!"

Or else too stupid. "Well then," I said, "will you excuse me too?"

"Yes, I will."

"Please don't come at me while I'm doing this, Theopard. It would not make for a dignified courtship."

"On my honor. (Such as it is.)"

So with more difficulty I peed out on my side. Being shorter, and

differently constructed, I had to get up with one knee on the seat, the
other hoisted against the front wall. In view of this, he behaved himself
well. He was almost perfectly quiet.

Zed moved us on a couple of paces more.

"Now there's only *that*," I said, pointing. A black watch around his
wrist was so much a part of him that he had forgotten it.

It was called Data Bank and besides telling Mean, Daylight-Saving,
Greenwich, and Sidereal Times and the Julian Date it included alarm,
stopwatch, calculator, pulse-monitor, telephone numbers, world map
with time-zones, and schedule of appointments. "I wouldn't throw that
out the window," I said. "You might never remember what you're supposed to do to me next."

He winced but on principle threw it out. (But he threw it forward
where Zed could see it.) He had a Virtual Watchstrap whiter than any
Virtual Clevel. I forgot to mention that had earlier abandoned what he
called his sung lasses.

I hoped we would settle again. I thought I had deserved peace. I
set the example by snuggling down, turning on my right side. He came
down beside me, and, space being cramped, I had to lay my cheek on
his shoulder and let a hand stray onto his chest, but I hoped this would
suggest an atmosphere of trust. My hand half hid from me what I did
not want to see: the creeping of his stalk, like a stinkhorn after the
rains, yet further up out of the black thicket, up toward the creasy
navel. I forgot to mention that had earlier abandoned what he called his
sung lasses.

"I'm impressed!" I murmured. No, I decided not to murmur it. I
meant I was ironically impressed by the sacrifices he had made for me,
of all his clothes. Shared bareness seemed to be the price of acquain-
tanceship with me. Yoryo and Saxie had been willing to give me their
only spares, so that we'd have had to go naked together on wash-days,
but he was the first to commit himself to join me week-round.

The rest of his body softened as in sleep. Could that single part be
so taut?—I almost felt it to see. But he was only pretending to relax,
being now pelvically comfortable, aroused by action, and, besides, as
vulnerable as me: if he had shut his eyes he might have awoken never
to be a father. His eyes watched mine, and the moment they closed his
hands came over to my upper arms to hold me down.

The ultimate battle of our two bodies was joined. "That virginity of
yours," he growled, "that flagrant virginity, I'm going to *slaughter* it!"

I made one last effort to spike his gun by staring straight at it. "-Aren't you ashamed?" I cried.

"Of course I'm ashamed. Shame is fun!"

In Which There Is More Talk than Action in the Coach

NOW I haven't explained that this coach was very narrow. I've mentioned it, but I haven't explained *how* narrow, or rather in what way it was narrow.

It was just under a Theopard in height and in width, so that it was more confining for my captor than for me. Its most generous dimension was from front to back. But here the design flaw was that the space in which Zed was sitting, just in front of us—the driver's seat—was taken out of the interior space of the coach. Since the seat inside, on which we were sitting or fooling, was also subtracted from that space, the space had a cross-section like a—well, like a chair.

You could sit up in it. You could sit slumped in it. You could even, if you really wished, sit on the riser—lie on the floor with your legs on the seat. You could sit in various ways, you could carry on a prolonged wrestle in a hundred variations of sitting-position, but one thing you could not do was turn around and, facing a person sitting, get on top of that person. To do so would have required folding back at the rump and forward at the knees, which was beyond even my flexibility.

This was a two-person coach, and it takes a four-person coach for two persons to misbehave in. I began to entertain a more charitable suspicion about Zed's obstinacy in not letting us out.

There was quite a lot of headroom and quite a lot of legroom, but no fuckroom. You would think that, with a will, positions could have been progressively modified until something was achieved. Believe me, we tried—that is, he tried. Much care had been put into the escape-proofing, springs, elegance, and painted insignia of the coach; not enough into its core purpose.

The nearest he came was to get his body almost straight, from heels at the front of the footroom to head curled into the back of the ceiling, and hold me applied to himself, and then if my navel had been my cunt he could have ridden into it.

"You seem to be rather stiff," I remarked.

"Stiff! I should say so! I don't just *have* an erection, I *am* an erection!"

But he had to collapse beside me for further thought.

(I was only pretending to be as baffled as he was. There was a solution obvious to the rankest erotopologer. But it required collaboration. I withheld it for use if I chose.)

"Applepeel," he said, "tell me, how can it be that you aren't afraid of men?"

"Oh, I'm scared enough," I said.

"You don't seem it. You seem perfectly fearless; it's—discouraging. A little terror would make you even spicier, you know. But another thing: with the amount of tussling you must have had to do, how come your arms are still the same calm shape?"

"I don't use strength, I use quickness."

"Very well. But—I guess I'm unwise to say this—if you're going to rely on tricks you ought to learn 'em all. Don't you know you're supposed to use your knee? You had plenty of chances just now."

"Of course I know. But I couldn't hurt you like that."

I re-expressed it, so he wouldn't think he was specially privileged: "I could never hurt anybody like that."

He looked at me, thinking of what a rough life I was in for, or maybe just of his tomorrow's work.

"All right," I said. "Enough for a day. Let's sleep on our problems."

"Sure! You're my problem!"

"I usually like to be able to stretch out," I said, ignoring him, "but I've had enough exercise, I believe I'll sleep fine."

And we snored through the night, sometimes getting involved in each other's arms. At least I snored; he woke me once to tell me how charmed he was by my little cry on each outbreath.

The coach's pleasant motion lulled us through the first few hours. When morning came it was standing in cold white ground-fog on a heathery highland which reminded me (I was kneeling up to look out of my window) of those that could be seen from the Tashartris temple—the Gog-Magog Hills.

Zed was stirring porridge outside. After breakfast, we moved off, and seeing his preparation I tried to tell him "Look, you can now claim that you've Slept With me, so honor is satisfied"— "Honor may be," he replied, and came matching his body up to me. But the problem hadn't gone away, and he gave up.

"Bitch!" he shouted. "Cockteaser!"

"I've been called both those names before," I said. "The first means, I take it, that I'm female, and the other means you can't get what you want. I could think of worse things to call somebody, and in a minute I will."

He recoiled. (And from outside I heard Zed's discreet chuckle.) "Sorry," he said, "forgive the insults. Result of frustration. You'd probably beat me at that game. But I *am* good at copulation, as you *will* find out when we finally disembark."

"Thank you for informing me of me that."

"Look, I don't mean I've—well—"

"You have a wife, I believe?"

"I had, but she gave up on me and married an admiral."

"I'm sure she had good reason. You've served many women, I expect."

I could see him not wanting to admit to nogamy, but not to too much flingamy either.

---

* Beautician, surely.

"Not many, really. I don't want you to think I'm polygamous."

"Just—oligogamous?"

He smiled; then scowled, thinking I was teasing him for his present agamy. He said: "In any case, I've got more to do than talking." He had an uneasy consciousness of letting me muddle him into leaving stages out.

So he came at me, trying to oppress my mouth with a kiss. But that's not something you can force me to; I kept my jaw shut—put him off by laughing at his whiskers—turned my head aside. He seized me by the back hair and twisted me to him. But the anger in my face took the sugar out of that for him. He let me turn away and was content to prey on my cheek and ear and throat and the tendon of my neck.

And then down his logical list to the next kind of struggle: the struggle for my breasts; the breastling.

As usual, he first demonstrated that he was stronger enough to out-struggle me, but not by enough to make it not a struggle, and so the struggle was maintained with me all the time losing but not uncondi-tionally.

He interlocked his legs with mine to fix at least half of me still. From our hips upward we thrashed and squabbled, and while his fingers continually won their way to their targets, and my fingers tore them away only to give them length for driving in again, his face with its channeled umber cheeks and short dense fringe of beard was hard up against the side of mine and this caused him to talk to me.

"You ruined me, Applepeel, you know. I paid my whole fortune for you." (Dusky baritone up against my cheek, crammed down to a groan.) "I was to have got it back by renting you out to others. But you got away from us and so I lost not only you but everything. You even stole my waterproof blankie—I haven't even been able to jerk off without getting in trouble for spoiling hotel mattresses! All I had left, except for sixty pieces of silver that I kept in my boot, was that band of men that wanted you as badly as I did and trusted me to lead them in the hunt for you. What a shour of jerks!—a battleship salesman, a cruise-ship mortician,* a public procrastinator, a bill-shuffler, a culture-monger, a gospelbanger, a contraptioneer, a garbage-distributor, a tree-butcher, a sprawlveloper, a greenwash-spewer, a major corporate land-scraper or landscape-scalper or scene-scarifier, a hardware-tweaker, a software-fondler, a systems-tamer, an image-consultant or people-pack-ager, a celebrity-inflator, a damage limitator or litigator, a grantgrubber, a Human Interface Network Designer, an Archmishap, two accredited tax-twisters, three knee-shakers, any number of thumb-twiddlers, a market strangulator, five licensed pseudologists, a talking head and a dozen middlemen, not to mention hacks, geeks, leftbrainers, nerds, gooks, wonks, mavens and even a few of the common trades (a lice assassin, a stripper and grinder, a man with a van)—and more and more of them joined, till we had every kind of fop and ugly and turdstool and walking dildo you could wish for. And all of them had at least something to live *on* as well as *for* except me, their leader, whom they expected to live on thin air and hormones and inspiration. The only way I could even eat was to persuade them they were to stick to apples and give anything else they had to me for safekeeping. So I've been subsisting on chocolate bars and chew tobacco and bubblegum and liquorice allsorts. Don't you think that might account for a lot?"

"Yes, I'll need to feed you up," I said. Sarcastically, but he did have a better chance with me now he was fallen from tycoon to pauper. "Would you go easy on that one for a while?" And he gave my left breast a rest.

"My finances weren't all you ruined," he went on (chasing my other udder), "you nearly drove me out of my mind!" "Nearly?" "All the more because that performance of yours told me you were no porcelain saint. You're—can I admit it?—sexier than me. But let me tell you, I'm sexy! You're worth exertion, and I'm going to exert myself on you. Oh my gog, I've got such a backlog of ideas! I'm going to make up for lost time, like a clock that chimes every ten minutes."

"Looks like I'm in for a treat."

"That's the worst part, carrying so much in one's head, and new things suggesting themselves every time I think about you, so that I'm afraid of losing the oldest and best. Losing my tradition of you. And you were the only one I could really share them with."

"You should have jotted them down," I said.

"I'd be sent to prison."

"That bad? Tell me some spicy ones."

"I'm afraid I'll disappoint you—(take your eyes off me, you're confusing me)—seems the worst ones are the ones I've forgotten—only recall primary ones—odd and sentimental ones, you'll think. I remember that after we dressed you in applerind and ate it off you I was going to have you always in nothing but clumsy black buskins (or gray, were they, or brown?)—"

"Green, wasn't it?" I said. "Green roots. Boots, that is."

"Yes, gal in green galoshes—galoshgal. But I think black is nicer—up to the thighs—brutal boots—maximal contrast with your fair body—leather—though furry on the inside. You'll like the feel. And

gloves too." "Kitten in mittens?" "Or maybe iron—" "Iron *mittens?*"
"Yes, and boots too. Magnetic, stick you to the floor. Then we can
come at you from either side or bend you over. And rename you
Adame—"

"You may have to rethink there. I'm already known by that name
up and down Peccadilly."

He looked at me in surprise, while his fingers went on mashing
nipple. But he didn't want to cope with any story from me, yet.

"Well, never mind. We'll invent another name or two for you, or
ninety. You deserve polynomy—"

"Polyonymy, you mean."

"Yes, polyonymy, you should be as polyonymous as Tashartris
herself. You should be clothed in names and only names."

"They better be long ones."

"All right—we'll make them *appellations*. We'll apply them to you;
wind you around in ninety narrow namesashes! (And then put you up
on a stage and spin you by unwinding them.) Meanwhile *Applepeel* suf-
fices. It covers the whole of you. —You know, it used to be that men
hankered for strangeness; such is, or was, the hankering for the stranger
that we wanted our targets not only naked but name-naked. Not now.
—But would it interest you to know that even your *parts* have names?"

"Well, of course they do."

"No, I mean *names*. For instance these nipples are Liz and Libby,
and your navel is Pam Flanders."

"Hell! You're kidding, aren't you?"

"No, I swear. Naming sharpens perception, you see, like when you
know that a dandelion isn't really a dandelion but a hawkweed. I knew
a fellow doted on little Libby here—mumbled to her in his sleep. There
are others who call the two of 'em Jot and Tittle, but I find that a little
obvious— 'Don't want to leave out a single Jot or Tittle,' you know?
Yes, and your face is Blanchild, and *its* parts have names. This corner
of your eye is something like Genevieve or Joidvive, I believe. And your
left glush is Sylvia, and your right glush, Charlie." "Oh, Charlotte,
surely!" I begged.

"In fact," he said, "the Thorotouch is being rewritten in these
terms— 'He worships Miss Boston with the first joint of his left middle
finger; the second joint . . .' Can you guess who Miss Boston is?"

"No. Yes, so don't tell me."

"She's just your—"

"No, no; *basta!* I don't want to know which or where Mrs. Bostock
or Miss Lechworthy is!" "But—" "I don't want to hear what my hang-

nails and my dandruff are called by slavering lips, d'you hear? Enough is enough." "Okay, okay." "Enough of it!" "Okay!" "Let's review the situation—"

(It was around here that I tired of it and just dropped my hands, and he dwelled freely on my breastery, with more peaceful slappings and liftings and groupings and helical traceries. It both raised and soothed me. Once he applied his mouth, and murmured, I think: *"Apfelsoft."*)

"Let's take stock," I sighed. "We're both pauperized, you and I. We don't have clothes, we don't have money. I have only my names, you have only your craze or your alibido—whatever it is, that's got from your gonads into your bloodstream. Other than that, we seem to have nothing, except this coach and its driver who shall be nameless. And what about the castle where we were all to live together? That's an illusion too, I suppose?"

"No, the castle is all I've got. One of the last followers was the old Count of Beth-Eden. He could never properly get the idea that this quest was not a spiritual quest. He believed that you are Life the daughter of Love, or Luck the bride of Folly; that you have come out in your seventeenth year, like Magicicada, to sing for a mate. He left me his castle. That's where we're going. It's up between the headwaters of the Windrush and the Evenlode. Actually it's little more than a wine cellar and a conservatory and a grape arbor and a stable (where this coach came from) and a little flag-shaped garden—what the Persians call a paradise—with an old wall around."

"And we're to look after this place together, you and me and Zed? Or are there any followers left?"

"There may be a few—the most useless ones. The ones who would go and wait there, while the rest did the hunting. But more likely they've all scattered. By now there've been sightings of Applepeel at John O'Groats, reports of Applepeel swimming the Straits of Gibraltar—"

"So and what will you and me do when the grapes and the wine run out? We've got to live as well as love, you know."

"*You* are my resource."

"I see. Hire me out. (You *hire* people, you know; you rent *things*.) Or rather I suppose send out brochures and invite the patrons in. With convenient map of the drive up through the woods. 'The new Count of Beth Eden throws his grounds open to the public. And his concubine.'"

He smiled, picturing it with equanimity.

"Theopard, won't you be jealous? This will be a bit of a dilution of your bliss, I'm afraid. Am I never to hear you roar 'Take your eyes off mah woman'?"

He sat up (his legs had gradually become disentwined from mine) and put his hands on the seat and rocked forward and back before turning to me again.

"Believe it or not, Applepeel, that's not the way I feel about you. You may find it strange, but I feel—the whole world feels about you in a way other than that. We do not want to keep you to ourselves, to any one of us. You are too much. There were some who did, at first, but that was before they understood who you are. Now I think of Castle Beth-Eden as only the temple where I will bask in you and in the court of all those who admire you. I claim no special place, I'm just first among equals, though you must admit I've been the most persistent in pursuing you."

"Nothing special about you, among my lovers? —But perhaps I shouldn't presume to think you love me. I should just be grateful that you think me beautiful."

"Did I mention beauty?"

"Oh—perhaps you didn't."

"What you have isn't so much beauty as sheer Mark 45 *sex-appeal*. Sex-up-*peel-l-l*-ah-oh . . . You've got it because you don't know it. You'll always have it because you'll never believe it. You have deep grace in spite of your klutzy self. You've got a body's worth of s-z-z-appeal in every bit of you from this hair down to this toenail."

I plucked out a hair and gave it to him.

He looked back at me and grinned. "Enough?" I said. "A good start," he said. I gave him one of the frizzy hairs. "That's almost the way it is!" he said. "Your fingers speak more truth than they know." (He tried to tie the hair around his stalk, then ate it.) "I alone couldn't possibly do justice to you." (With the other hair I helped him.) "We are manikins that exhaust ourselves in worship: you are space and time."

"Oh, bull," I said, getting up.

"Where are you going?"

"I'm tired of being on this side of you."

"You think your right side is your worse—so do I, so does everybody—

> I showed them the old and cruel
> Side of my face

—but you haven't got a bad side; your right side is lovelier than the whole world's left side. The Thorotouch was made for you."

"No, for you, it's just your sort of obsessive, systematic—"

"Though it is infinite, every one of us will attempt it with you."

"That will kill every one of us."

"Even a completed Thorotouch would not be enough—"

"Bull! I've heard this inflated stuff from your disciples. I've got one more name, d'you know what it is?—Hyperbole. The highclass hetaira Hyperbole. It makes me want to laugh but not be able, and I see it makes you forget your— Never mind. Let's bring it down to specifics: does it mean I'll be able to send a letter to, for instance—well, Tarquin?"

"Sure. Send him a brochure. Is he still alive? Does the race of Tarquin yet hold sway in Rome?"

"That's Mr. Quitetwice the teacher, that's his name."

"Oh, him. A slight Tarquin. He was in love with you too."

"Only with my glushes, really." (Only glust.)

"Don't blame him. Faultless taste, whether it was your glushes he courted or your kidney or the glance of the light on your temple. He was in love with you. You are a country—the humble worshipper has to choose a province."

"Bull," I repeated, but my head swam. I didn't know whether to picture myself as queen on throne, goddess on altar, or bitch under rutting pile.

"Well, more of the latter, but there'll be time for interludes of the queen stuff."

"And Henry Parolong? and—more acquaintances; you haven't heard my adventures yet. And there's Fortesant too, who used to have a claim on me. D'you think they'll enter into it?"

"They'll enter into it!"

"I mean, enter into the spirit of it."

"Into the spirit, into the body, into everything they can, all together and all at once. If the spirit too has more than one hole, they'll enter into 'em all!"

"Please be a shade less blasphemous, Theopard. If you were a little boy at Sunnymead I hate to think of the punishments you'd find yourself catching. Now, you're describing, apparently, a situation of polyandry."

"Polly, polly!"

"You think I ought to be pleased and flattered, I suppose."

"There could be worse fates. In fact I don't suppose I'm the only male who thinks wistfully of being female and having an ounce of your fun. Of course we'd have to be reborn with an atom of your appeal."

"Well, I don't think it's all roses," I said. "For instance, won't I get Harry-preggers?"

"Oh, leave that to Tashartris—let her look after you. She always has, hasn't she? Yes, you're probably as fertile as you are exuberant. But let her decide whether and when you have babies. You'll always be Applepeel."

"I see. Anyway, it appears you really would rather share me than have me to yourself. (I could have said, 'be alone with me,' couldn't I?) You didn't just hold this out to hold your followers. How noble. And quite practical, really. After all, you may need a crowd to manage me. And to give you a rest between orgasms. No, I'm not being critical, I'm moving toward sympathy with the view that it could be fun. Admitted, neither you nor I have a terribly high opinion of those followers of yours. But then, I've only seen their backsides; are their fronts any good?"

"They're potbellied," he said, "and hog-jowled. About as much use as a broken rubber band, and annoying as a clinging shit. Liars, too: one time a squad of them claimed to have come within three yards of you, and do you know what their excuse was for missing?—their own erections got in their way!"

My laughter stormed out through my nose. I doubled over, and gasped as soon as I could: "I'm sorry, I'll get a grip—oh God's grandmother!—talk to me about something else, quick—I know: try to put that into verse—please!" So he frowned, and I followed his effort, and by the time he came out with

> They say they failed to catch her—is it true?—
> Because their own erections blocked their view

I had quieted down. "That's better, I can breathe. Listen, perhaps they aren't liars: that Squad we must have, if only for curiosity. Ah! I know, Theopard, you're their king and they're liars and quality not quantity, but sometimes we need liars for light relief. What else will they think of? —Another thing, by the way: my appeal doesn't seem limited to males."

"What d'you mean?"

"Can I have females come—Saxie, and Granny Oe?"

"Of course, of course. We'll be delighted. We'll make special times. We'll—"

But while he was running ahead on viewing arrangements, mixed nights, combinatory postures, I thought of Zed, and my face darkened.

"Zed. Let's talk about her. I suppose you traced me to the school, I wonder how you did that—oh, I know, you heard my radio appeal." "That was only a night ago," he reminded me. "So it was" (it seemed like a century); "anyway, you tracked me down, and by then you hadn't got enough followers left to take Sunnymead by storm, so you sniffed your way back along my trail to my home and found Zed, and paid her the sixty pieces of silver."

"She's got thirty. (She's buying our supplies out of one of them.) The other thirty are waiting for her in the castle."

"And then you had to show her the way there, so that she could drive the coach."

"No. She knew it long before you or I were born. In her remote youth she was carried off by a nomad tribe. You didn't know that? She's wandered around all these regions."

"Zed!" I called out. "Zed! Can you hear me, you Judas?"

No answer from up there on the driver's seat.

"How old are you, Zed?"

Then I heard her: she gave a long rork and a hiccup in *D*. Then quickly she tried to cover it by saying "Excuse me" and and croaking her answer: "Ninety-nine, Miss Felicity!"

I realized!

"Zed, you're a Monger!"

No answer.

"You're a Monger! So that's why you couldn't resist a bit of money! Zed, are you going to enjoy it? What are you going to spend it on? What if you don't live to be a hundred?"

That was my lowest point. Of all the awful things I have said, that was the one I would most wish unsaid. And Zed couldn't speak.

Theopard, either to come to the aid of his ally, or because he had completed his program on my breasts, started working his hands down. I had to get back to my futile defences.

And as he conquered his way bellyward—my ribs, my waist—it geographically fed his imagination, and he whispered fiercely to me: "Oh, on hunt nights we're going to let you get away from the castle, we'll give you a start, my guests will be riding, you'll find yourself on a peninsula—" "Is there a peninsula up there in the woods?" "—a fine afternoon's hunting—" "I thought you said it was night?" "—a night and a day, many close squeaks, but you can't get away in the end—someone spots you from the cliff-top: 'Look, down there, it's her!'"—down to my navel— "they stalk you, you're on the beach, hide-and-seek among the rocks—trapped—you try to get away into the surf"—fur—"you run into a marsh—" "A marsh? But I thought—" "—surrounded—we dismount and wade in from all sides—"

This was getting dangerous: his fingers were stumbling through the shrubbery, wading into the marsh. "Interesting phenomenon," I splut-

tered, "have you ever noticed? try it: if you grip like that and just keep
still for ten minutes—quite still—you'll forget what actually you're
touching; interesting—aspect of sensory deprivation, I think—or even
just five minutes—can always resume movement—try it," but he didn't
try it. I cried out: "What's that book down there?"

"—we all close in on you together— Your exercise book, as you
know, don't try to distract me. —a last splashy tussle—"

"No, there's something under it."

"—wet fingers up-under-at you—we're going to have you in thigh-
deep water—"

"I think I know what it is!" And I broke half loose (out of his grip,
but dragging fingerclusters) and dived across and picked it up. Yes,
under the exercise book was something else: the Applepeel Coloring
Book.

The Coloring Book

66 HOW IN the world—!"

"Drop it!" he said, sparing a hand to snatch the book from me. The other hand remained at the attack but now outnumbered. "Have you seen this thing before?" he asked guiltily.

"Yes. You picked it up off Mr. Quitetwice's desk, didn't you?"

"Yes, the dirty old—"

"You spied it and put my notebook down on top of it so you could pick them up together. You stole even that from him. He could have comforted himself a bit with it. Turn around and take this right back to him!"

"Don't be absurd."

"And you were so mean to him, I hated you for that."

"I was nervous."

"You!"

"Yes, I was. I was afraid about whether I'd really come away with you—or what I'd do with you if I did. I was afraid of *you*."

"You'd better be. I promise you that unless you mail this back to him at the first chance, with a love-letter from me, I'm going to be as nasty to you as I damn well can."

"How fearsome. All right. I will, at the next post office. Well, I will tomorrow."

"Why not today? Haven't *you* looked at it before?"

"No, as a matter of fact I haven't. I never had a groat to spare for it, and my followers thought me beyond it. There have been sequels, but they say this original edition is the classic."

"Well, it's not worth bothering with. Especially when you've got the real—I mean, I never got far into it before it put me to sleep."

Curiosity about the book got slightly the better of the curiosities being slaked by his fingertips, and with his free hand he contrived to turn the book the right way up and open it in the middle.

"Here you are for sure!"

He momentarily spared the other hand to turn a page. Then, "Could you hold it for me?"

"Oh, of course!" I took it in both hands and held it at his nosetip, and he goggled into it while plunging both his hands back into my midst—one down the front, one excavating under.

I laughed sardonically: "You expect some silly things, don't you!" I snapped the book shut on his nose and threw it across the coach, and

tore his hands out. He kept one perfunctorily trying, but with the other
he reached over and retrieved it, and set about learning to turn pages
with his thumb.

"Put you to sleep—really?" he said. "Didn't it excite you in your
body, just a little?"

"It's not even me, how could it be? The fellow never saw me."

"It's you. Recognizable by blot of hair—how are we supposed to
color that?—and a glimpse of a figure, mostly leg—breathtaking leg—
shrill leg—leg six feet long—and nothing much but glushes imbe-
tween. Ever slavishly rendered, the perennial colliding curves, ever
traceable whether clad in fishnet or bearskin or fresh air!"

"To what are you referring?"

"Your bot-tom."

"Why, by the way," I asked, "is it called my bot-tom? It's at the
middle of me."

"That's true. Other people have shorter legs, and aren't so often on
them."

"And you can tell this is me just because it has—these features?"

"No, that's not all"—he waved his hand, shirking the effort to
explain what made a likeness of me.

Life began to be easier. It needed only half my mind and my right
hand to keep up the protection of my center.

I pushed aside the window blind and for the first time enjoyed the
passing cottages and spinneys, the rail fences and the ponies in the pas-
tures, and the berries on the brambles, which were coming ripe, hovering between red and black—it would now have been even easier for
me to live off the land.

I remembered how in May I had gone along the paths with my head
turned sideways, saying to myself "*Spurge—poke—privet—
catbrier—dayflower,*" sharpening perception by naming.

Lunch was coleslaw, succotash, hominy, and gumbo. "Zed," I said,
"where in the world have you been wandering to get these recipes?"

Theopard took scant interest; absently he let me spoon-feed him,
while he used one hand to hold the book and the other to keep in touch
with my thigh or waist. So long as he kept off the target, I allowed him
some freedom with my peripheries.

He surfaced again into words: "Obscenity will never be the same
again!"

"Hardcore Applepeel, is it?" I asked.

"Not quite; you're peeled for sure but I'm getting impatient to see you cored and eaten. But still this is enough to keep a whole culture healthy with lust."

"Tell you what," I suggested, "let's stop at a fair and get you a box of crayons, and then you can be nicely occupied for the rest of the journey."

"Thank you, no," he said, "who wants to color banisters and beaches and bedspreads? The essential areas are skin—and I don't mean appleskin—and coloring skin isn't practical, at least for the ordinary guy. Oh, I'm sure they'd sell me a flesh-pink crayon, but to use that for your eyelid, your burnished shoulder, your honey stomach—sick! Maybe that's why nobody's done any coloring in this book, though they've got as far as wetting it. —Tell me, how have you spent most of the story since we parted?"

"Happily."

"I mean, how dressed?"

"The same way as then, I'm sorry to say: defenceless from the waist down."

"I wouldn't count on your defencelessness whatever you're not wearing. —But that's it: they know: they give us you in every *other* predicament. Here you're running around in nothing but a hat. Here you're in the gymn on a cold day—in legwarmers! Waiting tables—in an apron! In gloves . . . No, gloves and socks . . . A bib . . . (Only, you understand. Always only.) A belt, wide and tight . . . Here you're in a tutu—and even it keeps getting flashed up. Now you're getting married—" "Getting married, eh?" "Yes, wearing a ring and a bridal veil." "Well, I would, wouldn't I?" "*Only* a ring and a veil. Applepeel on a bike; wearing goggles. Oh, and a bicycle clip, for your pants that aren't there. On the beach; in sunglasses. Here you're diving into the pool—lovely view!" "What am I wearing there?" "Hair! Oh, no, I see: earplugs. Applepeel wearing an earwig." "Ear . . . ?" "Applepeel on a fashion runway, wearing a diagram . . . Applepeel in social circumstances, wearing a drink in one hand and a sandwich in the other . . . Applepeel wearing a tie." "Like a man, eh?" "Yes, it's man's tie, all right." "What's the pattern? Is it an old school tie?" "A stalk! It's painted to look like a stalk." "I've always wondered that, about ties." "Shall I tell you which way it's pointing?" "No." "Mostly you're allowed your highheels too—" "Ain't got no highheels." "—that's just for their usual function." "What's their usual function?" "Why, making your legs and glushes look extra good, of course. Erecting them. Wearing a watch—you ain't got no watch either, you don't know what it's for. Princess Applepeel wearing—guess what?" "Something, I hope." "A crown." "Surely only a coronet." "What's the difference? Crown, coronet, cornet, trumpet, strumpet—ah . . . And a necklace (hardly visible) with one ruby to enhance the sunshine on the skin. And here— oh no, can't look at that page, that's too much!" "Wearing too much?" "I think I glimpsed that the item you're only-wearing there is a *frock*. That's just too feminine, it'd make me spill . . . What's it called when its absolute minimum area and *also* diaphanous?—a cobweb, I should think. (Here you really are in nothing at all, and making love to your- self—oh, I see, you're applying suncream all over. So you are wearing something; a suit of cream.) The ingenuity of these stories—but I suppose they're not the first in the world driven by excuses to get a sleeve caught in a fan or a hem in a mangle. And now you're in a shred—and the things that happen to it! Almost as if they'd been observing us—only I didn't think of—"

"What is this, a coloring book or a comic strip?" I asked, peering over.

"It's a skin flick!" he said, letting the pages fly through his fingers.

"I had no idea there was so much of it."

"It's printed on onionskin paper. And those Mongers saved expense by leaving the coloring to the buyer, but they found an artist they couldn't stop. He draws Applepeels like you or I clip fingernails— he draws Applepeels in his sleep." ("Hey," I thought, "that's something I could do.") "And his ideas! Who is he? He makes me blush. He should be hauled before the Lord Chamberlain. He must have thought it was his last chance to pour out his lifetime's ribald inventions. Perhaps it was. I should think he wanked himself to death before he finished. Every one of these scenes is worth pausing for a jerkoff."

Theopard had forgotten about me, or at least he'd taken his left hand away and was using it as he supposed the artist used his non- drawing hand.

I should mention that I had tried it: slipped my earrings off, had them in my left hand. After a while I secreted them as I had once done with the priest's coin, except that now two places were needed.

"'Applepeel and the Caveman'!" he barked out. "'Applepeel and the Pirates.' 'Applepeel on the Magic Carpet' . . ." And a bit later: "'Applepeel as Cheerleader,' o heaven! Here she is protesting she doesn't know how, and they tell her 'Just prance and we'll follow you'—throw her in the air—team unstoppable—but it's her they're rushing—the whole stadium—let's turn to the locker-room scene," and he fell quiet. I got only parts of each story. "Applepeel the Witch, sole properties a tall black hat and a broomstick between her legs—you have to agree that's pretty erotic." "Just rotic." "Applepeel on roller-skates. (Applepeel *wearing* rollerskates. We need a new word for only-wearing. How about soloing?—Applepeel soloing a blindfold.) Applepeel skateboarding, she's pretty good, most of the time she's upside down. Applepeel on St. Pat's Day, here you're supposed to color her tunic *anything but* the notorious green, so everyone can pat her or pinch her . . . Applepeel swimming in place—"

"Let me see that," I said.

"Yes, it's delicious, isn't it? You can see how the water would slap through and keep everything shiny." It wasn't the Cressfont: it was a glass tank with water pouring along, crowds on viewing-bridges.

"Now they're dressing her." "Dressing her?" "Yes, multiplying her earrings into jewelry all over. Bangles, navel-jewel . . . The ideal of Decorated Nakedness . . .

"A page that *has* been colored: an orchard of new Applepeel ear-rings, garnet and ruby apples, gold-filigree trees with emerald leaves . . .

"And now it's the ideal of Duplicated Nakedness: a whole chapter on that; tights, levis, leotards, wet shirts . . ."

(I was almost interested. I had not been entirely without girlish fan-tasies of dressing.)

"Now she's in the pillory! There, I told you I might forget all my oldest and best ideas and lose my copyright on them! Look at her (half of her), with the townspeople lining up behind . . .

"Now she's being made to wrestle with another girl . . . with two . . . they've got her by head and torso, a compound grip, they're passing her nethers along the circle of spectators—don't you love that!"

"Yes," I said, "one of my favorite parts."

"Favorite parts, yes, each indulges in his favorite part as it comes past . . .

" . . . she's in a little arena, strippling—"

"Doing what?"

"Stripping with lashings of lithe and lissom writhings and wrig-glings, that means."

"You know Applepeel can't dance."

"She can on paper, believe me! And the audience is clappling or lappling, and if you don't know what that means it means they're sup-plauding."

"Run that by me again?"

"They're clappling: they're using the glushes of their lapgirls to applaud on. They've all been served with supplausae."

"Now look, Theopard, these are just pictures. All this language of yours makes me think your imagination is more rabid than the artist's."

"No, the words are Applepeel's own! They're all here—stripple, supple, lipple, lapple—in these Confessions of hers, printed under the pictures."

"Oh, her Confessions. I'd forgotten about those. So there is some text in this book?"

"Yes, but it's nonsense, overblown stuff. You have an over-generous tendency to credit people with things they *should* have said. And you go off into digressions and philosophies at the most unlikely moments—it's all too reminiscent of the operatic heroines who sing an aria between getting killed and dying, hardly realistic." "Why, golly," I said, or would have if I'd had time, "on the contrary, that seems to me quite true to life." Don't we all at every turn think more than we can say? Unspoken words outweigh the spoken as the iceberg does the snowflake. — "The pictures," he was explaining, "are just illustrations of your Confessions, I suppose they sat gently cundling and stalkling each other—like we're doing now—while she reminisced and he sketched and she corrected him. Shall I read you some?"

"No, that's all right, I expect it'll come back to me. Just carry on looking."

The book and I between us had found a way to render Theopard harmless.

When the coach halted for the night, he was already asleep. I called out to Zed: "Zed, it's a little cold!"

"Yes, we're farther north," she said. "But we're nearly through the hills."

"Where are we going, anyway?" Through my window on the left I could see the starry Virgin going down on her shoulder. "It seems about the same direction as home."

"Yes, roughly," she said, coming to look in on me. "Wipe your nose, child," she said by old habit. And by old habit I'd have obeyed, if I'd had anything to wipe it with.

"Please give me a blanket or something. I want to lay it over him too, he's drenched, he'll catch cold."

"I'm sorry, Miss Fristy, all I can give you is this lamp."

"Well, I don't want to read any more."

"It'll make you quite warm in there."

And gradually the lamp did heat the interior of the coach. I was restless, I hadn't had nearly so much exercise today. In spite of myself I opened the coloring-book and flipped again through the pictures.

Yes, it was me.

Decorated Nakedness—

Duplicated Nakedness—

I ran my palm down my waist, and into my groin, and away down my thigh; pressing.

It became the first difficult night of my life to get through.

Two days and nights in this plush-padded cell, this traveling cage, I had a right to be jittery! I couldn't even stand on my head. I did find a few exercises to do. I had to divide them around the ungracefully inert body that shared the cage with me.

The body showed signs of stirring, but I pacified it.

As you know, sleep is important to me. I can usually, at need, sleep open-eyed while people are talking to me. (Or even pinching my sphincter.) Two previous sleepless nights had been forced on me: mending the statue, and cavorting in the sinbelt, state bordello, helicopter, and duckpond. They had been immediately followed by the two wildest days of trial to my virtue and endurance. What could a third such night portend?

All this and still before the beginning! Though I hadn't been a virgin very long, it was coming to seem long.

"Zed," I called out.

"What, Miss Chiff? It's still three hours off dawn."

"Could we move on? Then I might sleep."

"There's no moon." For indeed it was the very night between moons.

But I persuaded her, and somehow she and the mule found their way forward down the moorland paths. On the unsteady floor the lamp flickered, threatening to set fire to the coach, firing only the undersides of our limbs; over them my eyes by stages closed. And in my sleep I grew warmer and warmer. And I woke moaning from the heat-dream.

Moaning!—I was sobbing! Scarier than the lechery in me was the ferocity—the last thing I did was smash a teapot with my hand, and I woke scalded. And then, as day cooled and soothed me, the sob choked in my nose and turned into a snort of hilarity! Could that have been my mind, in which grew furniture never graced by Miss Elvet and Applepeel-predicaments beyond the imagining of the Master of the Coloring-Book? Even this torrid dreamworld, like any freshly left dreamworld, seemed where I belonged, I wanted to explore back into it—its devices were so witty, I must tell them to Theopard! But it grew hazy and vanished back into me.

The lamp guttered out, and the window-blind went back to admit daylight and breakfast. Even now I had woken before the man, so I ate some of his too, and slipped my earrings on again.

The book was lying open, at the Anatomical Charts of Applepeel. Plan, elevation, view southpolar intercrural. Glush Maximus, Glush Medius. The crunode where the curves collide . . .

I was about to tear myself away and take a look out of the window, to see if I could tell where we were, when he opened his eyes. I shifted the book out of sight. But he just said as if to himself, *"Applepeel."* I said, "Eat your breakfast."

"There doesn't seem to be much left."

"Don't you want it?—I'll have it," and I leaned over and finished it for him (a bowlful of VitaGlush and goatsmilk).

While I did so his hand came under my breasts, and followed the food down along my linea-alba. "Go ahead—eat," he murmured. "You need it. We need it. Turn it into new Applepeel." Then when I had finished he sat more upright and tried to catch me in a kiss.

"Wait," I said— "do you want to look at some more pretty pictures?"

"No." "I'll look with you," and I spread the book across both our laps. After a quizzical glance at me, he obediently joined me in studying it.

"So this book—this book, if you can call it that—got you interested?" he said, sliding his hand to me under it.

"Yes, it's quite gripping. I wanted to get to the dénouement."

"I think she's already denued."

"It doesn't mean that, it means solved—unknotted. The story."

"Is there a story?" He bent his head over it again.

Finally I just opened my knees and let the damn book slip through to the floor, and turned to him and laughed.

"What are you gasping for?" I asked.

"Pure—something; pleasure, I guess. But what are you laughing at?"

"I don't know. But by the ring of Tashartris, I think I'm almost ready myself! except—well, there's still my dratted virginity."

"I suppose that *is* important."

"Sometimes I wonder," I said. "Who exactly is it important to?"

He cleared a little timidity from his throat.

"I mean," I went on, "virginity is not quite the same as parenthood, not quite—"

"I have to tell you something, Applepeel. I'm afraid you're not a virgin any more."

"What d'you mean? You're stalk's been over *here* all this time. Surcly mating my hand doesn't count?"

"No, but—where *my* hand has been may have made a difference."

We looked into the matter. He was right. By easy stages and by the infantry action or trench warfare of many mere fingers my defensive membranes had been eroded quite away.

"Well, phooey," I said. "After all this time. What a pooting way to lose it."

Home, Coming

66 I FEAR so," said Theopard. "I'm sorry." He sat for the first time chastened, chaste, and slack-stalked beside me; we were a disconsolate pair. He tried to brighten me. "Pooting it is. Still, more comfortable, you know. Avoids quite a bit of mess. Recommended for young ladies before their wedding nights, actually . . ."

"That's all right, Theopard," I said, patting his wrist. "I'll get over it. No use crying over split milk."

"That's the spirit. Spilt, you mean."

"Right; thank you. Theopard."

"What?"

"Are you by any chance a wise man of at least fifty?"

"Certainly not."

"I thought not. You're such a goof, in fact, that I may have to initiate *you*, and perhaps not gently."

"What are you driving at?"

"My virginity's gone."

"Yes, as we said. In this, ah, nugatory way."

"And since it's gone—"

"What?"

"Well, then!"

"Well then what?"—bewildered.

"Well then, for heaven's sake!" And I actually took his stalk in a pentagon of fingertips and drew it out; but it retracted like a slug, thinking I was merely accepting its apology.

"For heaven's sake what?"

"For heaven's sake don't be so pooting yourself! I can't stand it!"

"I'm sorry, but I thought I was being rather decent."

"You are—and worse late than never!"

"I mean I thought I was being rather understanding."

"Well, think again! Make another effort!"

"What kind of an effort?"

"An effort together, you arthropod and apologogue! *Apa-pachamos!* Let's get ooling!"

"Doing what?"

"I just made it up; a word is so badly needed."

"But what does it mean?"

"'Fuck' is so bad and 'screw' isn't much better." (I forgot about "mate.")

At last he got the message. I thought I was going to have to turn to Monger language.

"Oh! Right away! *Ool!*"

And we turned toward each other like the halves of a clam closing.

We went at each other, and at the padded interiors of the coach, I'm surprised it didn't burst around us; Zed above must have kept her seat with difficulty. For the first time freely I threw myself to him, every piece of me—threw my breasts to him and his mouth gulped them while his hands gulped glush—threw back my head and welcomed his trunk to mine, but still there was no room to welcome him to me centrally. Oh, there were more roars of exasperation, there were absurdities of body-clashing, we tried the very longest diagonal, we made a connection but could not hold it. And Theopard crashed back sitting on the seat, thumping his fists on it in utter frustration.

His tower stood, but I saw that it was finally about to crumble. So I had mercy on the kid and on myself. I chose to pass over his stupidity. I turned around, giving him a lazy smile, and sat on it.

It sank up into me, or, no, I was fulfilled, the scattered parts of me rushed together at their fulcrum and in their hunger for uniting locked.

For ten measures, stretched mouths and shut eyes were the only expression we gave to our amazement—his amazement that joy had come, mine at the joy itself.

He could not move (as on a previous occasion). He could not move; it was I who measured time's pulses, dancing on his lap.

"Why the *hell* didn't we think of this before?" he moaned.

"Yes, you big holligog!"

"Call ourselves topologers! Idiots! Stopologists! Stupescences! I just thought of frontward for ooling and backward for—" "For other things that I'll think of words for later when I make you do them." "A A A Applepeel—don't promise me more—this is too much already!—A A A!"—for I had already found something to do more: I found with my hands the lower stories of his tower, and spread over us the rivers that were arising from our springs and sealing us together at our source.

I rose faster, and on every fall, though I gave myself the falls, I had to scream; there was a pressing forward on my despot or apogee—that spot inside me; one of his hands tried to keep up with my breasts and the other with my rosamound, but lipple me he could not because of the height of my bounces: his face was beside mine and turned to it, staring in amazement at my cheek and eye that flashed upward past him— "The jewel, your eye!" he said to its corner—he took my earring in his mouth as it passed; it came off; I turned my head and laughed at the man with the gold earring in his mouth!

"Hey," he gasped, "you're supposta look in agony when you come . . ."

And meanwhile this journey, having become our honeymoon, was coming to its end. For we were coming into his castle, we were on the cobbles of the carriageway, and outside the blinds of the coach I heard dimly the noises of crowds like the gravel by the sea; hunters there must be still in the castle; but only dimly they mattered, it could have been the sea that rose around us or a legion of eagles, we knew only of a pang of electric blue that rose ringing like bells and spread like the tide into all my capillaries and announced mate in two moves and opened the double gate of paradise and suddenly blossomed into the fountain in the garden of Beth-Eden in the core of me, and he was pinching me in three places and I had stopped in flight so that he could fasten on me his kiss and I

was striving to become less kissed than kisser.

(And the blinds had opened.) And the earring passed from his mouth into mine, and I crunched it up. And I opened my eyes in the light. But only to look at his huge brown eyes, like chestnuts. Then without turning anything else, body or kiss, I let my eyes deflect.

For a long moment I knew what I was seeing but I didn't care and I just existed angelically. Then the inside of me, the zesty spirit, did three somersaults and a handspring within the coach of my body and stood up and shook itself down and was ready to be sensible and face the outside and answer to it. We were in the forecourt of my house, and there looking in on us from the right were my mother and my sister and from the left my father and my brother.

How, Felicity Jane, are you going to get out of *this* one?

I couldn't.

"Dad," I said, "Mum: meet my fiancé."

* See Sàneval, A., "New Light on the Story of Samson and Delilah from Cult Figurines Found at Gaza," *Proc. Philist. Soc.* XVIII 1 ff.

The Deed

ZED OPENED the door. Theopard shrank into his place, but I climbed off him and tumbled out into her arms, weeping and laughing and stroking her and saying, "Zed, forgive me for the things I said! Thank you for bringing me home—my everlasting little sister!"

"Hush, child!" she said in embarrassment, "let me go in and fetch you some clothes."

My mother put her hands in front of the youngsters' eyes, and spun them around and directed them indoors. (As soon as they were behind her they stopped, not to be deprived of the scene.) She then reached into the coach and, since Theopard had no collar by which to be lifted, she grasped his ear and drew him forth. My father stood looking by turns pained and glad but mostly bewildered.

I let Zed go and went to hug him next. He shyly put his arms around my bare chest as he hadn't been allowed to since I was fourteen.

"My goodness," he said, trying to make a joke of it, "she's sold her shirt to get home . . ."

Then I tried to rescue Theopard from my mother by aiming a hug past him. "What a time the Count and I have had!" I said. "Those footpads!—they stripped us of everything, as you can see! They tried to beat us too, but they didn't get away scot free: the Count is quite a pugilist!"

Thereupon my mother released the supposititious Count, who drooped limply, but she looked down upon him with apologetic respect; she almost made a curtsey. My father kept his doubts to himself. "A Count!" said Clarence. "Why's he got such short hair?" "She's shorn it," Theopard muttered.* Zed returned with my maroon dress. For Theopard all she had been able to find was a set of Poppa Pepper's pajamas.

Yellow. Besprinkled with blue ducklings. He had to put them on; was spotted something like the pard; was less than fully at ease. I hung the dress over my arm for the moment because I was still talking.

"They took everything, didn't they, Zed, those footpads?" I said to her. "The Count's moneybox too, alas!"

"Oh—yes," she said. "Those footpads. Yes. Everything, the scallywags. (Put your dress on, Miss Fristy.)"

To please her I began drawing it on—at least, I prepared to, rolling the neck around to find the sleeves. Donaldine's gaze was narrow, but I noticed that my small brother was staring at me with eyes like moons. I got my thumbs through the dress and raised it over my head. Theopard studiously did not look at me. Until my mother demanded of him: "Will you be able to keep her in the style to which she has become accustomed?" "Absolutely!" he replied, raking me with a glance from the ribs down.

Turning hastily to Zed, he said: "I hope— Well, you did say they missed the most important thing, didn't you? In the secret compartment?"

"Yes, of course, sir. I have it."

"What are you talking about?" I asked.

"This," said Zed, using her key to unlock a box under the driving seat. "I brought it from the castle along with the coach, as instructed, and haven't had a chance to transmit it to the inheritor."

"Thank you for keeping it safe, Zed," said Theopard. "You can let me have it now."

But instead she handed it to me: a scroll with a ribbon around it.

"What is it?"

"The title deed."

I unrolled it, and became fascinated by the illuminated apple-tree that formed the first letter.

"Read it, Miss Fristy."

I read: "To."

An apple had dropped from the tree to form the second letter.

"Go on, Fristy, for land's sake!"—my mother.

"To my beloved daughter," I read . . .   "To my beloved daughter whom I call Lilith, baptized under the name of Philippa, and known in this life since childhood as Felicity Jane Pepper, or in recent times as Applepeel Curtis, Andatashartris, Adame Mounteve, Morning, Blackmarigold, Fantasy, Dove, Coronarerum, and likely as many names as you have schools of lovers: Because beauty such as yours not only is in itself a primal good, but must—"

Theopard drew it from my fingers and scorched it with his eyes. My father stepped up and looked interestedly over his shoulder. Theopard kept his mouth shut and handed the document back to me, and I flipped it back to Zed.

"And you're my real mother, I suppose?" I asked her.

"No, my Fristy. And he's only using Daughter in some such way as you used Sister to me. All those are just fond-words. It didn't take any special birth to make you beautiful. You're a proper Pepper. Your parents are who they've always seemed to be. But they'll be reconciled to everything now you're a countess." (And she added: "Felicity-shut-your-mouth-when-you're-not-talking-flies'll-fly-in-how-many-times-do-I-have-to-tell-you.")

I stood thinking, while everyone looked at me. (I shut my mouth at first but to keep it so would have required all my attention.) The children came back to the circle, along with two of their little friends from the street. (And there was a wall of other townspeople watching at the open gate.)

"I don't want to call myself Countess, Zed. That will be no use in the future. Besides, I'm too small. You can call me what you like, but I'll call myself Fristy of Beth Eden, and since the castle, I gather, comes with nothing but debts, I shall set up in business there as a sculptress. It's a trade that needs thick floors and a lot of space."

"Are you serious?" said my mother.

"Yes, she is, ma'm," said Zed.

We went into the house. "After you, Count," said my mother, still briskly polite. "Lunch at noon. Take a bath first, Countess Jane."

I had to walk in beside the only person I'm seriously in awe of, my little sister. One of those people so prematurely wise that they've never been stung by a nettle. "Have you actually been going about like that?" she said.

"Like what?"

"Nood."

"Only haffnood."

"Which half, if one may ask?"

"The right half!" I said, laughing nervously. I could have said "the outer half" or "the inner half." I didn't tell her that at times I'd been reduced to wearing, for instance, one boot.

She held the door for me, making it an expression of judgment. "Another thing: you should say sculptor nowadays, not sculptress."

"Sculptress," I said, in answer to her stricture, "because it sounds voluptuous even more than sculptor—nearly as luscious as sculpture. I shall sculpt structures and scribe on them scriptures. 'As some seg-mented skull a sculptor structured,'" I said, thinking of a Canova head of Napoleon. My fingers were curling in anticipation. Relenting, she gave me a chocolate to chew. "I'll call myself sculptrice if you don't look out! No, it's all right, I'll be plain sculptor—I'll be lucky if I can attain that. It's either that or masseuse—the only other way I can think of for utilizing my feeling for the body." "Why d'you need a job?" Donal-dine asked me, or rather I imagined her asking me, so that I could continue our dialogue in my head— "you don't need a job if you're going to get married"; "Well," I said, "that might need a feeling for the body too," etcetera.

While I was in the bath Zed, stooping over me, removed my left earring. "Let me keep it for you, Miss Fristy," she said. "Where's the other one?"

"Here. It's a bit bent, I'm afraid, in fact it's a little bit bitten."

"Well, your mother will be able to bend it back into shape if I can't." (My mother was strong enough to snap her fingers underwater.)

"Zed, am I going to have a baby?"

"You know you're not, Miss Fristy. It all fell out of you. Almost all," she said, teasing out a thread of scum which went eddying away between my legs. "In any case I've been feeding you for the past two days and— I'll give you the recipe."

I clambered out. (Donaldine was standing in the doorway watching, with her big brush ready to attack my hair.) "Zed, you don't really need to towel me. And I should have let you take the first bath. You must be so tired!"

"Don't you worry," said Zed, "I'm quite a chicken!"

"Take the next bath, anyway, and then that poor Count, or Consort!—if there's still time and hot water. —You do really think my plan will work?"

"Yes, I believe you'll break even in the first year."

"Are you a fortune-teller?"

"No, I'm a Monger."

The Solution

ZED, STILL toweling me, and Donaldine, brushing my hair, followed me into the bedroom that the three of us shared.

"Finished?" I said, and they stood back. "Which room has the viewhole—this or the bathroom?"

They gaped at me. No, that's not right, neither of them would gape, Donaldine with her tough little face or Zed with her century of learning control.

"Okay, let's put it differently. Which of you was his accomplice?"

"Whose?" said Donaldine.

"Come on, you know what I'm talking about. I've been thinking about it a lot. I've had to think about it so much that it's influenced me. You must have realized that, when I announced I'm going to be a sculptor. The sculptor—no, I won't call him that—the carver, the good-for-nothing lodger (dislodger, rather, since he set all this off), whose dribble is dripping through the hole even now."

Shocked, both of them let their eyes flick up to a cobwebby corner of the ceiling.

"Ah, I see," I said. "*Both* of you were in it. And it was the bedroom, not the bathroom. I guess I thought it would be the bathroom because it was while I was lying in another bath, gazing at the ceiling, that I realized."

To my relief, Zed and Donaldine both relented and started to giggle. With them, it was proof enough.

"I'm surprised at you, though," I said. "You let the fellow stare down at your skin too."

"We were safe," said Zed. "Whose eyes would waste time on an old woman and a little girl when they've got you to look at? Anyway, *we* sleep under bedclothes and don't let our nightgowns rile up around our necks."

"Zed is being wicked," said Donaldine primly. "We never lay here knowing that somebody was looking at us. We had no idea about this until the morning of your birthday. You were still in bed."

"On bed," said Zed; "she's never *in* one."

"It was a Sunday," I said.

"We did all the work for your party, remember? even though we didn't get to come to it. Zed and I went up to the attic to look for candlesticks and a bigger tablecloth. And we opened a trunk and found *your head* in it."

My little sister said this with deliberate effect, hoping to see my real head go the same color as the plaster head. I sat down on the bed.

"We bust out laughing: 'Fristy's head!' We were carrying it down the stairs when he opened his door and said Excuse me, that was his. It was just a birthday present he'd been making for you."

"Ah—he said it was a birthday present."

"Yes, so he asked for it back. We said, It's only her head you've made, right? Yes, he said, just her head. You're sure?—what's this? And Zed brought out from under the tablecloth what we'd found in another trunk: your left breast."

"For gog's sake, my left breast!"

"A sort of brick including your left breast. We said, Are you by chance making the whole of her, in her birthday suit? He had to laugh and say yes, he thought that would be a suitable birthday present. It all came out. He showed us the chink under the carpet, and the optical device he inserted in it to enlarge the view. He was making the figure in sections for hiding and transport. Eventually they'd be glued together or there could even be a mould made from them and you could be cast in bronze. There were bits of you under his bed and wrapped in his pajamas, one of your feet in his kettle—"

"Feet? Did I have feet? And legs?"

"Of course, why not?" (The sculptor had exceeded his mandate: Tashartris-of-the-Cart has no legs. Perhaps he would keep them as part payment.) "By the way, there's a squinthole to the bathroom too." I covered my face, at which Donaldine laughed drily. "But he told us he was currently working on your glushes, so he only used the bathroom for pleasure; but even at the bedroom progress was slow because you were in a phase of sleeping mainly on your back. In fact he invited us to take a look."

"And was I?"

"No, you were dived over to my side of the bed with only your head and shoulders out of sight; they were under my pillow."

"Oh, when *I* looked," said Zed, "she was on her feet and trying to juggle with the hairbrushes."

"That was another difficulty he told us about," said Donaldine. "He said it would be easier to make a statue of a hurricane. And he could only study you when the light was on or you lay late in the sunshine. But Zed told me afterwards she thought there were other reasons why it was taking him so long, something to do with another kind of hole she'd noticed thirty inches away."

Oh no, what a creep! All that time I had been lying while he scrutinized me and screwed the floorboards. No wonder I had started getting torrid dreams.

"We were sorry for him," said Donaldine, "because he wasn't going to have you finished in time: even if he got the glushes shaped to his satisfaction and the whole thing painted, the glue to join you together would have had to dry overnight. So it wouldn't be possible to carry you down the stairs and have you standing on the table at suppertime (as we suggested). He pretended it didn't matter, he'd just have to have you ready for your next birthday. I told him that was out, I didn't want to wait till next year to see the face you'd make. So I thought of the idea of standing you on the roof—an even funnier surprise. The pieces wouldn't have to be carried far and we could just *stack* you there. — He raised objections, but I made him spend the day smoothing and painting you and numbering the pieces. And when the boys arrived I told a couple of them about it and what the signal would be, and they spread the word so that you and Fortesant were the only ones that didn't know. Then while you were eating supper Zed passed the pieces to me through the dormer window and I carried them up the back side of the roof and built you on that skylight between the chimneys, which is almost flat. I'm a daredevil climber—I'm a monkey," said Donaldine smugly.

"How did I look? Was my figure any good?"

"No-o, you were in various stages of finish—every cunthair was chiseled out but he had a lot of work to do on your knees. Really he'd only blocked out your proportions, but that was enough for recognizing you at a distance. I didn't have much time to look you over after I popped your head on, because I noticed people starting to pause in the street. I ducked down and got out of there. But I thought I'd left you in good shape unless the skylight broke or a wind blew up."

"But?"

"But—I'd been a bit hasty with your ankles—one of them was numbered 9 and the other 6; and . . . Slowly the whole thing began to tilt."

"Ayhi!" I shuddered, imagining the crash. — "Where are the remains?—in the side alley, I suppose. Never mind, I hope you've swept them up, I don't want to see them. And he took it badly?"

"Yes, he looked stunned, and next day his room was empty. I don't know why, it was all just foolery."

"Of course."

I wondered whether the carver had first tried approaching my mother with a contract for posings. No, he'd have been kicked all the way back to the temple. Or perhaps she and he had worked out a secret deal—that could explain the stepped-up jealousy of her remarks to me. Could it just be luck that there was a room to let above the model's bedroom? What happened a century ago when the last incarnation was found?

"Is it still empty?"

"Yes, no need to worry! There's nobody living there, we don't need lodgers now—it's been taken by some people that pay a lot better, a tourist agency."

"I see. Well, come on," I said, getting up from the bed, "we'll be late for lunch. Do you know," I felt like adding, "you might have caused a saint to be torn in pieces?" And in fact Master Yoryo wasn't yet out of danger. I had only a week or so to save him.

Beth Eden

A LONG sleep was what I needed, and I luxuriated on my bed all next morning, sometimes conscious of the sunshine pouring on me, sometimes, too, of my father or sister or Zed standing near the door. Theopard afterwards told me they took furtive turns to look at me, though he wasn't allowed a turn.

We spent only three days at home before setting out for the castle, and I stayed in the house, hoping for the Applepeel fuss to die down. I needn't have worried overmuch: a goddess has but ironical honor in her own country. Fortesant didn't appear. They said he was now a naval ensign and trying to forget about me.

As for Theopard, there was nowhere to put him but in the room over our heads. "Are you going to slip up there with him?" asked Donaldine.

"Certainly not. We're not married—what would mother think! I'm looking forward to cuddling up with you two, like old times. Swear you won't tell him about the peephole?"

"I swear," said Zed, and let out a Monger swearword; but I noticed she didn't swear *that* anything. So I guessed she would later extract a bribe from Theopard— "Would you like to be tantalized some more?"— "Yes, if that's all I can get"— "Well, there's a certain plank in the floor . . . And if Fristy gets at all hot she'll work the bedclothes off herself, and the nightclothes too, if you're lucky."

And when my nursemaid and my little sister settled into bed either side of me, they hugged me with more than wonted affection, so that my sleep was equatorial, and the morning light found me in the state Zed had predicted. I began a slow dance on my back. Zed and Donaldine turned away, huddling under their blankets, until the first audible groan was elicited from the ceiling. Then hastily they got up, leaving me to sleep in. I did sleep in, for a while. Then I felt the sunshine dipping from the window, and I began to bask, sinuously, with my eyes shut, a sleeping dance.

The sunbeam touched my toes, and I lifted the tips of my breasts into it.

The ceiling whispered to me; tried to waken me; cajoled me. I kept my eyes shut, and if I felt a grin breaking out I writhed over. The ceiling resorted to language terrible but soft. It was a struggle, as I wasn't really asleep, to stay down. I basked variously, while the steepening sunshine crept from my feet to my eyes. Once I didn't writhe over quite in time.

"You're laughing at me!" said the ceiling.

"Not aloud," I said. — "Now I am!"

"Stop laughing at me."

"I'm not laughing at you."

"Yes you are."

"I'm smiling aloud at you. It's better than crying at you, isn't it? It means I like you, doesn't it?"

"Does it?"

"I should think so. 'Like' implies a smile, so just think what a laugh means! A laugh is a loud smile—a sonic smile!"

"Maybe," he said dubiously. "Is it my fate to be teased by you without end?"

"No, Theopard. You really will get me alone in that castle; I mean, almost alone. Alone enough. Here, look at this . . ."

With my eyes open I felt freer to move. Having invented the sleep-dance I went on to invent the all-out bed-dance. I swam over the bed, feeling him see me variously under him, pausing to show him this or that of the ways into me and to roll my elements around it.

"Fristy, I'm warning you! you're storing up such a head of—friction for yourself!"

"Good goodee—I'm not sorry—By Ramgod, I'm making myself too ready too soon—" (I was making myself incoherent with readiness, or the writhing of the sheet under my cunt was—or the rug, for I had spilled off the bed)— "shall I come up there?"—at that the ceiling wooed the floor as never since the Sky first rained on the Earth. "No, I can't, we'd be caught and thrown out on the street together—I'd better stop—Have you yet—?—Don't, then; save it up. You'll have to eat pineapplepeel just a little longer. Let's leave on Sunday not Monday, okay? Come down and join me at breakfast."

I swarmed into my clothes and went to the kitchen. My mother was keeping breakfast warm, not for me but for the guest. She told me to call him, but he didn't come.

"Theopard," I shouted, "do you have a middle name, I still don't know it."

"Holloway," came the gloomy answer.

"Theopard Holloway, come down at once!"

"Haven't you forgotten . . ."

"Oh, that's right, you still have nothing to wear. I'll bring your breakfast up to you."

"*I* will bring it to him," my mother told me. And when she returned—a shade grimmer than ever—she opened with me a discussion of how a set of clothes was to be found.

"I thought I might keep him without for a while," I said.

"I see: you're afraid he'll run away."

"Oh, you think he might? Well, sure, let's give him some clothes."

"You'll have to find a way to pay for them, Lady Jane. Trousers for financially embarrassed Counts are no part of our family budget."

I decided to raise cash by giving a travelogue. It was held in our front room, which has straight-backed chairs formally around it, never before used, like all respectable front rooms. I wanted to stage it on the porch, but everyone was terrified of what I might say. Don't worry, you couldn't be *certain* what my choices of words meant, unless you were Theopard nervously listening from upstairs. Burgher after burgher had to strangle his sniggers as his wife turned on him.

My mother took up their contributions, and Donaldine went out to make the purchase. She was hot for Theopard, she thought he was one snake of testosterone from head to foot, and she got him a tight-fitting Robin Hood suit.

I made him drive the coach; Zed and I rode inside. This was my first extended chance to tell her my story and see if she could explain the things I still found puzzling. I was wondering about the role of the earrings when at last she stopped me and said: "Earrings—pfutr! Listen to me. What good would any earring be without a cheek like yours to hang beside? You keep wondering which 'created' you, earrings, green shirt, maydew, tickling, Mongers, Theopard, Tashartris . . . Don't you realize that you created yourself?"

"But that answers nothing, Zed. What does it mean? It amounts to nothing more than luck."

"Will you write your memoirs, do you think, Miss Felicity?" she asked me.

"I could, if I got someone with the patience to take dictation."

"And what title will you give them?"

"Title? How about—*Barefristys-saga?*"

"Or *The Problem of Beauty*."

"Hounds and cows! Who'd want to read a treatise on aesthetics?"

"But that will be your general subject. It seems to be such a problem to you, even though you are the answer yourself. You have the charm and the skin of a child, but that isn't enough. No one stupid can be beautiful. No one can be beautiful who isn't truly fearless. No one can be beautiful who isn't truly open. No one can be beautiful who isn't truly delighted. And most of all, no one can be beautiful who isn't truly kind."

"Don't you think some of that is potential in me so far, rather than actual?"

"Yes. But so soon as you get a nausea you'll sympathize with the rest of mankind."

I contemplated this for a while. It seemed half reasonable. I didn't know what a nausea was, but I'd sprained my ankles and had stomach-aches from eating apples too fast, and I remembered thinking "Pain! So this is what it is! Hell, if I survive this, I must do some good." But as yet my attention-span was too young.

"But," I said, "can't there be other types of beauty? What about tragic beauty?"

"Yes," she said, "you're right, there can."

We talked so much that I did not notice where we were going, except that the sun stayed behind us. So we were going in a curve, west, north, east, because there was no direct road over the hills. And then looking up to the right I saw a profile of familiar shape in reverse: the back of White Daughter.

Not much of the day was left when we pulled through the brick arch—ivy-eaten and crumbling—onto the cobbles of the courtyard.

I jumped down to explore, but first Theopard detained me and gave me an arrival-present: bath-salts and a bottle of lavender. I've never been much for scents and perfumes, in fact I'm not sure of the difference. But I was touched. He must have got Donaldine to find them for him. "Is there a bath?" I ran in, through a faceful of cobwebs.

In the middle I found a room which at first I thought I was going to hate: it was surrounded by mirrors. Then I saw what to do.

Theopard had to start at once on his new job, that of clay-digger. He started with ill grace, but the exercise was good for him, and he collected barrowloads as long as he could see his way down to the spring. We lit the lamps, and set up a table in the mirror room, and I made a life-size image of myself from the woman-bulge upward.

I felt I was learning fast, and I had no model but myself to tax the patience of. Theopard hung around, outside the mirrors. I finished about two in the morning.

"Well, are we going to sleep together at last?" he said.

"Theopard! We're not married yet!"

"So we *are* going to be married?"

"I guess, if you like, since I told my mother so, and after you come back from your trip. But you do realize, don't you, that when this operation gets into swing we'll need more clay-diggers, as well as gardeners, cooks, business managers."

"Yes, I realize. And you'll marry them all?"

"I don't know, we'll see. We'll work something out. 'Marry' sounds so nice and moist, doesn't it? Good night, fella. I think I'll lie down on this bench. Howdja feel?"

"Pseudogamous."

As he turned dejectedly away, I pinched him. "Come on, of course we'll sleep together! Is there a bed? You've been a good lad for four whole days. There, you really *can* smile! I love you. But I'm going to love everyone too, it's my nature."

"I know."

"It's late and I'm tired, so don't ool me tonight. Well, if you like, but be quick and then just hold me."

"I'll sculpt you." And he stroked the whole of me sensitively to sleep.

It was a curious night, this first in my castle, in the room which Theopard had readied for us, and which he called the Mistress Bedroom. Actually it was the great hall of the castle; twenty painted barons and wide-eyed baronesses of Beth-Eden looked down from the walls, but on the sandstone floor there was nothing as yet except a stack of mildewy cushions, set out to dry before a fireplace in which there was as yet no fire. There was a blanket from the coach; I fell on top of it. Theopard began caressing at my temple and my toes . . . my lobe and my sole . . . my eyes, my heel . . . my cheek, my ankle . . . my lip and the hollow of my ankle . . . my necktendon and my calftendon . . . He was hoping to build a suspension-bridge to a summit within my mound. And I meant to reward him for his art, to writhe up to meet him, but I was unconscious before he had reached halfway. Yet my dream all night was of what was actually happening: he was stroking, on and on; and I under it was lying still. Once I dreamed—and it was true—that he floated over me as I had once over him, letting only our downispheres touch; but when I rose yearning through this teasing he sank through it gratifying. About each fifth of the night, I'm sure, it was that I rose into enough consciousness to feel him moving on me. If he dozed and ceased, my body began its habitual flowing and evolving, away from him, around him, over him; and he woke and braked it with stroking (stroking all over me, stroking within me). At last the long cool shallow of dreaming faded and he got some sleep.

But in the morning he had to wake with my toes in his face. "Quite

all right, don't apologize," he said, "everything is relative, perhaps it is
I and the bed that are the wrong way around. But could I be reawoken
with something softer?—something for instance toward the same end
but nearer the center—"

"Another time; now what is the time?—it's half past late—please
get up and help me start the furnace. It won't draw, and you'll have to
find us some drier kindling."

"And why's the blanket on the floor?" he said, shivering and reaching for it.

"Because if I get too hot I have foul dreams. I had one anyway,
because of your body."

"Oh, thank you."

"You were making me hot even after I kicked the blanket off. So I
had a heat-dream, the worst ever."

"Tell me it!" he said with a grin. He guessed the kind of dream and
was getting ready to accompany it under the blanket.

"I dreamt I was a MAN!"

He put his feet on the floor, grumbling; "Why do you want a
furnace anyway, if you're always so hot?" "Because we need to fire
Tashartris," I said, throwing the Coloring-Book in. Theopard leapt off
the bed and made a dive to save it. But it had done the trick; the furnace
roared.

He was upset about that for a while. (He swore that from those
lewd pages as they expired into ash arose naked images coiling in the
blaze.) But we soon had hot water, which comforted him. We found
on a shelf a set of tube paints and I began to use them—but one was
that same daft green of my shirt, that *happy* color, and as a pigment it
had the most irrepressible liquidity and staining-power. As soon as I
tried to use it on the headdress it ran down and colonized all the other
shades. I scrubbed them all off and painted her in earth colors—
currant juice on her hair, coat after coat.

"What d'you think of her?" I asked.

"A masterpiece," he said, for want of a better word.

We packed her in a box of shavings, from the bookshelves which I
had already had him start making, and he set off with her in the coach.
"Can I trust you alone with her?" I teased; "be careful how you use her;
she leaves us seamless. You can give her a bit of patina if you like." He
was away a week, during which we would have starved but for Zed's
knowledge of the plants of the woods.

I began a portrait of her. We didn't, of course, have to work in the
mirror-room; we carried a trestle table out onto the grass. "Zed," I said,

looking at her hair, which was still only grey, "you've got bangs, just like you've given me: under it your forehead is naked like mine."

"I'm only an adopted Monger," she said. "And so are you a little, you know? We pick up certain things from them. Earthiness, longevity . . ."

She started to teach me the Monger conjunctions (winks, blushes, and earwags) and the strong verbs (teeth-gnashing, finger-cracking), and what my several species of laughter meant, and I could see why the Mongers don't talk that way. "Also," she said, "though you've never had a cold, you sneeze about once each day. You should stop that." "But it's fun," I said.

"Do you know how to make it come?" she said (while I continued to build clay onto her spine). "Make what come?" "The sneeze. Tap the ridge of your nose. But if you want to stop it, press upward under your nose like this." "Hey, I'll try it," I said; it might help to give me a nose like Saxie's.

Winter

U P HERE already the year was rusting. We were in time to plant a fall garden of turnips and curly kale. The park is amazingly overgrown. Only yesterday I came on a little lake and waterfall, set into the hill at our back. We still haven't found the apple orchard, where the wild scion called Temptation is said to grow.

When Theopard came back from the temple we were famous and rich, and, more than that, I knew that my dear friend the priest was alive.

For he sent me a message: "I thank Tashartris that you have never, and will never, come to harm—foolkin though you are. She has condescended also, just in time, to preserve my inconsiderable life, by giving birth to her new incarnation, a figure almost as lovely as yourself. Watch her from where you are" (I took it he meant her other icon, the moon) "when she is full in the month of your birth."

Applicants began to arrive. We've taken on husbandmen, handymen, washermen, bedmakers, and guests, though there is really no distinction. I feel finer than ever—I regard them as giving massage to parts of me in turn. Some of them have imagined things that jar with my imagination, but so far I've expelled nobody except for chopping down a tree. Theopard, being handy with ropes, is responsible for our swings and hammocks and rope ladders, and furnishes the play-room— the gymnasium.

From time to time I would hear someone in the morning ruminatively, with eyes still shut, roll the soft trisyllable around his mouth, or while standing at a door looking out on the garden. *("Applepeel...")*

"Look," I said, "at home at least, surely I can be Fristy. It embarrasses me to be called by a name that I'm not."

"You may have a rebellion on your hands about this."

"Why?"

"If I, for instance, hear one of my mates tell a story about you and call you 'Fristy,' I'm jealous. Is he friends with you in a way I'm not? Fristy is a real little morsel—mortal—the kind that only one fellow can make a claim to. Whereas . . ."

"Don't say it. Please, speak to me, if you can remember, by the name I've been used to—it's quite a nice one, isn't it?—and say what you like behind my back." "May I call you Fristy?" "Please do." "Fristy." "There, you see, you're my most special friend. Kiss me. Now if all the others will do the same."

But still I would sometimes catch *"Applepeel,"* apparently a whole sentence, a quietly satisfied remark, just for the feel of it on the lips. It was explained to me: "I can make myself feel wonderful by just saying it. *Applepeel!"*

I tried it myself. *"Applepeel.* I don't know what you mean."

I treat them all equally, though the humble and elderly can't help having an advantage. They have only to say "Nookie?" as they approach (carrying their tubes or bottles of love-oil) and they can have it. Why not? It doesn't even wear me out much—they generally climax so quick they don't have time to do most of what they expect to.

I thought I had seen the last of the Coloring-Book, and yet it rose from the flames. That is, one of the new arrivals brought another copy of it; Third Edition, Fifteenth Printing. I tried to outlaw Coloring-Books, but found I didn't have the power. I had to overhear arguments about favorite scenes—

"What's yours?"

"Oh, the First Battle of the Britches, any day."

"No, the Second is better still."

"Well, why not the Third?"

"I love it, but the trouble with it is, it doesn't let you wank properly: you lose your grip for laughing."

I had to accept the presence of Coloring-Books; perhaps they diverted pressure from me. In fact I discovered that from the Fifth Edition, Coloring-Books were being published from inside my own bedroom.

More even than operational space, sculpture can use archival space, even dungeon space. The battlements (ornamental, around the southern terrace) are sprouting stone life, turrets have patient sentinels, arresting beings begin to be met with in the avenues and in the maze.

I made another Tashartris, but with legs, so she inspires people just too much and can't go to the temple, unless they dig a hole in the altar. I soon left naturalism to my apprentices: they make multiple groups involving me. It has to be said that these provide most of the revenue and I the reputation. I progressed to other materials and other subjects: archers, black giantesses, black armor for Amazons, roads tackling ridges, figures under water, intersecting waves, air structures, rising moons, harbor cities, planet-riders, smoke-mazes, scenes in the womb, imagined systems of root and rind, simultaneous people, altars, three-dimensional models of the Sixteen Sleeps, and now a further challenge: the attempt to represent in glass the infinite Thorotouch. The adventure ahead into wonderful countries that have no far edges is mine.

Among the lesser things I made were earrings, chair-legs, buttons,

fruit bowls, licking-wheels (for postage stamps), tin skirts to keep squir-
rels out of pecan trees, and Chimneystoppers, bas-relief ones, large
ones for the castle hearths and smaller ones for sale to the lowlands. But
I received a visit from a Monger. It was a cousin Monger I had only
slightly known, Carline Monger. He arrived long before a very cold
sunup, All Souls' Day (though to him it was the day of *Savin*). He
appeared as friendly as Mongers can appear, he said nothing threatening, merely spoke a word or two to me in stomach-rumbling, and we
gave him a good breakfast and exchanged news. But I understood him
and ceased to make things that Mongers make.

My home town is only a day's coach-ride away, or two days' walk by
straighter paths over the shoulder of White Daughter, down through the
forest and past the spring of the Poorlouis. My father now works as gardener of his own garden. My mother lives proudly as Countess-Mother,
giving teas and working as staff of her own house. Clarence and Donaldine, I'm glad to say, are unspoiled: they haven't lost a single obnoxious
trait—but they have only two or three, and they're still in school.

The first winter has passed; not all the parts of the castle are
repaired, but we kept warm together.

Spring

IT'S SPRING—late already, even here in the north!—and I began to be restless.

I was born on the last day of April (I'm not, as people expect, a Moonchild—that's what they call those born under the sign of Cancer that they shrink from naming). But this year the moons fell at the beginnings of the months, so I was unsure which to watch—the Egg Moon of April or the Milk Moon of May. But it wouldn't hurt me to watch both. The evening before last, the last day of March, the sky was covered with dark cloud. But when the moon climbed enough to be white, first she broke through in two places, like two ragged stars; then one of them grew more powerful and was really her, and other hazy moons sprouted, more and more, finding weak places in the cloud, analysing it into a mesh, with the moon as a fluff of light behind—a spirit shining through a ribcage. But it didn't augur well for next night. And next evening—last night—the cloud was continuous, all the way to the northeast horizon where there was a clear fawn slit.

They had all forgotten. When I got up from the bed, where Tarquin and Eugene had fallen asleep handwrestling over my glushes, and went out (looked for some clothes on the way but couldn't find any), the cloud had been peeled back like a blanket, all the way to the southwest where it was a fleeing remnant: a cold front had come across. There blazed Tashartris, brighter than I had ever seen her, a wild still explosion consuming the frost-clear sky. Only by its not warming me did I know this moonlight from sunlight.

I had come out by a side passage that led straight into a carters' lane. Over the lintel someone had nailed a sign intended to discourage tourists:

BEWARE OF THE GRRL

I sat awhile with my back to the door, and the doormat over me; I wrapped it around me like a skirt as I wandered down through a hawthorn thicket, but cast it aside as I came out into a glade and lay on a grassy bank. I was back in the temple, but the temple had no walls;

---

* "In those years when Indonesian volcanoes girdle the earth with stratospheric dust . . . the eclipsed moon is a drop of almost blackened blood, or an Arkansas apple." —Guy O'Howell, *The Astronomical Companion*, section on "Earthlight."

it was as wide as half the universe. I began to freeze and doze. Suddenly I saw that the bronzing and re-reddening of the moon was not just because she was going over lower into the west. The round shadow of my head—no, of the world—was falling up onto her. The ruin of all the world's sunsets was raining on her. She went dark to the upper edge; but then, this time, darker, and darker. She did not quite disappear but settled, like an ember, to the color of my hair.*

She set, and I woke in the sun, shivering.

And the blood-washed moon will rise again tonight, whole and white.

There were two new faces at breakfast. Leaving them all in each other's company for a while may be the only way to hold down the population here. I began to talk about a new journey.

"April Fool was yesterday," they said.

"Don't I know it. But I'm serious."

"Where, then, Fristy?"

"To India, maybe." (But first, certainly, to visit Master Yoryo. And have another play at seducing him?)

"Wonderful! You certainly must view the love-sculptures of Khajuraho. I have a picture book on them, I believe I can be a guide for you"— "Let's take in the Second Sexolympics at Murmansk"—and many another suggestion.

"I'm sorry, I was really thinking of going by myself," I said, "incognito."

This provoked the familiar and by now rather irritating storm of merriment.

"Well, by myself, anyway. Not with an entourage. I'll manage however I manage. I'm sorry."

Then they competed in accepting this philosophically, each hoping that I would notice his especial sensitivity and make an exception in his case. But I was adamant.

Theopard said: "Well, *some* of the wanting of Applepeel is slaked here; I suppose it's only fair to give the rest of the world its chance."

"That's not my idea."

"You'll be away for your birthday."

"Well, maybe someone'll throw a party for me. —And now I'll have to finish this commission double quick, so let's have all of you out of here till suppertime."

"You don't mean you plan to leave tomorrow?"

"Why not?"

"But it's not new moon."

"Who said it was? Everything else is ready." And I worked until, about the middle of the afternoon, a light plane landed in our horsepasture, bringing a delegation that had not been able to face the journey up by dirt road.

"There's a high official of the United Nations to see you."

He came in. He was a Top official; indeed a Mandarin. He wore a suit and white shirt and tie and other quaint accoutrements, such as a tiepin in the shape of a broken chain, and a hat which he graciously removed. He was flanked by nearly twenty others in almost identical costume. The pupils of their eyes widened, as I've noticed happens first thing when I see people. It was as if I was receiving them in a throneroom, though I was cross-legged on the floor and was dressed only in an apron splashed with plaster—and, today, by a fancy, my earrings.

I put my finger to my lips for silence till the music had finished. On a ring of chairs to my left, not looking at me but intently at each other's faces and fingers, was a small chamber group. Traveling musicians are always welcome here—the fast movements of Vivaldi concertos especially make me bustle on with my work. After the resolution of the last chord we allowed the Mandarin to speak.

He spoke in an elevated international tone: "You ah Fwisty Peppah?"

"Yes. You can call me Felicity if it's easier."

"Thank you. Now, it is believed that you also went about undah the name of Applepeel Cuh-tis; is this twue?"

"That wasn't my choosing," I said. "People (well, Mongers) nicknamed me Applepeel. And I've no idea where the Curtis came from," I added, realizing this. Perhaps someone just thought it sounded nice with Applepeel. But names, I feared, were not the issue. Which of Applepeel's acts was I in trouble for?

He came straight to the point:

"We want you to go to Wome."

"To where?"

"To Wome. The empyah is on the point of invading us."

I sat openmouthed. So, the empire was about to assail the United Barbarian Nations, as they were still called, though after all these centuries they had sunk to hypercivilization. What good would it do to send one little fallen virgin to be offered up in the arenas of the metwopolis?

But the Mandarin began to explain. "The situation is despwit, but we believe you may be able to help. Can we defend asselves? No: we now have none but cewemonial ahmies. Can we send a diplomatic mission? We have sent thwee, and they all failed, including the last,

though it was headed by none othah than Yoz Twooly. Can we just let
them come? It is an option to contemplate; it came close to being
appooved by vote of the Cicuity Council; but it would mean saquifice of
all aah daughtahs, enslavement of whom is undoubtedly the Woemans'
objective. As you know, they ah obsexed with cess—that is, they ah
sexquazy—all at least twigamous, but theah gweed knows no bounds."
(He might have quoted, if he could, the proverb "Better whoremonger
than warmonger.") "No, we must at all cost wepell the legions. But
what weapon is left to us? Only one: Epplepeel."

I, a weapon?

"We're ready to arrange your transportation to the border," said a
fluent younger official, in charge of the details; the Mandarin, having
finished the exposition of the principle, stepped back, but did not fold
his arms. There was a touch of informality, even disrespect, in this delegation that had come to plead with me, but this was only an appearance given by their having to keep one hand in their pockets. "After
that," said the junior official, "you will blunder along fine on your own,
as we know you're well capable of doing."

"But if they won't call off their war when you ask them, why should
they for me?"

"They even might, and you could certainly try just asking, if you
penetrate all the way to the presence of the Emperor, or if you happen
to have the Senate where you want it. (We have an idea that the
approachable officials might be the Prolifex Maximus, or the Gurule
Aedile—we'll give you their addresses. While you're about it, ask them
to release poor Pope Decent, held captive in the Temple of Vesta since
his bulls *Summa Cum Laude*, *Non Sequitur*, and *Status Quo Ante*.)
But such a position would presumably be arrived at only after you have
proceeded for a while along the lines of Plan T—which is what our
working group has called the primary scenario."

"And it is?"

"Why, that you should subvert the empire."

"Oh, just that? Just subvert the whole— I see." I was wiping my
hands on my breasts, I checked myself, and wiped them on my
pinafore. "Just burrow in like a maggot in an apple— My Goddess. But
they'll make me sign an immigration form: 'Will you seek by violent
means to overthrow the Empire?—Yes/No. Will you incite riots and
import illegal substances and establish houses of ill fame . . .' And then
they'll arrest me as a radical feminist for having *A* at the beginning of
my name instead of the end. No, I know. I'll be smuggled in. Simple.
Then just subvert the empire. Of course. By messing them up? I'm

afraid not even I can cause that much chaos. But I suppose you mean by seducing them. Just let myself be tickled, perhaps, in the Circus Maximus, or ravished by a lion—or suckle a pair of wolfcubs, how about that?—and they'll all die of refined sensation. But as you said, they're well supplied already; they've got stablefuls of girl, shiploads of glushery—"

"Glushage, you mean. Glushery refers to the assemblage on a given woman; glushage is the collective luxury."

"All right. They're rolling in it; they've got cargoes and provincial tributes of it from Syria, Lydia, Tumidia." ("Swimmin' in wimmin"—it was the Mandarin himself, I'm pretty sure, who murmured that.) "I'm afraid the addition of me to their stock won't even slow them down."

"Not exactly by seducing them, Applepeel. (That would be all too easy—would consume, in itself, less than no time. They're pre-seduced.) By *tantalizing* them. That's your talent, isn't it?"

I had to grin.

I was supposed to keep the empire—or its lechers, who presumably included its ruling clique—chasing me in small circles and forgetting the existence of the frontiers. I doubted that any run of luck, pluck, wit, agility, topology, and magic would be long enough to carry me past a million wolves, but it might be fun to try.

"Don't attempt to satisfy them," said another official. "Messalina couldn't; it would wear you out without wearing them out."

"Tease them," said another. "Play hide-and-seek with them."

"Contrive to keep your clothes on sometimes—that should drive them out of their minds."

"You may be able," said the Mandarin, "to twansfohm the whole Holy Woman Empiah into something new and moah benign." A shrewd appeal.

"And take your time," contributed another, "if possible. The longer you can absorb them the better. It may become a lifetime's work for you."

"I think not," I said. "I've got things to do here. I'd hope to be back by midsummer at the latest. And your daughters all better be waiting to greet me with presents, by Zantium! —Anyway, gentlemen, your scheme is lewd and totally ridiculous."

They wrung their hands.

"I don't say I'm one hundred percent against it. I'll send you my answer next week."

"We're afraid, Applepeel, you'll have to leave tomorrow. As Sir

Sheville said, the position is quitic— desp— catast— it's almost too late alweddy."

"I see." (How many times must the innocent say "I see"?) "Well, I suppose you've come a long way and you'll have to stay the night. Saxie, could you show them to their wooms?"

Saxie opened the door for them. But the youngest and longest-haired official stepped out of the group and sidled up to me. "Thank you, but first could you ask your servants to leave for a moment?"

"I haven't any servants—these are my friends and lords."

He shuffled, staring at my navel, and I realized he had been deputed to make the collective pass. But everyone was listening and he had forgotten his words.

"Do you want some encouragement?" I said.

Whisper: "Yes please!"

I let my nipples rise. "Can you fuck?"

Low gasp: "Yes *mam!* That is, I could with you!"

"Wouldn't you rather do something more special? Difficult—tough—good?"

He answered with blissful body-language, ending in a heated nod.

"On the spot, okay?" He took a breath, and eased his beltbuckle.

Two steps more to a naked masturbating Mandarinling. But I told myself, Enough, Dame Jane. No more vengeful scenes which will end, you know, in taking pity.

"Well, I'm sorry. Please accept this souvenir instead," and I stood up and took off the apron and tossed it to him. Forty diplomatic eyes hooked instantly to the mat of my nether hair. "We were thinking of not having an orgy this evening—I mean we weren't thinking of having an orgy this evening. Go to bed on your own like good officials. If I'm to start in the morning, I want to rest, and if I'm to tantalize the empire I'll get in practice by tantalizing *you*." And I walked away through them.

Now I must stop scribbling and pack, though all I can think of is Zed's powder, and a few clevels and chocolate bars, and my trumpet. (You didn't know I play the trumpet, did you?)

Appendix of Selected Fristiana

Fortesant to Applepeel:
Dismiss me, goddess, my kneecaps hurt,
I'm forgetting to be grateful for the view up your skirt

Eugene Bluejean on reaching puberty:
Peril,
Ice-jab,
Shy young knee,
The earth
Can see

When they are wearing skirts
Astonishments begin:
Isn't there some mistake?
We can see the ladies' skin!

But when they switch to pants
I gasp as each one passes:
Isn't there some mistake?
We can see the ladies' asses!

No matter what they wear
Belief is shot to Hades:
Isn't there some mistake?
We can see that they are ladies!

What do you take me for? Glimpses to masticate.
Woman. The shrill jelly. She-stranger, otherflesh.

Hipment and lipment and suchlike equipment and
Sheilas as sheets over which to spill fingerscript.

Skirt's silky shine shed down shimmying slope of hip.
(Naughty you, naughty you, naught that you ought you do!)

Supple as rubber the palmfulls are, simple as

Apples the round parts. Her smile is a simile.

Seas for eyes. Clouds for thighs. Step out of silhouette,
Come with prompt breasts where they plunder the orchard's fruit!

No, you are right. Even queens have their dank places.
Stay in your stays and your stretch—I in mine as well.

Sketch-strokes are simpler and therefore more beautiful.
Don't rashly grab apples: some may be crab-apples.

Theopard to Applepeel:
You are naked now, but I'll keep on stripping you,
From suit after suit of air unzipping you

Her eyes as wells or else as moons,
Her glush as liquid or as rock,
Her cunt as lifegiver or grave,
She as a queen or as a slave.
Parts if I choose from her to love
I purify to monsterhood.

Duplicity of women!—but are they duple
Or rather quintuple or septuple?

But try this gospel on a disciple
Who's lodging many a mile from chapel!

When I am wedding her mouth, I scruple
Does this one know the maypole, the maple?

Lip slips over lip, hips ripple,
And rhyme implies a space for nipple.

We're after all cut out to couple;
Cunt is our country and our staple.

I would not scruple to die, for example,
Between the columns of this temple!

She's treacherousbutlecherous
Truculentbutsucculent
Busybodylazybones
Chatterboxandcopycat
Longlegged, lightheaded
Untrustworthybutlustworthy
She flaunted her haunches I haunted her flaunches
I spanked her flanks she shimmied her shanks she laid
Herself open for a flanconade

Legend of Ishtar-Tashartris, according to the priests:
A garment at each gate she had to shed,
A garment or an ornament instead,
When down along the Underworld she sped
To seek and save her lover Tammuz dead.
Each porter at each portal, foot to head
Queen Ishtar gazing, and his hand outspread:
"One garment, lady, or no further tread;
One garment is the toll—pelisse or shred";
One more, and in fulfilment of her dread
The porter "That last jewel!" sternly said;
Till at the last before the King she pled
Without a speech, delivering instead
The body left unwed

Zhanga Starchick on Applepeel:
Not for a cubic prune   would this cherubic prude
Her pubic tuberance   imprudently protrude.

A rejected applicant:
On Friday,
I'll confide ye,
My emotions were untidy,
So I went into the high'wy seeking feminine soci'dy.
On Saturday
A battery
Of women bright and chattery
Received my adulation, importunity and flattery.
On Sunday

Or on Monday
Or at any rate on one day
They were free from me because I had some things to do in Lundy,
But on Tuesday,
Feeling woozy,
Not particular or choosy,
I went out to get a bird or bint or chick or broad or floozy.
Then on Wednesday
In a frenzy
I approached a Mrs. Menzies
Who until I got too fresh had been a friend of all my friends's.
Well, on Thursday
By the Mersey
When I ventured up her jersey
I discovered it was stitched by too ingenious a durzi.
Mr. Menzies,
Using lenses,
Brought my tale to where its ends is,
So I'll use my dying breath to bring you lejjers to your senzes:
Though his wife'll
Be an eyeful
You must hesitate to trifle
With the intimate possessions of a man who owns a rifle.
Keep your eyes on
The horizon
That he readies his surprise on;
The experience will sadden you but be too late to wisen.
Now, my wit withal,
Don't jitter, all,
Or take my words too literal:
I'm only building doggerel and finding words to fit her all.
This still you may distil from all my litany and ritual: if secretary won't
then usherette or babysitter'll!

An accepted applicant:
Now, Lust, don't be so shy: act like your brothers.
Does Hunger ever back away from bread?
Is Thirst afraid to taste a wholesome liquor?
Does Weariness refuse a decent bed?

"Let's get naked.

What do you say, kid?"

"Whoredom
Is better than boredom."

"How much will your pay be,
Baby?"

"It'll cost you plenty
If you want real obscen'ty."

The virtuous women are those
Who give their love to the poor.
My blessing is hers who'll be
The undeserving's whore.

The virtuous, loving those
They hate, as many they must,
Withhold not from the leper
The lively gifts of lust.

Saxie on Applepeel:
She listened to lectures delivered by lechers,
Lubricity laving their lips.

Henry Parolong on feeling better:
In the hot days I asked them
Why not work in the night,
Love and slumber in sunshine?
"Oh no, that wouldn't be right.
We must wear clothes in the daytime
For armor against the light;
Part with them only at darkness—
Change one for the other harness—
For love is a secret rite."

Make love in the daytime!
Make love in the light!
Make love in front of a mirror.
It makes a fine sight!
Have a mirror on the ceiling,

Have mirrors to left and right,
Make love standing or lying,
Make love swimming or flying—
Yes, like the gods, in flight!

Muezzins call from their towers
"Prayer is better than sleep!"
Men wake in the dark hours
And into their wives creep.
My minaret in the daytime
Standing for passions that leap
Declares without word
"Love is better than work,
Blood pulses won't keep."

From the Story of Hai ibn Yaqzan, by Ibn Tufail ("Son of a Little Child"):
There is an island of India, below the equator, called Waq Waq. A tree that grows in this isle produces women as its fruit.

Verse attributed to the wandering painter Jecon Gregory and assumed to be about Applepeel:
She's a girl so very frisky, making love to her is risky,
She's a girl so very sweet you wouldn't think she's made of meat

Applepeel on essences:
You interrupt and push on me
This act irrelevant to love

Applepeel on words:
"Love" is like loaves in ovens.
"Love" comes in dozens.
"Fuck" is ospubis slamming ospubis.
"Fuck" is shallow and scrofulous.
"Sex" is like scissors among legs.
"Sex" is one big complex.
Only "wed" and "ravish"
Are liquid as "she," as acid.

Applepeel:
All living things live anxious. Almost all.

If Applepeel
Is real
As we feel
She must be,
For if that coz
Never was
What's the point of lusting?
Then where and how
Is she now?
Time passes.
Wear and tear
Don't spare
Even the most fair
Of lasses.
But of her two components, beaty
Is exceeded by vitality.